Texas Fire

By Gerry Bartlett

Texas Fire

Texas Heat

Texas Fire

GERRY
BARTLETT

LYRICAL SHINE

Kensington Publishing Corp.

www.kensingtonbooks.com

LYRICAL SHINE BOOKS are published by

Kensington Publishing Corp.
119 West 40th Street
New York, NY 10018

All Kensington titles, imprints, and distributed lines are available at special quantity discounts for bulk purchases for sales promotion, premiums, fund-raising, educational, or institutional use. Special book excerpts or customized printings can also be created to fit specific needs. For details, write or phone the office of the Kensington Sales Manager: Kensington Publishing Corp., 119 West 40th Street, New York, NY 10018. Attn. Sales Department. Phone: 1-800-221-2647.

Lyrical Shine and the Lyrical Shine logo are Reg. U.S. Pat. & TM Off.

First Electronic Edition: May 2017

ISBN-13: 978-1-60183-984-8
ISBN-10: 1-60183-984-7

First Print Edition: May 2017

ISBN-13: 978-1-60183-985-5
ISBN-10: 1-60183-985-5

Printed in the United States of America

Chapter 1

Megan Calhoun paid the driver, stepped out of the car, and rolled her suitcase over the gravel parking lot. Her hand slipped on the handle when she hit a pothole. Sweaty palms. Then her stomach rumbled. No, she refused to be nervous. She put on her "I don't give a damn" face, and stared down a man slouched next to a pickup truck who made a comment about her butt in snug jeans. She kept going toward the building that housed the offices of CWC Industries.

This was all her daddy's fault. Conrad Calhoun's will spelled out the terms: she had to work in the oil fields for a year if she wanted her inheritance. It had been her own bright idea to pick the man who'd be stuck with her for the next twelve months. She'd already scanned the parking lot filled with dusty pickup trucks. No sign of him. If he was as thrilled as she was about what was coming, he was probably hiding out.

Who could blame him? Except for one summer when she'd humored her father and gone along for the ride, she had no clue what went on in the oil fields. All she really knew was that those dirty, noisy places had always paid for her cushy lifestyle.

Megan stopped in front of the office. It wasn't much, just a low-slung building that had seen better days. Not like the high-rise where the Calhoun Petroleum Headquarters reigned supreme. This subsidiary of Calhoun obviously didn't rate funding for frills. She wrestled her suitcase up the steps, then pushed open the glass door and cold air hit her face. It was hot outside, typical for Texas in early September. At least air-conditioning was in the budget here.

The man at the counter had those wide shoulders she recognized. Former football player. "Rowdy, I was looking for you outside."

Rowdy Baker turned and looked her over. "I'm signing us in. Why the hell did you do it, Megan? Request me to be your partner for your playtime in the field?" He threw the clipboard he held down on the worn Formica counter. "I'm used to working alone."

"I'm not used to working at all." Megan let go of her suitcase. Of course it flopped over, landing on her foot. "Damn it." She left it there and looked around, making sure no one was close enough to overhear them. A couple of clerks were nearby, but one was on the phone and the other was in an office behind a glass wall.

"I wanted someone I knew. My sister says you're a decent guy. Was she wrong?" She grabbed the clipboard and checked their names.

"Am I supposed to be flattered?" Rowdy looked like he wanted to pound the counter. "'Decent'. Wow, I'm overwhelmed. Thank Cassidy for me. Now, go outside and pick someone else. Anyone else."

"No." Megan breathed a sigh of relief when she saw her fake name on the list. "Listen, we're stuck with each other. You need to adjust your attitude. She's probably going to wind up running Calhoun Petroleum, you know. Cassidy is showing everyone at Headquarters that she's got Daddy's business sense."

"Whoop-de-do. So I could get a promotion out of this?" Rowdy got close to Megan and she almost backed off.

He was big and, at the moment, intimidating. Maybe this had been a mistake. Cass had broken it off with him. Maybe he was mad and would make Megan's life a living hell. But then the devil you know . . .

"At the end of the year, all four of the Calhoun kids could be in a position to help you out. If we get good evaluations and get our inheritances." Megan smiled. Rowdy clearly wasn't impressed.

"I'm sure Cass *will* do well and end up running things. Wouldn't surprise me at all." He finally backed off. "She called me personally to break the bad news that I'd be dragging you along with me. Begged me to take you on, because you can imagine how I feel about dealing with another Calhoun woman about now." He glanced around the room this time. No one seemed to be listening to them.

"I'm sorry." Megan really was. Rowdy had been with Cass until recently. He was probably still aching over their breakup.

"Sure you are, Ms. *Cochran*. An assumed name. Really? What's the matter, afraid the roughnecks wouldn't like Daddy's little girl coming by to check on them?" He picked up the clipboard and a pen from the counter.

"It could cause problems. I'm not naïve, Rowdy." Megan ignored his sarcasm. "I've got to succeed this year. A lot's on the line. You get that? You going to help me swim? Or sink me like the *Titanic*?"

"I don't know." He looked her over, his dark eyes skimming down her body until she wanted to tug at her T-shirt. "You going to work this year or float through it and then expect me to lie so you can get your big payday at the end?"

Megan wondered if a smart woman would leave right now and pick a stranger, someone more intimidated by the Calhoun name— or at least respectful. But Rowdy was still standing there, looking like he expected her to cut and run.

She picked up her suitcase off her foot and raised her chin. "I'll work if you'll give me a chance. Will you? Or am I going to get the fallout because I'm Cassidy's sister and you're mad at her?" Megan saw she'd struck a nerve when he signed the clipboard and threw it down again. Good. Let him prove he wasn't still smarting from Cassidy's rejection. Too bad Megan couldn't help noticing that her sister did have great taste. She'd always been a sucker for big men with dark eyes and washboard abs.

"Cass and I are history. The question now is your attitude. I heard you never stick with anything more than a week or two." Rowdy strode toward the door, then turned to look at her.

"Someone's been talking too much. My sister claimed you were a nice guy. Guess she overstated that." Megan wanted to storm out of there and slam the door in his face. But what choice did she have with a three-hundred-million-dollar inheritance on the line? One year. She had to stick with this and Rowdy for three hundred and sixty-five days.

"I'm nice unless I'm backed into a corner." He glanced at the office staff, which had suddenly taken an interest. "Let's get out of here."

Megan tugged her suitcase outside, grunting at the heft of it as she worked it down the wooden steps. "Come on, Rowdy. See reason. You're the only engineer working for Calhoun that I know.

Daddy thought I had what it takes to learn the technical side of the business, and I'm determined to prove I can. Why wouldn't I pick you to work with over some stranger?" And that was the truth. She exclaimed when her damn suitcase fell over again into the dirt. "Are we good to go?"

"I don't know." He frowned at her designer suitcase. "What's in there? More of the stuff like you're wearing now?"

"Why?" Megan tugged at her T-shirt. "I packed light. One suitcase. My sister Shannon would have brought six." When he just grunted and started walking toward a row of pickup trucks, she got the suitcase up again and rolled it awkwardly over the gravel parking lot.

He stopped next to a generic four-door truck and leaned against the tailgate.

"Hey, if there's a dress code, you could have let me know. What the hell's wrong with what I'm wearing? I'm pretty sure Cass sent you an e-mail that included my phone number."

Rowdy looked her over with eyes that were almost black and cold as hell. When he stopped his scrutiny at her shoes, Megan wanted to kick him. No, she'd be damned if she'd let him get to her like that.

"Tennis shoes? For the oil fields? Those will last maybe one day. You need work boots. Heavy-duty. And what's in the suitcase? More jeans and T-shirts?" He picked up the case, making it look easy, and tossed it in the back of the truck.

"Of course. They're comfortable and can wash and wear. Similar to what you're wearing, but from a designer you've probably never heard of." Great. Now she sounded like a snob. "I mean, you have on jeans and a T-shirt right now yourself." And that T-shirt looked painted on. Not that she was going to mention that. The guy must work out hours every day to keep such a great body.

"I don't have breasts that will make the roughnecks fall off the rigs trying to get a look." He pulled car keys out of his pocket and walked around to the driver's side door. "Is there a coat in there? We'll be going to West Texas, where it gets damn cold at night."

"No, I thought I could buy something later." Megan realized he wasn't going to open the passenger door for her and rushed around to get in the truck. He'd already started the engine and drove out of the lot with gravel flying out from behind them before she even had a chance to get her seat belt buckled.

"Where we're going you won't have a chance to buy anything. There's nothing out there. It's a wasteland except for oil wells, bars, a few motels, and, if we're lucky, a café where we won't get ptomaine." Rowdy turned onto the highway. "I'm taking you to get work boots. I hope you have money. They're not cheap. But if you did happen to find a store that sold such things out where we're going, they'd cost triple what you'd pay here."

"Fine. Bring it on." Megan frowned. She didn't have much money. Her old credit cards had been cut off when Daddy died. Her mother had given her a gift card. But that had been before they'd found out Missy had been terrorizing Cassidy because she didn't like the fact that Daddy had included her half sister in the will. Meg felt funny using the card, but it seemed like she had no choice. "When do we get paid?"

Rowdy laughed and slapped the steering wheel. "Have you done a lick of work yet? And you seriously want to know when you get paid?" He kept chuckling as he drove, reaching for the radio controls.

"Yes, it's important." Megan looked around the interior of the truck. It wasn't fancy. Simple AM/FM radio, no satellite. Vinyl seats, but it was a four-door truck. The thing wasn't even very clean, and this was the start of their trip. A Coke can rolled around on the floorboard, and she stomped it with her foot.

"We're paid every two weeks, on Fridays. I have my check sent straight to the bank, because the check-cashing places the guys on the rigs use keep a hefty cut. I use a debit card when I need cash on the road. I have a company credit card for our gas, propane, and groceries." Rowdy looked over at her. "It's too late for you to arrange direct deposit. You'd have to give your real name and information back at the office for it anyway, and that would blow your cover. Now that we're on the road, they'll mail the check to your home address." He grinned. "That'll be a problem, won't it? How are you going to get cash, Megan? For personal items."

Megan glared at him. Could he quit enjoying this so much? "I don't suppose you'd let me slip tampons and shampoo into the grocery cart on the company dime." She loved the way his cheeks flushed. Got him. "Then I guess I'll have to ask my sister for help."

She was getting tired of his attitude already, and they had a long way to go. "Oh, did you hear? Cassidy and Mason are engaged." Well, that certainly wiped the smile off Rowdy's face.

"You're shittin' me." He wheeled into a parking lot and cut the engine. "They've known each other less than a month."

"Sometimes that's all it takes." Megan saw they were at a shoe store. "Do I have to get steel-toed boots?"

"Yeah. Go on in. I'll wait here." He stared at his hands on the wheel.

Megan realized he was truly devastated. He and Cassidy had been high school sweethearts and had been together off and on for years. Cass had broken it off for good as soon as she'd met Mason MacKenzie, a wealthy oilman and family friend of the Calhouns. Rowdy probably still loved Cassidy. She touched his arm.

"I'm sorry, Rowdy. It was mean of me to just blurt it out like that. Sometimes—" She sighed. "Sometimes things happen. It's not your fault. Cass and Mason fell hard for each other."

"Yeah, I know. And it all happened as soon as money fell into Cassidy's lap, didn't it?" Rowdy's fingers tightened on the steering wheel. "Go on in, Megan. You're another spoiled rich girl, and I really don't feel like dealing with you right now." He looked at her, his eyes dull. "You hear me?"

"Yeah, I'm out of here." Megan opened the truck door and jumped out. She wanted to argue with him about the money. She knew it hadn't had a thing to do with how Cass felt about Mason. Love at first sight. Like something out of a romance novel. Rowdy would hoot at the notion. Most men would.

Well, he was hurt and needed space. She got it. So she took a good long while to pick out some of the ugliest boots she'd ever owned. There wasn't even a color choice. It was either light tan or dark tan. Jeez. After clomping around the store in them and deciding to buy heavy-duty socks when they immediately started making a blister, she noticed that this working man's place had a small section in the back corner that also catered to women. She hit the shelves to add thermal underwear and a pair of shapeless khaki pants with a matching shirt, and baggy jeans, too. A denim shirt came next. Did she really need a coat? It was a sweltering ninety degrees outside but she forced herself to add a down jacket and gloves to her growing pile. It would make serious inroads on her gift card, but she wasn't going to suffer later because of the weather. A heavy-duty duffel bag finished her purchases and she was good to go.

Rowdy was still where she'd left him when she lugged the duffel out to the truck. He actually got out and heaved it into the back.

"This is more than a pair of work boots." He looked at his watch. "We need to get going."

"I listened to you and bought weather-appropriate gear." Megan gestured at her work shirt. "And I'm covering my tempting tits. What do you think?"

"I'm thinking it's a start." He nodded, then started the engine. "Did anyone tell you about our living arrangements for the next year?"

"What's to tell? I know we're moving from site to site. I figured we'd stay in motels or hotels as we went." Megan threw open the shirt and aimed an air-conditioning vent at herself. It was too hot for the stupid cover-up. Was she seriously going to have to shield herself like a damn nun every time she was around the oil workers?

Rowdy laughed. "Motels? Hotels?" He turned into a large lot crammed with travel trailers. "Look around, Megan. We carry our home with us for the next year. I told you I usually do this alone. I wasn't kidding. It's tight with one person. With two?" He stopped next to a silver and white trailer that couldn't possibly sleep both of them. "Well, let's just say it'll be interesting."

Rowdy stayed busy getting the paperwork straight and supervising the hitching of their home for the next year. Yes, they'd come back to base every six weeks for a break. But the grueling schedule of six weeks on, two weeks off, was something he'd lived with for the past two years. He blamed it for the deterioration of his relationship with Cassidy. No wonder she'd fallen hard for Mason MacKenzie. The guy had a good line and plenty of money, not to mention time to give her.

He watched Megan stuffing her clothes into the storage areas of the trailer, cursing under her breath at the lack of space. He figured she wouldn't last on the road. The life wore on him, and he was used to it. The long hours, isolation, and rough conditions were just part of it. His job had changed since the oil bust, and now he was charged with figuring out which wells needed to be shut down. Layoffs, termination decisions, and hard feelings were the rule, not the exception. He had to fight the urge to drown his sorrows every night at the bars that were way too common near the sites.

But he'd seen too many of the men with his job wreck their lives because of addiction and affairs with the women who hung around the camps near the rigs. He had always kept a tight rein on his self-control. How would it work with a hot woman in the trailer during those long nights and lonely rides? He couldn't imagine it.

Of course, as far as he knew Megan was a free agent, too. He needed to check into that. Because he sure as hell was. Wait a minute. It would be stupid to get involved with another Calhoun. Megan might enjoy a little sack time with him, but he would just be convenient. A way to ease some tension. Then she'd walk away, back to one of her rich boyfriends. No, he'd do well to remember he wasn't in her league.

"You can't put your things in there. We have to load the groceries. We'll be going places where we'll need to cook for ourselves." Rowdy stepped next to Megan and pulled her pile of T-shirts out of the cabinet above the microwave.

"Cook? You're kidding." She tossed the shirts on the small dinette table. "And where the hell am I supposed to sleep? I only see one bed."

"Which is mine." Rowdy grinned. The reason he'd been given this size trailer was because the bed was long enough for his six-foot-five frame. "The table pushes down and you throw a cushion on top of it. Stretch out on top. That's your bed. From seat to seat. See?" He swept her shirts off the table, reached under the table, and lowered it until it was even with the built-in seats, then rearranged the cushions. "Should be okay. There are linens in the drawer under my bed. We may have to buy a couple of extra blankets. There's air-conditioning if it gets too hot, but usually it's the opposite problem. Cold at night."

Megan eyed what Rowdy knew was a pretty comfortable double bed in the forward section of the rig.

"I'm not sharing." He grinned at her.

"And I'm not interested, even if you were." She picked up her shirts and refolded them. "This is ridiculous. I looked in the so-called bathroom. Where do we brush our teeth, wash our faces?"

"In the sink next to the stove. And you shower right there next to the toilet. You're lucky we get hot water. Let's just hope it doesn't break down. That's happened." Rowdy waved the stack of papers he'd gotten at the check-in. "You're going to earn your keep. I've decided to let you be my navigator. Can you read a map?"

"Of course." Megan left the shirts on the cushion and took the papers. "Are we leaving now?"

"Yep. We have four hundred miles to go before we get to our stop for tonight. And we've got to get out of Houston first. Let's go." Rowdy looked around. "Make sure there's nothing loose that will fly around if I make a sudden stop or turn. Put those shirts away, Megan. And that bag. Makeup?"

"Yes." She set it in the sink. "Give me a minute. And I'd like to stop for coffee before we go too much farther. I didn't have time to have any before I got here this morning."

"I'm not sure about that. Coffee, then you'll want a restroom break. We'll never make any progress like that." Rowdy shook his head. She was starting to wind up for a comeback when he took pity on her.

"Relax, Megan. I could use coffee, too. I'm not the enemy. Let's get out of town and then we'll make a stop. Okay?" He picked up her shirts and stuffed them back in the cabinet where she'd had them in the first place. "And we'll hit a grocery store, too. One in the suburbs. Better choices here than in the boonies."

"Great." Her smile made her glow, and Rowdy looked away from it. Tempting. Curvy figure and shiny blond hair that looked like she'd just run a comb through it and didn't do much else. It was an easy look. The kind he liked. Damn it. He turned when he was on the ground and automatically held out his hand to help her down. She was a little thing and had to jump out. There was a step he could pull out for her. He should have . . . Shoot.

They'd have to work on a routine when they set up camp each night. Use the step, figure out shower schedules . . . He double-checked the trailer hitch to keep from staring at the tight fit of her jeans as she headed to the passenger side of the truck. This was going to be one long year.

By the time they were settled in the cab of the truck, he had made a decision. He couldn't live with a woman like Megan Calhoun and treat her like an enemy. But he wasn't going to jump her, either. No, they'd have to work out a friendship. So he told her where they were going, showing her their destination and the best route on the map. He even let her pick the place to stop for coffee. He was going to make this work somehow. And the best way to do that was to not ever touch her. Not even by accident.

Because, damn it, he liked women. Loved everything about them, except the way they could turn him inside out when they broke his heart. So he was going to be careful here. His heart was not going to be involved, that was for damn sure. But his body . . . it was way too interested in the way Megan Calhoun smelled—so freaking sweet and clean. Just standing next to her in that trailer, brushing up against her when he'd put her shirts away, had reminded him how all woman she was. Which was wrong on so many levels he couldn't count that high. Shit. Those close quarters were going to kill him.

This was what he got for not taking advantage of those free and easy women who'd come across his path when he'd been out in the field the past few months. He'd never been into free and easy. At least not before. And what had that gotten him? A permanent hard-on and no reward for staying true to the woman he'd always thought he might eventually marry. Instead he'd been dumped on his ass.

Enough of that whining. He and Cass were done. He'd known it even before she'd told him so. Part of their problem had been his own lazy ass. They'd been comfortable together. Yeah, how was that for a revelation? He'd liked the fact that he knew where he'd be on a Friday night. And that he had a girl to go home to on his breaks from this grind of a job. He should have moved on; they both should have, a long time ago. But it was scary out there in the dating world of online profiles and fix-ups. There were so many crazies and people with baggage. Neither of them had wanted or needed that uncertainty. So he'd been blindsided when Cass had actually found "the one" first.

Rowdy pulled into a drive-through at Megan's direction. At least they both liked the same kind of coffee, though she wanted special stuff in hers and he was happy with black and strong. But it was a start. When they settled on a radio station that suited them both, Rowdy relaxed even more. Okay, maybe the year wouldn't be a total disaster. Then Megan shrieked in his ear, and he almost jackknifed the trailer.

Chapter 2

"Pull over! Stop the truck!" Megan gripped the door handle and looked like she was about to leap out onto the road.

"What the hell? Are you sick?" Rowdy put on his turn signal and looked for a spot where he could maneuver out of traffic. He glanced at her. She didn't look sick, just in a panic. Thank God, there was an abandoned gas station coming up, and he slowed enough to make the entrance. As soon as he rolled to a stop, she was out and running back along the shoulder of the road.

"Megan! You're going to get yourself killed!" Rowdy shut down the truck, pulled out the keys, then took off after her. She was hunkered down over something in the weeds, totally ignoring the traffic whizzing by at seventy to eighty miles an hour mere feet from her backside. He stayed as far away from the road as he could without falling into the ditch that ran along the highway. It was filled with water from recent rains, and he couldn't tell how deep it might be.

"Come here and help me. I can't believe someone could be so cruel." She was struggling to untie the string around a burlap bag. "Do you have a knife on you? Cut this."

Of course Rowdy had a knife in his pocket. It was a Swiss Army knife that came in handy on the road. It even had a corkscrew that he'd used . . . Never mind. He flipped it open, figuring the sooner they got off this roadside, the better. He cut the rough rope holding the bag closed. When a brown and white puppy leaped into Megan's arms, she staggered and he grabbed her.

"I'll be damned." They both had almost fallen back in front of a semi, which let them know it with a long blast of its horn. "Get back over here!" Rowdy hustled into the weeds again.

"See? I knew it." She cradled the dog against her, not minding at all that it was getting her wet and muddy. "Someone in a truck ahead of us just tossed it out the passenger side window. I saw the bag moving. Can you believe it?"

"Must be the runt of the litter." Rowdy grabbed her arm and dragged Megan and her cargo back toward their truck and trailer. "Come on. This is dangerous, and we need to talk this over."

"There's nothing to say. I saved this baby's life. I'm not letting it go." She looked mulish, no surprise there. But she flinched when another big rig almost clipped them. She hurried behind him, her sigh of relief audible when they made it back to the parking lot.

"Megan, see reason. We're on a job. What are we going to do with a puppy?" Rowdy got a good look at the thing, which squirmed in her arms, trying to get loose. It was tiny and probably a pit bull. People weren't looking with favor on the breed lately, which he thought was a shame. He'd known people who owned them and they made great family pets, kind and gentle, if they were raised right. But if some local had bred pits to sell, this one was too little and didn't have the strong jaw buyers wanted. The pup licked Megan's face, and Rowdy knew it would take more meanness than he had in him to pry that dog away from her.

Well, hell.

"Get in the truck. We'll sort this out later. We've got to get moving if we're going to get to the first site by nightfall." He opened his door. "Set the little guy down in the grass and see if he'll do his business before we take off. I won't have the cab smelling like pee."

"Right." Megan's smile lit up her face. "He needs a name." She held him up and looked at his tummy. "Yes, he is a boy." She trotted over to a patch of grass, whooping with glee when the dog went straight to a bush and peed on command. "What a good boy!"

Back on the move, Rowdy knew he was doomed. Megan had crawled between the seats and fashioned a bed from an old towel he kept back there. She was trying out names and clearly not giving a thought to the reason they were on the road in the first place.

"He's a survivor. I don't care if he is a runt." She faced the front again and took a pull on the diet soda she had left over from their fast-food lunch.

"Fasten that seat belt." How had this gotten so out of control?

Rowdy let the miles go by while she chattered about dogs and names until he'd had enough.

"Damn it, Megan, don't you realize how impractical this is? He should go to a vet. Be checked out and get his shots. Can you afford that?" Rowdy the bad guy threw that at her.

"I have no idea what that costs, but surely I can after my first paycheck. And maybe you could go in on it? Don't you like dogs?" She turned on him, squinting those big blue eyes. Like she was daring him to be a dog hater. Maybe he'd also admit he liked to kick babies and cut the tops off of pretty flowers.

"Hey, I love dogs. Had one as a kid. But now I'm on the road too much. It's not practical." Rowdy concentrated on driving. The traffic had thinned out as they'd gotten farther from the big city. The speed limit had jacked up to eighty-five out here, but he couldn't do that with the trailer behind him. So he stayed in the right lane and got passed by people who shot him the finger or honked. He ignored them, uneasy at the look of the clouds ahead. He tried the piece-of-crap radio for a weather report, but just got static. They were moving into the part of Texas that was sparsely populated and mostly desert. The area could use rain, but it would be hell driving in it.

"We'll make it practical." Megan wasn't dropping the subject. "He can be good company and maybe turn out to be a guard dog. You did say we were going to some pretty isolated places."

"We don't need a guard dog, especially one smaller than my left foot. Besides, I have a gun in the glove compartment." Rowdy knew he was talking to himself when Megan turned to look back between the seats again.

"He's so sweet, and you know he'll grow, Rowdy. Why, it's a miracle that bag landed short, in the grass instead of in the ditch. He would have drowned." She sighed and settled back, facing the front again. "You're not talking me out of this, you know."

"It is a kind of miracle that you saw him tossed out of that truck." Rowdy knew when he was beaten. "That dog's lucky to be alive."

"Lucky. That's what I'll call him. It's not very original, but easy to say and it fits." She didn't gloat exactly, but gave Rowdy a pat on the arm, as if to say *he* was a good boy.

Hell, and he hadn't even peed on a bush.

* * *

Megan knew she was pushing Rowdy with the dog thing. She was impulsive. Always had been. But this time she'd saved Lucky's life. The idea that someone could kill an innocent little thing like that made her blood boil. And a dog! She remembered the dogs she'd had growing up. Unconditional love. She could really use some of that now, and she wasn't about to let Rowdy talk her out of keeping this tiny scrap of furry affection.

Lucky would be a comfort. Because inside she was scared to death of what was ahead. She didn't have clue one about the oil business or this engineering gig. That one summer with her father was a distant memory. Instead of learning about the rigs they'd visited, she'd been busy calling her friends and looking for a way to escape from what she'd considered a punishment because she'd flunked out of college. For the second time.

Now here she was on her way to that noisy, filthy hell again. She glanced upward, hoping her father's sins hadn't kept him out of the pearly gates. *Daddy, do you really think I can cut it in the field?* No answer. She refused to look down at her feet and ask again.

All she could do was try. At least now she looked the part of Rowdy's assistant in ugly clothes. She could trail along after him and hand him a tool at the right time, but how was that really going to help save her daddy's company? That was the three-hundred-million-dollar question.

It was hard to believe that Calhoun Petroleum, the company that had given her an extravagant lifestyle her entire life, was teetering on the edge of bankruptcy. It was up to her, her sisters, and brother to do something about that. Yes, the price of oil had been the start of their troubles, but then Daddy's death had come at the worst possible time.

Maybe the company could have weathered all of that, but then they'd found out a dirty little secret. Conrad Calhoun, the man she'd always idolized, who'd come up from nothing and built a billion-dollar company, had used fraud to get the company started. No one else knew. Yet. Her sister Cass was on top of it, trying to make things right. The big question was, whether once she did, there would be anything left for any of them to inherit after this year.

Megan glanced at Rowdy. She'd picked him before the ugly details of her father's double dealing had become apparent to the family. None of the people who'd been cheated knew yet that they probably had big money coming to them. Including . . . She looked away as the barren landscape whizzed past the truck window, sifting through what she knew about Rowdy Baker. He'd managed a football scholarship to college, served in the army in Afghanistan, where he was wounded so his dreams of playing professional football came to nothing. His single mother still held down a low-paying job in the small town where he and Cassidy had grown up. How different Rowdy's life might have been if . . .

"Hey, you ever think about what you'd do if you'd been the one to inherit a boatload of money like Cassidy just did?" Megan slurped the last of her diet soda and realized she'd have to find a bathroom soon. Too bad Rowdy seemed to have the bladder of a camel.

"What's the point?" Rowdy didn't look her way, his eyes on the road.

"Oh, come on. Play the 'What If' game." He was serious about his driving. She'd thought about offering to take the wheel, but figured keeping a heavy-duty truck pulling a trailer on the road with semis blowing past them couldn't be easy.

His mouth quirked. "You mean, like what if I were cruising along alone now, enjoying my favorite CD without you here complicating my life?"

"I'll put in your favorite CD, whatever it is, and shut up if you'll play along." Tough promise. She'd gone through his music collection in its zippered case already. It was heavy with traditional country. She liked it, but a variety would be better.

He tapped a finger on the wheel. "You'd shut up? Promise?"

"At least until the next bathroom break. Deal?" She unzipped the CD case. "Pick your poison."

He named an artist, and she pulled out a disc. Great. She'd be crying in her cola when this went on. "All right. So here's the game: What if you came into a million dollars tomorrow? What would you do?" She eyed the empty landscape. At last a billboard promised clean restrooms twenty miles ahead. Thank God.

"A million? Put it in the bank and live off the interest. Should be a nice income. Quit this miserable job, that's for sure. I'm sick of traveling." He grinned. "Of course, I never had a woman with me before. Might make the trip easier. We'll see how it goes tonight. More action, less talk."

Megan's jaw dropped. Was he flirting? Ha! No way. He was pulling her chain. She knew she looked like hell—hair windblown and paw prints on her shirt. And he'd been pissed at her from the get-go. This sudden charming grin and innuendo was just to throw her off her stride. It was working.

"How it goes?" Megan raised an eyebrow.

"I'm doing all the driving, so I figure you could do the cooking, cleaning. Woman's work."

Oh, he was so going to pay for that. "It goes like this, buddy. I'm nobody's little woman. I don't cook, clean, or take care of you." She leaned toward him and gave him a poke on his bicep. "In any way." Damn, but he was ripped. Didn't matter. Megan backed off. "We're traveling companions and coworkers. That's it." She heard the dog whine and unbuckled her seat belt to reach for him. "We need a pit stop."

"Defensive, aren't you?" Rowdy nodded toward the next billboard they whizzed past. "I'm all for a stop myself. But you don't issue the orders around here, Megan. Coworkers? Not exactly. I'm your boss. Or have you forgotten that?"

Megan cuddled the dog. "You hear that, Lucky? He's our boss. Let me see. How does that work? Should I ask permission for a potty break? Get a list of my duties?" She turned to him. "Or remind Mr. Macho Pants that my family owns the company he works for?"

"Seriously? You want to play that card? On day one? Threaten to get me fired?" His big hands gripped the steering wheel.

"Forget I said it. Low blow. And I'd never follow through." Megan stared down at the dog in her lap. The truth hurt, but she blurted it out anyway. "I couldn't if I tried. Get you fired."

"Way I understand your situation, Megan Calhoun, you not only have to work this next year to earn your inheritance"—his hands finally relaxed and he smirked at her—"you have to do a satisfactory job at it."

"Yeah, yeah." Megan stroked Lucky's head. "My father wrote the strangest will." She raised her chin. "So, I'm stuck and so are you."

"I have your evaluator's number on speed dial." Rowdy started humming. "Screw up and I'll let him know it. Then we'll see who's stuck."

Megan wanted to shoot him the finger but knew that was childish. So she stared out the window, giving him the silent treatment.

"Put in that CD. I believe I've played your game."

Megan shoved it in, gritting her teeth as the music filled the cab. Damn him for being right. Messing up this year with Rowdy would be just plain stupid and could cost her everything. She took a breath and turned down the volume.

"Rowdy, seriously. You usually do this trip by yourself. Surely you get takeout or eat out every meal." That woman's work thing was not going to fly. Not in her lifetime.

"No, I cook for myself. At least at night. A lot of the food on the road is crap or fast food that packs on the pounds." He gave her an inspection. "But if you don't care . . ."

"What the hell does that mean?" Megan knew she was curvy and didn't apologize for it. They rode in silence. Obviously Rowdy knew better than to touch that question.

"I can't cook. Never needed to learn." She hated that she sounded a little pitiful when she said that.

"Would you like to know how?" Rowdy shook his head. "Calhoun Petroleum is in trouble, everyone who reads a newspaper knows that. You might end this year with a share of nothing. Knowing how to feed yourself could come in handy."

"Oh, please. Even if we have to file bankruptcy, there are enough assets for me to come out just fine." Lucky yelped, and Megan realized she was squeezing him. "Sorry, pup." She sighed. "Oh good. There's the truck stop. My bladder is about to burst." She looked down at the puppy. "And we need to find a patch of grass for this dog."

"Fine. Take care of him then lock him in." Rowdy pulled into a parking space with room for the trailer, then tossed her the keys. "See you inside." He bolted out of the truck.

"Well, Lucky, guess we aren't the only ones needing a bathroom." Megan realized she was going to have to dip into her gift card again when the dog scampered across the parking lot and she had to give chase. This was a big truck stop, part of a chain, so hopefully she'd find a collar and leash inside as well as puppy food. By the time she caught up with Lucky, she had two burly truckers interested in her and the dog. It did her ego good to have the men flirting with her. She sure wasn't charming Rowdy.

"Looks like a pit to me." A trucker named Bullseye took her elbow as she carried Lucky across the busy lot. "But he's a tiny thing."

Megan told him how she'd saved the dog from a watery grave.

"That just tears me up." A big bruiser named Leroy growled. "Sons of bitches. There's rescue groups that woulda found that pup a good home." He glanced at his big rig. "I got two goldens in my cab right now. You can't keep Lucky, I'll take that sweet little critter."

"Thanks, Leroy, but I can't let him go." Megan grinned up at the man. "You two are restoring my faith in mankind, that's for sure. I've got to go inside and get him a few things. Collar, leash, food."

"Don't let that boss of yours try to talk you out of keeping Lucky. But here's my number if you need me." Leroy handed her a business card. "I'll take the pup and make sure that man knows your value before we part ways."

"Now, hold on, Lee. I saw her first." Bullseye gave Leroy a shove. "I got a card, too." He dug in his pocket, then set a card into Megan's hand. "Honey, put up the dog, then run along inside. Leroy and I are going to get this settled. Man to man." He grinned, a gold tooth gleaming in the sunlight.

Megan looked from one to the other. Were they going to fight?

"Go along now, little gal, and keep an eye on this weather. There's storm warnings ahead." Leroy popped open the passenger door of her truck and took the dog. "Lucky will be all right. I'll watch the truck for you. I'm sure I'll be seeing you again, if you're going west." He winked when Megan nodded. Leroy then took Bullseye's arm and dragged him away but still in sight of the truck.

"What the hell was that?" Rowdy strode across the pavement.

"New friends." Megan shook her head and ran inside, straight into the women's restroom. It was sticker shock when she started shopping. Everything was ridiculously expensive. Thank goodness she and Rowdy had done their grocery shopping at a discount store while still on the outskirts of Houston. She had to settle for a sad-looking rope leash, not the leather she wanted, and generic dog food for Lucky. She complained about the prices to Rowdy.

"It's the convenience you're paying for, Megan." Rowdy started the truck and eased out of the lot, ignoring the two men who waved at Megan from beside their rigs. "Did you notice we left civilization a while ago? Now we're in the middle of nowhere. You need something, you pay the price."

"Obviously. For gas, too." She'd noticed the price at the pump was a good dime a gallon higher than it had been when they'd filled up at the edge of Houston. They'd driven several hundred miles since then.

"Transportation costs make everything out here more expensive. Just wait till you see the prices in the town where the drilling is going on. Renting a room in a house costs so much the roughnecks sleep two to a room and work long shifts just to get ahead."

"I remember visiting some of the well sites with Daddy one summer. Dirty, noisy, and dangerous." Megan sighed. She'd loved those times with her father. He'd obviously thought it was the oil business she was showing an interest in, if you could believe his will. Instead, it had been the undivided attention she'd had from her dynamic dad. She'd pretended for a while to care about drill bits and rig counts. But it had been the way Conrad had treated her, like they were pals, riding along together in a company truck, that had kept her by his side for most of the summer.

She stared out the window at the bleak landscape—desert, tumbleweeds, and a few cows looking for decent grazing. Not much to see. It was lonely, and the tune coming out of the stereo wasn't helping her mood. She missed larger-than-life Conrad Calhoun with a sharp pain in the region of her heart. Yes, she knew now that he'd had a dark side, but he'd never shown that to her.

For a while she'd shared her dad's enthusiasm for the whole thing—hunting for black gold, the excitement of bringing in a good well. But, just like it always did, her interest flagged, and she'd found herself desperate for an escape. Looking back, she honestly couldn't remember much of anything she'd learned that summer, not about oil. Now she remembered how her father had laughed when she'd been scared of a tarantula. And that he'd loved finding little local cafés and had called all the waitresses "Darlin'" while he'd left big tips that had made them gasp. The landscape blurred and she sniffed.

She also remembered Daddy's face when she'd told him she was off to Mexico to look for designer jewelry to help a pal start a little boutique. Yep, she'd left him in the lurch without a backward glance, because there'd been something new and shiny beckoning. And when that had begun to bore her, she'd gone on to the next new thing. She couldn't even remember what that had been now. God, what was wrong with her? Why couldn't she stick with anything?

"Hey, if this music is that depressing, I'll turn it off." Rowdy reached for the stereo controls, and Megan realized a tear had escaped down her cheek. Just then rain hit the truck hard, and he switched on the windshield wipers instead.

"Don't be ridiculous. Keep your music on. A deal is a deal. Leroy warned me the weather looked bad. Obviously he was right." Megan frowned as the wind howled and the rain made it almost impossible to see the road.

"Yeah. The trailer is making this tough driving." Rowdy was frowning, both hands gripping the wheel.

"You're doing good. Toss me a what-if. It'll pass the time. Take your mind off the weather." She scrubbed off the tear and snuggled Lucky against her. He shook when thunder boomed. "Surely you can think of one."

Rowdy frowned. "I'm not really into games. But, okay, let me think." That finger tapped the wheel again. "Okay, here it is. What if you could be anywhere in the world right now? Anywhere but here. Where would you be?"

Megan liked the question. It was the kind one of her friends would have tossed at her. She studied Rowdy with new respect. Maybe he had potential. So she thought about it. She'd been plenty of places. Had been fortunate that way. The rain stopped as suddenly as it had started. Weird.

"Right now?" She stared out at the desert. It had soaked up the brief rain, and you couldn't tell it had even gotten wet. The thermometer on the dashboard said it was ninety outside, though the sky was a strange dark green and that should have made it cool down. At least the air conditioner in the truck was doing its job. "I'd be next to the pool at home, one of our housekeeper's Bloody Marys in my hand and something cheerful on the stereo." She grinned at him. "You? Where would you like to be?"

"In a ditch. Shit, Megan." Rowdy pulled the truck to the side of the deserted highway and turned off the motor. "Get out of the truck. Hurry and bring the dog."

Megan gasped when she saw a huge funnel cloud dancing along the desert toward them. It was hopping up and down, pulling up shrubs and stirring up the sand into a cloud that looked to be taking up everything in its path inside it. She wrapped Lucky in his towel and flung open her door, following Rowdy as he ran away from their truck and trailer. The land was flat except for a slight dip a few dozen feet from the edge of the asphalt highway.

"Lie down here and cover your head!" he yelled over the scream of the wind as it came closer. Sand flew around them, stinging her skin everywhere it touched. Lucky wiggled frantically, trying to get free, when Megan fell into the depression next to Rowdy. She pressed her face to her forearm, the other protecting the dog. Forget about her head. The storm came closer and she was battered and scraped, sand-blasted. She shrieked when a piece of cactus hit her leg and stuck, going straight through her pants.

When Rowdy's arm came around her, she pressed her face to his chest, the dog between them. Were they going to live through this, or be picked up and taken to Oz? She fought back a hysterical giggle. Breathing was next to impossible, Rowdy's cotton shirt giving her nose only a little filter against the endless sand swirling around them.

Finally, finally there was silence. Rowdy moved first. A heavy layer of sand slid off of him before he helped Megan get up and try to stand.

"Ow!" She looked down at the spines still in her leg and backside. It hurt like a thousand knives were sticking her.

"You're bleeding." Rowdy didn't reach for the cactus. Smart move. Then they'd both be bleeding.

"What hit me?" Megan stroked Lucky with a shaking hand. If all that was hurt was her leg, she was as lucky as this little dog.

"Cactus. Don't touch it. You'll just make it worse." Rowdy pointed toward the highway. "Holy shit. Would you look at that?"

Megan turned and swayed on her feet. No, this couldn't be happening. Oz would have been a better outcome. Mother Nature had just played a cruel trick on them. The truck and trailer were scattered along the pavement like broken toys.

Lucky wiggled free and scampered over to a bush to lift his leg. As a statement, it pretty much summed things up.

Megan swayed but was afraid of falling down on the cactus. "All we need now is a rattlesnake."

Rowdy grabbed her arm when Lucky started barking. "You just had to say that, didn't you?" He nodded toward the dog. "Can you stand on your own long enough for me to get my gun?"

"Yes, go. Lucky! Come here!" Megan clenched her teeth and managed to stand on both legs. It hurt like hell, but she had to stay still and stay put. She knew about rattlesnakes. Her late uncle Buck used to come to South Texas every year for the Rattlesnake Roundup. He'd shown her his hatband and belt made of snakeskins and had even made jewelry out of the bones and rattles. The damn snake was poisonous, and her brave little dog was determined to take it on. She could hear the rattle going when Lucky paused for breath between frantic barks and growls. "Lucky!"

The dog was just like every male she'd ever encountered—stubborn as hell.

Chapter 3

Rowdy ran toward the truck, which had been pulled apart from the trailer and had landed several feet away. The truck was on its roof, the passenger door popped open. That was a great piece of luck. He crawled inside and managed to get the glove compartment open to pull out his gun. He kept it loaded and he took off the safety as he hustled back to Megan's side. The dog was still barking like it wanted to take on the rattler.

"Any developments?" Rowdy touched Megan's shoulder. She was pale and shaking but still on her feet. He could see the back of her jeans was soaked with blood. Damn it. The cactus spines had to hurt like hell.

"No, Lucky hasn't gone any closer. Just keeps barking like he's telling the snake he's a badass." She tried for a laugh and failed miserably. "As if."

"Call him again." Rowdy stepped slowly and carefully closer to the dog and snake.

"Lucky, come here, baby." Megan sounded on the verge of tears. She patted her good leg. "Come on. Leave it!" She firmed her voice. "That's what they teach in dog training. I think he's had some training, the way he sits and heels. Leave it!" To their shock, the dog actually looked at her and moved toward her.

"Are you a good shot?" Her voice trembled.

"We'll see." Rowdy steadied his aim, not surprised that he was pretty shaken up himself. Tornado. Rig in a mess. Woman bleeding next to him. But he remembered his training from the army. Aim and shoot. The snake had its mouth open, fangs ready to strike. He blasted its fucking head off.

"Good shot."

Rowdy did a fist pump, then looked back to see Megan swaying like she was going to fall over. Well, shit. He grabbed her, careful of her wound. "Steady. It's dead."

"Lucky!" She held on to Rowdy's shoulder. "Don't let him do that."

Of course the dog was on the snake's body, grabbing and shaking it now that it was no longer any danger to him. "Let him go. It's not going to hurt him. Rattlesnake meat is good eating."

Her eyes filled with tears. "Damn it, Rowdy. He, we, could have been killed."

"Yeah, well, you're right." He checked to see where the cactus spines were, then decided the only thing to do was to put her in a fireman's carry over his shoulder. "Sorry about this." He heaved her up and over.

"Hey!" She beat on his back. "Stop. What the hell?"

"You rather I put my hands under your butt? Poke those spines in harder?" He stalked over to the trailer. One look and he knew there was nothing to see there that would help much. But a cushion was within reach. He carefully set her on her feet next to the metal shell that looked like a giant had stepped on it.

"Lean on this while I pull some things out for you to lie on. Can you do that?" He figured she didn't have much choice.

She was breathing through her mouth, rapidly. "Yeah, yeah. I'm trying not to be sick. Upside down like that wasn't so great. But, hurry." She waved him off when he reached for her again. "Cushions. Lots of them. A bottle of water would be nice, too." Lucky came up to them dragging the snake carcass. "Get that away from me."

"It's a prize." Rowdy did take it away and tossed it on top of the trailer. "Here, Lucky. Dog treat." He picked up a can of Vienna sausages that had rolled out of the smashed door and popped it open, pulling one out and handing it to the dog. "Good, brave dog."

"Stupid, brave dog." Megan waved a hand in front of her nose. She sighed when Rowdy dumped a pile of cushions next to her. "Oh, thanks. Let me see if I can sit." She eased down on her good hip. "Should we pull these spines out now?" She craned her neck, trying to see the place where the cactus had bit into her.

"Later." Rowdy looked at the mess the tornado had made of their rig. He pulled his phone out of his back pocket. "Thank God I had my cell with me. The trick is to get reception." He waved it in the air. No bars.

"Lucky! Come back here!" She'd let go of the dog, and he scampered around them, sniffing everything and watering a few bushes.

"Let him go. He's the least of our worries." Rowdy looked back at the wreckage of their home on wheels. The tornado had obviously picked up the truck and camper and taken them for a wild ride. Sometime during that, the two had come unhooked. Now the RV was on its side in the middle of the highway. It was a totaled mess. The door had been ripped off and interested vultures were already circling in case there was food to be had. He did manage to get a bottle of water out of the fridge and passed it to Megan. She opened it with shaking hands.

He walked back to the truck a few yards farther down the highway. He'd noticed that Megan's purse was still safely stowed in the side pocket of that open passenger door and he grabbed it for her.

"What are we going to do? You know I can't just ignore these needles." Megan had wrapped Lucky's towel around her fist and was trying to reach part of the cactus stuck on the back of her leg.

"Hope someone comes by soon. But this debris is a road hazard. I need to hunt for flares." Rowdy knelt next to her. "Careful. I'm telling you, if you try to pull it out, you might just make it worse." There were tears in her eyes. "Hurts like hell?"

"Yeah. When I got hold of one sticker, I think I took out a chunk of my skin." She let him take the towel, hissing when he wiggled a long spine free. "You're good. That only measured an eight out of ten on my agony meter."

Rowdy patted her shoulder. "I've had a little practice. I've had my own close encounter with a cactus. The needles can have barbs on the ends. We don't want to just jerk them out. So the rest will have to wait." He jumped up when he heard a motor in the distance. "We've got company. I hope they can stop in time without hitting anything. But if they try to go around, they could run off the road and get stuck in the sand."

The truck driver slowed down with a *screech* of brakes. He blasted a warning with his horn when Rowdy ran toward him, waving his arms. The trucker had probably been going over eighty when he'd seen the mess in the middle of the road. He was clearly skilled to be able to stop before he hit any of the debris. The guy put on his emergency flashers, threw open his door, and stood on his running board with a CB radio microphone in his hand. Then he hopped out of the truck and hurried toward them.

Lucky barked, a pint-sized guard dog, ready to tear the man apart and snapping at the trucker's pants when he got close to Megan.

"Now there, Lucky, don't you remember your buddy Leroy?" The man touched the brim of his gimme cap. "Little gal, this is quite a mess here. The weather must have caught up with you." He peered down at her. "What the hell? You look like you lost a battle with a cactus."

"I'll live." Megan waved him back when he squatted down like he was going to make a stab at pulling out the needles. "I'll deal with my wounds later. What about the road? You did a good job braking so quickly."

"Thanks, it wasn't easy." Leroy got up and frowned at Rowdy. "I knew the weather was going to be bad, but this is obviously from a twister. How'd you two keep from getting hurt worse?"

"It wasn't easy. The thing came out of nowhere." Rowdy picked up an excited Lucky and thrust him into Megan's arms. "We didn't have time to do more than find a low spot and hunker down."

"Thanks for stopping, Leroy." Megan gave the trucker a strained smile.

"Didn't have a choice, Megan. 'Course I would have stopped anyway, once I saw people needed aid. It's what we do." He cast a worried glance at the wreckage. "Hell of a thing. I called for help. You'll need a couple of heavy-duty tow trucks right away. This is my regular run, so I knew who to contact." He pulled off his cap and scratched his head. "But, hate to tell ya, the nearest town's a good hour away."

"Thanks for calling." Rowdy shoved his phone in his shirt pocket.

The trucker hit his cap on his jeans, then locked eyes with Rowdy. "That thing all you carry?" At Rowdy's nod, he spit on the ground. "Cell phone's useless out here. If you're going to drive or do business in these parts, you need to have a satellite system or a CB radio. Only things that work in these isolated areas."

"You're right. Lucky for me this is the first time I've had any trouble and I've been years on this job." Yeah, Rowdy would like a freaking satellite phone, but his company was too cheap to spring for one. He glanced at Megan. Now that the beloved daughter of the late company owner was with him, he should push for that. And he would. If he could get a fucking signal to call Headquarters.

"Leroy, settle down." Megan struggled to her feet, Lucky under her chin. The trucker was instantly by her side, holding on to her elbow to steady her. "Rowdy saved my life. He saw the tornado coming and got me out of that truck and running to a safe place just in time." She pointed at their smashed vehicle. "Look. If I'd been in the cab when the tornado struck, I'd be roadkill." She pushed her hair out of her eyes. "Then we ran into a rattlesnake. Rowdy shot its head off!" She pointed to the carcass still sitting on top of the trailer, a vulture pecking at it.

"If that don't beat all." Leroy nodded at Rowdy. "You've had a rough day, sweetheart, and it ain't over yet. What say I ease you over to my rig while I see if that help is on the way? I've got the air conditioner going. It's nice and cool inside." He glanced at Rowdy. "You got flares you can get to? We need them out both directions to warn oncoming traffic."

"I was about to get them out when you drove up." Was this man issuing orders? Rowdy noticed he hadn't been included in that invitation to cool off, either. Megan had obviously made a conquest. Good for her. Too bad it was hot as hell where he was standing. And—wouldn't you know it—ants were swarming over his boots. Rowdy stomped them away, then went back to survey the RV to see what could be salvaged. He knew where the trailer flares should be, but there was no getting to them in this mess. He found some in the back of the truck, though, and went to work setting them out. Leroy helped Megan and Lucky into his truck and got on his CB again.

Back in the RV, Rowdy spotted Megan's duffel bag. It took some work to dig it out, but he managed to fill it with most of her stuff and threw it outside. His own clothes had been put away neatly in drawers that were now jammed closed or blocked. So much for being organized. He pried open one cabinet and found a trash bag, dumping cereal boxes and canned goods inside. He tossed the full bag out and hopped down beside it. He pulled his gun out of his waistband and tucked it in the garbage bag. He didn't like the solution, but he didn't want to walk around with a loaded gun, either, even though he had a permit to carry.

"Hey, Rowdy!" Megan leaned out of the cab. "That's my duffel bag. You got my stuff? Seriously?" She smiled at him.

"Yes. Don't get too happy. It will be a long time before we rest tonight. We've got to get this mess off the road and hitch a ride to the next town. Then find a place to stay." Rowdy saw his schedule blown to hell. He heard a siren and realized the highway patrol had been alerted. At least they'd make sure traffic wouldn't be a problem.

He talked to the officer who climbed out of his vehicle. Apparently the twister had damaged some of the ranch houses nearby, but no one there had been hurt. They were still finding more problems on the highway, including one fatality. Rowdy decided Megan didn't need to hear about that. Unfortunately, the resources for getting them on the road again were stretched thin in this part of the state. Rowdy walked over to Leroy's truck, pretty discouraged as the patrolman roared off, responding to an emergency call.

Megan threw open the passenger door. The blast of cold air was a welcome relief.

"Leroy says tow trucks are on the way, but it'll take them a while before the first one makes it. He's getting behind on his delivery schedule because of us. I told him to let me out and go on, but he insisted he's going to wait with us." Megan turned to say something to the trucker, then turned back. "Get in with us. It's nice and cool and I can see you're sweating."

Sweating? Rowdy had moved beyond that to soaking wet. He was so hot he felt sure you could fry an egg on his forehead. To add to his misery, sand had crept into every part of him. When he brushed a hand through his hair, more sand flew out, stinging his eyes. Sunglasses. It was too much to hope they'd survived in the truck, but he dropped the bags and went back to climb inside. Hot damn, they still sat securely in the built-in case over the rearview mirror, which was now on the floor. Rowdy slipped them on, then walked back to the big rig. He had to admit that Megan's ability to make instant connections with people had come in handy.

Of course the trucker would have had a tough time driving around the wreckage anyway. Rowdy shoved that uncharitable thought away as he climbed on board, careful not to touch Megan's injured hip. It wasn't easy since it was a tight squeeze. Lucky greeted him with a yip and a lick that just missed his chapped lips. He'd obviously made friends with the trucker's golden retrievers who were happy to have him join them in the small backseat.

"Rough luck, running into that twister. If it had been a wet one, you'd have been in real trouble." Leroy pulled a cold bottle of water from a cooler next to his feet and passed it to Rowdy. "Megan showed me where you told her to lie low. Put you smack in the middle of an arroyo. Water fills those up quick as a wink, causing flash floods in these parts. Lying like that, the three of you would have been pushed in front of the flood, tossed about like pieces of tumbleweed, and drowned for sure."

"I could tell when I saw it coming that it was kicking up dust and sand, not water." Rowdy couldn't believe he was defending himself to this guy. "I know about arroyos."

"Sure you do." Leroy got on his CB again. "Come in, Simon, what's your position?"

"About twenty minutes out. Quit nagging us, Leroy. We're pushing as hard as we can."

"Over and out." The trucker opened his door and jumped down out of the truck. "You two sit tight. I'm going to put some more flares out behind my rig and let my dogs take a leak. Doubt there will be anyone else along, now that I put the word out, but you never know." He gathered his dogs after snapping on their leashes then slammed the door.

Rowdy and Megan sat in silence, staring out the truck window at the wreckage of what was supposed to be their home away from home.

"Say something." Megan was almost in Rowdy's lap because of their close quarters.

Rowdy twisted off the cap and took a deep swallow of cold water. "I wouldn't have let you drown, Megan. Your trucker is an asshole." And with that, they both lapsed into silence.

It was dark when they finally got to Fowlerton, which was less town and more a scattering of houses that included a yard owned by the tow truck driver and the E-Z Rest Motel. It didn't take an insurance adjuster to know that both the truck and RV were a total loss.

Rowdy was on the phone to CWC Headquarters. Megan tuned him out. She knew he was getting some grief about losing his ride. The company couldn't afford any losses at this point. But they did carry insurance. She was on her stomach on the queen-sized bed, She needed a shower, but first she had to get those pieces of cactus out of her butt. Lucky kept jumping on and off the bed, every movement sending darts of pain through her. The desk clerk hadn't liked the idea of a dog in the room, but seeing a company credit card and the request for two rooms in this dusty town had made him look the other way.

"Okay, we're set. They're going to arrange for us to have a rental car. We'll drive it to Sparkle City, which is close to the well sites, and get another truck and RV. Not sure what will be available, but we'll have to 'make do'." Rowdy shook his head. "Don't like the sound of that."

"But that's not until in the morning, I hope." Megan didn't think she could go anywhere like this. She reached down and unsnapped her jeans. "Do me a favor?"

"What? You heard me arrange for a room next door." He stared as she attempted to pull down her pants. "Careful, you're just making things worse."

"Then for God's sake, help me! Pull those bastards out of me before I rip off my pants along with half my thigh!" Megan bit back a sob. How could he just stand there when she was in so much pain? And he looked like barely surviving a freaking tornado hadn't even phased him. Instead he was preoccupied with his damn schedule. If he mentioned it one more time, she was going to pick up the nearest object, which in the E-Z Rest Motel was an ancient clock radio, and cram it down his work-obsessed throat.

"Calm down and lie still. Let go of your pants and I'll see what I can do." He removed her fingers from her jeans with a surprisingly gentle hand. "Your pal Leroy left some first aid supplies before he took off. I'm going to wash my hands in antibacterial soap, then go to work on you. Can you be patient and wait for me to do that?"

Megan dropped her head back to the pillow. "Fine. Scrub up. Thoroughly. All I need is an infected ass. But speed up. It feels like a thousand bees are stinging me back there."

He chuckled, proving now *he* was the asshole. "Only about six.

But I know it hurts. You want something to take the edge off? Leroy left you a bottle of premium tequila. As a love offering."

"Crack that baby open and pass it here." Megan reached out a shaking hand. She'd love to be roaring drunk when Rowdy started digging cactus needles out of her butt and leg. When a bottle hit her palm, she leaned up enough to get it to her lips. A swig made her gasp as it burned its way down her throat.

"Holy hell, what is that?" she asked when she could talk again.

"Mexico's best. I'd say it's part of Leroy's regular run. He skirts the border and pops over there to get his supply." Rowdy sounded farther away, then she heard running water. "Take another drink. I'm ready to start."

Megan did just that with a couple of swallows that probably permanently scarred her esophagus. "Go on, get it over with."

"I've got some antibiotic salve for your wounds once these are out. Lie very still." He braced a hand on the back of her knee, holding her leg down firmly on the bed. Good thing, because when he worked the first needle free, she jerked.

"Son of a bitch!"

"I'm sure. Five to go. Keep drinking." He kept one hand firmly on her leg.

"You bet." Megan swallowed, then bit her lower lip when he pulled out another one. This went on for what seemed like centuries until he finally announced that he was done.

"I'm going to pull down your pants and look at your skin now. Put some salve on the wounds and make sure there's not any part of the cactus spines still in there." He suited action to words, not wasting time as he slid the denim, along with her panties, down to her knees. "Nice ass." He said it clinically.

"Thanks. I work out." Megan straightened the bottle, now half-empty, before it fell over onto the dirt-colored bedspread. "Well, sometimes. I like to swim." She realized he hadn't touched her yet. "You going to do something or just enjoy the view?"

"Both. Give me that damn bottle." He grabbed it and she heard him swallow. "Shit. That's strong." She heard the *clink* of glass on wood, so he must have set it down. "You got tweezers in your stuff? There are a few barbs I'm going to have to fish out of your skin."

"Oh, great. More torture." Megan closed her eyes.

"Megan? Did you pass out?" He squeezed her shoulder.

"No, unfortunately. Go ahead. Do your worst. Tweezers. In my makeup bag in my duffel." Megan didn't care if he'd also see her underwear, tampons, and birth control. Right now her head was swimming from pain and tequila. "It's the pink flowery zippered thing." She waited, hearing him cross the room and dig through her stuff.

"I see it. You really need eye shadow and mascara on a job like this?" The bed sagged when he sat beside her leg.

"A girl should always be ready for anything. Who knows? My prince may come along on an oil rig while I'm riding with you." Meg smiled into the pillow. Prince? Ha. She knew a hell of a lot of toads, but the closest she'd come to a prince had been Eli, who'd wound up marrying one of her best friends. Megan had to admire her pal's single-minded determination to get her man. Robin had been one of those girly girls who had no dreams in her head except snagging the richest bachelor in the dating pool. So, after an extravaganza wedding with a dozen bridesmaids, Robin and the prince had jetted off to Europe for an extended honeymoon. They'd come back with her old pal expecting twins.

Stupid to be jealous. Domestic bliss had never been her dream. Of course, she had never pinned down a dream at all. Damn it.

"You falling asleep there, princess? I'm almost done. Didn't realize I was so good at this. You haven't even flinched." Rowdy braced her leg again.

"Tequila haze. Works every time." Megan realized she was buzzed. "Finish this so I can pass out. And don't call me princess."

"Why not? Rich girl, slumming with the working class. You think I don't know you'll wind up with a pile of money at the end of this year no matter what I say about you?" Rowdy had lost his teasing tone.

"Hey, *I'm* not counting on it." Megan felt cold steel against her leg. "And if you don't get this over with, I'm going to . . ." No threat came to mind. Stupid tequila.

"Quit talking and brace yourself. This is the last one, but it's the worst." His grip on her bare leg tightened. "Hold still, I'm going in."

"Ow! Ow! Motherfucker! Stop torturing me!" Megan arched her back, her head up. "What the hell are you doing? Drilling for oil?

Digging a tunnel? Let me go!" She reached, hoping to grab his hair and pull it out of his head. She missed and flopped back on the pillow.

"Got it." He held the tweezers in front of her face, and Megan could see a nasty bit of cactus barb, shiny with her own blood, in the grip of them.

"Oh, I think I'm going to be sick." She fought the wave of nausea and lost just as a blue plastic trash can was shoved under her face. She heaved until she had nothing left in her stomach. Lucky had watched all of this from the floor, clearly upset by all the yelling and noise. When she finally collapsed back on her pillow, the dog nosed her hand where it dangled limply off the edge of the bed.

"Well, that was disgusting." Megan gladly took the wet washcloth Rowdy handed her and wiped her face. "Am I still bleeding?"

"A little. I'm going to cover these wounds with the salve, then slap a bandage over the whole thing. Can you skip a shower until in the morning?"

"I couldn't stand long enough right now to do it anyway." Megan patted the dog, trying to ignore Rowdy's skillful fingers running up and over her thigh. Had she really been stuck *there*? Didn't matter. His touch was unexpectedly soothing and she let it happen.

"Okay, applying some of these really big Band-Aids now. I should run out and get us something to eat and more first aid supplies." He stood and loomed over her.

Megan tried to roll over but gave up when it took too much effort. Instead she lifted her head enough to look at him. "No food for me. Just a cold drink. A Coke with lots of ice. Take the dog with you. Please? I just want to lie here. Undisturbed." She wasn't altogether sure she wasn't going to hurl again and didn't want an audience.

"Whatever you want." Rowdy took the trash can out of the room and she heard running water again. He came back and set it close beside the bed.

He stood there for a minute. "You were brave. Most women . . . Well, you didn't cry."

"No, my go-to is cursing a blue streak. Our housekeeper says I have a potty mouth. No apologies for that." Megan had to point that out.

"I would have done the same." He reached down and brushed her hair out of her eyes. "Rest up. If you want that shower, I'll help you when I get back."

Megan heard him talking to Lucky as he snapped on his pitiful rope leash, then left the room, the door clicking closed behind him. He'd help her with that shower? The thought should not, absolutely should not, make her feel warm in all the wrong places. Her stomach rumbled and she closed her eyes, willing the nausea away. Tequila. It had never been good to her. But she couldn't blame the tequila for the mental picture she was drawing in her head of Rowdy stripping her down and standing her in the shower stall. Then she'd lose her balance and he'd have to come in to help her stay upright. Oh yeah. The water would be warm, he'd be hot, and there would be a lot of touching, getting all the sand out of the places where it still made her itch like crazy.

Restless, Megan forgot that her right hip was on fire and rolled over. She screamed when she landed wrong. Shit. She settled on her stomach again but that was a mistake, too. The room swirled and her gut jerked. Trash can.

Oh God. Had she ever been so miserable before? Yeah, once. At that bitch Robin's reception. Megan had been forced to wear a strapless lime-green taffeta number that had made her look like a bowl of guacamole. Then she'd made a speech as maid of honor, toasting the happy couple. That night daiquiris had dulled her pain. Damn and double damn. When would she learn? Alcohol might work temporarily, but the payback was so not worth it.

Chapter 4

The loudest country song she'd ever heard jerked Megan out of bed. She'd been sleeping hard. She looked around the room. What the hell? She was alone. Oh yeah. She must have conked out after Rowdy left to get food and slept straight through until . . . five thirty in the morning? What an ungodly hour. She smacked the radio silent and fell back on her pillow.

A quiet knock on the door was her only warning before she heard an old-fashioned key turn in the lock. Rowdy peeked inside, bringing with him an exuberant Lucky and the smell of coffee.

"Time to get up." Rowdy had the nerve to look wide awake and freshly groomed.

Megan just stared at him while Lucky bounced around the side of the bed, trying to get to her.

"Coffee?" He stayed well back. "Or is your stomach still upset?" He glanced at the trash can next to the bed and shook his head. "That's not a good sign." He set the Styrofoam cup on the dresser across the room and picked up the can. "I'll just wash this out."

"Thanks," Megan managed to say when she really wanted to dive under the covers again. Her head hurt, along with her hip, and a squirming, happy-to-see-her puppy who finally managed to get up on the bed and throw himself on her uneasy stomach just made everything worse.

"Lucky, get down." She gave up and patted him. "I stink."

"Yes, you kind of do." Rowdy set the clean can beside the bed again. "I'd like to get an early start. That's why I set the alarm. If you feel like it, hit the shower and change clothes. What do you say? Then we can go get some breakfast." He smiled, unaware that she really, really wanted to throw that clock radio at his head. "Nice little diner attached to the motel. Homemade biscuits, the waitress said."

Megan's stomach rumbled. "Give me a minute." She crawled out of bed, noticing that she'd lost the jeans and wore only her panties and T-shirt. Whatever. He'd seen her butt. And she wasn't eager to put anything heavier than nylon over it just yet anyway.

"You going to make it? Need help in the shower?" He said it matter-of-factly.

Megan stopped feeling her way to the bathroom and held on to the door frame.

"Seriously? You offering to hose me off?" Megan stared at him over her shoulder. He didn't look excited by the prospect. Which was a good thing.

"It would be better than riding with you for a hundred miles like you are." He stayed well back. "Hate to hurt your feelings, but you have sand in your hair and I can smell vomit from here."

"Yeah, I see how much you hated to say that." Megan knew she was a mess. At least he'd stopped short of saying she was disgusting. "I'll manage. Where'd you get clean clothes? Last I knew you were stuck with what you had on you."

"Tow truck driver helped me pry open our RV. I salvaged what I could of my stuff. Now that heap is on its way to a junkyard." He settled in the room's single chair. "I'll wait here. You can't go back to bed, Megan. We're way behind schedule. Got to get moving."

"Yes, sir." She gave him a mock salute, then slammed the bathroom door before leaning against it. It took a lot out of her, but she did manage to get showered, using the generic products provided by the motel to wash her hair. The jumbo Band-Aids on her hip actually survived the water. When she turned off the shower, Megan realized she hadn't brought clean clothes in with her. Obviously her brain wasn't firing on all cylinders yet. She was just about to risk stepping out in nothing but a flimsy towel when there was a *thump* on the door.

"Megan! I put some clothes on the bed. Lucky and I are going for a walk. We'll meet you in the diner. It's at the end of the sidewalk. You have ten minutes or I'm coming in after you." Rowdy gave the bathroom door one more brisk knock before she heard him leave the room.

"Ten minutes?" Megan wiped off the steamed-up mirror over the sink and stared at her reflection. An hour wouldn't make her look any better. He'd left her toothbrush and toothpaste next to her makeup bag on the bathroom counter. The unexpected kindness brought tears to her eyes, which she quickly blinked back. Kindness? No, he was in a freaking hurry. So she slapped on minimum makeup, slicked back her wet hair and clipped it, then threw open the door and saw a pair of loose yoga pants on the bed. Thank God. Those she could tolerate over her throbbing wounds.

Then she noticed the underwear. If that wasn't a typical guy thing. Rowdy had found a pair of black thong bikini panties and a matching push-up bra. For a car ride? Megan threw the bra back into the duffel and pulled out a sports bra. A big T-shirt that showed absolutely none of her figure went over it. The thong, at least, was great because it didn't press against her sore hip.

She stuffed her feet into flip-flops and threw all her stuff back into her duffel, glad to find a plastic laundry bag in the closet for her sandy clothes and shoes. With that bag over her shoulder, she did a room check, then headed out the door and down the sidewalk. A glance at her watch showed she had hit the ten-minute mark on the dot as she limped into the diner. What should have delicious smells hit her as soon as she opened the door. Too bad they were making her stomach twitch instead of making her mouth water. She spotted Rowdy at a corner table. When he saw her, he jumped up to grab her duffel and the laundry bag.

"I'll put these in the car. Lucky's out there with the windows down. The morning breeze is cool enough that he's okay." Rowdy looked her over. "Feel better?"

"Not sure. Maybe almost human. What's all this?" Megan saw the table loaded with food—bacon, eggs, pancakes, and those famous biscuits, along with a bowl of gravy. Oh God, the smell. She was relieved to see a glass of water among the clutter and grabbed it. A long swallow helped.

"I ordered us both a big breakfast. Eat what you can. We have a long drive ahead of us, and I'm not stopping for anything." With that Rowdy stalked to the door.

"Dictator." Megan sipped more water. She bet he'd stop if she puked all over the front seat of the rental car.

"Coffee, hon?" A waitress with a pot in her hand stopped at the table. "Nice-looking man. Is he single?"

"Yeah, but he's a tyrant and my boss." Megan gingerly sat in a chair, very careful of her hip. "Coffee, lots of cream and artificial sweetener."

"You got it." She filled a cup in front of Megan and gestured to a pitcher and container of sweeteners on the table. "You should see my boss. Five feet tall and three hundred pounds. Voice like a hog caller. Which he is when he competes at the state fair." She laughed and glanced toward the door again. "I'd be tapping that if *my* boss filled out a pair of jeans like yours does."

"It would complicate things." Megan stirred cream into her coffee. "But he does do his jeans proud." She frowned. "He doesn't like me, though."

"Honey, you can do something about that." She glanced at Megan's outfit. "Show him the goods. What man doesn't like that? I'd wear a shirt about three sizes smaller if I was you. V-neck. And a smile." She winked as Rowdy came back through the door. "Know what I mean? Might make your job go smoother."

"Not sure it would be worth it." Megan added sweetener and stirred some more. But she had to admit she was attracted to Rowdy, physically anyway. Big man, football player shoulders. She'd always liked the type. And he'd been decent when he wasn't focused on his time management. The spoiled rich kids she'd grown up with acted entitled. The men were the worst. They expected women to fall at their feet, or somewhere a little south of their belt buckles. She'd grown tired of their games a long time ago.

Rowdy had the tough, self-made quality like her daddy had worn proudly. It made a man sometimes difficult but always interesting. A challenge. She realized she was smiling before she looked down at her loaded plate.

"You'd better eat. I'm warning you. I want to leave here in fifteen minutes." Rowdy drizzled maple syrup on his stack of pancakes, then cut a wedge out of them.

"You and your time limits." Megan picked up a piece of bacon and took a careful bite, not sure it would stay down. "I'll be ready, but don't make it so hard. You start putting an egg timer on everything I do and I don't think I'll be able to handle it." She sipped her coffee. "It's just not in my nature to be ordered around like I'm in boot camp."

"You need to get over your 'nature,' Megan." Rowdy frowned as he picked up a biscuit. "I'm pretty sure your father set up these strange tests in his will because he wanted his kids to learn something this year." He frowned. "But . . . when did he make his will?"

"Why?" Megan set down her cup. There was something in his tone that made her worry.

"It must not have been recent. Because this job has changed since the price of oil started going down." Rowdy stuffed another huge bite into his mouth.

"I guess he made the will a year or so ago. I know that's when his heart trouble started." She sighed. She and her father had been close, even after she'd made it obvious that the oil business wasn't exactly in her wheelhouse. She'd realized Daddy was slowing down and looking tired, not like himself. She'd blamed it on Alexandra, Daddy's third wife, and their marriage falling apart. Alex had been a bitch on wheels and made the divorce messy, even with a prenup in the equation. Daddy had moved back into the house with his kids. They'd been happy to have him. But he hadn't looked well.

"That was when the price of oil was still high. So, putting you out in the field was no big deal. Now . . . This job is about shutting down wells. More than half of them are already idle. It causes problems. We're announcing layoffs and letting the royalty owners know the money is no longer going to be coming in." Rowdy signaled for more coffee. "Tension will be high where we're going. Seems like all I do these days is bring bad news. You have no idea what we might run into. That's why I carry a gun. It's no place for a spoiled rich girl, Megan."

The waitress filling his coffee cup gave Megan a wink before she walked away.

"Excuse me? You don't know me. You have no idea whether I'm spoiled or not." Megan waved her fork at him. "I can shoot. Buy me a gun. I'll watch your back."

"That's all I need. You think I want you armed and possibly dangerous?" He picked up his biscuit.

Megan could almost see him thinking: She couldn't handle a little trouble, because she was pampered and entitled. Damn it. This was one of her hot buttons. People took a look at her "profile" and pegged her. Father a billionaire and her mother . . . Well, she really didn't want to be classed with her mother who was batshit crazy and still in a mental health facility that the family euphemistically called "rehab." If only what was wrong with Missy Calhoun could be fixed with a twelve-step program. Her mother had problems distinguishing right from wrong. She'd recently gone too far doing what she thought was right for her kids. Mom was lucky she wasn't locked up in a prison instead of a cushy hospital.

If he'd heard how her mother had gone on a rampage with her own gun and almost killed someone, he'd never trust Megan with a weapon. Especially since that someone was Cassidy.

I'm not my mother. But she didn't say it out loud. Because inside she was terrified she might be someday. Megan took a steadying breath when tears suddenly threatened. Her stupid, crazy mother. She should have quit loving her a long time ago, but Megan was a little too much like Missy—acting, then trying to talk her way out of the mess she'd made. Megan stabbed at her eggs, aware of Rowdy's thoughtful gaze on her. He probably saw her blink back those tears.

"I'm not dangerous. You have no reason to think I would be." She ground that out, then forced herself to take a bite of the eggs. It almost gagged her.

"You're right. All I know is what I see—a woman from a family that owns the company I work for. You think I don't know how much money Calhoun makes even in distressed times?" He stabbed his fork into his pancakes until he hit the plate with a *screech*. He dropped the fork and picked up his coffee cup. "I've had to work my ass off for everything I've ever gotten—school, job, car, all the things that you've had handed to you your entire life." Rowdy leaned across the table, his cup poised like a porcelain Frisbee he'd like to cram down her throat. "You going to deny that?"

"No, you're right. My dad paid for all of those things. I never had to worry about getting a car. Even wrecked the first two he bought me and a new one magically appeared the next day. In my favorite color." Megan was a little ashamed to admit that. "Clearly we're very different, Rowdy. I can't change where I came from any more than you can. But that doesn't mean we can't work together. We have to, whether we like it or not. Now, shut up so I can eat. I'm suddenly

starving, and my asshole boss says my time is running out." She
stuffed more eggs into her mouth. Too much, too soon. So she slowed
down, chewed, and finally managed to swallow.

Rowdy gave her a narrow-eyed stare but kept eating. Finally he
lifted his hand and signaled for the check.

"You through?" He glanced at Megan's plate. She'd put down
her fork.

"Yeah. I'm going to the bathroom." She got up, still nauseated,
and barely made it back there before her breakfast came up. Oh, the
misery. There was a knock on the door.

"Honey, you okay?" The waitress pushed into the two-stall room.

"Sick. Drank too much last night." Megan came out of the stall
to rinse out her mouth at the sink.

"I thought you looked a little green when you came in here almost
at a run." She wet a paper towel and handed it to her. "I made you a
Coke to go. Take it with you to sip in the car. It'll help settle your
stomach."

"Thanks, I appreciate that." Megan took a steadying breath. Day
two. How the hell was she going to survive a year of this?

Rowdy finished walking Lucky, then stuck him in the backseat
of the car just as Megan finally emerged from the diner. Her face
was pale and she limped, favoring her hip. He actually felt sorry for
her. But when he tried to take her elbow, she jerked away from him
and got in by herself.

"I can make it. Wouldn't want to slow you down." She set a drink
in the cup holder between the seats, fussing when Lucky almost
stepped in it trying to get to her. "Watch it, pup. I need this drink."

"And in about thirty minutes you'll be hollering for a bathroom."
Rowdy pointed that out as he slid behind the wheel.

"Well, by then the cup will be empty." She smirked at him. "I can
pee in it and you won't even have to slow down."

Rowdy ignored the jab and started the car. "That won't be necessary. We're only ninety miles from where we'll pick up our new rig.
Hopefully you can hold it until then." He knew he'd been hard on
her. But, hell, she was a pampered princess. Wrecking cars and
rewarded for that by getting a new one? More than once? He shook
his head as he pulled out of the parking lot. Megan had no idea what

it was like to really struggle for every dime. He reached for the radio but hesitated when he saw her rub her forehead. Hangover. No, they'd travel in silence. She buried her nose in Lucky's fur.

"You gave him a bath." She glanced over at Rowdy. "He's tan, not brown like I thought he was."

"Yeah, he showered with me. Had to get the sand and dirt off him." Rowdy got them on the highway and set the cruise control. The rental car was easy to drive, and they'd make good time. "He took the bath pretty well."

Megan smiled and settled the dog in her lap. "He certainly looks and smells better. Thanks."

"I did it for me, too. Didn't want to travel in close quarters with a stinking mutt." Rowdy leaned back, glad there wasn't much traffic this early. "So, why do you think your father gave you this particular job to prove yourself?"

She wrinkled her nose. "He wanted one of his kids to take over Calhoun Petroleum one day. But he could never get any of us to even work in the office." She sighed. "Oh, I spent a summer vacation with him once, touring some well sites, but couldn't imagine making a career of it. When a chance to do something else came along, I jumped on it."

Rowdy waited her out, figuring there was more to the story. She glanced at him.

She stroked Lucky's fur. "I guess Daddy was desperate when he made that will. He knew he was dying. Heart trouble. And none of us had ever worked seriously at anything. Except for Cassidy, of course. And none of us knew about her before that day we heard the will read." She turned to face him. "She seems like a hard worker. Daddy obviously felt bad that he wasn't able to acknowledge her while he was alive."

"If he had, her life would have been a hell of a lot different." Rowdy knew he'd never have ended up spending so many years dating Cassidy Calhoun. He would have figured she was as beyond his reach as this woman sitting a few feet away from him right now. But Conrad Calhoun had abided by a divorce decree that had terminated his parental rights and forbid him from contacting his first child. So Cass had been raised like Rowdy, in a tiny town with a single mother and a no-frills lifestyle.

But she was one of the oil-rich Calhouns now, thanks to her father's will. He didn't doubt she'd successfully fulfill her year working at the job her father had picked for her. About five minutes after that will was read, Cass had found a man who also belonged in a rich man's world. Damn, but it still stung that she'd found it so easy to move on from her high school sweetheart.

"You're looking awfully solemn over there. Still brooding about Cass? They haven't set a wedding date yet." Megan must have been reading his mind.

"She can marry anyone she wants. I just hope the guy's good enough for her." Rowdy realized he was holding the steering wheel way too tight and eased off. "You know him. What do you think?"

"Mason MacKenzie is a good guy. I grew up with him. And he's crazy in love with Cass. If you're worried about him breaking her heart, don't." Megan patted his hand. "He'll treat her right. You can safely move on."

"Thanks for the permission." Rowdy wanted to grind his teeth. He didn't know how to feel. Relieved? Mad? Hurt? "Look, Cass and I loved each other. It'll take me a while to figure out where to go from there." Oh shit. He *was* hurt. That his lady had moved on so fast and never looked back. Had his voice betrayed him? Megan's hand still rested on his. "I'm fine. Need to get laid, I guess." He forced himself to give her a wolfish smile. "What do you think?"

That got her hand back where it belonged quickly enough. And the pity out of her bright blue eyes.

"I think I have no interest in being your rebound, if that's what that look means." She gently shoved Lucky into the backseat again. "You need to get your rocks off, check around the rigs where we're going. You may have to pay for it, but at least you'll get your problem handled."

"Women around the rigs? Yeah, there are plenty of them who are ready and willing. Not necessarily whores. Some of them live in the small towns that the oil boom changed." Rowdy shuddered. "It's a damn shame, but those gals can get desperate to move out of the middle of nowhere and they see the roughnecks as their ticket to ride."

"You're kidding." Megan shook her head. "I'd never depend on a man to take care of me."

"You've never had to, if we don't count your father." Rowdy tapped the radio on but all he got was static. Yeah, middle of nowhere. He turned it off again. "Sometimes that's all a woman can see as her future. And the rigs pay good money."

"Can't women work on them, too?" Now she had the light of a defender of women's rights shining in her eyes.

"It's hard physical labor. I'm sure there are some who could handle it, but it really is a man's world. You'll see." He realized they were coming into a small town, speed trap, and he slowed down. "I wouldn't sleep with any of the women hanging around the rigs. That's the bottom line."

"So I guess you're stuck with your frustration, Rowdy." She smiled like she was happy to watch him suffer.

He kept his eyes on the road but couldn't help remembering Megan's really fine ass when he'd been working on her cactus wounds. "Guess it wouldn't be a good idea for you and me to hook up anyway. You'd fall in love with me, and I'm sure not going to get seriously involved with a woman in the foreseeable future. Certainly not a Calhoun."

"*I'd* fall in love?" She angled to face him, wincing when she must have hit her sore hip. "You think I couldn't just have an affair with you and not become emotionally involved?"

"Women aren't like men, Megan." Rowdy laughed. "I've learned that much in thirty-two years. You would never be able just to relieve a little tension at the end of a long day and then let it go. You'd get all caught up in 'feelings.' Try to make it into a relationship. Admit it."

"I'll admit no such thing. You want to have a no-strings affair? I wouldn't mind it. I was dreading a year with nothing going on but this job looking at oil rigs. Even worse, pretending I knew what the hell I was doing. A fling with you would certainly add spice to things." She said it like she was discussing what to have for lunch.

Rowdy glanced at her, sure she was joking. "Not interested. I told you. It would be complicated. I'm your boss. Next thing I know, you'll be yelling sexual harassment."

"Get real. I guess someone could make a case for it—you boss, me underling." She reached down and unclipped her seat belt. "But I'm a Calhoun. A lawsuit against a worker for my company hurts me, too. Not going to happen." She squared off to face him, a look on her face that made him uneasy.

"What the hell are you doing? That's not safe." Rowdy had left the small town and was going eighty-five again, the speed limit. He always wore his seat belt—and not just because it was the law. Megan had a light in her eyes that spoke of challenge and mischief. All this talk of an affair and no strings was just that—talk. He wasn't buying it for an instant.

"Showing you the goods." She pulled off her loose T-shirt and tossed it over her seat. It landed on Lucky, who barked and tugged at it, clearly thinking this was a game.

"I've seen the goods. Not interested." He tore his gaze back to the road. At least she wasn't wearing that lacy black bra he'd picked out. He'd done it as a joke. Had she put on the thong anyway? No, he wasn't going there. He couldn't keep from glancing over again, though. Shit. She had on one of those stretchy bras. The kind women wore to the gym where he worked out when he was in town. A sports bra. It covered more but was almost as bad as the black lace. Because it clung. The bright pink clearly outlined the sharp points of her nipples straining against the knit. Yeah, it was cold in here, because he kept the air-conditioning on high. He reached to throttle it back.

"Watch the road, Rowdy." She mocked him after there was the telltale bumping sound that meant he'd wandered too close to the edge of the highway. "Thought you weren't interested."

"Put your shirt back on." He didn't need to look again to know she had generous breasts that were high and firm. Her stomach tapered down to where those loose pants hung low. He'd noticed the edge of a colorful tattoo above the string that tied those pants. Red, white, and blue. Not the stars and stripes but the Lone Star. He didn't figure her for a flag-waving type. He swallowed, his imagination waving a flag of its own. "Cover up."

"Can't. Lucky's sitting on my shirt." She reached forward and adjusted the AC vent so it was aimed at him instead of at her. "You're flushed. Feeling the heat?"

"Yeah. It's hot outside." He was relieved to see a sign for the town where they'd pick up their truck and RV. "Fifteen miles to our stop. Quit showing off, Megan. I'm not having sex with you."

"That's a relief." She reached over and ran a fingertip down his arm to where he gripped the steering wheel so tight it was a wonder he didn't crack the plastic. "Because, while I can have a simple affair, I'm pretty sure you'd get all tangled up in those 'feelings' you're so worried about. Your history with my sister suggests you like relationships." She leaned closer, her womanly smell pushed at Rowdy by that damn air conditioner.

"Stop it. You trying to make me run us off the road? My history is none of your damn business. You and me? I'm pretty sure I wouldn't be the one who would make a big deal out of it." He wanted to slap her hand away.

"Please. This isn't my first rodeo, Rowdy. I love 'em and leave 'em all the time." She sighed and sat back. "I told you, I have a short attention span. With jobs, men, you name it. A month, two at the most, and I'm always ready to move on."

Damn him, Rowdy couldn't keep from watching her chest rise and fall as she took another deep breath. "I don't live that way. I was with Cassidy for over a decade." Almost two, but he wasn't going to admit that. It made him sound like he'd never . . . Well, shit. What did he care what this woman thought?

"That's nice." She laughed softly. "Forget I mentioned it. I'm used to men who've been around. Clearly you would have no idea how to please me." She patted his knee, then sat back, a sassy smile on her face. "Come on, boss. Admit it. You hate me. Hate everything about me. The last thing you want to do is to fuck me."

"Son of a—" Rowdy jerked the steering wheel and jammed his foot on the brakes. The rental car wasn't going to like it, but it managed a squealing stop, rocking in place on the gravel shoulder. He unclipped his seat belt and turned to her, dragging Megan into his arms.

"Maybe it's the last thing I want to do, but damn it, right now it's all I can think about." He kissed her with an open mouth and all the hunger she'd been deliberately stirring in him.

Chapter 5

Megan kissed Rowdy back. He'd started it, but she wanted to finish it. He seemed angry, because she'd goaded him. Well, she'd give him something to think about. But then the way his mouth moved over hers became more than she'd bargained for, and she lost the point she'd been trying to make. *Mistake.* She finally shoved him away from her.

"What the hell was that?" Megan sat back. Of course she knew the answer. She should feel satisfied. He'd lost control. Hadn't that been her goal? Stupid. Since when were high school games part of her jam?

"Shut up, Megan." Rowdy clipped his seat belt and put the car in gear. A car hauler blasted its horn, warning him to watch what he was doing. "Now see what you did. I almost got us killed." He looked both ways, then carefully eased them onto the highway.

"What *I* did." Megan fastened her own seat belt. "Yeah. Bad Megan. Taunting you until you couldn't help yourself." She grinned. "I'm not sleeping with you."

"And *I'm* not sleeping with you. Worst idea ever." He kept his eyes on the road. "Grab your shirt and put it on. We've got to deal with the people in town about the car and RV. You need to look more presentable."

"Yeah, right. *That's* the reason you want me covered up. Not that I'm a distraction or anything." Megan stretched her arm between the seats and managed to snag her shirt. After a brief tug-of-war with Lucky, she got it and wiggled back into it. She was *not* going to think about that kiss, even though the cotton shirt brushing past her sensitive nipples made her sigh. And then there was the way she still tasted him—coffee and maple syrup mixed with warm male who knew his way around a kiss. Oh damn, but this seat was uncomfortable.

A billboard whizzed past on the right side of the road. Gas station ahead. Business. Good idea. "Tell me more about these issues we'll be dealing with at the rigs. We have to close more wells?"

"Afraid so." He looked as relieved as she felt at the subject change. Then he frowned. "We'll be announcing layoffs. Towns like the one we're coming into are being hurt by this shutdown. The oil money meant a lot to them and most of it has already dried up. Going back to the way they were before the boom can be painful. I've seen it happening around the state, and it's not pretty." Rowdy slowed the truck. "Speed trap. We're almost there."

"Do we have to shut them down? The price of oil has been climbing lately." Megan had downloaded an app before she'd left home that let her check the figures on her phone. "I know it's not back to where it once was, but the price of crude isn't at rock bottom anymore."

"This isn't our call, Megan. I've got orders. We're shutting down three wells. We stay until they're contained. Then we go on to the next site." Rowdy dug between the seats. "Look at this. It's all right there."

Megan opened the folder, but it might as well have been written in Chinese. She had so much to learn it was overwhelming. She closed it and stuck it between the seats again. "I'll study it later, when you can go over it with me. Just tell me what I'm supposed to do. You said you're usually by yourself when you handle this job, so I guess I'll just be in the way."

"Exactly." He glanced at her. "So stand around, watch, and make sure no one knows you're a Calhoun. The laid-off workers find out you're part of that family, you'll be on their shit list."

"I get it. I don't want the credit or the blame for anything we do here." Megan swallowed, thinking about all the bad news they'd be delivering. It was easy to say it was just a business decision, but people's *lives* were going to be affected.

"Trust me. It would be all blame." Rowdy nodded at a sign advertising a used car lot as they crossed the city limits. "That's where we'll be picking up a rental truck and RV. Not sure what they have available, but at least this town is bigger than the one where we spent the night. They had nothing right for us there." Rowdy slowed to a crawl when they hit a thirty-mile-per-hour zone. "If you ever take the truck, keep in mind these little towns are notorious for ticketing outsiders."

"Got it." Megan had been through plenty of small Texas towns in her life, and this one looked pretty typical. They passed some fast-food restaurants, then came to an old-fashioned square with a charming vintage courthouse in the middle of it. The big stone building had been lovingly restored, and there was an antique store and café facing it. She also saw a few vacant shops with their windows boarded over. Seemed like hard times had already hit here. Too bad.

"You told me we might face problems when you announce the layoffs. I bet tempers are short when you bring the bad news." She turned to face him again.

Rowdy stopped at the single red light. He rubbed his jaw and finally looked at her. "Yes, it's hard. The roughnecks are cut loose without much notice, and finding another job in this economy will be tough. The superintendent will be given severance, and we usually can transfer him to another job. Not so sure about that this time."

"How hard? You ever have anyone come after you?" Megan jumped when a horn honked. "Uh, green light."

Rowdy hit the gas. "It's just a lot of tough talk. Once I remind them I can fire any one of them for cause so that they'll lose their unemployment benefits, things settle down pretty quick."

"That's good. Unemployment. Is that a decent amount?" Megan sympathized with these unknown workers. She was beginning to see what it was like to need money and not have it. But she realized she'd never been desperate for a paycheck. Even now she could ask any one of a number of people for cash and they'd give it to her, no questions asked. Of course, she'd have to be awfully hard up before she'd go begging to her rich friends. She could imagine how they'd laugh behind her back.

"Unemployment?" Rowdy shook his head. "It's a fraction of what they're used to making. So tempers flare when I bring the bad news. The roughnecks know it won't cover the payments on their fancy-ass trucks and their other bills, too." Rowdy glanced at the glove compartment. "It hasn't happened yet, but I do like to be ready for trouble. That's one reason I carry a gun, Megan." He grinned. "And to protect myself from the occasional rattlesnake."

"Don't remind me." Megan shuddered. "What if the other man had a gun, too?" She popped open the glove compartment. Yes, he'd put it in there. Like she'd told Rowdy, she knew how to use a pistol and a rifle. She checked to see if this one was still loaded. It was.

"This is Texas. The other guy usually *is* armed. But we're not about to get into a gunfight, Megan. I'd call the cops if I thought a hothead was about to get that crazy." Rowdy shook his head. "Put that damn thing away."

"Maybe you should carry it. Won't do you any good in a glove compartment."

"Don't be ridiculous. I have the power of the company behind me. Tempers burn hot but cool down fast when I threaten jail time and no benefits at all." He glanced at his phone. "The rental place with our RV and truck should be right up here."

"Thanks for scaring me half to death. We'll be in isolated places. It took a long time for the police to respond after that tornado, re-member? We were lucky it was Leroy, a nice guy, who stopped. We were on a highway that heads to the Mexican border. It could have been a drug runner who'd found us stranded on the side of the road, you know. Maybe I should have a gun, too." Megan jumped when he stepped on the brake so hard the car bounced on its shocks.

"Put a gun in your hands? No way in hell." He glared at her. "I know you claim that you know how to use one, but what does that even mean?"

"I'm an excellent shot. My daddy taught me and Mason when we were old enough to hold a gun." Mention of Mason MacKenzie didn't help her case. "I'm sure there's a place in this town that will sell me a pistol. Put it on the company card, Rowdy. Necessary busi-ness expense. I can call my sister and clear it."

"Don't get your sister involved in this." He used his car key to lock the glove compartment. "One gun is enough. Drop the subject."

"Then drive. What are you waiting for?" Megan was sick of not having money. Damn it, being poor didn't agree with her. She needed cash or to get hold of that company card. She eyed Rowdy's fat leather wallet that he'd tossed on the console when he'd gotten into the driver's seat. Typical male. He didn't like to sit on it for any length of time. "Well?"

"We're here." He nodded and she saw they were sitting in front of a car lot.

"You could have said so." She jumped out of the car and snagged Lucky's leash when he tried to take off. "Oh no, you don't." She led him to a bush and watched him take care of business. "How far to the first well?" Maybe she could take the truck later and come back to town. Do a little shopping of her own. She could claim she needed "feminine products." That should kill Rowdy's interest in coming along. She did have a little left on her gift card. Was it enough? She'd never bought a gun before.

"Not far. We're going to a ranch about twenty miles from here. At the Rocking S spread. We have orders to shut down three wells, then we'll move on to another section of the ranch to turn the spigot on another five." Rowdy waved at a man who'd walked out of a tin building on the car lot. "My company called about some rentals. CWC Industries?"

"Sure. Got 'em out back. Did I hear you say you're shutting down more wells?" The man spit on the ground. "On the Rocking S this time?"

"Afraid so. Rowdy Baker." Rowdy held out his hand, but the man ignored it. "It's a job. Not my decision."

"Hell of a job." The man shook his head. "Follow me. Rig's out back." He looked at Meg. "This for the two of you? And the dog?"

"Yes." Meg stepped up. "Is that a problem?"

The man laughed. "Not for me. Just thinkin' it'll be tight. Of course, maybe you two won't mind that." He walked on, winding his way through dusty cars and trucks in the gravel lot to a tree-shaded yard behind his office. "This is all I had when I got the call. Heard you had a close encounter with a twister."

"Yes. We're lucky to be alive." Megan stopped in her tracks. "This is what you expect us to take?" The silver trailer was a throwback to the sixties. If it had been refurbished, it could have been cute in a retro way. Instead, it was dented, rusty, and way too small. "Tight squeeze is right. And, yes, we'll mind. We're coworkers, not a couple."

"She's right. Surely you can find something else." Rowdy

struggled to open the door on the side of the trailer. It finally gave way with a screech. He peered inside. "I see only one workable bunk. What shape is the air conditioner in?"

"Like I said, this is all I've got. AC works, from time to time. If you're careful. Don't turn on the microwave when you're running it. The electrical is a little dicey. Got propane, of course, but the refrigerator ain't worth a damn. I'd take an ice chest for your cold things. Put it in the back of the truck." The man who hadn't bothered to introduce himself held out keys. "Now, the truck runs good. AC is plenty cool and, as you can see, it's a four-door. Room for the dog."

"I hope to hell you aren't charging the company too much for this." Rowdy stepped inside the trailer to look around. They heard a *thump* and a curse. He came out rubbing his head. "There's no headroom and, Megan, I guess you'll have to sleep on the floor."

"I don't think so." She climbed inside. The wood paneling was peeling. There was a fairly new microwave on the counter, but it wasn't anchored. A sharp turn would probably send it flying. The matted shag carpeting was dirt-colored and smelled like dirty socks.

She opened the door to what proved to be a tiny bathroom with a showerhead in the curved ceiling. The black stuck between the tiles might very well be toxic mold, and she knew for sure she wasn't going in there without shower shoes. Rowdy wouldn't be able to stand up straight in it. No sink in there. When she turned the spigot in the mini kitchen, rusty water sputtered out of a pipe that wobbled and almost came off in her hand.

"It's a disaster." Back outside she took a deep breath of fresh air. "I think we'd do better sleeping in the truck."

"Sorry. Head on to San Antonio and they'd have a new outfit for ya. Of course, that would set back your timeline for shutting things down here." The man smirked. "I coulda done the ordering myself, but it's hard to feel the love for anything to do with CWC, which I know is just another name for Calhoun Petroleum."

"Now, listen here." Megan put her hands on her hips. "Seems to me Calhoun has done a lot for this town. Courthouse looks cleaned up recently."

"Yep. Sandblasted last year. Jail, too. Good thing, since Saturday nights, the cells are full of them oil people so drunk they can't drive. Or shouldn't." The man spit again and kicked a boot toward Lucky when he sniffed at him. "Don't get me started on how the roughnecks treat our sweet little gals." He scowled and looked toward the town square. "You expect us to be grateful to Calhoun? Not on your life. Oil ruined what was a nice little town before they came in here bringing strangers and big money. Now we got roads full of potholes, young'uns with ridiculous expectations, and a fancy courthouse that'll soon be nothing but a reminder of how some people like to act the fool when they've finally got a few extra dollars to spend."

Megan didn't know what to say to all that. Rowdy just strode back to their rental car to unload their bags. Obviously they were going to have to take this RV and truck and make the best of it. She shook her head, already thinking ahead. The Rocking S. She'd heard of it, unfortunately. She just hoped the owner wasn't around. Because that could get awkward with a capital *A*. Well, she'd worry about that if and when she had to deal with him. She grabbed her duffel and helped Rowdy stick their stuff in the tin can they'd now have to call home. She hoped it was temporary. The car dealer announced that the rental car was to be turned in at his lot, so they were soon ready to roll.

"We need to stock up on food again. But not much. Eating meals at night in town makes sense with the rig we're stuck with now. Breakfast and lunch out at the site. I'll buy us a big cooler and ice. Damn, but this is going to screw up our schedule. I usually work long hours, twelve-hour shifts. Can't do that if we have to keep running into town for ice and such." Rowdy started the truck, frowning at the sound the engine made. "Runs good? Doesn't seem like it."

"Twelve-hour shifts?" Megan wondered if they got overtime for that. "That's ridiculous."

"It's how the roughnecks work, so I've always done the same." He looked her over. "Maybe I'll change my schedule this trip. If it sounds like you can't handle it."

"Who'd want to? Seems like an eight-hour day is more reasonable. Blame me for shortening your precious schedule. I don't care." Megan couldn't imagine spending half of every day doing a job she was sure to hate. She turned around to watch the trailer as they left the lot. It didn't even roll along like it should. Bad springs? She was sure Rowdy was noticing as he frowned at the rearview mirror. "Seriously, the trailer he gave us is a joke. Maybe we can trade it in when we get to a bigger town. How far is San Antonio, anyway?" Megan had been there many times and knew the big city would have everything they'd need.

"Too far to get sidetracked. We'll have to make do with what we've got until all our work at this ranch is done." Rowdy pulled into the parking lot of the local grocery store. "Grab what you want for breakfast and sandwich stuff for lunch."

"How long are we going to be here?" Megan trailed him into the store. Her stomach had settled down, and she was actually hungry now.

"A couple of weeks if things go smoothly. We'll see." He turned to study her face. "You feel like eating lunch in town before we go out there? Think you can hold it down?"

Megan tossed a couple of bags of chips into the basket. "Hope so." She was eyeing the sodas when her phone rang. "Oh, we have cell phone service." She dug it out of her purse and glanced at the caller ID. Her sister Cassidy. "Hello."

"Are you okay? I heard you were in a tornado!" Cass sounded a million miles away, and the call was full of static.

"I'm fine except that a cactus bounced off my butt. I'm sitting very carefully." She waited while Cass exclaimed. "No, really. Don't worry about me. But the replacement RV they set up for us here in Nowhere, Texas, is horrible." Megan smiled at Rowdy. "Way too small for the two of us, and ancient."

"I'm sorry. I was told that was all they had. The good news is that I arranged for you to have a satellite phone. Today. So you can get service anywhere. I can't believe you were stuck in a storm with no way to call for help. That can't happen again."

"Hey, thanks, sis. Does Rowdy get one, too?" Megan winked at him since he was obviously trying to eavesdrop.

"Yes. It's a safety thing. He should have always had one. Now that I'm in charge, some things will be changing. So hang in there with the RV. Trade it in when you get to San Antonio. You sure you're all right? Maybe you should see a doctor."

"I'm fine. I just have a sore butt." Megan walked a few feet away and turned the corner to face the milk aisle. "How are Mason and the wedding plans?"

"We're great." Her sister laughed. "Fantastic, actually. We're thinking about a Christmas wedding, but every night feels like a honeymoon if you want to know the truth." Big sigh.

"You're making me jealous." Megan looked to make sure Rowdy couldn't hear her. "I'm glad you're so happy with Mason. Don't let our business problems ruin things for you."

"I'm trying not to, but we're so busy. I'm neck-deep in the financial mess here at Calhoun, and Mason's got his own company to worry about. We're trying to get everything worked out with the people our father defrauded without too big of a scandal hitting the news. Shannon and her lawyer friend, Billy Pagan, are doing damage control with the public relations department and working on the legal angle."

"Really? You're calling Billy her 'lawyer friend'?" Megan laughed. "Those two have quite a history and it didn't end up with them as friends. I can't imagine that they're getting along now."

"So far they are. Only a few explosions that I know of." Cass could be heard talking to someone in the background. "Shannon says hi. She's here working with me in the office."

Megan felt a wave of homesickness. "Hi to both of you. I wish I was there, helping . . ."

"Right. So, how are you and Rowdy doing?" Cass was back in business mode. No sign of any feelings for Rowdy in her voice.

"We're okay. He's my boss and acting like it. He's not exactly a fan of the Calhouns. No one is."

"That's not good. Have you told Rowdy about his—"

Megan heard the cart coming up behind her. "No! What would be the point if we don't have exact figures for what's owed? You don't have them yet, do you?"

"No. But we're talking about offering each person our father defrauded a settlement. It's cheaper than dealing with possible lawsuits. But we'll still be out millions, Meg." Cass's regret was obvious, even over the phone. "Rowdy deserves to know. I know we agreed to wait, but if you want to go ahead . . ."

"Sure. Eventually. When we have solid numbers. Not now, though. Got to go. I'm on the job, you know. Take care." Megan could feel Rowdy's eyes on her.

"The mobile phone office where you'll pick up your new phones is on the square facing the courthouse there. It's supposedly the only

one in town. And *you* take care. I'm sorry you're stuck out there."
Cass ended the call.

"So, that was Cassidy." Rowdy stopped next to Megan as she
slipped her phone back into her purse. "She okay?" He asked it
nonchalantly, like he didn't care about her answer.

"She's fine. Great. She's arranged for us to get satellite phones,
one for each of us. How about that?" Megan watched his face. Did
he want to know whether Cass was still with Mason? Did he hope
they'd broken it off?

"Look, quit waiting for me to burst into tears or something. I'm
not pining for your sister. I'm glad if she's happy. I'm getting on with
my own life." He frowned down at her, his mouth firm. "She *is* still
happy, isn't she?"

"Blissful. A Christmas wedding is in the works." Megan laid her
hand on his arm, but he shrugged it off. "Glad you're handling it so
well. Nothing worse than a whiny male, I always say. So, breakfast
food. That cereal looks way too healthy for me. I'm going back for
some Captain Crunch." She was glad to see she'd almost made him
smile.

"Hey, thanks for the satellite phones. I've been asking for one for
years." He put a gallon of milk in the cart next to two boxes of cereal.

"Well, there's the power of being part of the family." She winked
and rounded the corner, after her favorite cereal. "When we leave
here, we look for the cell phone office across from the courthouse."

"All right, then. Finish your shopping and let's move." He pushed
the cart toward the front, grabbing a couple of loaves of bread, the
healthy kind. Megan met him there, loaded down with cereal, white
bread, and peach yogurt.

"Not too much perishable stuff. We have to put it all in a cooler."
Rowdy grabbed a big one from by the door and told the cashier to
charge them for a half-dozen bags of ice, too. Soon they were on
their way again.

Rowdy drove straight to the square and griped when he found it
was impossible to park a truck pulling an RV in front of the cell
phone store. He let Megan out and took off to hunt for a long stretch
of curb away from the center of town. Megan pushed her way inside
the small store that represented every cell phone carrier she'd ever
heard of and some she hadn't. A bored teenager in a cowboy hat

lounged behind the counter, his boots on the wooden table next to him. When the bell tinkled above the door, he lifted the hat brim and studied her.

"What can I do you for?" He had a slow drawl that matched the lazy way he looked her over from the top of her messy hair to her toes. His name tag declared him to be "Jason."

"I'm here to pick up a couple of satellite phones. For CWC Industries." Megan figured they could be charged on Rowdy's company credit card if they weren't already paid for.

"Can I see some ID?" He stood and pulled a pile of invoices from under the counter. "I got two names here. You need to match at least one of them." He frowned. "You don't look like a Rowdy Baker, but then you never know." He leaned an elbow on the glass countertop. "ID?"

"We can wait for my boss." Why, oh why, hadn't she thought of identification? It was one thing to put a fake name on her paperwork at Headquarters, but she sure didn't have a driver's license to match. Maybe her sister had remembered to stick with her phony name on this order. But she was so busy, it would be a miracle if she'd handled it herself and not passed the chore on to an assistant. "What's the other name, Jason?" She leaned in, trying to soften up the guy. "I'm Megan. Bet one of the names on those invoices is mine."

"Yeah, it is. Megan Calhoun. If you're claiming that's your name, then I'm not giving you a damn thing without a look at your driver's license." He wasn't smiling. "Never met a Calhoun before. If you're her, then I'm damn disappointed. Figured you'd be dressed in diamonds or at least in something better than what looks like the shit my sister wears to wash out the horse trailer."

"What's going on here?" Rowdy had pushed through the glass door and now stood behind Megan. "You got a problem, fella?"

"I need to see some identification before I hand over these expensive phones." Jason held out the invoices. "Company paid for them in advance. Surely you don't expect me to just pass them over to the first person through the door. I expect you'll say you're Rowdy Baker. But you'll have to hand over your driver's license to prove it."

"Got it right here." Rowdy pulled out his wallet, then dropped his

Texas license on the counter. "Now, pass them both over. I'll vouch for us. Megan works for me."

Jason made a big deal out of examining Rowdy's license, then laid it back down. He shook his head. "She works for you? That's a good one. A Calhoun. What's she doing out here? Checking to see that you get all the wells shut down right and tight? Wouldn't want an extra drop of precious oil escaping, now, would you? Might have to pay the folks here another dollar or two." He slapped two fancy-looking phones on top of the papers. "Sign for these and get out of here. If my dad didn't need the business, we wouldn't be selling to a fucking Calhoun, and that's a fact."

"Hey, you did sell to the company, so watch your language in front of the lady." Rowdy suddenly had a grip on Jason's shirtfront, his face inches from the clerk's. Jason's cowboy hat hit the floor. "There's no need to be rude."

Megan waited while Jason stammered out an apology.

"Rowdy's right. You were happy enough to take our money, so watch it." She picked up one of the phones. "Are these fully charged?"

"Yes, ma'am." Jason suddenly found his manners. "Good for twenty-four hours before they have to be charged again."

"I want a car charger thrown in for free." She grabbed the invoice, her eyes widening at the cost of the things. A cell tower of their own would have been cheaper.

"Sure." He glanced down to where Rowdy still held his shirt. When Rowdy let him go, he grabbed a car charger from a rack to his left and tossed it on the paperwork. "Phone numbers are on the invoices. You're supposed to call your company and let them know the phones are active now. We were told to pass on those instructions to you."

"Oh, we will." Megan studied his flushed face. "What do you have against the Calhouns, personally?"

His eyes filled, and he seemed horrified that he had to clear his throat. "Daddy bet on that oil boom lasting. Bought the mineral rights to a piece of land with my college fund. Right before you people quit drilling new wells." He leaned over and grabbed his hat. "But that's our luck for you. Guess if it hadn't been the Calhoun outfit, it would have been Texas Star or another of the big companies that come out here looking for oil." He wiped his nose on his shirtsleeve. "I'll get to college, one way or another. Just take me a little longer, that's all."

"I'm sorry, Jason. I'm betting oil will come back. Tell your daddy to hang on to that property." Megan thought about patting his hand, but he turned, getting busy with a pile of accessories and avoiding her eyes. She glanced at Rowdy, but he was on the phone to the office. She could hear him talking about the town where they were now and his stupid schedule.

She stepped back from the counter and hit a button on the phone. Nice loud dial tone. She punched in a number, and a familiar voice answered after just one ring. "Janie, it's Megan. This is my new number if you need me for anything."

"Got it on the caller ID. How you doing out there, honey?" The Calhoun housekeeper sounded so normal and familiar, Megan was surprised to feel tears fill her eyes. She blinked them back. Janie had run the Calhoun household since before she was born. At times she'd been more of a mother to her than Missy had been.

"I'm okay. But I miss your cooking. Will you call my sisters and brother and give them this number?"

"Sure thing, hon. You need me to send you something? I can make up a care package. Some of my cookies or a few things from your closet if you forgot something."

Megan had to take a breath before she could answer. "I'd love that. But I don't have any way to get a package. We move around." She glanced at Rowdy. "If I figure out how to receive anything, I'll let you know. Love you." She heard Janie echo it along with an admonishment to take care of herself. It was all she could do not to burst into tears. Stupid. She hadn't been gone that long, and she was already homesick?

"Will do. Got to go. My slave driver of a boss is giving me the evil eye." She ended the call. "Works great. Clear as if I was back home in Houston."

"All right, then. Let's find someplace to eat lunch." Rowdy had ended his call. He signed some papers and passed them to the clerk.

"If you're looking for good food, the café across the square features home-cooked meals, Mr. Baker, Miss Calhoun." The clerk had decided to cooperate now that Rowdy had shaken some sense into him.

Rowdy's frown made Jason cringe. "I'd appreciate it if we kept her name our secret."

"It was on the phone order." Jason jammed his hat on his head. "If it's supposed to be a secret, it's too late. News that a Calhoun was coming was too good to keep to myself. I already told my mama. She told her bridge group and"—he shrugged—"you might as well put up a billboard on the highway saying, 'Welcome, Megan Calhoun' after that." He looked down at the counter. "Or maybe something not so welcoming, if you know what I mean."

"I know, all right." Rowdy grabbed Megan's elbow. "Come on. Let's eat lunch and then go out to the site."

"Is it true you're shutting down more wells? This time on the Rocking S Ranch?" Jason pretended to straighten what was left of his paperwork.

"How do you know about that?" Rowdy turned at the door.

"This is a small town, and what Calhoun, or CWC, whatever you call yourselves, does is big news. I ate breakfast at the café and heard you were picking up an RV over at the used car lot. Most of the wells still pumping around here are on the Rocking S. Last man through here from CWC shut down six wells on one of the other ranches. Figured this time it would have to be the Rocking S. How many are you shutting down?"

"None of your damn business." Rowdy gestured and Megan walked out ahead of him onto the sidewalk. "Man, I hate little towns. There are no secrets."

"Obviously. Are we still going to eat?" To her surprise, she really was hungry.

"Might as well. Just don't be surprised if we run into more attitude. I'm sure Jason isn't the only one who doesn't see Calhoun Petroleum as the town sweetheart it once was." He led the way to the crosswalk. With no traffic coming, it was simple enough to walk to the café, which was doing a good business.

"Lucky staying in the truck?" Megan was glad that there was a nice breeze blowing, but it was still a warm September day.

"Yes, and I parked in the shade. He'll be all right with the windows down if we don't take too long over lunch." Rowdy looked through the plate-glass window. "Brace yourself. It's a full house, and they're staring at us already."

Megan took a breath and inhaled what had to be chicken fried steak. "I can handle a few hard looks if that tastes as good as it smells." She grabbed the door handle. "Let's go."

Of course, every eye followed them as they settled into a red vinyl booth in the back. The waitress slapped two menus down in front of them.

"Today's special is chicken fried steak, mashed potatoes, cream gravy, and green beans. Homemade yeast rolls come with it." She had a weary slump to her shoulders and recited it like she'd said it at least fifty times already that day.

"Sounds perfect." Megan smiled. "Sweet tea, too."

"I'll have the same." Rowdy handed her their menus. "Thanks."

"You got it." She managed a smile and headed back toward the kitchen.

"You the folks here to shut down more wells?" A burly man in overalls stopped next to the table.

"We're here with CWC Industries. What we do here is our business." Rowdy got to his feet and faced the man. They were about the same height, but overalls guy outweighed Rowdy by about fifty pounds.

Megan picked up her fork, the only weapon at hand. She slid her dull-looking butter knife toward Rowdy, but he was too busy puffing out his chest to notice.

"No need to get your back up." The man stuck out his hand. "Clem Eastwood. I'm mayor of Sparkle City."

"Rowdy Baker." Rowdy didn't introduce Megan as he shook hands.

"This little gal must be Miss Calhoun. A pleasure to meet a member of the famous family. I met your daddy once." He pulled off his John Deere cap and put it over his heart. "You have my deepest condolences, ma'am. Your daddy was a fine man."

Megan shocked herself by tearing up. "Thank you. Not everyone around here seems to like the Calhouns."

"Sour grapes. Some got big checks when all the wells were

pumping. Acted like it would last forever." He slapped his cap back on his balding head. "I knew better. Yes, I got money from it, but I invested my windfall." His smile showed off what had to be a nice set of false teeth. They were large, startlingly white, and perfectly matched. "Anyway, I picked up plenty of good property in San Antone. Rent houses. No matter what oil does from now on, I'm sitting pretty."

"That was smart of you, Mr. Eastwood." Megan dabbed at her wet cheeks with her paper napkin.

"Call me Clem." He looked around the café. They were certainly the center of attention. "If anyone gives you any problems while you're here, you just give me a holler. I'll have the sheriff out there at the well site as fast as you can say jackrabbit. You hear me?" He dropped two business cards on the table.

"We appreciate that, Clem." Rowdy smiled and sat down when the waitress approached with a full tray. "We don't anticipate any trouble, but it's good to know we have backup."

"There you go. Enjoy your meal." He patted the waitress on the shoulder. "Emma, honey, you put this on my tab. And add two help-ings of Polly's banana pudding, made fresh this morning. Can't be beat, I'm telling you." He tipped his cap again and headed for the door.

"That was nice." Megan inhaled the delicious aromas coming from the plate in front of her.

"Hot rolls in the basket with honey or butter there on the table." Emma leaned down and stared at Megan. "You really a Calhoun?"

"Yes. I'm sorry if the wells going down are making it hard on you." Megan set her fork back on the table, not sure what to expect.

Emma ran her hand over her swollen belly and Megan realized she was pregnant. "It's not the wells' fault I guessed wrong on a man. My own stupidity. My mama is right about that." She sighed. "What's a Calhoun doing out here in the middle of nowhere?"

"I'm working. Learning about oil drilling." Megan picked up her fork again. "I'm a little late to the party, but I have to figure things out or we could lose everything."

"Hmm. Guess even rich folks have problems." She nodded. "Don't let that food get cold."

Megan dug into her mashed potatoes. "This looks good."

"It is. My mama is the best cook in the county. Good luck with your job." The waitress gave Rowdy a serious once-over. "And be careful. I learned the hard way that a girl's got to watch out for herself. You know what I mean? 'Cause sure as shooting, no one else will." She grabbed a tea pitcher and moved on to give refills to a table full of men.

Rowdy leaned forward. "You think she spit in my mashed potatoes?"

Megan choked on the bite she'd taken. When she could finally speak, she shook her head. "I hope not. Because this is the most delicious thing I've tasted in my life. Take a chance, Rowdy." She grinned, then cut into her steak. Heaven on a fork.

A big meal should be followed by a nap. Of course, Rowdy didn't think that way. Instead he ordered her to dig out her work boots and change shoes before they headed for the well site. He drove over a bumpy road that ended where there were at least a dozen oil wells in a muddy field, all of them still pumping. And they were going to have to shut some of them down? It made Megan sad. Her daddy would have said they were leaving money in the ground. Had Conrad Calhoun seen this coming? Had he had any idea that the oil boom would go bust? She was almost glad he hadn't lived to see all his hard work going to waste.

She missed her daddy so damn much. Every time she saw the Calhoun logo on a truck or building, she felt a sharp pain near her heart. Her family *had* to save Calhoun Petroleum. She'd told that waitress she was here to learn. She hoped to God she could. First she'd have to overcome Rowdy's hostility and get him to teach her what she needed to know in plain English—in simple terms that a girl who had flunked out of the University of Texas, twice, could understand. So far he'd acted like she was a burden he was required to drag from one end of the state to the other. She had to change his attitude. Prove to him she was going to take this seriously, and then . . .

Well, hell. As they drove into the well site, she saw the man she'd hoped to avoid once they arrived here. He waved at her, a smile on his face. Was there anyone in Sparkle City who hadn't heard that Megan Calhoun had arrived?

"That's King Sanders." She nudged Rowdy across the console. "He owns the Rocking S ranch."

"You know him?" Rowdy kept driving, the truck and RV kicking up a cloud of dust that blew over the two men standing in front of the rigs.

"Unfortunately. Oh, he's nice enough. He was best man at a friend's wedding. I was maid of honor. We were thrown together a lot until . . . Let's just say it didn't end well." She tried to shove what had happened to the back burner of her brain while Rowdy parked the RV behind the office trailer for the well site. While he was maneuvering the vehicles, she kept her mouth shut.

"What went wrong?" Rowdy put the truck in PARK and looked at her.

"I had a crush on the groom, got drunk, and made a fool of myself, hanging onto King and trying to make Eli jealous." She forced a laugh. "Clearly I wasn't thinking. As if Eli would notice me with King, during his own wedding." Megan wasn't about to admit that the next morning she'd woken up in King's bed. King had taken her act seriously, convinced they could be a couple. She'd just wanted to run far and fast. Oh God, but that had been a low point in her life. She couldn't bear to look at Rowdy and what would surely be disgust in his eyes. Finally she made herself face him. No, he was thinking about the business implications, of course. His eyes were on the precious oil rigs.

"Relax. If he's a successful businessman, then Sanders is here for one reason. He'll try to talk us into keeping his wells going. It's money in the bank for him." Rowdy nodded and focused on her. "You used him? Now he'll use you if he can. We can't let him do that, Megan. Don't let him get to you. This is our job. We have orders. Personal feelings can't sway us, and your being a Calhoun shouldn't be a factor."

"Got it. That's the line I'll take. If he tries that." Megan grabbed the door handle. Really? Would King want payback? She owed him for stringing him along, but the company didn't. If that was his game, she'd set him straight, in a hurry. "I have orders. No control when it comes to the rigs." But then she saw King grinning at her from the other side of the door. He pulled it open before she could hit a lock or even prepare a speech.

"Megan, sugar, what are you doing here?" King grabbed her around the waist, swung her out of the truck, then spun her around. "Aren't you a sight for sore eyes?" Then he did the unthinkable—he kissed her, catching her mouth open when she started to tell him to put her down before she knocked him into next week.

Chapter Six

Rowdy watched King Sanders paw Megan and realized he was going to have to do something or this workday was going to be a total waste. Before he could speak, Megan pushed Sanders back.

"King, is this your land?" She smiled like she was happy to see him. Must have been a hell of a kiss.

"Sure is. I made a deal with your daddy to let him drill here. Now there's all this talk about shutting down." He gestured toward the field. "I'm telling you, that's not going to happen."

"You know the oil business is struggling, King." Megan kept her distance.

"Not my problem." The good old boy with his cowboy hat in his hands showed a hint of steel. "But that's what I have lawyers for." He settled the hat back where it belonged and made a smooth move, capturing Megan with his arm around her. "Beats me why you're here, Megan. This is no place for a little gal like you."

Rowdy waited for the explosion. "Little gal"? Sure, Megan Calhoun was small, but he didn't think she'd like that description.

Megan pushed away from King again and lost her smile. "King, you'd better buckle up, because I'm here to work. I'm surprised the gossip hasn't reached you. I have to learn the business in the oil fields if I want to inherit my piece of Daddy's fortune. It was spelled out in his will."

"Well, that's a damn shame. What was your daddy thinking?" He wasn't getting the message and reached for her again. She put out a straight arm that stopped him.

"That I could handle shutting down half your wells. So, you'd better take me seriously." She waved Rowdy over. "King Sanders,

Rowdy Baker. Rowdy is the engineer who's my boss for the next year. I'm working for him. Learning about how we drill oil, kind of from the ground up, you might say."

Rowdy put out his hand and the rancher shook it. "Sorry about this, Sanders. But we're going to be taking out three rigs here and another half dozen on your western field."

"That's ridiculous. I've got a contract that says not only do my wells keep pumping, but Calhoun owes me even more than have been drilled here so far." Sanders frowned. "Honey, we need to talk. Where are you planning to stay? Surely not in that rusty tin can." He glared at the trailer. "Why, it wouldn't hold your shoe collection."

"I didn't bring my shoe collection, King. Unfortunately." Megan rolled her eyes. "And I'm staying there because that was all your little town had to offer."

"Sugar! No way will I let you suffer like that. Come home with me." King poured on the charm.

"I'm not your 'sugar'. And if you think you can talk me into keeping your wells going, King, forget it. I'm taking orders from Rowdy, and we're both getting them from the head office." Megan turned her back on the tin can. Clearly she didn't want to stay there any more than Rowdy did. He had to admire her for resisting the offer.

"That office is run by your family. At least it was, last I heard. And they'll be getting an earful from me about this plan to shut down wells, you can be sure of that." Sanders wasn't going to take no for an answer. "But, like I said, let the lawyers handle it." He walked over and pulled open the trailer door. "While you wait for more *orders*, it's clear you can't stay here. Why, it's filthy and hot as hell." He strolled back to them and waited.

"Look, King. We know it's horrible, but that's part of the job, staying near the site. Isn't it, Rowdy?" Megan looked resigned.

"I usually stay near the well sites. But it's going to be tight in the RV we're stuck with now." Rowdy shrugged. Letting Megan stay with the rancher might not be such a bad idea. The only problem would be transportation every day. He glanced at the truck, where Lucky was going crazy in the backseat.

King noticed. "Whose dog is that?"

"Mine. A rescue named Lucky." Megan walked over and opened the door so she could grab Lucky's leash and let him out of the truck.

Rowdy watched her butt twitch under the soft material of her yoga pants. Not exactly work clothes. And they looked foolish with the heavy boots he'd made her put on in town. She no more looked like she belonged on a well site than feathers on a cow. Lucky was barking when she let him down and Rowdy smiled, pretty sure the dog would attack the rancher. Instead, King knelt down and made friends with the mutt, who was soon licking his hand.

"Now, isn't he a cute thing? You rescued him? I always knew there was a kind heart in there, Megan Calhoun." King stood and winked at her. "Now, show me some of that kindness and agree to stay with me. I'll put you up in an extra bedroom and even loan you a truck so you can drive back and forth over here. Or is that against the rules, boss man?" He turned to Rowdy, as if daring him to make Megan suffer in the hot tin can.

Rowdy glanced at the trailer. Even he didn't want to sleep there. "That's up to her. But Megan does need to be here most of the time. On call."

"How long does it take to get here from your house, King?" Megan bit her lip, apparently ready to take one for the team. A room in what was probably a luxurious ranch house or stuck here in tin can hell?

"About twenty minutes, give or take." King smiled when Rowdy stayed silent. "Now, look at that. Your 'boss' is going to being reasonable. He didn't say no, did he?" Sanders glanced at his watch. "I don't know about you, but it seems silly to start a workday in the middle of the afternoon. Why don't we head on to the house? I'll fix us something cool to drink, and we can catch up on old times." He slapped Rowdy on the back. "What say, boss man? Isn't tomorrow morning soon enough to get this little gal into the trenches?"

"I can speak for myself, King." Megan must have seen how close Rowdy was to losing his temper at the rancher's high-handed tactics. "Two o'clock isn't the middle of the afternoon when you're on the clock. I bet you don't see it that way when you're the one signing the paychecks."

Sanders laughed. "You've got me there. So, how much longer you going to be?"

"We planned to work till five or six, didn't we?" She waited for Rowdy's nod. When a happy King tried to hug her, she held him off.

"I'd appreciate a better place to stay, but I won't do it unless you offer both of us rooms." She smiled at Rowdy.

"Well, I guess I could do that. I have a bunkhouse with plenty of space." King nodded. "I don't know who foisted that hunk of junk on you, Baker, but I wouldn't ask my least-favorite hunting dog to sleep there."

"We were desperate. Got caught in a tornado south of here, and our old rig was blown to pieces." Rowdy thought about the offer. Hell, why not? He bet even the bunkhouse in this man's place was a damn palace.

"What? Megan, you weren't caught in that twister outside of Tuleta, were you?" King grabbed her shoulders and studied her face. "Honey, that's the talk of South Texas. Fella was killed when his truck and trailer got caught in crosswinds down there. His truck rolled and flung him into a ditch. Broke his neck."

"No! I hadn't heard." Megan let her fear show on her face for a moment when her lips trembled and she grabbed the rancher's hands.

"Why, you must have been scared to death." He glanced at Rowdy. "What the hell happened?"

"Rowdy saw it coming and got us out of the truck in time. We hunkered down in a low spot until the tornado passed. I was terrified." She closed her eyes as if she was remembering the scene. "We had to lie there while the sand hit us from all sides and we couldn't breathe. The dog was under us. It was crazy." She opened her eyes and looked up at him. "You should have seen what it did to our truck and trailer. If we'd been inside? Well, I'll never forget it."

King pulled her in and she let him hold her. He stroked her hair, his eyes meeting Rowdy's. His voice was rough when he spoke. "Good on you, Baker. To get her to safety. Thank God you're okay." Megan eased back from him and he crossed himself.

Megan sighed. "Yes, thank God."

"Just goes to show. Live for the day, sugar. You never know what tomorrow will bring." King looked up at the cloudless sky, then shook his head. "So, how about that offer? Stay with me while you wait for new orders. I'm pretty sure there's no way you're going to be shutting down my wells." King's confident smile proclaimed he was used to getting his way. "I'll even feed you breakfast and supper while you're here. Wait till you meet Carmelita. You'll think you've died and gone to heaven when you taste her cooking."

"I guess it wouldn't be a conflict of interest. As long as you understand, Sanders, that putting us up won't influence what we're here to do." Rowdy figured the air-conditioning in the trailer wouldn't be worth a damn and it was still hot here. Not unusual for September in these parts of Texas. Great food? He wasn't stupid. "Let me talk to the super here and get things lined up to start inspections tomorrow, then we can follow you to your place."

"Sounds like a plan." King straightened his tan Stetson. He'd pulled it off as soon as he'd seen Megan. A gentleman. Rowdy had to like him for that, even if he was arrogant. "I'll get out of your way. Be in my truck with the AC going and making some phone calls. Can Megan come with me, or does she have to stick with you?"

"I'm learning the job, King. I'll stick with Rowdy." She patted King's arm. "Thanks for the invitation to stay. I'll admit I was dreading tonight and figuring out our sleeping arrangements."

"Just relax and do your little job, sugar. Leave those sleeping arrangements to me." King winked, then sauntered over to his truck, an expensive model that seemed to resist the dust that covered everything around them.

"What are you looking at?" Megan wiped sweat and dust from her forehead, then gave Rowdy a narrow look.

"Me?" Rowdy grinned. "Are you getting defensive? Your buddy there is imagining sleeping arrangements that'll make him happy. How that shakes out is up to you. I'm just glad we don't have to stay in that trailer. Thanks for including me in the plan to go to his ranch." He strode over to the office trailer, where the superintendent of the well site stood anxiously waiting on the top step. "Listen while I discuss the plans for the next few weeks with the super here. This is the kind of thing we'll be doing at every site. We inspect what's going on, even if we don't have orders to shut down wells."

"Rowdy! How are you doing?" A tall man with salt-and-pepper hair held out his hand. "Come on in where it's cool. This must be our honored guest. Rumors are flying in town, I have to tell you. Never expected to see another Calhoun out here after Conrad died." He jerked open the metal door behind him, smiling and gesturing for them to precede him.

"Megan, this is Vince Claypool." Rowdy shook his hand, happy when cold air hit him. "Glad to see your AC is working."

"Not that I get to hang out in here when the roughnecks are sweating outside. That wouldn't be great management." Vince bent down and patted Lucky. "You brought a dog." He smiled. "That's new."

"He's mine." Megan followed him up the wooden steps. "Megan Calhoun. I'm sorry if Lucky is a problem."

"Happy to meet you. You can bring in a herd of camels if you wish, Ms. Calhoun. Your company, after all." He took off his hard hat, stuck it under one arm, then held out his hand. He shook Megan's as if it were made of glass. "Sorry I didn't greet you when you drove up, but I saw King Sanders approach you like he was an old friend. Didn't want to interrupt." Vince shuffled his feet, clearly nervous.

"Has he been giving you a hard time?" Rowdy looked around the office. It was in pretty good shape. Typical. There was mud on the floor, a mass of paperwork on the desk, and a table full of charts. A map on the wall showed where the current wells and future well sites were scheduled. He hated the fact that one of his best superintendents was acting like the queen was visiting. Vince had walked over to the desk and was busily trying to straighten a pile of papers.

"He's anxious for us to drill more wells, of course, not shut any down. It's money in the bank for him." Claypool jumped when the phone on his desk rang. "Sorry, but I have to take this. You know we're not drilling new wells. Be surprised if you weren't here to shut some down. Sanders pitched a royal fit when he found out that might happen. Make yourself at home." He answered the landline, which was connected to a computer on his desk.

Megan frowned at Rowdy. "If King has a contract . . ."

"That could cause us problems. Usually we can do what we want once we arrange for the oil leases. He and your dad must have worked out some kind of sweetheart deal." Rowdy heard his name called.

"Rowdy Baker's right here. Yes, sir." Claypool held out the phone. "He wants to talk to you. It's a lawyer at Headquarters." His smile was strained as he slapped the receiver into Rowdy's hand. "Seems Sanders got on the horn right away."

"This is Rowdy Baker." He wasn't surprised when a lawyer introduced himself.

"William Pagan. King Sanders had his lawyer call us and raise holy hell. We're going over the Sanders contracts now. Don't do a thing yet about shutting down any wells. Wait for word from us. Apparently you have a new number?"

"Yes, got it an hour ago. You can reach me anytime." He told him the number. "We can do our usual inspections while we wait to hear from you. But that shouldn't take us more than a day or two." He saw Vince pulling cold drinks out of a mini-fridge. Then he set a bowl on the floor and poured a bottle of water out for the dog. Megan was drinking a Coke and trying to put the super at ease. You'd never take her for an oil heiress in her loose pants and T-shirt with those clunky boots. Her hair was loose around her head and her face pink from the sun she'd gotten the day before. She shouldn't look beautiful but, damn it, she did. He realized Pagan had been talking about legal clauses and lease agreements and he hadn't heard a word.

"Are we clear? You don't stop drilling."

"Got it." Rowdy made himself look away from Megan and concentrate on the phone call.

"Fine. We'll know by tomorrow whether you can proceed with the shutdowns or if you should move on. Apparently Conrad cut quite a deal with Sanders. There are cash penalties if we don't drill a certain number of wells on his place. We're treading close to that now. Price of oil isn't mentioned as a factor. It's a damn shame, but there it is."

"You're right about that." Rowdy was ready to hang up when the lawyer asked if Megan was with him. "Yes, she is."

"Put her on the line. We're old friends. Tell her it's Billy Pagan."

"Of course. Megan!" Rowdy handed her the phone. Another man who'd been "friends" with Megan. Had she run away from this man's bed, too? One of her legion of lovers? And how many had Rowdy had in *his* past? The number could fit on one hand. Damn it.

"What? I don't know anything about contracts." She took the receiver as if it might sting her hand.

"An old friend. Billy Pagan?" Rowdy frowned when her face lit up and she grabbed the receiver eagerly. Was there any man whom she didn't have a history with? He picked a hard hat from a line of them on hooks by the door. "I'll leave you to him while I take a quick tour with Vince. Stay here with the dog. You're not dressed for the rig." He stepped out of the trailer and into the heat. Stupid to feel like the whole world had been with Megan Calhoun at one time or another. He had just made it to the bottom of the steps when Megan called his name.

"Wait up! I'm going with you. I can change pants in the trailer." She hurried to join him.

"Not so fast, Ms. Calhoun." Vince was on her heels, a brown grocery sack in his hands. "Can't go anywhere on the site without a hard hat. When we heard you were coming, the fellas decided to make you something special. Pedro, one of the hands, has a little artistic talent. I think he did a fine job, especially considering he only had one day to put this together." He thrust the sack into Megan's hands. "See what you think."

Megan peeked into the bag. "Oh, I couldn't." She flushed. "Really. I want to be one of the guys."

Rowdy exchanged looks with Vince. "Megan, there's no way you could ever be mistaken for one of the guys. What is it?"

She pulled a hard hat out of the bag and handed the empty sack to Vince. Rowdy bit back a laugh, pretty sure work was stopping nearby as the men watched her reaction.

"Now, that's a hard hat." Rowdy clamped down on his tongue hard enough to draw blood so he wouldn't laugh.

"It's beautiful." She lifted it up for the men on the closest rig to see, then set it on her head. "Honestly, tell Pedro he has real talent. It's really too pretty to mess up on one of these sites. I'd be sick if I scuffed it up when I climbed on a scaffold."

"Oh, he sprayed it with polyurethane. It should be pretty indestructible." Vince laughed. "You really like it?"

"Love it." She turned to Rowdy. "Seriously. Did you see the way he wrote my name in fancy lettering? It's not easy to keep it even on a round surface. I used to own a boutique, and I could have sold things decorated like this for big bucks."

Vince turned to give two thumbs-up to the watching crew, who broke out in a cheer. "I'll be sure to tell him. He does all kinds of artsy-fartsy stuff. Maybe you'll have time to see some of it while you're here. Let him know if you think he has a way to make money with it." Vince cleared his throat. "The oil business being what it is, he might need a fallback income, sooner than he thinks. He's got a wife and three kids at home."

"I'd be happy to take a look if he has some samples. I have connections in Houston who could help out if he has pieces ready to go." She laughed. "Not hard hats, but jewelry, boxes, the kinds of knickknacks that people use as decorations."

Rowdy held out his hand. "Let me see that." He took the hot pink hat with its design of trailing vines with exotic flowers in all the colors of the rainbow. Examining it, he could see that the workmanship was meticulous. "What does this man do on the job?"

"He's our mechanic and electrician. Pedro can fix just about anything. Keeps our generators running, that's for sure." Vince pointed with a blunt fingertip. "I told him I thought it was art, too, so I made him sign it. On the back. He put his initials. *PG.*"

"Yeah, it is art. Obviously he's good with his hands." Rowdy reached for the bag. "Give her a regular hat for when we get on the rigs. It would be a shame to get mud on this one." He laughed. "Now you have a dressy hard hat, Megan."

"Don't put it away." Megan reached for it and put it on again. "Can we go meet Pedro and get a picture? I want to send it to my sisters at Headquarters. They'll get a kick out of it and wish they had one. Just give me a few minutes to change into jeans."

Rowdy figured that would shoot the hell out of the workday, but he went along with it as a morale booster for the workers. Picture taking and introductions took another hour, then King Sanders hunted them down.

"Well, would you look at this?" He smirked as he checked out Megan in her pink hat. "If it isn't Oil Rig Barbie." He whipped out his own phone. "With mud on your boots and a smear on your chin, the gang at the country club is going to have a fit over this."

"King, stop it!" Megan turned to Rowdy. "Seriously? Mud?"

"Just a little. Shows you're taking this seriously." Rowdy pulled out a handkerchief and wiped it off. He wasn't going to notice how her smooth skin felt against his fingers or the way she laughed when he explained how his mother made him carry the piece of cloth.

"You really care what those slackers sitting by the pool back home think?" King busily added text to the picture and sent it off. "A gentleman should always carry a handkerchief." He pulled a snowy one out of his own back pocket. "See? I was taught the same thing."

"Okay, you two. And those slackers are the very ones who might notice the workmanship and start clamoring for Pedro Galvan's fine hand-painted pieces." Megan pulled off the hat and shook out her hair. "Can we go now, Rowdy? Those derricks are the filthiest places I've ever seen—and noisy! My head is pounding."

"You'd better get used to that, Megan." Rowdy remembered his first exposure to a rig when it was in full operation. He'd find some aspirin for her.

"I know. First, I need a shower." She looked down at her mud coated boots. "How do you ever get your boots clean?"

"Come over here, Megan." Vince had finally relaxed enough to call her by her first name. "Wash them off at the faucet here." He was spraying mud off his own boots. "My wife would tan my hide if I came home with my boots full of mud." He handed her the hose and nodded at Rowdy. "I take it you're done for the day?"

"Guess so." Rowdy followed Megan and soon had his own boots clean enough to get into his truck after Vince helped him unhitch it from the trailer.

"All right, then. Heard from my lawyer. Looks like you won't be shutting down any wells this trip." King slapped his jeans with his hat. "Sorry if that disappoints you. But I guess you have other things to attend to here. So, let's get going. I called Carmelita and she's cooking up a feast for us, Megan. Baker, you can come join us. My sister is at the ranch this week, and I think you two might hit it off. Unless, that is, you have a wife waiting for you at home?"

"No wife. A feast sounds good." Rowdy didn't like the way King gloated as he steered Megan to his truck. But he was hungry and he wasn't turning down a chance to have a decent meal. A fix-up with a millionaire's sister? Hey, maybe he'd see where that went. Certainly his ex had found love with a rich man. What did they say? What was sauce for the goose, was sauce for the gander. Or maybe he had it turned around. Whatever.

He could see at every turn the power that money bought. Lawyers on speed-dial. Feasts, too. Sanders was even telling Megan about his private plane as he helped her into his truck. Rowdy glanced back at the wells pumping oil nearby. Even at historically low prices, they represented money. Whoever owned the land got a nice percentage. Vince had told him the Sanders ranch had been in the family for generations. They raised cattle and farmed spinach, of all things. When oil had been discovered in these parts, it must have seemed like hitting the jackpot.

So, what the hell? He'd give this rich woman a chance. Pride had bought him nothing but a bruised heart. As he followed Sanders's truck along a bumpy road through fields that were dotted with cattle and past a surprising orchard with rows of some kind of fruit tree, he decided to keep an open mind about this sister. Why not? How bad could she be? He turned to the dog, sitting happily in Megan's seat for a change.

"If I'm lucky, I'll fall in love with this rich woman and she'll fall for me. We'll raise rich little kids and spend our lives together traveling the world and throwing her money around."

The dog just gave him a look, then licked his hand. Yeah, it didn't sound right to him, either. He wasn't cut out for the easy life of the idle rich. Couldn't imagine it.

"Don't tell Megan I talked to you." He patted the dog on the head. "I still don't think we should have a dog with us when we're working."

Lucky whined and lay down on the seat. He'd gotten the message.

Megan listened to King carry on about his ranch, his cattle, and—surprise—his olive grove, and wondered if she was going to have to fight him off later. She clutched that paper bag with her pink hat in it, still simmering about that crack he'd made. Oil Rig Barbie. Jerk.

"So, Karen is here. I thought she was in Europe."

"She's going to be heading to Italy with me next week. I've made several trips there, to study about this olive oil business. Since she speaks Italian, I asked her to come along." He grinned. "Now, if you want to take her place, I can always tell her to forget it."

"I don't speak Italian, King." Megan stared at the trees planted in neat rows. "Seems like it will take years before these trees yield olives."

"Not too long. Some varieties take less than three years to produce. I'm trying several different ones. You know, this area is known for growing spinach. I have fields of it. Because the soil here is good. But I decided it was time to diversify."

"Spinach. I saw a statue of Popeye in the town square." Megan laughed. "So, that's why."

"It's big business in these parts. But oil pays better. Then the oil crisis came along. When the price per gallon dropped, so did my royalties. Thank God I'd made your dad sign a contract. Connie wasn't paying much attention to the details when we hammered it out and I got such a deal." He had the good sense to flush. "Well, let's just say I have clauses in there that will keep the wells pumping, but the royalties will always be tied to the price of oil. That's a damn shame. It sure has hurt my income from the wells."

"Yes. You have to know I am keenly aware of what a shame that is." Megan knew it would do no good to antagonize him when they might have to shut down his wells anyway. Of course, he was a shrewd businessman, she'd always admired that about him. What surprised her was that he had pulled something over on her father, who'd always been shrewd himself. Her daddy must have been suffering more with his heart problems toward the end than they'd all realized.

"I'm sorry, sugar." King reached for her hand. "I liked your daddy. He could wheel and deal with the best of them. But our contract stands. It's just business. You understand. Don't let it come between us."

She slid her hand out from under his. "There is no 'us,' King. We had a moment. Okay, maybe an hour or two. I made a fool of myself. Won't happen again. But it was sweet of you to offer us a place to stay. I'm happy to be your friend."

"Now, honey, don't say that. Friend? We went further than that. So, please say you'll relax and enjoy the time we spend together here. Let me remind you why you went home with me that night. Give me a chance, Megan." He reached out and took her chin in his hands. "Or do you have something going on with that 'boss' of yours?"

"Don't be stupid. I barely know Rowdy. He used to be with my sister. If anything, he hates the Calhouns because Cassidy dumped him."

"I'd heard you discovered you have a new sister. So, this Baker is her ex?" King looked thoughtful. "And you just happened to be working with him this year."

"Yes, well, I needed to find someone who could teach me about oil, and Cass introduced us. Right after she broke up with him. It wasn't because she was in line to inherit some of Daddy's money, but because she met someone else. Still, the timing has to haunt Rowdy. And Cassidy's new guy is Mason MacKenzie."

"Ha! Another rich oilman who happens to be a good friend of mine. We went to college together. He's a stand-up guy. But all Baker probably noticed was that Mason's got a butt load of money. I bet that killed your boss, who's just a working stiff." King didn't exactly look broken up about that.

"Can you blame him? Guys like you and Mason with your ranches and planes and expensive toys are impossible to compete with. Rowdy would have to be bitter about how his relationship with Cass fizzled when it did." Megan felt guilty even talking about Rowdy with King.

"Well, then. I have a shot. Because, you're right, any woman with the Calhoun name will be poison to him." He leaned in and kissed her lightly on the lips. "Now, promise you'll be nice to Karen. I know you and she never did get along. For God's sake, don't show her that hard hat. She'll laugh to bust a gut."

"Didn't you post the picture on Facebook? You going to tell me she doesn't follow you?" Megan had good reasons for not being one of Karen's fans, but she'd never tell King what they were.

"Oh, shoot. Of course I did. So she's already seen it. Might as well put the thing on and play it out. If you don't, she'll make sure you suffer." King unlocked the doors. "Your boss just pulled in behind us. I'll get Karen to show him to the bunkhouse. That should help distract her."

Megan took King's advice and slapped the hat back on her head. She let him help her out of the high-riding truck, then realized Karen Sanders had come out to greet them. King must have called her before they'd left the well site. The two were twins, both tall, dark, and handsome. Karen had a voluptuous figure that she always showed off in expensive designer clothes. King was a masculine version of his sister and clearly spent plenty of time working out and in the sun if his tan could be believed.

"Oh my. That hat! It looks even more ridiculous in person." Karen laughed until she had to wipe a tear from her eye. "Megan Calhoun, you are just too funny." She grabbed Megan's shoulders and gave her air-kisses. "Welcome to the Rocking S Ranch."

"I knew you'd want to see it. Check out the workmanship. They have this man out there on the oil rigs, working in all that mud and heat, who is an absolute genius with a paintbrush. I'm going to get him under contract to do some special designs for that little boutique I used to own. You remember it, I know. You were one of our regulars." Who had rarely paid her bill on time. Or, worse, had complained endlessly if a salesperson didn't treat her like visiting royalty.

"Yes, I still shop there when I'm in Houston. 'Treasures'. A cute little place." Karen held out her hands. "Let me see."

"I still enjoy hunting for things to consign there." Megan handed Karen the hat. "Imagine custom jewelry and painted denim outfits for the rodeo. My sister Shannon knows everyone on those rodeo committees. She could certainly spread the word."

"I wonder if he could paint on leather. I would love a vest and matching skirt with some of these vines and flowers painted along the seams. In turquoise cowhide, I think." Karen's eyes were alight with the avarice of a dedicated shopper. Megan had known this about her for years.

"I'll make sure you have first dibs on any orders. How's that?"

"Perfect. And I'll expect a discount. You did find this artist working on one of my wells, didn't you?" She turned as Rowdy walked up. "And, speaking of workers, who's this tall drink of water in the truck bringing what I guess is your luggage?" Karen licked her lips. She shopped for men like she shopped for clothes, though she had only just dumped husband number three. She always went back to her maiden name after the divorce. Rumor was that she had her eye on an Italian prince for number four.

"Rowdy Baker. He's my boss since I'm working for the company now. Rowdy, Karen Sanders." Megan watched Rowdy's eyes widen as he dropped her duffel in the dirt to take Karen's hand in his. Karen wasn't listening to her. She was too busy making sure Rowdy got a look at her cleavage in the barely buttoned red silk blouse that flowed over her tight designer jeans. And he was taking full advantage of the sightseeing opportunity.

"Let's all go inside and get out of this heat and dust." King took Megan's arm. "Sugar, where's your luggage?"

"It's that bag at Rowdy's feet." Megan wanted to laugh at the way her so-called boss was being treated to Karen's manhandling. She had latched on to him and wasn't about to let go, asking him questions and barely waiting for the answers.

"King! Surely you don't expect Rowdy to sleep in the bunkhouse with those cowboys, do you?" Karen dragged Rowdy with her as she stomped up to her brother. "These two are our guests. Why, we have plenty of room in the house. I have a wing to myself, Rowdy. A room right next door to mine is empty, in fact. Come on, honey, I'll show you."

"The bunkhouse is fine by me." Rowdy did finally speak up.

"Nonsense. And we're having cocktails in the living room right after you and"—there was a delicate sniff—"Megan have a chance to shower and change." Karen's orange-painted nails made dents in Rowdy's tanned forearms. "You're not going to disappoint me, are you? I do own half of this ranch. Seems like you're drilling on my land."

"No, I wouldn't want to disappoint you." Rowdy smiled down at her and let her lead him away.

"A hundred bucks says she has him in her bed before midnight." King grunted as he hefted Megan's stuff and headed into the house.

"I'm not taking that bet." Megan refused to admit that she didn't have a hundred bucks. Or that she was very afraid a man who needed to get his rocks off might be happy to enjoy what Karen had to offer. Not that it was any of her business. The ache in the pit of her stomach was obviously hunger. What time was it, anyway?

"Smart. Why bet on a sure thing?" King pointed her down a hall.

"Karen has her ways, and Rowdy's a healthy, single male. They can have at it if they feel the urge." Megan said it breezily and patted herself on the back for pulling that off.

"So, you really don't care what he does." King threw open a door to a large bedroom. "Good to know." He dropped the bag and gestured. "Here's a bathroom, and I'll be cleaning up myself. Yes, right next door. I have hopes, too, Megan." He laughed at her expression, then moved closer, suddenly serious. "I told you, I remember every single detail of our time together. I want another chance. With you sober enough to remember, too." He put his finger under her chin and dropped a kiss on her lips before she could step out of reach. "Now, I'll be waiting in the living room whenever you're ready. Dinner in about an hour. Okay?"

"King." Megan didn't know what to say. If she shot him down now, she'd be hustled right back to that junk heap of a trailer. And he did look tempting. Handsome, sure of himself, and kind. She cleared her throat.

"Thanks, King. I appreciate your hospitality." Megan stopped him by the door. She kissed him on the cheek. "No promises. It's not your fault that I might have sent out mixed signals in Houston, at Eli's wedding."

"No, I got your signals. You were carrying a torch for my best friend. I knew it, didn't care. I wanted you, sugar, and set out to get you. When you agreed to come home with me, I knew I'd hit the jackpot. So I didn't look too closely at the situation. My bad." He folded her into his arms and rested his cheek on her hair. "Damnation, woman, you smell like oil and gasoline. You sure you have to work in that shit for a year?"

Megan laughed and pushed back. Thank goodness King still had his sense of humor. She'd always liked that about him. She'd gone home with him that night for the wrong reason, needing comfort from a friend. And King *had* been a friend to her. Unfortunately he'd pushed for something more than she was willing to give then. Now? Well, he was still a man with a lot going for him.

"Yeah. I want my piece of Calhoun. If anyone should understand, it's you, King. It's a family business. Like this ranch."

"Yep. I get it. But it's a hard way to make it. What if I offered you a different way? I could buy your part for you." He rubbed her cheek and then frowned at the trace of mud he came away with. "Marry me and I'll spot you the cash to do just that."

"Stop it, King. You're being way too generous. Trust me when I tell you that I'm no prize." Megan touched his cheek, rough with his evening scruff. He was darkly handsome, with a toughness that ranch life had given him. It hadn't been so obvious when she'd met him in the city. Out here, she could see it. And the intelligence in his dark eyes appealed to her. But the essential chemistry, that *zing* that she felt with . . . No, not going there. Anyway, she couldn't encourage this.

"Don't put yourself down, sugar. You have no idea what I want. You're scrappy, tenacious." He grinned. "Oh, look at you, surprised I know big words. I did go to college, you know. And Wharton School of Business. You keep trying to put me in the friend zone. I'm not settling for that this time. You need to relax and give me a shot. There's more to life than oil rigs and family duty. Let me show you the world." He gathered her in and gave her a world-class kiss.

Megan leaned into it. Giving him that shot. She closed her mind to everything but this man in front of her, holding her against a rock-hard body that fit surprisingly well. She opened her mouth, tasted him, let him taste her, and even relaxed enough not to mind when his hand smoothed over her jeans and caressed her bottom. Oops. She felt it when he got close to her cactus wounds. She flinched, but he took it as encouragement and made a move toward her breast.

No, she just couldn't. So, she stepped back and patted his chest.

"I'm sorry, King. You *are* a good friend. Now I'd better hit that shower."

"I could scrub your back." His smile didn't fade when she shook her head and shoved him toward the door. "I'm not giving up."

"I'll give you points for persistence." She smiled but wondered why she didn't feel the *zing*, the thrill, the *got to have him* ache between her legs.

"I'll take them. Later, Megan." He held on to the door and winked. "And keep that hard hat beside your bed. Did you think "Oil Rig Barbie" was a slam? Sugar, I had fantasies about my sister's Barbie dolls back in the day that would make a hooker blush. So, think on that, why don't you, while you're naked in the shower?" He eased the door closed with a laugh.

Megan leaned against the wood and fanned her face. Well, she had that ache between her legs now. Too bad it wasn't King Sanders she was picturing easing it.

Chapter 7

Dinner was the promised feast. Megan sat at the massive mahogany table with a crystal chandelier hanging over it while a young woman brought in platters of roast beef in a wine sauce, buttered new potatoes, and creamed spinach, along with a salad. While inhaling the tantalizing smells, Megan also admired the heavy silver at her place setting and the fine china. This ranching family knew how to appreciate the finer things, even though they were miles from the nearest big city.

"That's beef from our own stock. I guarantee it will melt in your mouth." King opened a bottle of wine and frowned at the server. "Where's Carmelita, Angela? I wanted to introduce her to Megan."

"She was tired, complained of a headache, and took to her bed." Angela smiled. "She will be all right. I think she's pouting because you didn't bring your guests to her right away." She studied the table. "You want bread? I can bring out some hot rolls. It will only take a few minutes."

"No, I think this is enough." Karen held out her wineglass to her brother to be filled. "You sure she's okay? It's not her blood pressure, is it?"

"No, she's taking her pills." Angela shook her head. "She says eat your spinach, Mr. King. No excuses." She hurried away from the table.

Megan saw him grin. "Your housekeeper orders you to eat your veggies?"

"She's more than just our housekeeper. You'll see when you meet her tomorrow." He filled everyone's wineglasses and then turned the talk to Houston and people they knew there.

By the time Megan pushed away from the table, she'd concluded that someone who cooked as well as the mysterious Carmelita could name her terms. King had certainly eaten two helpings of the delicious spinach, even after Karen had explained that they'd been raised on the vegetable since it was their biggest cash crop after cattle. They were both pretty tired of it, no matter how Carmelita dressed it up.

When Megan stood, the room spun for a moment and she had to hold on to the edge of the table. Oh. Maybe the glass of wine she'd had before dinner and the second one with it hadn't been a good idea. She was exhausted, and this day had been endless.

"Let's adjourn out by the pool. I think it's finally cooled down, and I'm sure there will be one of Carmelita's fabulous desserts and coffee ready for us out there." Karen latched on to Rowdy's arm, urging him to walk out there with her. He'd been pretty quiet during the meal. Of course, he didn't know the people the Sanders twins had insisted upon talking about.

"I should check on Lucky." Megan hoped her words hadn't slurred, but she was afraid they had.

"Your dog is fine. The cowboys are enjoying him. Don't be surprised if they try to keep him." King kept his arm around Megan. "You okay? You look a little wobbly."

"I am. It's been a long day. Remember, it was only yesterday that we barely survived a tornado. No wonder I'm still reeling." On top of that, it was only two days since she'd left home. Didn't seem possible.

"She was hurt then, too." Rowdy hadn't gone far. "She took a bad hit from a cactus." He ignored Karen, who kept pulling on his arm, determined to get him outside. "She still can't sit without wincing. Or didn't you notice, Sanders?"

This got Karen's attention. "Are you kidding me? You got cactus needles in your butt?" She laughed.

"Not funny, sis." King looked Megan over, as if he could see through her long dress. "Sugar, you should have said something. Can I get you a pillow? Have you had a doctor check you out?"

"I'm feeling better. Just tired. I didn't get much sleep last night. Or not good sleep, anyway." Megan liked King's obviously genuine concern. She should probably give him a real chance to charm her.

"Rowdy had to ply me with liquor so he could get those damn cactus spines out without me leaping off the bed."

That got the Sanders twins exchanging looks and what must be a secret signal. Because Karen got busy. Before he could blink, Rowdy was sitting beside the pool with a coffee cup in his hand and a plate with a giant wedge of *tres leches* cake in his lap. King practically carried Megan to a well-cushioned chaise lounge chair at the opposite end of the pool. He made a show of seeing to Megan's comfort, fixing her coffee just the way she liked it and serving her cake before he sat at her feet.

"I'm fine. Really." Megan sipped her coffee. "I feel better already. Not so tired. Guess I needed the caffeine."

"That's decaf. It's all Carmelita serves after nine o'clock at night." King laughed. "I know. It's obvious that we're run by our staff." He slipped off her sandals and began to massage her feet. "You've had a near-death experience. Let me take care of you."

"Death by cactus? Please don't Tweet about it. Now, that would really make the country club crowd hoot." Megan took a bite of cake. "This is delicious. But I can't eat another bite of anything. Here, you finish it. I don't want to hurt Carmelita's feelings."

King set the plate aside. "She'll get over it. Now, tell me how Baker took out those cactus spines. You know it's making me jealous as hell imagining that scene."

"Nothing to it." Megan glanced across the pool when she heard the merry tinkle of Karen's laugh as she got up and pulled off her flowing dress to reveal a yellow string bikini. "Seems like there's going to be swimming."

"It's the perfect night for it." King stood. "Baker, you want to borrow some trunks?"

"I think I've got some in my room. A swim sounds good. Be right back." Rowdy disappeared into the house.

"You feel like swimming? I'm sure Karen has a suit you can use from the stash we keep on hand for guests if you didn't bring one." He pulled Megan to her feet, still being careful.

"I think I've got mine. Rowdy repacked for me. My suitcase took a hard hit when our trailer rolled so he took whatever he could find and stuck it in that ugly duffel bag. It might take me a while to find my suit, though, if it survived." Megan looked at the gleaming blue water with the pool lights shining through it. It was a warm, clear night with a thousand stars in the sky. The idea of relaxing in the pool was tempting. "Yeah, I do love to swim. Give me a minute."

"I'll meet you at your door." King grinned. "I'm warning you now. The idea of seeing you in a bikini has me hot and bothered."

Megan put her hand on his chest. "Stop it, King. This isn't going to happen."

"I don't want to be your friend, Megan. That would truly suck." King plucked off her hand and kissed her palm. "Stop fighting this and give me a chance, sugar. Think about letting me kiss your hurts and make them all better."

Megan shivered and hurried to her room. King did know the right things to say. Sexy talk. She'd always had a weakness for it. Rowdy seemed perfectly willing to play Karen's games. Not that he was a factor here. So, why was she so determined to keep King at arm's length?

She dug in the crammed-full duffel and found her bikini. It had been a last-minute add at home because she always liked to be ready for the unexpected when she traveled. This lean year coming up would make her wardrobe work hard. Thank God she'd bought quality pieces that should hold up. If there were no more natural disasters. At least the caftan she'd worn to dinner had survived. It didn't wrinkle and looked smart in a casual setting like the ranch. Guys like Rowdy probably didn't have a clue that it had cost what would be a month's salary to him. Her thong sandals with the stone embellishments had set her dad back about the same. Karen had looked her over approvingly when Megan had joined them for dinner.

Of course, the woman didn't care that Rowdy had only changed into fresh jeans and a knit shirt that showed off his broad shoulders. As long as those jeans hugged his butt and the yellow had flattered his tan, Karen had approved of his outfit, too.

After her shower this afternoon, she'd taken off the big Band-Aids and her wounds looked better. Still, Megan grabbed a towel from the bathroom and wrapped it sarong-style around her hips, trying to cover as much of the redness as possible.

"You do know how to rev a guy's engine, lady." King was leaning against the wall across from her room when she opened the door. He wore black swim trunks that left little to her imagination.

Megan swallowed. King was ripped, with the kind of body most men had to work hard to get, if they ever could. His washboard abs were lightly dusted with dark hair that arrowed down to a flat navel, then to a bulge that kept growing while she watched. Megan tore her gaze from the spectacle.

"Behave." She stepped past him to head down the hall.

"Can't help myself. You're just too damn sexy. You think I don't remember what little you're covering up?" He moved behind her and snagged the towel. "Well, hell. I can see where that cactus got you. Maybe you shouldn't get in the water. It looks inflamed." He stopped her with a hand on her shoulder, then went down on his knees.

"What are you doing, King? Get up from there!" Megan gasped when she felt his warm breath against her hip. The turquoise bikini didn't cover much. Of course, he could see the places where the spines had bit into her.

"I just hate to see you hurt, sugar." He gently traced her wounds with his lips. "This must have hurt like a son of a bitch. No wonder he had to get you drunk to take them out."

Megan hit him on his head with her hand. "King, you need to stop now. No, don't untie that." He was working on the side ribbon that held the bottom of her suit together.

"Well, would you look at that? Take it into her room, brother. Rowdy and I are on the way to the pool." Karen's voice made Megan jump and grab at her bikini tie.

"Couldn't find my trunks, so Karen found some for me in your room, Sanders." Rowdy's voice was rough, and Megan turned to see him staring at her. "Guess they're still in that trashed trailer. I knew some of my clothes didn't make it."

"King got carried away when he saw where the cactus hurt me." Megan licked her lips. Stupid to be embarrassed. And look at Rowdy, wearing next to nothing himself in navy trunks stretched to the max. So he had a great body. What did she care? Karen draped herself over him as she pushed him down the hall.

"Come on, Rowdy. That water is waiting, and I'm dying to jump in."

Jump in or jump him? Megan kept that comment to herself.

"Don't splash her, Baker. She'll chew you out if you get her hair wet. Just warning you." King had hopped up as soon as he'd realized they had company. "Megan, you sure you want to get in the water?"

"Yes, even a shower felt great against my wounds. Let's go." Megan picked her towel up off the floor and rushed down the hall. Outside, the moonlight reflected on the water, music played from hidden speakers, and a bottle of wine and glasses had been set out poolside. The magic of a well-trained staff.

Karen settled into a float that allowed her to set her wineglass into a holder. She paddled around aimlessly while watching Rowdy swim laps. When he accidentally sent some spray her way, she playfully kicked water at him, silently begging him to come closer. He glanced at Megan as she eased down the steps in the shallow end, then he swam over to hang on to Karen's float and sip from her glass.

"Those two seem to be getting along." King stepped down into the water, then put his arms around Megan so she could float in front of him. "How do you feel?"

"I told you I'm fine. Really. Don't hover." She realized she was being churlish. "Sorry. But I'm tired. A few minutes of this, then I want to go inside and conk out. We'll have to be at the site early."

"Not to shut down the wells." King glanced at Rowdy.

"Just inspections," Rowdy answered him. "The lawyers are figuring things out. You can relax and let them handle things. I'm sure you're paying them well to do just that."

"You're so right." King pulled Megan closer. "Wrap your legs around me, sugar. I'm taking you to the deep end."

"That's what I'm afraid of." Megan sighed and laid her head on his shoulder. She was too comfortable resting in King's gentle arms. Before she knew it, she'd closed her eyes.

"It's the damnedest thing. She's sound asleep." King Sanders was pissed.

It took all Rowdy had in him not to laugh his ass off.

"Just carry her to her room and put her to bed. I hope you're too much of a gentleman to take advantage of her in this situation." Rowdy had his hands full with the man's sister. Karen seemed determined to have him in her bed. She was certainly hot. There was something wrong with him that he just couldn't get with her program. Instead he kept glancing at Megan. When he'd seen her in that bikini, showing off her curves, he'd taken a hard hit. He'd also finally gotten a good look at her colorful tattoo. It was low on her stomach, below her belly button, and featured the Texas flag with TEXAS FOREVER emblazoned under it. It was both ridiculous and sexy as hell.

But what had really punched him right in the gut was the way Sanders had put his mouth on her, tasting that creamy skin and making his moves. Rowdy wanted to pound the rancher until he was nothing more than a stain on the tile floor in his fancy hall. Shit.

"A gentleman? Well, hell. Of course I am. Oh, I'll get her out of that wet suit. Enjoy a look-see. What man wouldn't?" King aimed a glare at Rowdy. "That what happened when you got her drunk and took those cactus spines out of her ass? After she passed out?"

"Hey, a gentleman wouldn't take advantage." Rowdy yelped when Karen hit him on his bicep. "What was that for?"

"My brother is a gentleman, but he's human. You saying you wouldn't look at me, if I passed out on you?" She put on a pout.

"I somehow doubt that you ever pass out, Karen. Or that I'd have to resort to playing Peeping Tom to see more of you." He rubbed his arm, but grinned. The woman was clearly aiming to make his night interesting.

"Well, that depends. On how things go here." She held out her empty wineglass. "Get me a refill?"

"My pleasure." Rowdy took the glass. Seriously, didn't these folks see the danger of glass around a swimming pool? He climbed out, then helped a frustrated Sanders juggle a boneless Megan as he climbed out of the water with her in his arms. She was down for the count. "You sure you don't want me to take her for you?"

"In your dreams." King growled as he stomped off toward the door leading into the house. "Fuck!"

"Not tonight." Rowdy laughed as he filled Karen's wineglass, then poured one for himself. Maybe that was what was wrong with him. He needed to loosen up. He turned to Karen, grunting when he saw her yellow top floating away from her. "Looks like you had a little accident. Aren't you afraid your brother will come back?"

"No. He's too smart for that. Come here, Rowdy." Karen slid out of her float and walked into the shallow end.

Her breasts were flawless. Of course, he'd noticed that right away.

Too bad he could see they weren't natural. Guys weren't stupid. The size and shape were a dead giveaway. He'd been in enough strip clubs to . . . But, hell, he was still impressed. What guy wouldn't be?

"Here's your wine." Rowdy figured she'd noticed he wasn't immune to seeing naked boobs. Double Ds, even with surgical help, weren't to be ignored. He took a deep drink and then set his glass on the edge of the pool. "You trying to tell me something?"

"I've been trying to tell you something since before dinner." Karen moved in, brushing against him. "You wouldn't believe how scarce men of quality are around here. I'm sure not going to get involved with one of our employees. Too messy if and when things went south."

"I can see that." Rowdy ran his hands down her bare back. "You're in fantastic shape. Yoga? Pilates?" He knew women appreciated having their work acknowledged. She obviously spent some time in the gym. Surgery couldn't account for her body being so perfectly toned. He didn't think so, anyway.

"A little of this, a little of that." She smiled. "And thank you. I didn't think you'd noticed." She looked at him through her lashes, then teased a path across his chest with her fingertips. "I have to work out, with Carmelita feeding us like we're starving kids who'll never get another meal once we leave here." She laughed and tweaked one of his nipples. "Now, you. I do like your body. Megan told me you used to play football. Guess you keep up the workouts."

"If I didn't, I'd probably run to fat. I have a big appetite. Wouldn't want to develop one of those beer guts like some of my friends have now."

"Tell me more about your appetite. Better yet, quit talking and let's get down to business." Karen slid her hand down the front of his trunks and squeezed.

Business. A cold word. Not one he liked to use when thinking about a woman. There had been no kissing yet, and he really had no urge to touch his mouth to hers. She wore bright red lipstick and he'd be wearing it, too, if he leaned in and tasted her. Her lips were a little too pumped up, maybe more fake stuff. He knew from experience that they wouldn't be soft, and he really didn't even want to check and see for himself. Then there was a plastic quality to her face that was either some kind of waterproof makeup or more surgery.

Did Karen really think she needed all that to make herself desirable? His mind drifted to Megan, all natural. She'd certainly had the money to do everything this woman had done, but she hadn't bothered. He'd felt her against him when he'd lost his mind and kissed her. She'd been soft, yielding. Nothing plastic about her. He realized his hands had fallen to his sides and he'd leaned away from Karen.

"What the hell are you thinking about, big boy?" Karen let go of him and stepped back. "You either get with the program or say good night."

"I'm sorry. I just broke up with a woman whom I thought I'd be with forever. Maybe I'm crazy, but I don't just fuck, Karen. I make love." Rowdy sat on the top step and took a swallow of wine. "Guess that makes me some kind of pussy. But there you have it."

"Seriously? You can't just have fun? Fuck me and move on?" She stood in front of him, those damn bobbing breasts taunting him. She crossed her arms over them. Like he might change his mind if he had to work a little harder for a peek.

"I don't know. Maybe. But I don't really know you, Karen. And I think any woman deserves more than a man who has his mind on someone else." Rowdy cleared his throat. To his surprise, it had been days since he'd given Cassidy any serious thought except to hope the guy she was with now treated her right. No, his "someone else" was a lot closer than Houston, Texas.

"She broke your heart." She studied his face, then turned away.

"That's part of it." He touched her back and she faced him again. "But you should have a guy who will want *you*, make you feel special. You're a beautiful woman, and any man would be lucky to have you. And not just for one night, either." Rowdy knew he'd said enough, so he polished off the wine and looked out at the gleaming water.

He jumped when he felt the pressure of her breast against his arm. She'd sat beside him on the step. Well, hell. Was he an idiot? He didn't want to hurt her further by pushing her away, so now what? Oh yeah, he could take what she offered. But this really didn't sit well with his conscience. He'd be using her and picturing someone else. God damn it. He gripped his wineglass, fighting the urge to smash it on the tile. Then he heard her sob.

"What is it?" He turned to see her crying with big tears running down her cheeks, her face flushed. "Karen? I'm sorry if I hurt your feelings."

"No, it's not that." She slid her arms around his neck and kept crying, her tears wetting his shoulder.

"Talk to me."

She finally lifted her head, her lashes wet. Waterproof mascara. He'd learned from his years with Cassidy that she must have used it or she'd have what Cass had called "raccoon eyes."

"Would you get my top for me?" She sat back and put her hands over her breasts.

"Sure. Stay there." He swam out and dove to rescue it from where it had been sucked down against a drain in the deep end. When he got back to her, she'd found a towel and was mopping her face with it.

She slipped the top back on and tied it at her neck. "There. Now I'm decent again. Sorry for ambushing you. I always think about what *I* want. I figured you were a healthy male. What would be the harm?"

"Hey, I'm flattered. Beautiful woman, moonlight. Most men . . ." Rowdy shut up. What else could he say?

"No, you're a gentleman. Like my brother. And you're right. I give myself away too cheaply. Always have. I even marry for the wrong reasons, looking for someone who'll finally value me, not my money. So I marry rich assholes." She shuddered. "I do want someone who will really love me. Not just fuck me for the fun of it. Then move on and forget me." She blotted her face again. "You actually turned me down."

"Call me crazy." Rowdy leaned over and kissed her cheek. "Forgive me?"

"If you'll do me a favor." She brushed a hand down his cheek. "Play along in front of King and Megan. I have a reputation to uphold. If he knew you rejected me, my brother would laugh his ass off."

"Surely not." Rowdy couldn't imagine what kind of relationship the twins had that they could be so casual about sex with strangers.

If he had a sister, he'd punch out any guy who thought he could use her and just walk away.

"Trust me, King thinks I can get any man I set my sights on." She pulled the towel around her shoulders. "I'm not going to admit it's not true."

"So you want them to think we're sleeping together." Rowdy didn't like the idea of lying to Megan. Of course, Ms. Calhoun wouldn't care. She was probably going to play her own bedroom games while they were here. And it wouldn't hurt for Cass to hear he'd moved on, now, would it? And to a woman who was probably even richer than she was. Take that, Calhoun heiress.

Rowdy breathed and hated that he'd even thought that. He was ready to refuse her when Karen poked his arm.

"Please? I do have my pride." She grinned suddenly. "Or I could say you couldn't get it up. Too broken up over your ex-girlfriend."

"Threats?" Rowdy stood. Damn it, he knocked over the wineglass and it shattered. Before he realized what he was doing, he stepped wrong and cut his foot. "Shit!"

"Oh God. Look at the blood." Karen threw her towel down on the glass. "Let me help you inside. We have a first aid kit in the kitchen."

Rowdy limped after her while she offered to call a doctor. "Forget it. Let me wash it off and see if there's a piece of glass still in there." They settled at the bar while she found the kit, then took care of what turned out to be a minor wound. "You have your pride and I have mine. So I'll go along with your lie. I don't think we'll be here long if the lawyers say we can't shut down your rigs. This fake affair of ours isn't going to last past our leaving here."

"Thank you!" Karen finished putting a bandage on his foot, then looked up at him. "You really are a nice man."

"I'm not feeling nice right now. I'm feeling manipulated." Rowdy got up and looked around the massive gourmet kitchen. Rich folks. Karen left the mess they'd made—a bloody towel, bandage wrappers, and broken glass—without a second's thought, murmuring about leaving it for the help to clean up in the morning. It was careless and not his way of dealing with things. When they ran into her brother in the hall, she giggled and grabbed Rowdy's hand, tugging him toward her bedroom.

"Out of our way, King. This one's in a hurry!" She laughed and shoved Rowdy inside a room that was a nightmare of pink and lace and smelled like a perfume factory. Then she leaned against the door. "Give him a few minutes to get to his office. He'll probably work for hours before he goes to bed. King is a night owl."

"Well, I'm not. I have an early morning." Rowdy jerked open the door, looked both ways, then limped to his room, easing the door shut and locking it. He'd had quite enough of the Sanders twins. He never thought he'd hope the lawyers figured out that they couldn't shut down those wells, but now he was wishing for a speedy departure. The sooner, the better.

Megan moaned when the bed shuddered. "Go away."

A wet tongue hit her face and she was suddenly wide awake. "That is not sexy."

"Good to know." Rowdy laughed. "Lucky, did you hear that? Licking Megan's face is not sexy."

"What time is it?" Megan pulled the covers over her head. Too damn early, that was for sure.

"We need to get out to the rigs, and there are breakfast smells coming from the kitchen. Biscuits. Bacon. Get up and get dressed for work." Rowdy shook her.

"Get your hand off my boob."

"Oops. Thought it was your shoulder. I'm taking Lucky out for a quick walk, then one of the cowboys is watching him until we leave. His name is Buck, and he sure would like to adopt this hound. Think about it. It would make our life easier."

Megan threw back the covers and sat up. "He's my dog. He is not getting adopted. Now, go away so I can get dressed." She gave Lucky a head rub, then watched them go. Once the door *click*ed shut, she analyzed the look on Rowdy's face as he'd closed the door. Then she looked down at what she was wearing. Oh hell. King had obviously put her to bed and decided to have a little fun while he was at it. The sheer white top was supposed to be a bathing suit cover-up. She hadn't found it last night, or she could have put it on over the bikini. Worn over her naked body made it an invitation to play. And Rowdy had read that message loud and clear. Damn.

With a groan that meant she was still feeling the effects of the cactus, Megan rolled out of bed and into a quick shower. Minimum makeup and work clothes got her down the hall to breakfast faster than she would have thought possible. Rowdy sat at the table looking at the Houston newspaper, the business section. The rest of the paper, along with the *Wall Street Journal* and the San Antonio and Austin daily papers were on the table, too.

"Good morning. Are you Carmelita?" Megan sat carefully.

"Yes, I am. Coffee, *señorita*?" The housekeeper brought over a pot. The woman was probably in her sixties, gray streaking her black hair and with a comfortable figure that showed she enjoyed eating her own delicious food. She had intelligent black eyes that roved over the kitchen. She snapped out orders in Spanish to a young woman who scurried about behind her, working at the massive stove.

"Coffee. Yes, please. I'm Megan Calhoun. That was a delicious dinner last night. Thank you." Megan held out her cup. Cream and every kind of sweetener imaginable were already on the table.

"I'm glad you enjoyed it. This morning we have eggs, bacon, biscuits, and anything else you might want, Miss Megan. Or I can fix you *huevos rancheros*." Carmelita set the pot on the table. "Butter and honey are on the table."

"I'll just have whatever Rowdy is having, only half as much." Megan stirred her coffee. "It smells wonderful. I guess King is still in bed."

"Oh no. King is out in the horse barn. One of the horses is having a baby. He is very worried. It is an important foal. Anyway, it started in the middle of the night. Should be over soon. The vet was called. We pray the mama horse is going to be okay." Carmelita carried over two plates, one piled higher than the other.

"Yes, I tend to forget this is a working ranch." Megan picked up her fork and dug in. "This looks fantastic. I love *huevos rancheros*." She tasted the Mexican-style egg dish. "Perfect. Not too spicy."

"It's one of King's favorites." Carmelita smiled.

"Thanks, Carmelita. We are certainly lucky Megan and King are friends and he invited us to stay here. This is a treat." Rowdy set aside the newspaper and grinned at the housekeeper, then turned to Megan. "Price of oil is up a few cents. That's good."

"So, maybe it isn't so bad if we can't shut down these wells." Megan buttered a biscuit. It fell apart in her hands. "Though I wouldn't mind hanging around here with food like this."

"Did I hear you say you can't shut down the wells?" King came in through the back door, smelling of horse and morning sunshine. "Dish me up some of that and a big coffee. Did you meet everyone, *Abuela*?"

"Yes, I did. How is the *yegua*, King?" Carmelita handed him a mug.

"The mare's tired but she did well. We have a fine new colt in the barn." He took a swallow, then walked over to the sink and washed his hands. "Thought we'd lose them both for a while there. Breech birth. But the doc handled it. Can't say I'd want my hands up in that business." He laughed, clearly in a good mood. "Megan, you didn't answer me. No shutdown?"

"We don't have orders yet. Too early. We were just talking about the price of oil. It's still inching up." She smiled at King, liking this side of him. He walked over and kissed her cheek, before sitting at the head of the table. He glanced at the headlines on the newspapers before shoving them aside, then concentrating on his breakfast.

"Let me know as soon as you hear. Not that I'm in a hurry to lose you two. Or at least wouldn't want to lose you, sugar." King winked. "Baker, can't you let her stay here today while you do whatever it is you have to over at the rigs? Megan was a champion rider as a teenager. Bet you'd love to ride out with me later, wouldn't you, Meg?"

Megan smiled at him. "Gosh, I haven't been on a horse in years, King." The idea of a ride was tempting. "I would love that."

"That wouldn't satisfy her father's will, would it, Megan?" Rowdy reached for another biscuit in the basket the housekeeper had set in the middle of the table.

"Wait. You called Carmelita '*abuela*'. Is she your grandmother?" Megan stared at the housekeeper busily directing the young woman who was now loading the dishwasher.

"Yes, she is." King got up and put his arms around Carmelita. "*Abuela*, come sit down with us. Megan just figured out why you run this house and Karen and me. Believe me, it's her choice, Megan. I would have her in a rocking chair, but she insists on working."

"It's true. I have been here since the children's mama, my sweet Cecilia, and their papa were killed when their plane crashed when the twins were *pequeño*." Carmelita brought a cup of coffee to the table. "It was terrible. I will never ride in one of those tiny airplanes. Of course, King insists on flying one now. Worries me sick." She shook her finger at him. "I tell you. It was a tragedy. Both their parents in love and gone so young." She crossed herself. "*Que descansen en paz.*"

Megan leaned forward and patted her hand. She spoke words of sympathy to her in Spanish, glad she'd learned it when she'd had a nanny who'd helped care for all the Calhoun children until they were in junior high school.

Carmelita thanked her, then got up from the table. "You speak very well, Miss Megan."

"*Muchas gracias.*" Megan picked up her fork again. "I'll say it again. Your cooking is delicious."

"You're right about that. Yes, I'd like for her to retire, but she'd still have to do kitchen duty when I'm home. No one cooks like my *abuela*." King smiled and nodded at Rowdy, who echoed the praise as he cleaned his plate. "I forgot Megan could speak Spanish. It's a helpful skill around here between San Antonio and the border. On the rigs, too. A lot of the workers near here are Hispanic. Do you know the language, Baker?"

"I'm not good with foreign languages. Suck at them, if you want to know the truth. The few words I know in Spanish come out wrong, and the hands who speak it just laugh at me." Rowdy shoved his empty plate away and tapped Megan's shoulder. "We need to get going."

"He's right. It was nice to talk to you, *Señora*, but I have to go to work." Megan stirred around the pile of scrambled eggs on her plate, suddenly losing her appetite. What the hell did she know about the oil business? Yesterday she'd seen men with work gloves using chain and enormous tools to push pipe into the ground. It was part of the drilling process, but she didn't have a clue why they were doing it or what made them run around spraying water with a hose to create so much freaking mud. Then there was the generator that made such a hellacious noise she'd thought her head would explode.

Even getting to where the men were working was treacherous, with scaffolding and ladders, and boards laid across to get from one section to another. It was a miracle there weren't more accidents on the rigs every day. It was a hazardous job. She and Rowdy were supposed to climb up there, too, and "inspect" what the men were doing. She got filthy just watching from down below. Wading in for a closer look didn't bear thinking about. To top it all off, they were supposed to see whether the crew was following the safety rules outlined in a thick book that Rowdy had threatened to make her read.

"Sugar, you look like you want to give up. My offer still stands. We can take off for Italy and let your family company go hang." King reached for her hand. "The oil rigs are no place for a lady."

"You sound like a fifties throwback, Sanders." Rowdy frowned at King. "Megan wants to prove she can handle her job. Why don't you relax and let her try?" He nodded at Megan. "She hasn't had a chance yet. Her father thought she could cut it, why don't you?"

Megan's mouth fell open. Rowdy was defending her, showing faith in her. Where had that come from? So far she'd done nothing but drag down his precious schedule.

"Thanks, Rowdy." She smiled and took another bite of eggs with Carmelita's ranchero sauce, feeling a renewed interest in food.

"My God, what time did you people get up?" Karen trailed in wearing what Megan knew was a designer-label lingerie set in red silk and lace. "Rowdy, baby, I didn't think you'd have enough energy left for an early day after what you put me through last night." She leaned over and nibbled on his ear.

Rowdy's face turned red. "Karen, don't exaggerate. It was nothing."

"I wouldn't say that." She smirked at Megan and leaned over his shoulder to snag a piece of bacon from a platter on the table. "You'd better fill your plate again, big guy. You'll need your strength later." She ran a hand over his chest, then up to ruffle his hair. "Carmelita, I'll take my coffee and toast in my room." She yawned. "I didn't get much sleep last night." She waved and headed back down the hall.

Carmelita muttered some things in Spanish that Megan was tempted to translate to Rowdy. It would make his face turn even redder. "That girl. If she is waiting for room service, she will starve. This is not a hotel." She gave everyone at the table a stern look. "Or a *burdel*, even if my children try to act the *childre traviesa*."

"What's that?" Rowdy looked from Carmelita to King.

"Naughty children, of course. Now Karen's gone and done it. Gotten *Abuela* stirred up." King laughed. "Calm down, *mi dulce*." He jumped up and gave Carmelita a hug. Then he leaned over Megan and squeezed her shoulders. "See what you did, speaking Spanish?

She's on a tear now. I'll hear it all day unless I get on a horse and go out to check the fence line."

Megan laughed and finished cleaning her plate. "That fence probably needs checking anyway." She pushed back from the table.

"It can wait." King put his arms around her. "Megan, honey, I didn't sleep last night, either, but mine was from frustration. So, I'm going to bed. See you tonight. You be careful today." He kissed her on the mouth, attempting to deepen it but failing when Megan gently pushed him back.

"King, blame your exhaustion on your night with your horse, not frustration with me." Megan patted his chest. "I'd like to see that new foal tonight. So, get some rest. I'll see you later."

"You sure will. And we should know by then the status of the wells." King let her go, then turned to Rowdy. "My sister is dear to me, Baker. If you think she's your golden ticket, think again. She has an Italian prince on the hook, and I expect she'll reel him in once we get to Tuscany next month."

"I hope he's worthy of her." Rowdy stood and tossed his napkin on his empty plate. "I like Karen. I know she's just playing. Megan, I'll get Lucky. Meet me in the truck." He thanked Carmelita for the breakfast and walked out the back door.

"Was that necessary?" Megan faced King. "Warning him off Karen?"

"You never know who might turn into a fortune hunter. If they're burning up the sheets, he might be getting ideas." King pulled Megan against him. "Baker's not like us. You think I didn't do a quick background check as soon as I invited him into my home? He's from nothing, Megan. Onetime football hero, college on a scholarship. Tore up his knee in the army in Afghanistan, so his dreams of the NFL fell flat. Of course that makes him something of a hero in my book, so I give him props for that. Still, he might hold on to some of those big dreams he had before he got hurt. Marrying a rich woman could make them happen."

"Oh, please." Megan did not like this line of thought.

"Hey, he didn't dump your sister, did he? She drop-kicked *him* for Mason MacKenzie. Remember, you wouldn't even know the guy except that he dated your new half sister for most of his adult life. Is that really a recommendation? How well do you even know Cassidy?"

"Stop it. She's family now, and she told me all about Rowdy before I decided to do this year with him. I trust that she's steered me to a great guy who has no ulterior motives. I'm the one who hijacked his career and made him take me with him. He hasn't been exactly thrilled with any of it." The truth of that was undeniable. The fact that a few sparks were now flying between them was probably due to the fact that they'd been through tornado hell together. And that they were stuck in close quarters and had to look forward to the next eleven months and twenty-something days of more of the same.

"Honestly, Rowdy doesn't seem to be dazzled by money. In fact, it puts him off. Look what happened when his girl found out she was a Calhoun. She dumped him for a billionaire. That had to leave a bad taste in his mouth."

"Or a craving for a sugar mama of his own, Megan." King glanced at Carmelita, who was watching them. "We'll talk more tonight. When you've had a chance to see just how this new job doesn't suit you." He looked her over and frowned. "Work boots and baggy jeans? Sorry, that outfit doesn't do you justice." He pulled her closer. "I like you in silk, like what you had on last night. You were made to wear fine things and to be taken care of. I'd like to do that."

Megan studied his handsome face. He meant it. An easy life. Strange that the promise didn't move her more than it did. She felt Carmelita's eyes on her and looked past King's shoulder to see her approving nod. Why? Because Megan spoke Spanish and had a similar background to the wealthy rancher? It was more than a lot of couples she'd known who'd jumped into marriage had going for them.

Unfortunately, the divorce rate in her crowd was sky-high. Take Karen's third strike in the marriage game. She was typical, unfortunately. Megan had seen bad marriages up close growing up, and it had made her shy away from committing. At twenty-eight she was beginning to wonder if she'd ever risk a permanent arrangement.

King grinned. "Keep thinking, sugar. Remember, I can take you away in a heartbeat and still buy you a piece of Calhoun Petroleum if that's what you want."

"You're pushing me, King. Stop it. You're a good friend, that's all.

I wish you'd remember that." She eased away from him. Too bad he was way too used to getting his own way. Spoiled rich boy.

Who'd lost both his parents when he was young and been raised by his grandmother. He also worked hard to keep his ranch running. Not so spoiled, then. Shoot. She was a little too tempted by what he was offering, and that rankled. No, she wanted to earn her inheritance, didn't she?

"See you later." She finally got out of there and walked to the waiting truck. Looking around, she thought about what King was offering her—affluence, a man who wanted her desperately, and a life of ease that would be familiar. King would let her do what she wanted because she could wind him around her finger, and he made her laugh. But then there was the chemistry—or lack of—between them. Okay, she did feel a little something with King. He was an attractive man, after all. She'd have to say it was a slight sizzle. Would it come to a full boil with time?

She climbed into the truck, laughing when an exuberant Lucky hopped into her lap and licked her chin. Rowdy ordered the dog into the backseat with a firm voice, and the dog obeyed instantly.

"So, here we are. Are you ready to find out if you can hack it as an employee of one of your father's companies?" Rowdy started the truck but didn't put it in gear. "Or will you let some rich rancher rescue you?"

Megan didn't know the answer, so she did the only thing she could think of to do. She aimed a middle finger at him and buckled her seat belt.

Chapter 8

"Megan, watch this." At Vince's signal, all of the men stripped off their shirts and got busy around the pipe in the center of the rig.

"This team is proud of the fact that they are one of the fastest crews pushing pipe in the state. Look at them go." He put his hand out when Megan tried to get a closer look. "Stay well back. When they get moving, it can be dangerous. With the chain, the drill collar, and the turntable going, there are a lot of factors at play."

"Vince, it looks like a safety issue to me." Rowdy frowned, obviously not happy.

Megan was just glad the men had quickly moved from "Ms. Calhoun" to "Megan." Didn't hurt, either, that they were showing off their bodies, glistening with sweat in the hot Texas sun.

"Maybe Rowdy's right. I hope they're careful. It looks slippery up there." Megan couldn't believe the way the men worked together to keep sending pipe down the hole. They kept attaching more pieces with the so-called collars as water was added to make the drill bit slide down into the mud.

"We've got a great safety record, Rowdy. Otherwise, I'd put a stop to their little show. And, yes, it *is* slippery. These men are experts, though, and have this routine down to a science. Watch and be amazed." Vince glanced at Lucky, who was barking as if he were a cheerleader for the men. "You keep a good tight hold on that leash."

"I will. If it wasn't so hot, I'd keep him locked in the truck." Megan had thought about putting him in the office trailer, but he might have gotten too interested in the paperwork scattered around there. They should probably invest in a good-sized dog crate for their future stops.

Rowdy frowned. "We should have left him at the ranch."

"He's okay. Give it a rest, Rowdy." This was the fifth time she'd heard him say that. Megan turned to Vince. "Tell me more about what they're doing." She listened carefully but couldn't take her eyes off the men working smoothly together. What they did looked dangerous. A generator roared, chain whipped past them, and the heavy equipment surrounding them rumbled. One man was in charge of a water hose, keeping the pipes wet. It splashed them all, which made their tanned bodies even more appealing.

"You're licking your lips." Rowdy leaned close to say that. "Not a good idea to encourage them."

"I'm not!" Megan gave him an elbow. "I'm admiring their strength. I can't believe they can pick up those pipes and collars so easily. I tried to lift just one end of a pipe and couldn't budge it."

"Yep. They're good men. They have hard jobs." Vince glanced at Rowdy. "Would sure hate like hell to have to lay off this crew."

"What's Carlos doing?" Megan had quickly learned the names of the men on the rig after Vince had introduced them. "That looks scary." The man was walking on the edge of the scaffolding holding a long piece of pipe over his head.

"Son of a bitch. Pardon, Megan. But the idiot's showboating. For you." Vince frowned and shouted at the crew, but Megan doubted he could be heard over the roar of the generator used to send the drill bit into the ground. "I've got to put a stop to this. Stay here." He stalked off to climb the rig, his face red.

"Vince is right. With you standing here, the men want to show off." Rowdy looked grim.

"This isn't my fault. I'm just doing what I have to do to learn about the field." Megan gasped when the worker suddenly lost his balance and plunged over the side of the rig to land on the dirt many feet below. "Oh God!" She thrust Lucky's leash at Rowdy and ran to see if the man was all right. He wasn't moving.

"Carlos! Are you hurt?" She squatted next to him and laid her hand on his muddy cheek.

"I am now, *querida*." He opened his eyes and smiled, then tried to sit up. "Stupid mistake. Knew I should have joined the circus."

"What?" Megan stood out of his way as he slowly pushed to a sitting position.

"Always wanted to be a tightrope walker. Couldn't you tell?" He hissed when he tried to put his weight on his left foot, then cursed in Spanish. "*Estoy tan jodido.*"

"You are, if that's broken." Megan tried to help him when he started to get to his feet, but Rowdy was there first, offering help.

"You understood me?" Carlos shook his head. "I'm okay."

"What did he say?" Rowdy took his arm and got him to his feet, but it was obvious Carlos had seriously injured his left ankle.

"He said he's screwed. Which he is, if that ankle's broken." Megan took Lucky's leash and stepped out of the way. "I'm sorry, Carlos. What can I do?"

"I've got him. You take the dog and go sit in the office. Read the safety manual." Rowdy sounded furious.

"What did *I* do?" Megan lifted her chin at his tone.

"You just ruined this outfit's safety record." Rowdy nodded toward a big board next to the office door. "Three hundred and thirty-nine days without an accident. Close to a year. Gone in an instant, thanks to you."

"Hey, don't blame Megan. It was my fault. Lost my head and didn't watch where I was going." Carlos shrugged away from Rowdy's helping hand and glared at him. "You didn't do a thing, Ms. Calhoun. Don't let him treat you like that. Last I heard, it's your family's company. Not this guy's." He gestured for another man who'd been hovering nearby, and with his help, he hopped away.

"No, he wasn't watching where he was going. Instead, he was watching you, Megan. Standing there in a T-shirt that clings like plastic wrap and jeans that do the same. These men don't need you as a distraction. They're doing a dangerous job."

"I—I'm sorry. I know it's dangerous. And I hate that he's hurt." She looked down at herself. "Wait a minute. Clings like plastic wrap? Are you kidding me? Everything I have on is at least two sizes too big. Besides, I can't help what the men watch when I'm around." Megan flexed fingers that had been in fists so tight they ached. Boy, did she want to plant one of those fists right on Rowdy's arrogant chin.

He didn't say anything, just pointed to the office trailer.

"Wow. For a man who got his rocks off last night, you sure are in a bad mood." Megan patted Lucky on the head and tugged him toward the wooden steps leading to the office. "Come on, pup. At least it will be quieter in there."

"Megan, stop." Rowdy took off his hard hat and stalked over to her. "Don't discuss our activities at the ranch around here. I'm sure there's been talk already. That we're hanging out with the Sanders, who are big shots in this part of the state."

"'Hanging out.' Yeah. You and Karen got right to it, didn't you?" Megan stared at him. "I noticed you're limping today. She ride you a little too hard?"

Rowdy flushed. "Broken glass around the pool. I stepped on it. And what I do or don't do with Karen is my business. Just like what you and King do is none of mine."

"Trust me, I have no desire to get into your personal affairs. But how can I learn anything about the oil business when I'm shut inside the office?" She pushed Lucky into the sit position.

"Memorize the safety protocols outlined in that book. And keep your dog out of the way. Until it gets cooler, he's a problem. If we had a decent trailer, we could lock him in there with the AC going. So you study. Something a real hand would have done before I'd have hired him as an assistant in the first place. Right now you'd just be in the way. And a dangerous distraction, as you just saw." Rowdy shoved on his hard hat.

"Let me remind you that I didn't want to come along in the first place." She stepped closer and jammed a finger into his chest. "I had no choice. It was take this job or lose my inheritance, buddy. And, trust me, there are millions of dollars at stake. I could either choose you or a stranger to follow around the next year. For some reason Cassidy thinks you're a great guy. You sure had her fooled." Megan tugged on Lucky's leash. "Come on, pup. Let's get cool and sit down with that book. Vince said there are more Cokes in his re-frigerator. And he's got that bowl I can use for cold water just for you. How does that sound?" She turned her back and stomped up the stairs, slamming the metal door for good measure.

"She's a firecracker." The superintendent had come up behind Rowdy. "The Calhouns all have a temper. You really have to take her around the drilling sites for a full year?"

"That's what I've been told. Don't have much choice in the matter, unless I want to quit my job in this economy. Don't think I haven't thought about it." Rowdy turned to Vince. "Sorry about your accident record."

"Yeah. Me, too. I have bonuses tied to that record." He walked over and erased the chalk number on the slate and drew a big zero.

"It won't be in my report." Rowdy saw a truck pull out from the dusty lot. "Carlos going to town?"

"He needs to get his ankle x-rayed. For workmen's comp. I may not like the way that happened, but we're still liable for the injury." Vince spit on the ground. "Let's get this inspection done. No word yet from the lawyers?"

"No. But you know paperwork and contracts. Could take a while to untangle." Rowdy followed Vince as he led the way, the superintendent describing his safety measures. He was a seasoned employee who had worked his way up in the company. If what he said he did proved to be the case, Rowdy knew he'd have a good report to send into the home office.

"Hey, guys," Megan called from the office door. "The phone in here was ringing so I answered it. Billy Pagan, he's the lawyer currently serving as in-house counsel, is on the line. He needs to talk to you, Rowdy." She stepped back inside, letting the door slam again.

"Guess it didn't take as long as I thought it would." Vince stared at Rowdy and shook his head. "Let me know how it shakes out. I'll be up on the rig, checking on the crane. Looks a little off center to me. Plus I'll be chewing out that entire crew. Showboating don't have no place on an active rig. Carlos is lucky he didn't get hurt worse than he did." He strode off.

Rowdy headed into the office and picked up the phone. He noticed Lucky happily chewing on a bone from the ranch Carmelita must have slipped to Megan.

"This is Baker."

"Megan says you're not happy with her out there." The man chuckled. "You ready to burn her, write up a bad evaluation, and make her lose her inheritance?"

"No!" Rowdy certainly didn't want to deny Megan what he considered her birthright. He might not trust rich women, but he wasn't going to be the cause of her losing her money.

"Well then, what's going on out there?"

"Honestly?" Rowdy turned to Megan. "Why don't you take the dog for a walk?" He pointed to the door.

"So you can talk about me? Swell." She huffed, then slammed out of the office, the dog in tow.

"You have a dog with you?" Pagan chuckled. "Is that normal?"

"Not at all."

"Then I'm sure it's on Megan. She's always been a dog nut. Can't believe she brought a dog with her to work, though. You should have shut that down, Baker."

"You try telling a Calhoun woman no. I don't seem to have figured out how to do it yet." And wasn't that a pisser. Rowdy couldn't believe he'd just admitted that to a total stranger.

"I hear you, man. And I've had more experience with just that than you know." There was a brief silence. "Well, fill me in. What the hell's happening out there?"

Rowdy thought about the accident they'd just had. He could blame Megan, but it was really the man's fault. If a worker couldn't keep his mind on his business, then a broken ankle was what he deserved.

"She got us a nice place to stay, anyway. I'm not complaining about bunking at King Sanders's ranch." Rowdy decided to let it go at that.

"Okay, then. Conrad's will is pretty clear. I've gone over it. He wants her to have field experience, end of story. So be sure that happens."

"You think the man was firing on all cylinders when he made that will?" Rowdy was beginning to wonder about that. "The contract he signed with Sanders is way over the line as far as what he let the rancher get away with. Even King Sanders admitted that. The super here has a copy, and I looked it over. The guarantees are ridiculous."

"I hear you." Pagan was silent for a few moments. "You have a point. But do not ever say that again. Trust me on that. You give even a hint that Conrad was not of sound mind toward the end, and all hell will break loose here. If that will's not valid, it'll open the door to all kinds of financial complications. Corporate raiders might have a shot at taking over Calhoun Petroleum while we figure things out here. Also, there are ex-wives with their own lawyers who would like nothing better than to get a bigger piece of the pie, if you know what I mean."

"No idea. But you're the lawyer. I need to know now if we're staying here or moving on. The safety inspection will only take a day or two. Are we shutting down wells, or not?"

"You're not shutting down any wells for the foreseeable future, especially not on Sanders's property. Maybe not anywhere. We believe the price of oil is now steadily on the rise. Stockpiling oil and gas is the smart move for now. What we need from you is to check on a fracking snafu getting out of hand in West Texas. Now, that shit, we can stop. It's a public relations nightmare, and the mess Conrad made when he started the company is going to be bad enough without fracking complaints on top of it."

"Fracking doesn't have to be a problem. If it's done right, it doesn't have to harm the environment." Rowdy wondered if the problems were with the people running the job there.

"There you go. It'll be your job to make sure that it *is* being done right. I have no idea what has the community out there stirred up. All I know is that you need to get to that site and see what's going on. Take Megan and use her as a representative of the family. Might make an impression." Pagan laughed. "Her sister is the public relations expert and that's her idea. I don't get it. When someone hates Calhoun Petroleum, do they really need a target to shoot at? But Shannon seems to think Megan has it in her to handle this situation."

"I'm an engineer. I don't give interviews. I hope to hell no one shoves a microphone in my face." Rowdy had been approached by reporters before and had stuck to "No comment." "As to the fracking, if there are problems with the way it's being handled out there, it may take some serious money to fix the issues. I know Calhoun is having a tough time, but let the people holding the purse strings know that I may have to ask for big bucks to make things right." Rowdy tried not to imagine the worst. "No need to panic yet. Let me get out there and see what's what."

"What's what is a bunch of unhappy locals trying to make noise. So, tie up the job where you are and grab a new truck and trailer in San Antonio. Cassidy's arranging things. Then head for the field west of Pecos. I'll be e-mailing you the details." Pagan shuffled some papers and named the well site. "I believe you've handled that area before with some success."

"I've been there." Rowdy had a lurch in the pit of this stomach.

Unfortunately, that was close to some natural resources that anyone would hate to see ruined. Fracking could be a headache and unpopular with the people who lived near it. Earthquakes. Chemical smells. Water pollution. The list of complaints were many, and all it took was one fuckup and environmentalists would be all over it.

He looked out the window and saw Vince waving his arms at his crew and pointing down to the pipe where Carlos had dropped it on the ground. This well site was as clean as one could be. If supervision out west was the problem, maybe he could transfer Vince and find someone else to run this field. Vince wouldn't thank him for the assignment, but maybe he could talk the home office into agreeing to a bonus for the man. He'd earn it. Rowdy realized Pagan had finished his rundown of logistics and was waiting for a response.

"Okay, we'll head out there as soon as we wind up our inspection."

"You don't sound excited." Pagan laughed. "Tough shit. If you and Megan can get this thing handled, it will be important for the company. We're facing a lot of issues here, and we didn't need this on top of everything else. Showing these people that a Calhoun cares about their concerns might just calm them down. It's certainly the kind of thing Megan needs to know how to do. Teach her about fracking and why we like it."

"I don't like it unless it's done right." Rowdy turned when the door opened and Megan and the dog marched in. "Thanks for the update. I'll be looking for an e-mail confirming the details."

"You've got it." Pagan ended the call.

"So, are we staying or going?" Megan let go of Lucky and poured a bottle of cold water into his bowl.

"Two more days, then we're going. I think we should head into town and turn in that hunk-of-junk trailer—the truck, too, if we can get the rental car back. Pagan says we'll get everything we need in San Antonio." Rowdy hung his hard hat on the peg next to the door. "We need to give Vince time to cool down. You don't realize how hard he's taking the loss of his perfect safety record."

"I apologized to him outside." Megan hung up her plain one, too. She'd left the pink one at the ranch. "He was fine with it. Suggested we eat lunch in town. Which I guess was his way of saying to stay out of his sight for a few hours." She sighed and her shoulders slumped.

"Yeah. Vince is too nice to tell you outright to disappear and too aware that you're a Calhoun." Rowdy opened the trailer door. "I know you didn't mean to cause the accident, Megan. Men are stupid sometimes. Carlos lost his head over a pretty woman. We should dock his pay, not give him workmen's comp."

"No, please!" Megan followed him outside. "I should have left my work shirt on. But it was so freaking hot."

"He acted the fool. He was using the railing like a tightrope, and the pipe like a balance bar." Rowdy laughed. "Didn't you notice?"

"Not really. I was watching how the pipe was going into the ground. But he did say something about the circus." Megan laughed. "My father would have been impressed by the fact that Carlos tried that trick. You have no idea how much Daddy loved the circus."

"Yes, I do. Cass showed me the master bedroom at your house in Houston." Rowdy hadn't believed the strange collection Conrad Calhoun had put together in his place. The man had been obsessed with anything to do with the circus. Maybe he *had* been losing his mind toward the end of his life. That would certainly help explain why he'd pushed his daughter, a woman who had no chance of doing well, into this ridiculous charade of learning the business on the road.

Megan climbed into the truck. "Forget Carlos for now. You know, I don't think the company should pay a dime for that trailer, do you? And not much for this truck."

"Nope. I'm going to give that dealer a piece of my mind. Then I think we should hit the café in the square again. Vince says today's special is fried chicken."

Megan leaned back in her seat. "The only good thing to come out of this trip so far is the food. I never thought I'd say that." She sat up again. "Wait. Where *are* we going next? You didn't sound too happy about it."

"I'm not. Let's just say they have places out there the roughnecks lovingly call the Devil's Asshole." They both shut up after that.

Two hours later, they were finally in the café. It had taken that long for Rowdy to get the trailer turned in and for them to make sure the company wouldn't be charged for it. The same waitress served them the daily special—fried chicken and fresh corn with sweet potatoes. Megan was already buttering a yeast roll.

"I'm going to gain weight on this trip if I don't start running or something every day." She took a bite and smiled. Bliss.

"My foot is killing me. I won't be running any time soon if I don't get it looked at. I'm afraid there's still a piece of glass in there." Rowdy picked up a chicken leg and took a bite. "You're right. So far the food has been outstanding."

"You want me to look at your foot when we get back to the office this afternoon? I saw a first aid kit there." Megan smiled. "It would be my pleasure to dig a piece of glass out of your foot. With a dull knife or tweezers."

"I see the gleam of payback in your eyes. No, thank you." Rowdy sipped his iced tea. "Maybe the doctor the company uses for its workmen's comp claims can fit me in this afternoon. You should let him look at your butt while we're here."

"I'm fine. I barely feel a thing now." Megan wasn't about to show her hip to anyone else. And it was true she was healing well. "But I know you can't afford to take a chance on an infection when you're on the road."

Rowdy told her a story about getting sick once when at a site in far West Texas. The lunch went by quickly as they laughed over his sad plight.

"Hey, it wasn't funny." He pretended to be insulted. "I lay on that bathroom floor for two days until the super found me and took me to the hospital. Which was an eight-hour drive away."

"Wow. Such isolated places. I'd go stir-crazy if I had to stay so far away from civilization for long." Megan pushed back her plate. "But you've gotten to see a lot of the state. Do you enjoy it? The traveling?"

"I did at first. Now I'm pretty sick of it. I'm going to ask for a transfer to another kind of job after our year is up." Rowdy threw his paper napkin on top of a plate that was clean except for chicken bones. "I'm ready to do something else. I hope I can do that within the company. I know this is a bad time to change jobs in the oil industry, but moving around so much is getting me down. I'd like to see what it's like to stay in one place for longer than a two-week stretch."

"I see your point. But for now this lifestyle seems like an adventure to me. If I didn't have to learn about oil, I'd think it was cool to pull a trailer around the state and see so many new places and meet new people."

"Well, you're going to see new places anyway. Day after tomorrow is my best guess." Rowdy pulled out his phone. It was a text. "Just got the confirmation from my boss."

"Seriously?" Megan sat up straight. "King will be disappointed."

"I'm sure." Rowdy didn't look broken up about it. He was busy texting back. "This is going to be a mess. We're going to West Texas, where there's an issue with fracking. Outside of Pecos. There have been problems, protests, and environmental issues. Someone is getting the protesters organized which is where you come in. You're supposed to diffuse the tension while I see what's up with the rigs. Says here your sister Shannon is going to e-mail you some articles about what's happening there. She wants you to be the face of Calhoun. Doesn't that sound like fun?" Rowdy grinned, clearly glad he wasn't going to have to meet the press.

"Fun?" Megan looked down at her jeans and T-shirt. "Not if I have to stand next to one of those noisy rigs and pretend like I don't think fracking is an assault on the environment. Daddy and I had fights about it." She leaned forward, elbows on the table. "Shit, Rowdy. We should shut those wells down, no matter what the company wants us to do."

Chapter 9

"The foal is a beauty, King." Megan leaned against the stall where the mother horse nursed her colt. "It always amazes me how they can stand so quickly."

"This is fine stock." King went on at length about horse breeding and bloodlines.

Rowdy wasn't really listening. He looked around the huge barn. It was clean, well-organized, and looked like it must have cost a fortune. There were at least ten horses in different stalls, and all of them had the look of champions. Not that he knew much about it. He'd ridden a few times back in college when he'd been lucky enough to score invitations to the working ranches where some of his football buddies lived.

This was a different world. One where Megan fit right in. Seemed that the Calhouns had a ranch somewhere, too. She'd already mentioned that it would probably have to be sold because of the problems in the oil industry. That had set King off. He was always offering to buy Megan things—the Calhoun ranch, her dad's company. Shit. What had happened to candy and flowers?

King's phone rang. "I've got to take this. I have a man in Montana bidding for me at a big cattle auction. There's a bull I have my eye on. A prime breeder. They must have put it last in the lineup." King stepped away from them, his phone to his ear.

"You ride?" Megan turned to Rowdy where he'd stopped in front of a big black horse who'd stuck its nose over the fence. "Careful. He might bite."

Rowdy jerked back his hand. He'd actually forgotten you weren't supposed to pet a horse.

Megan laughed. She pulled a carrot out of a cloth bag Carmelita had given her at the house. "Here. Offer him this. Put it in the palm of your hand so he can take it from you and you can avoid those big teeth of his. That's King's horse. He probably *would* bite you. He's a one-man horse, according to King."

"She's right." King watched Rowdy offer the carrot, which was snatched out of his hand before the horse devoured it. "Sorry, sugar, but I have to go inside and get on the computer. There's a bidding war going on, and I can see things better on FaceTime in there. I want a closer look at that bull before I go too high." He waved over a man working at the opposite end of the barn. "Juan can saddle up a couple of horses if you two want to take a ride. He'll point you to a nice little trail out to the tank in the western pasture, too. It's about an easy thirty-minute ride if you think your butt can take it." He looked Megan over and gave her shoulder a squeeze. "What do you think?"

"I'd like to try it." She smiled. "I do miss riding. Don't know why I quit. Got too busy in town, I guess." She turned to Rowdy. "You didn't answer me. Can you ride? I won't go by myself."

"I'm rusty, but I'll give it a shot." He listened to King give Juan orders, in Spanish of course. The man pulled a horse out of a stall, then pointed to another, waiting for King's nod of approval. "Speaking of shots. Sanders, did Megan tell you we went to the doctor today?"

"No! Did he examine your cactus wounds?" King shifted on his feet and clutched his phone, obviously in a hurry, but he couldn't take his eyes off of Megan.

"Yes. Rowdy pushed me into it. He had glass in his foot after he played games with Karen." She arched her brows at Rowdy. "So he needed a tetanus shot. Then my boss here opened his big mouth and mentioned my encounter with the cactus. The doctor made a big deal out of it." Megan rolled her eyes. "I don't think the doctor likes the Calhouns for some reason. He must have said my last name ten times. 'Yes, Miss Calhoun. Bend over, Miss Calhoun. Oh, did that hurt, Miss Calhoun?'" She popped Rowdy on the arm when he laughed. "Not funny. Anyway, I got a tetanus shot, too. With a dull needle. It hurt me worse than that cactus ever did."

"That would be Mickey Murakami." King glared at Rowdy, who was still chuckling.

He couldn't help it. Megan was right. The doctor had clearly had it in for her. Rowdy stopped laughing when King wrapped his arms around Megan and kissed her cheek. "I'm sorry he took his disappointment out on you, sugar. He's a good doctor, but still bitter because he owns land and the mineral rights under it. Seems his wells were the first that your company shut down. He still makes money doing workman's comp for Calhoun, but it's not much compared to those lost royalties." King let her go. "Damn, I wish I didn't have to see about this bull right now. But leave old Mickey to me. He doesn't realize that if he holds on and oil comes back up, the money will start flowing again."

"That's what we're all praying for." Megan sighed.

"I'll have a talk with him. He should have realized that if he makes you mad, you could tell the main office to keep him shut down no matter what oil does." His phone buzzed, and he glanced down at it. "Shit, it's a text this time. The price just keeps going up on that bull. I sure wish I was riding with you, but I'll be damned if I'll let some fella from Wyoming steal this bull out from under me. If I get things settled in time, I'll join you." He hurried out of the barn.

"You haven't told him we're leaving yet." Rowdy walked down to where Juan was saddling a brown and white horse. "Why not?"

"You know why not. He'll make a big deal about it and try to keep me here. For some reason he thinks he's in love with me." Megan talked to Juan, then finished saddling the brown and white while he went to get a second horse.

"He *thinks* he's in love? Maybe he really is. The question is, how do you feel? He seems like a decent guy." Rowdy moved out of the way when Juan brought out a dark brown horse. Rowdy had no idea how to saddle one of the beasts and just tried to stay out of the way.

"He *is* a decent guy. And he's been wonderful to me. I've told him I just want to be friends, but he won't accept that. He thinks he can wear me down, make me love him. Maybe over time . . ." Megan checked the cinch on her saddle. "If he's serious about me, then he can just cool it for a while. I have this year to work for the company ahead of me. He should understand that and quit pressuring me."

"Good point." Rowdy realized Juan was probably taking this all in with interest. "We'd better get a move on." He followed Megan out of the barn, leading his horse the way she was leading hers. It was obviously something she'd done many times, while he felt awkward getting the horse where it needed to go. When they were finally outside, she let Juan give her a boost before she vaulted into the saddle. At least he remembered which side was the right one, then got on without help. It actually felt pretty good once he was up there and settled in. Juan adjusted the stirrups for his long legs.

"Ready?" Megan grinned, obviously eager to get started after Juan gave them directions to the trail they'd be taking.

Rowdy nodded and followed her lead. It was a cool night, the sky was clear, and the moon looked almost full. Once they left the lights around the house and barn and their eyes adjusted, it was easy to see the well-worn path they would take toward the glistening water that King had called a tank. Cattle grazed beyond a barbed-wire fence.

In the distance he could see the sky lit up by the fiery flare next to the drilling site where they'd spent the day. They were burning off the natural gas produced by the wells when the oil came to the surface. He needed to explain that to Megan. It was a good reminder of why they'd come here in the first place. He took a deep breath of the clear air and appreciated the quiet, though if he concentrated he could still hear the persistent rumble of the generators at the well site. It was good that they were far enough away that it was possible to pick up the sounds of an occasional birdcall, the *clip-clop* of the horses' hooves, and a cow lowing mournfully. Rowdy wondered why it sounded sad, but he knew even less about cows than he did about horses.

"So, I wonder why Karen took off for San Antonio?" Megan broke the silence as they rode side by side.

"Shopping emergency? She told me last night she needed to get ready for her trip to Italy." Rowdy hadn't been surprised when Karen didn't show up for dinner. King had explained that she'd taken off for the big city right after lunch and wouldn't be back for several days.

"Oh, you had time to talk?" Megan twisted in the saddle to look at him.

"Maybe." He wasn't going to elaborate. He wasn't comfortable with Karen's deception and sure wasn't going to invent details.

Megan shook her head. "Don't play dumb, Rowdy. King told me what really happened last night. Seems Carmelita came down hard on Karen for acting like a slut, so your *lover* broke and told the truth. That there was nothing going on between you two. When Karen was packing her bags, she even admitted you'd turned her down. Apparently you hit her right in her ego." Megan steered her horse close. "Why didn't you take what she offered, Rowdy? She's attractive. The kind of woman who wouldn't have tied strings to a little affair. And she certainly wouldn't have sprung the baby trap."

Rowdy shrugged. "Maybe I'm stupid."

"Seriously?" Megan eyed him. "Most men would have jumped on her offer."

"Can we stop talking about this?" Rowdy tightened his legs and his horse went faster. Good. At least he'd remembered that much about riding. He passed her on the trail and enjoyed the cool wind on his face.

Megan rode up beside him again, looking like she'd been born on a horse. "She claimed you couldn't get it up." She must have seen Rowdy's horse dance when he did something with the reins. "Relax. She didn't tell Carmelita that, but she tried to bluff it with King. He laughed in her face." She sighed. "That's when she broke down and told him everything. Those two are really close. Karen actually thinks you're a nice guy, but she couldn't face you again after you rejected her. You hurt her pride. She likes to think she can get any man she wants."

Rowdy, the nice guy. It burned him that the three rich people had been discussing him, maybe laughing about his uptight, old-fashioned morals. He uncurled his fist from the reins and sat back in the saddle. He gave a gentle tug when they reached the gleaming pond. To his relief, the horse did stop and he slid off, letting the reins drop to the ground when he saw Megan do the same. He walked over to the water's edge, then turned to face her.

"So, she was hurt? What a pity. But I didn't like what happened last night. Part of the reason I turned Karen down was because I don't want to be used. Especially by some spoiled rich woman who brags that she can get any man she wants." He looked Megan over, from head to toe. "Is that how you think, too, Megan? Wiggle your butt, bat your big blue eyes, and men fall right at your feet? Well, I'm sick of it. Because when your type is done with a man, you don't give a shit what kind of wounds you've inflicted or the pain you've caused. Cass sure didn't look back when she was done with me." God, he sounded like a character from one of those fucking soap operas his grandmother had loved. He turned away from her, disgusted with himself and her. What was she thinking now? *Poor, pitiful Rowdy?* Better that than him being too "nice." The word made his teeth hurt.

Her laughter got his head up fast enough.

"What's so funny? You don't believe me? That I got hurt?" He blinked, trying to work up a tear. Of course, he was ·bone-dry. "Women. They think they can just run over a man and we won't feel a thing. Look at what you're doing to King Sanders. The man is offering you the world. Laying his heart at your feet. And what's your reaction?" He dusted his hands in front of him. "You tell him to quit pressuring you. It would be kinder to just give him a firm yes or no. But I haven't heard that. Oh no. Instead you let him put his hands on you, play the flirt, and plan to leave him without a backward glance. *Adios*, King. Thanks for the offer, but not now. Maybe I'll get back to you after my year is done. Or maybe not."

She stared at him, her mouth open.

He shook his head. "Hell, you tell me to use Karen for a meaningless fling, but I don't see you taking your own advice. Why won't you at least sleep with the guy to put him out of his misery?"

"Why you . . ." Megan stepped closer. "You really have no idea—"

"I know what I see. You're leading him on. Have since the day we ran into him here." Rowdy looked up at the stars. "Shit. Why am I wasting my breath? You obviously expect him to just tough it out. To wait until you figure out if he's the best you can do. You think he'll wait? Let's make a bet on it." He held out his hand, dropping it when she just stared at him. "No?"

She lifted her hand then and placed it right over his heart. "I'm sorry."

"What for? You apologizing for being a woman? It's in the genetic code, baby. You're all alike. You lure us in with your bodies that won't quit, and then there's your smell." He inhaled and almost swayed. "Jesus, the smell of a woman is the one thing they can't bottle. It'll drive a man to his knees every time. Like you had King on his knees last night. Right there in the hall. He was begging you for it, and you just, what, put him off until you fell asleep in his arms? Like you couldn't even be bothered to stay awake for him."

"I'm sorry you've been hurt, but don't take it out on me, asshole." She shoved him then.

Caught off guard, his feet flew out from under him and he hit the water. Just like that. He came up sputtering. At least he'd left that expensive satellite phone back in his room at the ranch house. His wallet, too. So all that was hurt was *his* pride. He sat there—the water was only a foot deep—and glared at her. She was laughing, of course. So much for sympathy. Something in his eyes must have warned her, because she started backing away. Not fast enough.

"No, Rowdy."

"Yes." He vaulted out of the pond to grab her around the waist. Then he walked her right into the water, which got deep pretty fast. He threw her in, happy to see her come up spitting. When she stood, the silky shirt she'd worn to dinner clung to her body, leaving nothing to his imagination. Not that he needed to imagine what was under there. He'd seen her this morning in that see-through white thing she'd slept in. Tonight she wore a skimpy white bra underneath the silk and they were both transparent. Her nipples were dark and point- ing right at him, begging him to come closer. Before he could stop himself, he'd taken a step.

"No, Rowdy." She said it again. Clearly she saw something in his eyes. Her hands were up by the time he got there. "This is a bad idea."

"I know it." He touched her then. God, she felt good.

Her eyes closed. Bad idea. She knew it, too.

He slid his hands over the silk and held those breasts, feeling the shape of them, savoring the pressure of her hard, and soft against his palms.

"Don't you dare kiss me."

She sounded breathy, as if she couldn't think straight, talk right, work this out in her head. He was right there with her.

"I always take dares." He pulled her up until her body was flush against his. Holy shit, but it felt right. Even wet, they seared each other, her arms coming naturally around his neck so that they were molded tight. He leaned right while she took left and their mouths clashed. Hunger fired through him. He was pretty sure it was blazing through her, too. It had been building, and now they finally let it go. Rowdy staggered in the water, his hurt foot in wet tennis shoes landing funny on a rock and knocking him back on his butt. Didn't matter, he wasn't letting her go.

She didn't release him, either. She straddled him, her knees on either side of his hips, and he knew she could feel how much he wanted her. He was ready to rip open his jeans and hers and do something about his long, hard abstinence right now.

Megan pulled back, panting as she looked down at him. Her mouth was swollen, and she looked well kissed. Then she glanced behind him while the water lapped at his chest and her eyes widened. "Oh God, I hear something. Horse." She dragged herself off of him and struggled out of the water. "It's got to be King."

Rowdy lay back until his face was covered with cool liquid. Pain. He deserved it. What had he been thinking? He knew Megan Calhoun wasn't for him. And now he'd be found in a situation that could bring them all a world of hurt. He came up and wiped off his face with both hands. He wasn't a coward and couldn't let Megan face King Sanders alone. So he dragged himself out of the water, too, shaking off like a dog. He was just in time to face the rancher as King rode up.

"What the hell happened here?" King slid off his horse. "Megan? Baker? Did I interrupt something?" He looked from one of them to the other, his eyes hard. "This explains a lot."

"No, don't jump to conclusions, King." Megan had found a blanket in the saddlebag on the back of her horse and wrapped it around her. "I fell in. Rowdy jumped in after me."

"I'm not stupid, Megan." King wasn't calling her "sugar" this time. "That tank isn't more than five feet deep anywhere. You didn't need rescuing." He got back on his horse. "I'll see you back at the barn. The lawyers say the drilling continues. My contract is solid. So, I expect both of you to be gone in the morning." He turned the horse and rode away.

"I hurt him." Megan leaned her head against her own horse. "For real, this time."

"Maybe what happened is for the best. You said you didn't love him. Stringing him along wasn't kind." Rowdy didn't touch her. "I wanted a couple of more days here, but we can leave tomorrow. Vince has his drilling sites in good order. I really don't need to do any more inspecting. Today's accident was a onetime deal and that man's fault. The other site has gone almost a year without an accident, too. So I'm going to give Vince a pass on the other site near here that we haven't visited yet."

"All right, then. I'll pack and we'll leave first thing in the morning." Megan faced him, her eyes swimming with tears she didn't let fall. "We need to forget that kiss, Rowdy. You know it's not a good idea . . ."

"You're right. We have to work together." And he could fill in the blanks. Rich owner, employee. Karen had said it best—it came with complications. Rowdy knew that. King Sanders was out of the picture, but that didn't mean there weren't a few other men in Megan's league who would line up to fill his spot. He shivered as a gust of wind hit his wet clothes.

"Let's go." Megan gave him one last look before she mounted her horse without help.

Rowdy just watched her, wishing he could say something to take that look off her face, as if she'd lost a friend. Of course she had. "I'm sorry if I messed things up for you. With King."

"No, you're right. I needed to finish things with him. Not like this, of course, but before we left here. I'll try to talk to him. Let him know you and I . . . Aren't. But I'll make it clear that I'm not going to be his, either. You may not believe me, but I told him from the beginning that I just wanted to be friends. He wouldn't listen. Yes, he put his hands on me. I guess I wasn't rude enough to him about that." Megan stared down at him.

"You don't have to explain yourself to me, Megan." He mounted his horse.

"So, we're headed to San Antonio tomorrow." Megan started her horse moving.

"Yes. I'll send a text that we'll be getting there sooner than expected. I need to straighten out our reservation anyway. Someone made a mistake. I usually stay at the same low-budget motel there, but they've got us booked into something on the River Walk. It'll cost the company a fortune." He rode beside her down the trail.

"No mistake. My sister made the arrangements. She texted me, too. We'll be staying in style. It pays to know the acting chief financial officer." Megan laughed, but he could tell it was forced. "We'll be in a two-bedroom suite while we wait for our trailer and truck to be ready. Let's hope it takes days or even a week."

Rowdy couldn't hope for that. San Antonio on the River Walk. It was one of the most romantic cities in Texas. Hell, maybe in the country. He hadn't traveled much, except to Afghanistan with the army. He and Cass had splurged on a weekend in San Antonio once. They couldn't afford one of the fancy hotels on the river. But their budget digs had been within walking distance of the bars and restaurants there. It had been a great weekend and one he should definitely not be remembering right now, especially since he was still trying to come down from a kiss with Megan that had stirred him to life in a big way. He shifted in the saddle, trying to get comfortable.

"Well, tonight proved one thing," Megan said as they neared the lights of the house and barn.

"What's that?" Rowdy pulled his thoughts back from that hot kiss in the pond, and that long-ago sex-filled weekend, and back to the present.

"You're definitely recovering from Cassidy." With that, she urged her horse into a trot and left him in her dust.

Rowdy just watched her go. Damn, but he was in trouble. How was he ever going to survive a year with this woman? He'd thought losing Cass had hurt. Now he was getting his head filled with dangerous thoughts about another Calhoun sister. There was no way this could end well. Workplace romances were never a good idea. And with one of the owners of the company? God, he had to be out of his fucking mind to have ever touched her at all.

A smart man would harden his heart, maybe play the player. At least build walls too high for her to climb. But that kiss. Their second one—but who was counting? Obviously he was. Damn him for a fool. He couldn't stop replaying the way she'd looked coming out of the water, as good as naked. And her taste . . . He needed a cold shower and a reality check. He wasn't a kid, desperate to get laid.

And fantasizing about a woman he couldn't, shouldn't, have was stupid beyond belief.

If there was one thing he'd always prided himself on, it was his problem-solving skills. Time to put those to work on this situation. It wouldn't be simple, but he was going to have to figure out a way to let go of this fascination with Megan Calhoun. Mind over matter. Logic. He was an engineer, damn it. He could do this. A chart, a spreadsheet. Surely there was a way . . .

He saw Juan waiting by the barn door and checking his watch. Rowdy urged his horse faster. He was keeping the man from his bed. Too bad they'd be leaving the Rocking S in the morning under a cloud. But he was glad to go. At least he wouldn't have to watch King paw Megan anymore. That thought had him smiling as he rode into the barn. Yes, one problem out of the way. His competitive edge had always driven him. Now he could check that off as no longer an issue. King Sanders. Done.

"King, please talk to me." Megan leaned against his door. She knew he was in there. She'd heard noises through the wall, like maybe he was throwing things. Now that she had showered and changed, she knew she couldn't go to sleep until she tried to mend things with him. He didn't deserve what had amounted to a slap in the face when he'd ridden in on that scene next to the pond.

The door suddenly opened, and she almost fell into his bedroom.

"All right. I'm listening. What do you have to say, Megan? Get in here. I don't want *Abuela* to hear about this. She really liked you." He didn't sound like he wanted to hear it, but a chance was a chance.

"What you saw—"

He cut her off with a gesture. "I said come inside." He pulled her into the bedroom and shut the door. "Don't bother making up a story. I know what I saw. You and Baker obviously have something going on. I was a fool to not pick up on it before. The fact that he turned down my sister was a red flag." King leaned against the door. He wore jeans and nothing else. Did he think she'd be tempted by his blatant masculinity? Another woman might be.

"There's nothing between Rowdy and me." Megan didn't like being in King's bedroom. "Can't we talk in the living room? Or outside?"

"Here is fine. Say what you came to say, but don't bother lying to me." He wasn't budging and his hurt was clear to see. He'd convinced himself that he loved her. "For the record, I don't believe you. Didn't look like nothing to me."

"Okay, we kissed. Big deal. I've kissed a few men. More than a few. It's chemistry. Got out of hand. But never went further. Never will, either." Megan ran a hand through her hair. It was still damp and would be unmanageable tomorrow. *Concentrate.*

"So you're kissing the guy whom you're going to be working with for the next year. I know where that will lead. Have at it, Megan. I get the message. If you and I were going to turn into something, you wouldn't be kissing anyone but me." King stalked over to his bed and sat on the side of it.

Megan followed him, but kept her distance. "That's the point, King. You and I aren't going to turn into something. I know that's what you wanted. I told you up front that I didn't see us together, even though you did your best to tempt me." She looked around the room. He had a big bed in a masculine bedroom that was done in burgundy and dark brown. The padded headboard was brown velvet, the comforter a dark print. He'd obviously emptied his bookshelf with a temper tantrum. There were books all over the floor.

"That obviously didn't work. Not if you'd already decided to play with the hired help." King sounded bitter. And why not?

"King, I'm really sorry. I never wanted to hurt you. You've been wonderful to me. Letting us stay here and being so kind." She sat beside him and put her hand on his knee. "I *am* stupid for not taking you up on your offer. You're just too good for me."

"That's a pile of shit. 'Too good'?" He grabbed her hand. "That sounds like an excuse."

"You don't really know me, King. Yes, we used to hang out together in Houston, but that was a while ago. I'm a mess. I never stick with things. I have family problems I really can't share, but they are nothing you want to be involved in." Megan wiggled her fingers when he just held them tighter. "And I'm not in love with you."

"I can make you love me, Megan. Stick around and you'll see." He tried to kiss her, but Megan finally wrenched her hand out of his and jumped up and away from him.

"Stop. You know love doesn't work that way."

"Are you sure?" He stood and looked down at her. "Don't you see how perfect we'd be together? We have the same kind of background. *Abuela* approves of you, and you have no idea how far that goes with me. And you're good with horses, a rider. All these things make us fit. Imagine the kind of life we'd have." He ran his hands up and down her arms. "Maybe you aren't feeling our chemistry right now, but I'm feeling enough for both of us. Let me take you to bed and show you how I can make you feel. I can make it good for you. Give me that chance."

"King, no. I'm sorry. Now, I have to go." She hated the fact that she had to shove herself away from him. But honestly, she'd felt more chemistry in that kiss with Rowdy than she'd ever felt with King. And no matter how many months passed, no matter how hard either of them tried, she knew it wasn't going to happen with this man standing in front of her, even if she wished it would.

King looked at his hands. "If you have anything else to say, go ahead. I'm tired. Of this conversation and of being played for a fool."

"You're not a fool, King. You're a fine man, an honest man. And I respect you. Thanks for letting us stay here." Megan walked to the door. "I'm sure we'll run into each other in Houston. I hope you'll remember that I did want us to be friends." She eased out of the room and shut the door. She would never forget the look on his face as she left him. She bit back a sob and staggered into her own room. How had she let this get so out of control? Rowdy had accused her of encouraging King. She tried to remember every conversation, every touch. *Was* it her fault? Didn't matter. She'd have to live with it now. Hurting him. And she would see him again. They ran with the same crowd when he came to town. She lay on the bed and stared at the ceiling. But maybe they wouldn't after this year was over. Maybe Megan Calhoun wouldn't run with the country club set ever again. Somehow she didn't feel too broken up about that.

Chapter 10

"The trailer will be ready tomorrow. So, this is our last night in San Antonio." Rowdy hung up the phone and collapsed on his comfortable king-sized bed. Forget the rest of the city. He'd never stayed in such a nice hotel. After several days of overseeing the RV prep and making sure the truck they were getting had what they needed, he was tempted to just plant himself in the bedroom and watch the big screen. Hell, he might even go wild and help himself to a beer from the minibar on the company dime. He'd let Megan go her own way, and they'd seen little of each other until now.

"Too bad, but just as well. Lucky must be anxious to see us again. The vet says he's healthy. She gave him all his shots and everything he needs. We can pick him up in the morning on our way out of town." Megan stood in the doorway. She'd left him a note this morning about some spa treatments her sister had scheduled for her in the hotel. Now she glowed from a facial and some kind of massage with hot rocks.

"Glad he's healthy, but I bet that's going to cost a bundle." Rowdy knew it would be a problem bringing the dog without a license into the fancy hotel, even though it did allow pets. The concierge had been glad to help them find a vet who could take care of Lucky during their stay.

"Expensive? I didn't have the nerve to even ask. But it had to be done. Now, get up and let's go. I'm not wasting our last night here." She stood over him. "There's a great Mexican restaurant close to us on the River Walk. I'm starved, aren't you?"

"You want to go now? The Aggies are on the ten-yard line." He wasn't about to leave until he saw if they scored.

"You can watch football any time. That spa lunch they brought me upstairs wasn't much more than a lettuce leaf and a piece of grilled chicken so tiny I had to get out a magnifying glass to find it." She moved closer and poked his shoulder. "Come on. I need real food. Tex-Mex. There's some of the best just a short walk away. It's the least you can do for me before I'm dragged out to the back of beyond." She dove for the TV remote, but he hid it behind his back. She put her hands on her hips. "Rowdy! Are you listening to me? I need to enjoy civilization while I can."

He did a fist pump when his team scored. "Civilization. Okay, I get it. I can leave now that the Aggies made another touchdown. No way those Sooners can score twenty points with only two minutes on the clock." He pulled the remote from under the pillow behind him and killed the TV after the kicker made the extra point. "Make that twenty-one. Yeah. I'm hungry, too." Rowdy swung his legs off the bed. "We haven't seen much of each other the past few days. I guess you've stayed here on the river before."

"Many times." She must have hit the hotel gift shop, because he didn't recognize the white Mexican-style blouse and skirt she wore as something he'd stuffed into her duffel after the tornado. This top hung off both shoulders and she'd cinched it at her waist with a fancy silver belt that he did remember finding on the floor of their old trailer and sticking into her bag.

"Did your sister send you an advance on your salary? Those are new clothes, and they look expensive." He walked over to the mirror above the dresser and ran a comb through his hair. Megan would have to be satisfied being seen with him in his usual jeans and knit shirt. He hadn't brought dressier clothes, not for this job, and she looked ready for a night on the town.

"They were on sale and I couldn't resist the colorful embroidery along the edges." She did a turn, holding out her skirt. "Found this downstairs in the shop off the lobby. You like?"

"You didn't answer me. You can't go charging stuff like that to the room, Megan. And quit looking at me like I'm the devil. I'm the one who'll have to explain this expense account back at the office."

She *was* glaring at him. "Relax, boss. I didn't charge it. Cass and I had a little talk. I told her I was running short on funds so she wired me some money. Yes, it was an advance on my paycheck. She sent it here to the front desk. They called me while you were at the trailer dealership." She stopped to admire herself in his mirror. "For the record, Cass will be approving this trip's expenses personally now. Because of Daddy's will and my being with you, this trip isn't your run-of-the-mill business trip. These are special circumstances. Mason MacKenzie himself suggested it. Our evaluator?" She smiled. "I know you don't want to hear this, but he's a nice guy."

"Nice to the Calhouns, anyway." Rowdy really *didn't* want to hear about the man who'd stolen Cassidy's heart in record time. "Just wait till you see the trailer we'll be picking up tomorrow. We'll be living in style for this trip." Rowdy had been shocked at the size of it. The thing would be hard to tow, but much more comfortable than his usual rig, thanks to Cassidy's orders to give them a larger deluxe model. Another of MacKenzie's ideas? Or was Cass feeling guilty about the way she'd dumped Rowdy? Did she think giving him a nice bunk would make him feel better? Didn't matter, he was going to enjoy the hell out of the luxurious accommodations. Just like he'd been enjoying this nice hotel.

"Forget the trailer." She looked over her shoulder. "How do I look?"

"Fine. Very pretty." Too pretty. That blouse showed off her tan and a lot of skin. "If you bought that outfit here, you probably got ripped off. When I was in San Antonio before, I found little markets away from the tourist traps on the river where you might have gotten that stuff for ten cents on the dollar." Now he sounded like a penny-pinching asshole.

She almost danced over to the doorway that led to their shared living area. They had a suite, for crying out loud. "I've shopped those markets, too. You can't trust some of their goods. Colors run. Seams come apart. Believe it or not, I'm an expert when it comes to shopping." She stopped and looked back, playing with the neckline that dipped low enough to show the swell of her breasts.

"I believe it. But I doubt you ever had to follow a budget."

"I used to buy for a boutique I owned with a friend. When you're reselling, you have to watch what you spend." She looked defensive. "Anyway, I'm happy with my purchase. It was a good price and this is quality fabric. Preshrunk. I'm sure it will survive our imminent trip to hell and back." She picked up a small purse and walked to the hall door.

"I wouldn't wear white anywhere near the rigs or near Lucky when he's been running around in the dirt. If you're smart, you'll pack that away and save it for when we're on our way home again." Feeling out of sorts, Rowdy let her lead the way to the elevators. He'd never had the nerve to ask for an advance on his paycheck, even when his mom had struggled to pay for cancer treatments and he'd needed to help her out financially. He'd gone to the bank for a short-term loan instead. But then he didn't have the connections Megan had. It was a good reminder of who she was. He sure as hell shouldn't be wondering whether she did or did not have on a fucking bra.

Their hotel sat right on the river. The lower level featured a patio where they could step out onto the stone walkway that ran alongside the waterway. They could catch a water taxi or just stroll along the well-lighted area to one of a dozen or more restaurants and bars. Mariachis played catchy tunes somewhere nearby, and it seemed like they were on their way to a party instead of just out for an early dinner.

Megan led the way, chattering about a school trip in fifth grade to the city to tour the historic Alamo. Then there had been other visits with her girlfriends for spring break when she was in college. She'd even gone to some basketball games here with a former boyfriend whose father had been part owner of the Spurs. It was more evidence that she'd had a privileged life. The only field trip Rowdy could re-member taking in elementary school had been an hour-and-a-half ride in a non-air-conditioned school bus to see the San Jacinto Mon-ument and the Battleship *Texas*. He'd been thrilled with that at the time. He mentioned it.

"Hey, we went there, too." Megan grinned. "I guess every student in a school around Houston goes there at least once. Fourth grade. Texas history unit. Am I right?"

"Yep. That was it." Rowdy laughed. "I didn't get to see the Alamo until much later, when I was old enough to drive here myself."

"Loved the battleship, but they didn't let us stay nearly long enough as far as I was concerned. The worst part was being herded around like sheep." She pulled a face. "I got in trouble because I slipped away from the teacher and climbed up into one of the forbidden sections of the ship. They had to hold the bus until they could find me."

Rowdy stopped in his tracks. "You're kidding. I did the same thing! I was determined to get up in what I thought would be the crow's nest. I'd always had a thing for pirate stories. Of course, it was a battleship, not a sailing vessel. I got turned around, lost my way, and ended up where the captain steered the ship. Mrs. Yates, the teacher, found me holding the ship's wheel and pretending I was the commander yelling, 'Battle stations!' like I'd seen in a war movie once."

Megan laughed, hit his arm, then linked hers through his. "Who knew we were so much alike? That's the place I was looking for when I sneaked away from the group. I wanted to be the captain of the ship."

"I can see that." He could also see that her smile lit up her face. Her eyes shone in the gathering darkness, and the way she leaned against him with another chuckle made something catch in his chest. Oh, he was so screwed.

"Are you saying I'm bossy?" She tilted her head as she looked up at him. "Well, maybe I am. My sister Shannon will tell you I always have been, even though she's two years older than I am." She stopped. "Look, there it is. Las Flores. I thought I remembered the way. See all the gorgeous hanging baskets of flowers everywhere? They have bouquets on all the tables, too." She tugged him toward the entrance. "And the most delicious margaritas. Do you like a good margarita, Rowdy?" Megan smiled.

"Sure. But I have a limit." He realized he was grinning, too, as she steered him into the restaurant and spoke Spanish to the woman at the front desk.

"Relax. You're not driving. We get too sloshed, we can catch a water taxi back to the hotel." She said something else in Spanish to the hostess, and they were soon seated at a table for two out on the patio where they could watch the boats go by. Some were packed with tourists on sightseeing tours, while others were those water taxis taking passengers up and down the busy river.

As the sky darkened, the businesses along the river lit up with thousands of tiny lights. Megan declared the way the reflection hit the water magical. Rowdy had to agree. When frosty salt-rimmed glasses were placed in front of them, he took a cautious sip. "Man, that's strong."

"Otherwise, why bother?" Megan grinned and reached forward to wipe salt from his mouth with a fingertip. "Rumor has it they put something illegal in these drinks."

Rowdy took another sip. "Doubt it, but it's delicious." He was determined to ignore the way she'd so casually touched his lip. Then he saw her put that same finger in her mouth. Oh God. "Megan, what the hell are you doing?"

"Hmm? Enjoying my drink. Let's get a menu." She smiled innocently.

Rowdy raised his arm and a waitress hurried over with two large menus. He used his like a wall. He didn't want to look at her. Innocent. Yeah, right. Maybe she was as frustrated as he was. Sanders had made all kinds of plays for her, but he was sure she'd resisted. Didn't matter why, the fact was she hadn't slept with the guy. So she was feeling an itch that needed scratching. He was not, *not* going to help her out.

He let her order first. She had a hearty appetite, and he could tell she did know her Mexican food. He'd grown up on it. Anyone from their part of Texas ate it about once a week unless they had dietary problems, because it was usually cheap and delicious. He ordered a deluxe combination plate and sat back.

"If we eat all of that, we'll have to walk along this river two or three times to work it off." She was halfway through her drink. "But it'll be worth it. Wait and see."

"I'll take your word for it." Rowdy picked up a tortilla chip and dug it into the red sauce that had been put on the table as soon as they'd arrived. He took a bite, then gasped. "Holy shit, that's hot." He gulped margarita. Not a good idea. At this rate he'd be drunk on his ass by the time the meal was over. He raised his arm again and asked the waitress for a glass of water.

"Too hot for you?" Megan ran her hand around the neckline of her blouse.

"Uh." Rowdy grabbed the water when it came and took a gulp.

"The sauce. Yeah. Pretty spicy. But I can take it. In smaller doses, maybe." He made himself look past her as a boat went by. "Bet it's cooler on the water. You ever take one of those tours?"

"A long time ago. They're all right. Plenty of history in San Antonio. It's interesting." She picked up a chip and slid it into the sauce, then licked it with the tip of her tongue. "Whoa, you're right. They've really amped up the chilis in it tonight." She dropped the chip on the small plate in front of her. "I think I'll wait for my food to come."

Rowdy was still staring at her mouth and seeing the way her tongue had . . . *Get a grip, Baker.* His margarita glass was empty. Without his asking, the waitress brought him another one. Had Megan signaled for a refill? He didn't ask, just took a sip. The drink was tasting better and better.

"History. You're right. Cass and I took the tour once." He threw that name out there. It was a good reminder that he was not going to get tangled up with another Calhoun sister.

"Cass." Megan finished her drink, but shook her head when the waitress came by again. "You still pining for her, Rowdy? Is that the real reason you turned Karen down?"

"No." Rowdy jumped when a plate of food was suddenly placed in front of him. He thought about letting the distraction get him off the hook. But maybe it was only right that he tell Megan and himself the truth.

"I loved Cassidy. It started in high school. She was my first, for a lot of things." Rowdy smiled, remembering two teenagers fumbling their way through sex. They'd been damn lucky they hadn't sprung the baby trap on themselves a time or two.

Megan didn't say anything, waiting for more.

"Cass was patient and waited for me while I went off to college on a big football scholarship. She had to stay home and work her way through the local schools." He sipped his drink when his throat went dry. "I played the football jock to the hilt. Racked up good stats, even had pro scouts looking at me. All that attention goes to your head, and I went a little wild. She found out about it, so we took a few breaks. But when I came home she'd always be there, so sweet and happy to see me. We'd get together again. What we had was easy. Comfortable." He stabbed a tamale but didn't take a bite.

"You joined the service instead of playing pro football after graduation." Megan stirred her refried beans but she wasn't eating yet, either.

"You know that?" Rowdy put down his fork. "Yeah. I'd done ROTC. They call it 'the Corps' at A&M. It also helped pay my way through school, so I didn't have to get student loans like Cassidy did. She ended up drowning in debt. Naturally, after graduation I felt an obligation to serve." He ran a hand over his face. "Got sent to the war zone." He shook his head. "It sure wasn't like playing on the Battleship *Texas*." He looked down when Megan covered his other hand on the table. "The jeep I was riding in got hit by a roadside bomb. Tore the hell out of my knee and I was the lucky one. Two of the guys in my squad didn't make it."

"I'm sorry, Rowdy." She squeezed his hand. "And you weren't so lucky. No more football." She sighed.

"Right. The point is, Cass was there for me when I got home. Helped me deal with the disappointment and the, shit, trauma I guess you'd call it, of seeing death up close. She was loyal through it all, even when I was mean as a snake to her." He leaned back, thinking about it. He'd been in a dark place back then. Cass had stuck with him and kept him from drowning himself in a bottle or putting a gun to his head, like some guys he knew had done. She'd made him get counseling, and it had helped.

"Rowdy?"

"Eventually I got this job. Which, you have to admit, has a hell of a travel schedule. She put up with it. No complaints. I owe Cass a lot, Megan."

"I'm hearing loyalty, patience, and caring. And I know you were mad when she dumped you for Mason." Megan squeezed his hand. "But are you truly broken up about it?" She stared at him until Rowdy had to look away.

Was he? Did his heart hurt, or was it his pride? What the hell did it say about them, *him,* that Cass could throw away the fifteen years they'd been together after knowing that rich oilman for less than a month? Whoa. He'd just had a fucking epiphany. One of those aha moments like he'd seen people on TV talk shows scream about. Should he tell Megan? He turned over his hand to grip hers, then looked her in the eyes again.

"Well?" She had a calm gaze, like she wasn't going to judge him, whatever his answer.

"Pride." He nodded. Yeah. Nailed it. He smiled at her, liking the fact that she didn't say anything, just gave his hand another squeeze. "Thanks for helping me see that, Megan." He dropped her hand and picked up his fork. "Now, let's eat before this gets cold. It looks and smells delicious." He dug in.

Megan ate but didn't really taste the food. What was it about Rowdy Baker that fascinated her so? Sure, he was handsome and had a great body. But those things were superficial. If all she wanted were good looks, then King Sanders had filled that bill in spades. Maybe the fact that Rowdy considered the Calhoun women off-limits made him irresistible. Was she so messed up that she needed that kind of challenge?

Rowdy had said it himself when talking about Karen—he didn't want anyone who was too easy. Hooking up with Rowdy sure wouldn't be that. An affair with him was a recipe for disaster. Rowdy was technically the "hired help," as King had put it, but their position was unique. While he worked for the company her family owned, he was also supposed to be her boss, with that stupid obligation to report to her evaluator, Mason MacKenzie, on her job performance. So far she'd done zip, *nada*. Of course, there was plenty of time left to prove that she'd probably totally fail this test. Because it was clear to her that she couldn't handle what her father had set out for her to do in his will.

On that depressing thought, she ordered another margarita. She might as well quit thinking and just relax. It was a beautiful night. And after he worked his way through his dinner, Rowdy's mood had lightened so much that he was sharing misadventures from his college days and trips to San Antonio with his buddies. It didn't hurt that she felt pretty in her new outfit and had noticed his eyes lingering on her shoulders and the place where her loose top dipped low.

She sipped her drink and thought about running her hands over Rowdy's broad shoulders and his powerful chest. God. And when he smiled? She shifted in her seat, pretty sure he had no idea how the flash of those white teeth in his tanned face made her desperate to feel his mouth on hers again.

They each stopped at two drinks and switched to water. By the time they pushed back their plates and ordered coffee, neither of them could claim to be drunk, just pleasantly buzzed.

"Dessert?" Rowdy leaned across the cleared table. "Or how about a boat ride?"

"I'd love to get out on the water." Megan grinned at him. "Don't throw me in this time."

"Not unless you give me a reason." Rowdy pulled out a credit card and handed it to the waitress. "It's too dangerous, anyway. Seeing you in wet clothes makes me lose my mind. Remember?"

Megan caught her breath. How could she forget? That hot kiss. His hands on her breasts. If King hadn't ridden up when he did . . . She stared at Rowdy and saw the same memory in his dark eyes. He took the folder from the waitress, grabbed his credit card, and quickly signed the check.

"Ready?" He stood and held out his hand.

Megan knew he was only talking about leaving, but her thighs clenched. He walked with her to the nearby taxi stand and flagged down a boat. Soon they were sitting on cushioned seats next to each other. The twinkling lights on the sleek watercraft made it seem like a Mexican version of a Venetian gondola.

"Can you give us a nice long ride before you drop us off at our hotel?" Rowdy passed the driver some folded money, then scooted closer to Megan, who shivered. "Are you cold?"

"Maybe a little. The wind *is* cooler on the water."

There was a blanket folded on the other seat across from them but Rowdy ignored it. He put his arm around her instead. "That better?"

"Much." Megan leaned against him and enjoyed the ride down the lazy river. They were both silent, as if afraid talking would break the spell that had started over dinner. They'd become friends as they'd shared experiences. It was a good feeling, and she didn't want to ruin it. She savored the cool weather after a long, hot summer and watched the trees lining the river go by. They also passed many busy restaurants and bars. Laughter drifted across the water along with music from different venues. It was a romantic vibe. But none of that intrigued her as much as the solid strength of the man next to her. He ran his hand up and down her arm, warming her, but he never said a word, not even when, finally, the boat landed in front of the hotel patio. Rowdy helped her climb out.

"That was lovely. Thanks." She took his hand and walked beside him to the elevator. What would happen when they got to their rooms was up to him. She knew what she wanted.

He opened the door with his key card when they got there. Megan almost held her breath when he looked at the door to his bedroom. Then he walked over to the balcony in their shared living area and opened the glass slider. Okay, so he wasn't quite ready to call it a night.

"You want something from the minibar?" She opened the tiny refrigerator and peered inside. "I—" Warm hands came around her waist, and she slammed the door shut, then straightened.

"What I want is standing right here." His voice was low, husky. He trailed his lips over her bare shoulder. "This has been driving me crazy all night. I need to know." He pushed the top down her arms. "No bra. Woman, that is just plain cruel." He cupped her breasts in his palms and pressed against her from behind.

"Rowdy." Megan raised her arms and reached back to run her fingers through his thick, crisp hair. "God, that feels good. I've wanted your hands on me ever since the pond. Even before that." She sighed when he circled her nipples with his fingers. "Are you sure this is a good idea?"

"You going to stop me?" He turned her around and looked into her eyes. Another man might have just checked out her breasts, but he was waiting for her answer.

"Stop you?" She grabbed his shoulders. "Are you going to stop *me*?" She stretched up, reaching for his mouth with her own, needing to taste him again. He let her in to explore with her tongue, then took over, making her wild for him, for more.

He picked her up and carried her to his bedroom, still kissing her. Only when he stood next to his bed did he set her on her feet and lean back to take a breath.

"Let me." He unhooked her silver belt and dropped it on the floor. Then he lifted up her blouse, drawing it up her arms and off before he tossed it aside. "Beautiful." He leaned down as he held her breasts, stroking one with his tongue, then taking a nipple into his mouth. When he drew hard, she gripped his hair again and gasped his name.

"My turn." She pushed up his shirt, desperate to get it off of him. He finally cooperated so he could throw it aside. It hit the dresser, landing in front of the mirror. Megan glanced that way and saw them together. He was much bigger than she was, but she didn't mind it. She reveled in his strength, his broad shoulders and the muscles that rippled in his arms when he slid his hands inside her elastic waistband to tug her skirt down her legs, along with her panties. She stepped out of them and kicked off her shoes, leaving them all on the floor. He ran his hands down her legs as he dropped to his knees while Megan held on to his shoulders again.

He laughed and kissed her tattoo. "Bet there's a story here. Texas forever?"

"Of course. But that story's going to have to wait." She sighed as he trailed his lips across her stomach and aimed farther south. "You headed somewhere?"

"Damn straight." He gently shoved her back on the bed, his hands under her thighs as he pressed open her legs and eased between them. He pulled her toward him, then sat back, smiling before he traced a line where she knew he could see she was desperate for him already. Then he leaned forward and slid his tongue along the seam, just enough to make her moan.

"Rowdy?" She looked down at him.

He touched her again, opening her so he could take a long look. She'd been waxed in the spa upstairs. Her recent swim had reminded her that she'd needed to keep herself tidy in case she had to get out that bikini again. He must have liked what he saw, because he kissed her there until her head fell back and she forgot how to breathe.

"This something you like?" He sounded like he was laughing at her.

"Depends." She wasn't going to let him get away with that. So she wiggled her butt. "This something you're really good at?"

"You tell me." He bent his head again and proved that he was not just good at it, he could make her scream his name and her hips come up off the bed.

"Oh my God!" She gripped the comforter in her fists. "Stop it. You're killing me, Rowdy."

"So you didn't like it." He grinned and shucked his jeans after toeing off his shoes. "Well, that'll never happen again."

"Damn it." Megan sat up. "Come here." She was quivering after what had to be one of the most intense orgasms she'd ever experienced. And he just stood there? Like he was king of the bedroom? Oh no. And clearly he was hurting. It would serve him right if she walked out of there right now and let him suffer. But there was a better revenge. Megan Calhoun knew her own power and how to use it.

"Where?" He stared at her. "You want me to lie on the bed? Next to you?" He looked down at his erection. "I seem to have a problem, Megan. I'm in pain. Can you help me?"

"It hurts? I can see you're swollen. Too bad." She looked him over. Yes, she just bet he hurt, since he'd been doing all the giving and none of the taking. "But I'm done for the night." She slid off the bed. Her knees almost buckled. God, but he'd put her through her paces. "Thanks for the nice time." She picked up her silver belt and began to gather her clothes.

"Wait. You can't leave me like this. Not when you're responsible." He'd dropped to the bed, but now he leaned up on his elbows.

"Me? What did I do? I just lay there on the bed. You did all the work. If you can't control your body, fella, it's not my fault." Megan bit her lip to keep from laughing.

"But just seeing you naked caused me pain." He touched himself. "And I think I'm not the only one who needs help now. Look at you, you're flushed. Face, breasts. And it's not whisker burn. I shaved this afternoon. Must be something wrong, Megan. But I've got the cure right here." He lay back and patted his stomach. "A ride on the Rowdy Baker love train will help you feel better. Me, too. Guaranteed. If it doesn't work, you can have a do over."

That did it. Megan burst out laughing and jumped on the bed, landing next to him. "The Rowdy Baker love train?"

"All aboard." He pulled her on top of him, lifting her easily with those strong, strong arms until she straddled his hips.

Megan settled onto his erection, taking him in until she gasped, still incredibly sensitive from that first orgasm. She had a feeling more were ahead. God, he felt good inside her. She looked down and thought his eyes might have rolled back in his head.

"Rowdy? Are you with me?" She hit his chest. "This train needs to leave the station."

"I'm waiting for the conductor to give the signal. That's you, lady. Set the pace. Fast, slow, any way you want it." He reached for her hips. "I can help if you're too weak to get us moving."

She laughed and leaned down to kiss him. She'd never had a lover who was this much fun. "Maybe you can help this time, but I do have a few tricks of my own." She squeezed her inner muscles and his eyes widened. "Do you like that?"

"Shit, woman! Do that again and this trip may be the shortest one ever." He slid one palm up to her breast and held on to her hip with the other as they began to move.

Megan leaned forward. He smiled into her eyes as he began to shift with her, finding that angle, that spot that made her gasp again and shudder. She held on to his shoulders, the pressure building inside her again almost too intense. Harder, faster. He slid both hands down to her hips, no longer smiling as he drove into her. Megan held on, her breasts brushing against him as she matched his strokes, their bodies slamming together. She rode him toward a release that quaked through her until his own climax pulsed hot inside her. A moment later, she collapsed on his chest, out of breath and totally spent.

"Wow." That was all she could manage.

"You feeling better, Ms. Calhoun?" Rowdy murmured against her hair as they were drifting off to sleep. "I think you reached your destination."

"Some better. But I may need a do over in the morning." She sighed and snuggled closer.

"You know this was probably a bad idea." He pulled her leg over his and settled his hand on her breast.

"Probably. And I don't give a shit." She kissed one of his nipples, then pulled up the sheet when the air-conditioning cycled on.

"Me, either. Good night, Megan."

More comfortable than she'd thought possible, Megan closed her eyes and slept.

Chapter 11

"This trailer is certainly a step up from the one the tornado took out." Megan looked behind them as Rowdy negotiated the turn that would take them to the vet's office. "It's huge."

"It's a blessing and a curse." He shook his head. "Look at the size of that parking lot. I can't get this thing in there. I'll have to leave it out here on the curb. At least this neighborhood seems safe."

"A little too high-end. I should have known anyone recommended by that hotel wouldn't be cheap." Megan sighed as she realized she'd soon be broke again. "The vet told me what the bill is going to be. It'll just about wipe me out again."

"I'll pay half." Rowdy looked surprised that he'd said it.

Megan stared at him. Had he lost his mind? Maybe he'd offered because he was still in a good mood from two rounds of the best sex she'd ever had in *her* life. Wow, Mason must really be something in the sack for Cassidy to have given up this guy for him. Then again, her new sister claimed to be "in love." Since Megan had never been hit by Cupid's dart herself, she really had no idea what kind of thought or lack thereof made a person decide they'd met "the one."

"What did you say?" Maybe she'd misheard.

"I like the dog. And I can afford it. My paycheck's a lot bigger than yours. I checked before we took off, when we were back at the office. You're getting the same pay an entry-level hand without a college degree and no experience would get."

"You don't have to look smug about it. So I didn't finish college. Hell, it's already obvious I don't know a screwdriver from a drill bit. And, yes, I know you'd never have hired me in the first place."

Megan ignored him when he stretched out his hand as if to comfort her. "But I'll accept your help, Rowdy, and thank you." She unbuckled her seat belt when they came to a stop. "I'll pay you back if I manage to pass Daddy's stupid test and get some money at the end of the year. That's a promise."

"Okay, then." He turned off the motor. "It's a loan. No interest, unless you want me to add that, too."

She opened the truck door without saying another word. By the time he joined her at the entrance to the vet's office, Megan had figured out that pouting was stupid. He was being nice. She had to get over herself.

"Seriously, Rowdy, thank you. I know you were against bringing the dog along. Add the interest. It's only right." She stuck out her hand.

He shook it. "That's a deal." He held the door into the office open so she could precede him. They could hear a familiar barking coming from the back. The veterinarian herself came out to talk to them after they paid several hundred dollars for Lucky's shots and license. Not that they'd be staying in San Antonio again, but apparently it was a requirement in this office.

"He's a little thing, but healthy and seems like a smart fellow, already knows a few basic commands." The doctor smiled when her assistant brought an excited Lucky out from the back.

The dog lunged at Megan, almost knocking her down when she squatted to greet him. She laughed and shoved him back when he tried to cover her face with dog kisses.

The vet grabbed the leash off the floor and handed it to Megan. "Nice leash. Hand-tooled leather."

"We just came from a ranch where one of the cowboys made it. He really wanted to keep Lucky for himself. If my dog goes missing, I'll know where to look." Megan rubbed the dog's ears. "But I won't give him up. I told you how I found him. It seemed like fate."

"He was one lucky dog, all right. I put a chip in him as you asked. Just fill out the paperwork and e-mail the registry. If he gets away from you, he can be traced." She shook hands with them. "If you need me again, my information is on your copy of the bill."

They thanked her and headed for the truck. Lucky sprang into the backseat, where they'd put down a new beach towel for him. They'd already stopped at a big box store for supplies, using the company credit card to replace a lot of the things they'd bought before the tornado had wiped them out. Also on their list was a laptop computer for Megan and a new tablet for Rowdy. He had explained that they both were essential for the next job they'd be tackling.

"Thanks again for helping with the vet bill. I'm still in sticker shock." Megan pushed Lucky back when he tried to ride in her lap. "I guess you want me to navigate again. Do you have a map?"

"No need. This new truck has a nav system and satellite radio. Plus we're heading straight out I-10 until we get near Pecos. Then we skirt the Davis Mountains."

"I've never been there." She realized there was a lot of Texas she'd never explored.

"Wait till you see them." He smiled at her. "I don't know about you, but after being raised in the flatlands around Houston, I'm crazy about mountains."

"Me, too." Megan leaned toward him. This was something else they had in common. It continually surprised her that they liked so many of the same things. "One of my favorite vacations is skiing, just about anywhere. Not that I'm any good at it. I just love to sit in the lodge with a good view of the mountains and gaze at them."

"I get it. I went skiing once. A little too cold for my taste. But being in the mountains? Hoo boy. That's amazing. I'm with you. A spot next to the window, a roaring fire, and one of those hot toddies." He laughed. "Nothing like that where we're going. You'll see desert one minute and mountains the next. The site is out of town on a county road. Maybe I'll use the nav system then." Rowdy eased them away from the curb. "Cassidy made sure we had all the bells and whistles in this truck. For once I'm not dreading going out west."

"She went overboard, Rowdy. I never expected any of this." Megan stared out the window, all thoughts of romantic nights in the mountains overwhelmed by the reality of what this rig must have cost. "The company really can't afford this kind of extravagance right now." She knew things were getting better for the oil industry as a whole, because the price of oil had been rising. But she couldn't forget the dark cloud hanging over Calhoun Petroleum that had nothing to do with that price. How could Cass justify this kind of expenditure? Rowdy claimed the dealership had thrown in extras, hoping for future business from Calhoun, and had given them a fleet rate. There was insurance money from the first set of wheels, too. So maybe her clever sister hadn't spent as much as Megan thought. Of course, Cass was probably feeling guilty, too.

And not just about her relationship with Rowdy. Conrad Calhoun had defrauded a lot of people. Stolen their mineral rights. He'd even tricked Rowdy's senile grandmother into signing away her rights thirty-something years ago. Now the family held that secret and felt horrible about it. Megan had been warned not to tell anyone until Cass was ready with numbers for the victims of the fraud. Even hinting about the scandal to King had been dangerous. But how could she just sit back and ride west with Rowdy like she didn't know . . . ? Once he found out, not only would he be pissed that her daddy had deceived his family, but he'd also be furious that she'd played ride the love train with him and never said one word. Not to mention, he'd hate anyone who carried the Calhoun name.

Megan was having a very hard time handling what she'd learned about her father herself. She fought back sudden tears. It was impossible to believe that Daddy, the man who'd called her Pumpkin and thought she could learn the oil business, had been a lying, cheating scoundrel. She sucked in a shaky breath and knew she wasn't nearly ready to tell Rowdy the truth about Conrad Calhoun and what he'd done.

She watched Rowdy steer them onto a freeway headed west. He was competent as usual. They had miles to go yet, and months more in close quarters. No way did she want to ride that long with a furious man who felt betrayed. Especially after what they'd just discovered about each other. So she'd keep her secret and pray he wouldn't find out from anyone else—at least not until a big wad of money could take some of the sting out of the betrayal.

Because last night had been . . . amazing. And this morning he'd turned to her and rocked her world again. No wild rides on the love train this time. Instead he'd made slow, tender love to her. It had still ended with her losing her mind in his arms. The man was a genius when it came to finding just the right places that made her body hum or shout hallelujah. A quick shower together had made a third round tempting. But Rowdy always had his schedule in mind. So they'd grabbed breakfast from the buffet in the hotel dining room, then used a cab to get to the dealership where the brand-new four-door truck and RV were waiting. A two-bedroom RV. Megan smiled, hoping that only one of those bedrooms would be used, unless they could train Lucky to sleep in the other bunk.

"What are you smiling about?" Rowdy glanced at her. "Couldn't be thinking about a train ride, could you?"

She laughed and leaned across to rub his knee. "How did you know?" She sighed. "Just wait till tonight. I want to christen that new trailer properly. From one end to the other."

"Woman, don't talk to me like that while I'm driving." He grabbed her hand when she started to slide it up his thigh. "Play with the radio, not with me, or you'll get us both killed."

"Yes, sir." She grinned and began to hit buttons, finally opening the glove compartment to check for a listing of channels. There was his gun and extra ammunition. "You think we'll have *this* kind of trouble out there?"

"You never know. I hope we won't need the gun, but trouble is waiting for us. You should check your e-mail. Your sister is supposed to send you more information about that group of protesters at the well site determined to stir up the locals." Rowdy glanced at her. "Put the gun away."

"I am." She glanced at the radio listings and picked a station. "Tell me what you've learned about the problem we'll be facing."

"A retired college professor, environmental studies, moved out west to enjoy the fresh air and open spaces when she quit teaching." Rowdy studied his mirrors, then carefully changed lanes. "Just her luck that her new home is near a site where our company is doing some heavy-duty fracking now. Similar to what you saw at Sanders's ranch."

"It was noisy with the generators running day and night. And every once in a while you could get a whiff of rotten eggs or something that smelled like raw sewage. Yeah. I wouldn't want to live next door to that. Or to the flares and bright lights at night. So, why did she move there?" Megan settled back in a leather seat that felt like a comfortable easy chair.

"I don't have the whole story yet. But what you saw was a well-run site, Megan. With only one well seeing action, the rest were already complete and pumping. Imagine if there were several wells being drilled at a time."

"It would be deafening and it would reek."

"And you'd be able to hear and smell it from miles away." Rowdy tapped his fingers on the steering wheel.

"You say she's protesting now. What good will that do?" Megan also remembered how the roads were torn up by the heavy equipment and big trucks that were part of the process.

"It's bad publicity for the company. Shines a light on how we do things. If a site doesn't dispose of its wastewater properly, it can cause local well water to be polluted. Then there's that stench from the chemicals we use. The source of those smells you described. It can travel for miles. I'm guessing that the man running the site near this lady isn't being careful or the smells wouldn't be too strong. Last time I was out in that part of Texas, they hadn't started drilling yet. The man in charge there is new to me." Rowdy frowned. "This woman's screaming to high heaven that we need to shut down. That we're ruining the environment out there. Even found some lizard she's saying we could cause to become extinct."

"Do you think she's right?" Megan pulled out her smartphone. "What's the name of this lizard?"

He told her and she began a search. "You can look but we always do an environmental impact study before we ever dig the first well. There are several lizards indigenous to that area. She can cry about the thing but in our state, we aren't worried about it."

"Seriously? You think she's lying about a lizard to bolster her case to shut you down?"

"It's not *me*, Megan, it's *us*. Calhoun is you and me. But mostly you, remember? No matter how you might feel personally about fracking, it's your bread and butter. And the trouble your company is in will only get worse if you give in to this fringe group and begin shutting down because of the noise or the smell." He hit a button on the steering wheel, and the channel on the radio changed. "Sports talk. Now, that's cool."

Megan leaned back with a groan. If she had to listen to men discuss tailbacks and tight ends for hours, she might as well take a nap. She looked down at her phone. Yes, Rowdy was right. That lizard was ugly as sin and only its mother would love it, but it wasn't endangered. She ran another search and found the latest news about fracking and the problems it could cause. Lots of negative articles and very few positives. She checked her e-mail next and found a long one from her sister Shannon with attached articles.

She started to write a long e-mail back, then decided it would be easier just to call her sister.

Shannon answered immediately. "Hey, sis, how goes the road trip? I heard a tornado almost got you. Are you okay?"

Megan told her the story. She listened to her sister's platitudes, then cut her off. "Save it. I just spent a great weekend in San Antonio at our favorite hotel. Cassidy even set me up with spa treatments. So I'm cool." She glanced at Rowdy. "She's really throwing money around. You know why?"

"Don't worry about it. She was shocked at the salary our old chief financial officer was making. I think she's using some of the money from the bonus he left behind when he quit." Shannon sighed. "Our new sister is some kind of financial whiz kid. I try to stay out of her way. Numbers make my eyes cross."

"Okay. Good to know. Now, what's with all the stuff you sent me about fracking? You really think I should go out there like I'm all for it? I've never been a fan."

"In a minute. Tell me about Rowdy. You two getting along?"

"You could say that." Megan noticed he'd turned down the radio. Of course he was eavesdropping. "He hasn't fired me yet."

"Well, he sure let Cass know, before you even showed up, that he didn't appreciate being stuck with one of 'those Calhouns'." Shannon laughed. "But I know you, little sister. He's probably already in your bed. Right?"

"I called you about the fracking." Megan felt her cheeks burning. She didn't dare look toward Rowdy. "Seriously. What am I supposed to do with these articles, Shan?"

"So I'm right. Go, Megan. Anyway, study up. You and Rowdy are headed to a site where this woman is getting people stirred up against us. This was my idea, and Mason okayed it."

"I know about the protesters. Rowdy told me. We're on the road right now."

"Good. We had to pull some strings. You know he technically works for one of our subsidiaries. This CWC Industries. Cass is doing something about that. His supervisor had other ideas about where he should go, but we 'borrowed' him for this."

"Oh, really. I hope Rowdy's okay with that. That your idea, too?" Megan loved her sister but knew she had as little experience working in the business as she did.

"We need you to be the face of Calhoun Petroleum out there. Calm down those people. Rowdy can make sure the drill site is doing what it should to protect the environment. Clean up some things if we're at fault. Then you read all that stuff I sent you and be our advocate. It'll impress this Wallace woman that a member of the family is handling her concerns personally. Isn't that a brilliant idea?"

"Well, aren't you the PR princess?" Megan grinned. "Are you impressing Mason?"

"I'm doing my damnedest. Too bad I'm having to work with . . . Never mind. Just do your thing and make this problem go away. You always could talk your way out of just about anything."

"Yes, except this year in the trenches." Megan sighed.

"Now, don't get discouraged. At least you're not here in the office, where it's all doom and gloom." Shannon had started whispering. "Cassidy's got us scared shitless about money. Enjoy that fancy RV, because we may all end up living in it after this year is over. This company may go under, Meg!"

"Don't say that!" Megan bit her lip. "You're right. I can do my thing, and you can do yours. Cassidy will work her magic with the numbers, and Ethan is probably reprogramming the computers there. If we all work together . . . Oh hell, what do I know? Love you, Shan."

"Crap. I'm sorry I said anything. Now I've got you really worried. Back at you, little sister. Take care. I'm glad that twister didn't get you. And you have fun with Rowdy. He looked like a good time to me." Shannon ended the call.

Megan turned to Rowdy. "Um, Shannon says you're working for Calhoun now, not CWC Industries. I expect your old supervisor will let you know."

"Are you kidding me?" He jerked the steering wheel, then corrected. "How did that happen?"

"They seem to think it's best. Because you're stuck with me. Makes it easier to coordinate." She ran her hand down his arm. "I'm sorry. If it's any comfort, I'll make sure you don't lose any benefits, vacation time, whatever. Maybe I can get a raise for you out of this."

He stared at the road ahead, his jaw tight.

"Rowdy?" Megan played with her phone, realized he wasn't in the mood to talk, and finally started reading Shannon's e-mail again. Swell. She was supposed to be the spokeswoman who was going to convince everyone out there in that sad, polluted wasteland that Calhoun had done nothing wrong and everything right? Oh boy, was she the wrong person for the job. Because the more she read, the more Megan realized that she'd like to meet this professor and join her group of protesters. Too bad she was doomed to be on the other side.

She jumped when a paw hit her arm from between the seats. "Rowdy, Lucky needs a potty break, and I wouldn't mind one, either. And a cold drink." She looked around. Where had the city gone? They were already out in a desolate area where towns were few and far between. Rowdy was going a sensible seventy-five with smaller cars and trucks passing him like he was standing still.

"Fine. Watch for signs. I think there's one coming up in about fifty miles." He frowned. "Damn it. The Texans have got to spend money on their offensive line this year." Football. The talk show, of course.

"Fifty miles, Lucky. I hope you can hold it." Megan watched open land, brush, and wide-open spaces pass by. They'd been steadily climbing in altitude, and she sometimes saw mountains in the distance. She knew they were on a famous plateau—flat, of course.

People who'd never been to Texas probably didn't understand how vast the state was. She'd spent some time on the East Coast. It had amazed her that if you were driving in the northeast, you could cross several state lines in the time it took her to get from Houston to San Antonio.

"I give up. Damn talk show hosts take calls from anyone, even idiots." He punched a button and it was quiet in the cab.

"Are you okay?" Megan had to ask. "About the change."

"That was your sister telling you all that?"

"Yes." Megan told him what Shannon had lined out for them to do in West Texas.

"It's probably for the best. You do the public relations, and I'll handle the technical side. I really don't like the idea of you crawling all over a rig anyway, if you want to know the truth." He smiled at her. "If Mason MacKenzie thinks it's all right for you to do this other stuff, then I'm glad. And Calhoun does have good benefits. Just make sure they follow through. Get my 401K where it needs to be."

"I'm sure Cassidy will handle that. Shannon says she's setting the office on fire there. Impressing everyone with her financial wizardry." Megan relaxed.

"Doesn't surprise me."

"Thank God I can quit pretending that I can learn everything about oil by following you around for a year." Megan plugged her phone into the car charger and set it aside.

"Hey, maybe you could. You're smart enough. But it's not safe or the right way to do it." He pointed to her stomach. "Why don't you tell me the story? About your tattoo."

"Really? Now?" Megan felt a flush crawl up her neck. "It's not my proudest moment."

"Even better." He grinned at her. "I have a tattoo, too, but you probably didn't notice it."

"No. You must have it well hidden. Or maybe I was way too distracted last night and this morning." She reached out and took his hand. Lucky hit her arm again. "Is someone jealous?"

"That dog can be locked in the bathroom if he causes a problem when we touch each other." Rowdy was still grinning as he pulled her thumb into his mouth. He gave it a gentle bite before he released it. "I'll let you look for my tattoo tonight. Now, tell me the story. We just passed a sign that promises twenty miles to a clean restroom. Is that enough time for your tale?"

"Okay. For the short version." Megan sifted through her memory. How to tell it so she didn't sound like one of those idiots Rowdy couldn't stand? Oh well. "I was living in New York."

"The city?" He sounded appalled. "Why?"

"I loved it. Attended a design school for a while." Until it got too hard and her lack of creativity became obvious. "I went up there with a friend who had a real talent for it. Me? Not so much. So I dropped out and tried acting." She laughed. "Trust me. Not my thing. I felt like a wooden puppet. Looked like one, too. So I quit that and just played for a while." She let her hand drift to his thigh again. "I'm really good at playing."

"I can testify to that." He covered her hand with his. "Lucky, stop it." He pushed the dog's paw back. "We're going to have to cure him of that."

"Definitely." Megan shoved the dog into the backseat and raised her voice. "Stay!" Lucky just looked at her, then put his head on his paws like he'd been kicked. "Oh, knock it off. Take a nap."

"The tattoo, Megan. You have ten more miles to finish the story."

"So, everyone was always making fun of my accent." She poked out her lower lip. "Do you think I have an accent? Seriously? Sure, I say 'y'all' once in a while and 'fixin'.' What's wrong with that? Compared to those folks from Boston, I speak easy-to-understand English. At least I pronounce my 'r's.'"

"Hey, I'm with you on that. I got razzed in the army for the same thing." He laughed. "So, that's why you got a tattoo? Did people call you Tex?"

"Some of them did. But then I met this guy . . ."

"Now, how did I know this would be about a man?" He hit the steering wheel. "If you tell me his name was Tex, I swear I'll pull over and . . ."

"No, you won't. But it was. Texas Rafferty." Megan sighed. "At the time it seemed like fate. Tex and Tex. His parents named him that because he was born here when they were stationed at Fort Hood in Killeen. Anyway, I was homesick and it seemed like he was meant to be mine, even though he didn't know a thing about Texas. They'd lived all over the world, because his dad was career army. Tex was so darned cute and sweet, too."

"Megan, I have a feeling that if you got a tattoo with the name of every guy you ever had a crush on, you'd be covered in ink." Rowdy slowed down the truck.

"You're probably right. I was very drunk the night I got my tattoo."

"I can believe that. You'd have had to be, because I bet it hurt like hell." He was the one rubbing her thigh this time. "But it's beautiful."

"I think so. And I do have vague memories of some screaming and a lot of tequila shots." She grabbed his hand when it crept up toward her front pants zipper. "Don't mess with me, Baker. I need a pit stop." She laughed. "So, no more tattoos for me. But at least I'm not stuck with George or Fred Forever. Texas Rafferty is history, of course. Turned out he also loved a gal from that damn Boston whose 'cah' was a Mercedes convertible." She leaned back, laughing. "Can't regret the tat, because I do still love my home state." She saw a busy truck stop coming into view. "Ah, relief is in sight."

Rowdy carefully steered them into the parking lot and found a spot near the grass. As soon as they were stopped, she grabbed Lucky's leash and jumped out of the truck.

"He's really gotten the hang of that." Rowdy stood by while she walked the dog over to the grass and a couple of bushes. Lucky immediately took care of business, then sniffed around for a minute or two before finishing up. "I think he'll be all right if we leave the windows down a few inches and lock him in the truck."

"Yes, it's cool today. A front must have blown in." Megan handed Rowdy the leash. "Will you do it? I'm hitting the restroom."

"Fine. Go. But now I'm trying to figure out how I can talk you into getting my name on you somewhere." He looked down at her, his gaze traveling a path that left her no doubt where he'd want it. "Think about it. Rowdy. It's not only a name, it's the way you like to play." He stepped closer.

She put her hand on his chest, too tempted to stretch up for a kiss. "You're right about that. But I'm done with ink. The only way I'll let a man lay claim to me now is with a ring on my finger." And with a grin and a twitch of her hips, she headed into the large building across the lot.

Rowdy watched her go. A ring on her finger. He couldn't believe the idea didn't send him into panic mode like it should. One night of hotter-than-hot sex, and she was throwing out challenges like that? Didn't mean a thing, of course. She was playing. And she was damn good at it. He put the dog into the truck, checked to make sure he'd be cool enough, then went inside himself. He wished he had a good story for her when she found his tattoo. But the two names on his wrist under the watch he always wore had been there since he'd come back alive and his buddies hadn't. He'd promised himself he'd never forget them and he wouldn't. It certainly wasn't the fun and colorful tale Megan told.

He used the facilities and bought a soda. He'd given up driving straight through without breaks like he did when he was alone. He had to admit, it was a pleasure to have company on these long trips. Or at least company like Megan. And to think he'd fought having a Calhoun with him. When he got out to the truck, Lucky greeted him with a bark and he took the dog out again, found a bowl in the trailer, and gave him a good, long drink of water, a treat, and another walk around the grass. Okay, he had to admit it, he was enjoying the company of the dog, too.

"Lucky, we're getting ourselves into a real situation here. You know it?" He saw Megan walking across the parking lot with a large soda and a bag of snack mix, his favorite kind. He'd only mentioned it once, in the big box store. But she'd remembered. She tossed it to him, then climbed in the truck when he opened the door.

"I have a theory. If we're moving, calories can't catch us. What do you think?" She grinned at him, then pulled a large Snickers bar out of her jacket pocket.

"I think we'd better hedge our bets and do some workouts tonight." He slammed the door and walked around to get in the driver's seat.

"Hmm." She bit into the candy. "What kind of workouts do you have in mind, Mr. Baker?"

He leaned over and kissed her, tasting chocolate, nuts, caramel, and Megan. He was across the console and close to doing something foolish when the dog barked. Making love in a parking lot. He'd lost his freaking mind. He pulled back and licked his lips.

"Delicious. Why didn't you get me one of those?" He sat back and pulled on his seat belt.

She looked a little dazed, the candy bar hitting her leg when her hand fell into her lap. "A Snickers? I did." She looked down. "Shit. Chocolate on my jeans." She pulled off the napkin she'd wrapped around her soda and dabbed at it. "I hope it comes out."

"You can wash them tonight." Rowdy started the truck. "That dog needs obedience school." He looked back at Lucky, who was grinning at them, his tongue hanging out. "And he sure doesn't get chocolate, it's bad for dogs."

"I know that." Megan tossed Rowdy a candy bar. "How am I going to wash my jeans in an RV?"

"Didn't you notice? Not only do we have two bedrooms, thanks to Cassidy, but there's a stackable washer and dryer in one of the closets. Free samples of detergent inside the washer." Rowdy laughed. "Your sister is out of control, Megan. I know there was insurance, but not enough for what she paid for this trailer."

"Cass went overboard." She sighed and looked out the window. "You think she's feeling guilty for dumping you?"

"Maybe. Or sorry you're stuck with me doing what will surely be a nasty, dirty job for the next year. Our own washer and dryer? I'm stoked." After he got them safely on the highway again, he steered with one hand and ripped open the candy bar. "Either way, I say we relax and enjoy it all." Rowdy took a bite and savored it. He rarely let himself eat this kind of sweet treat. Maybe Megan was a bad influence on him. But then again, he'd be working it off later.

He glanced at her as she wiped her fingers on that napkin and sipped her soda. She'd put on her tight jeans and form-fitting T-shirt for their trip this morning, since they'd probably not make it to the rigs in time to do more than set up camp. It had been chilly, so she'd thrown a jean jacket over it, but he could still see her curves from where he sat. And he remembered . . .

Megan had been all fire and fun last night and this morning. She was up for anything, and her zest for life had pulled something new out of him. Cassidy might be feeling guilty, but Rowdy realized that he was feeling liberated. Damn. It was as shocking as it was crazy to realize that he'd been holding himself back in his relationship with Cass for way too long. Yes, he'd loved her, but it had been a comfortable kind of love that he'd obviously needed to be blasted free from.

He smiled, thinking about how he'd let all his inhibitions go last night and just played. It wasn't how he'd ever approached love-making before. Why not? Beat the hell out of him.

Rowdy finished off his candy bar, looked around for a place to put the wrapper, and ended up cramming it into the side pocket in the door. Well, hell. He was disorganized, and that was just not like him. Usually he had everything figured out well in advance. In a new truck he would have brought along a sack for trash. Also would have picked up a handful of napkins when he'd bought his soda to have ready for spills or to wipe off his messy hands. Clearly Megan had screwed up his routine and his mind. Because in that truck stop all he could think about was hurrying back to her. Getting on the road fast so they could reach their destination and set up. And then the night would come, and she'd make good on her promise to "christen" that trailer "from one end to the other."

He reached forward and hit the radio again. Talk shows. Sports. Maybe that would calm down his body. Because he couldn't drive another two hundred miles with a hard-on. He glanced at Megan and damn if she hadn't dozed off, her head against the door. Not that he would have asked her to do anything about his problem. He adjusted his jeans and thought about football. Yeah. Like that was going to ease his pain. Eventually he calmed down. But then he noticed a smear of chocolate on the brand-new tan leather steering wheel.

Megan Calhoun. What was she doing to him? Worse, what was he letting himself be pulled into? An affair with a Calhoun woman. He knew where it was headed. He would save himself a lot of pain if he just drove this rig into a tree right now and got it over with.

Chapter 12

"Rowdy, we can't stay here." Megan pulled her T-shirt up over her nose. The smell was so much worse than it had been at King's ranch. The generators roared, chains rattled, and it was all too much. The pounding might as well have been against her skull.

"I usually just deal with it. But I see what you mean." Rowdy turned off the engine and jumped out of the truck. He looked back at her. "Stay here. I already don't like what I see, and I haven't even begun to inspect this place." He slammed the door and stomped off toward what she recognized as the office trailer.

"Lucky, I hate to tell you this, but if you want to pee, it's going to have to be here—on those dead bushes or that sand." Megan clipped on his leash and ignored Rowdy's orders. She needed to stretch her legs after a long ride. Sure, they'd stopped for lunch and another bathroom break, but sitting for over three hundred miles was flat-out exhausting. She tried to breathe through her mouth when the smell from a foul-smelling and greenish pond got to her. The dog sneezed and shook his head before tentatively stepping over to bushes that were obviously victims of the horrible conditions. Megan kept a tight grip on Lucky's leash, but he seemed to realize the pond wasn't drinking water and steered clear on his own.

"I thought I told you to stay in the truck." Rowdy came up behind her.

"The dog needed to take a leak." She turned and saw he wasn't alone.

"Ms. Calhoun. My, oh my, but this is an unexpected pleasure." The man was tall and bulky, looking more than capable of joining the roughnecks on the rig and handling a chain and collar himself. "Clint Stephens, supervisor here." He extended his hand.

Megan shifted the leash to her left hand so she could shake his. "Thank you, Mr. Stephens. I think I will get back in the truck. This smell is getting to me." She tugged Lucky, who was growling at the supervisor, toward the truck.

"Perfectly normal. I'm sure Baker here has explained that the chemicals we use in fracking are necessary." He smiled and gestured toward the three wells with men working on top of them doing what she actually recognized. There were six other wells already capped and pumping nearby, and they weren't exactly quiet. "This has been a good field for us. Very productive. And we're actually ahead of schedule. Your daddy would have been proud of the progress we've made here. He came out personally last year, when we started the first well." Stephens frowned. "Didn't have crazies trying to shut us down then. No, ma'am. Local businesses welcomed us with open arms. We brought employment opportunities and money to this town."

"I've heard that happens. Small towns like us until reality sets in." Megan opened the car door and shoved Lucky inside when he continued to growl at Stephens. "We need to find a place to set up our RV. Forgive me if I'm hoping it's not next to this"—she waved her hand toward the polluted water—"pond."

"Perfectly understandable. I rent a nice little house in town myself. It's only about ten miles away. Close enough to get here in an emergency, but far enough so I can draw breath, if you know what I mean." He laughed, seemingly not a bit concerned that Rowdy looked unhappy.

"So, where's the nearest trailer park?" Rowdy had told Megan he wanted to get them settled somewhere before dark.

"There's a tidy little trailer park about six miles due west. Has a nice view of the mountains and good hookups. No problem taking your dog in there, and good water you can use to fill your tank. Propane available, too." Stephens checked out the trailer, now covered with dust from the road. "Good to see the company set you up in style, Ms. Calhoun. Must mean the price of oil coming up has us in good shape and my job's secure. Right, Baker?" He slapped

Rowdy on the back, and Megan almost jumped between them at the look on Rowdy's face. But he held it together.

"We'd better get going. I'll expect to meet you here on-site first thing in the morning, Stephens. I want to see your accident reports and environmental studies. All of them, including readings on the well water in a five-mile radius from as recently as yesterday. Am I clear?" Rowdy motioned to her, and Megan climbed into the truck and slammed the door.

Whatever Stephens said wasn't good enough, because Rowdy got in his face and said a few more things that made the super's face flush. Finally the man nodded and turned on his heel, marching toward the office building. Rowdy strode around the truck and got in.

"Is he the problem here?" Megan slid her hand over Rowdy's fist on the steering wheel.

"At least part of it. I'll know more tomorrow." He turned to her. "This may be worse than we expected. If the company is entirely at fault because of shoddy work conditions, then you're going to have quite a time calming down the protesters."

"Well, let's see what you find out tomorrow before I panic, okay?" Megan sat back. "Please get us out of here and turn on the air conditioner. I know it's chilly outside, but I can't stand to breathe this air another minute."

"I know what you mean, and I'm fairly used to those chemicals. I didn't like the looks of that pond. He should have disposed of his spillage better than that. I'm going to be insisting on some changes here right away." He hit some controls, and soon had cold air hitting her cheeks. "Better?"

"A little." She wrapped her jacket around herself and shivered. "Now, find that trailer park. I can't wait to get our new home set up." She smiled at him. "You know what I have in mind, don't you?"

"Dinner?" He punched the address Stephens had given him into the navigation system, then pulled out of the site and onto the rutted county road that ran next to it.

"Dessert." She rubbed his thigh in his worn jeans. "I wouldn't mind skipping dinner altogether."

A woman's voice told them to turn left at the next intersection. Rowdy stopped the truck, looked around, then pulled Megan to him.

His hungry kiss let Megan know that he believed having dessert first was a fine idea, too.

Rowdy stopped when they got to the trailer park. It was no Disney World vacation spot, that was for sure. The line of trailers appeared at the end of a road behind a sign naming it RAY'S RECREATIONAL PARK. The only indication there might be any actual recreation was a netless basketball hoop nailed to the back of the post holding the sign. Megan didn't think it looked welcoming since there was a cluster of prickly pear plants near the entrance. All she needed was another dose of cactus spines.

"Maybe we should look somewhere else." She stared at the desert around her and the mountains in the distance. Not exactly picturesque.

"I'm tired, you're tired, and there's a sign on the trailer marked 'Office' that claims they have free Wi-Fi. I see what you're worried about. Just stay away from the cactus. I doubt it'll chase you down the road, Megan." Rowdy grinned and climbed out of the truck when a woman stepped out of the office trailer and looked them over.

Raylene, the manager, shook her head when he asked if she had space for them. "I'm pretty full right now, if you want to know the truth. But you can try to fit down there." She pointed to the end of a dirt and gravel road. Then she quoted an outrageous rental rate, both daily and weekly.

"Isn't that a little high?" Rowdy frowned.

She pointed to the RV. "Fact is, I can't really accommodate you. You're too damn long for the one space I've got left. I'm doing you a favor by letting you try to squeeze in there. Of course, there's always Fort Stockton. That's the closest RV park that I know of."

Rowdy shook his head. "Too far. That's fifty miles away."

"Well, then. I guess you'll have to try to put that rig down there on the end. You'll kind of poke out in the scrub grass, but it should work." She eyed the RV, then took a drag on her cigarette. "That's a sweet setup you've got there, I have to say. Just be careful if you try to back it in. It'll be tight. But there's water there and a plug for electricity." She frowned down at her dog, which had been barking nonstop. "Butch, shut the hell up."

"He's probably barking at our dog." Megan had climbed out of the truck and stood beside Rowdy. Any chance to stretch her legs was still welcome, and she'd wanted to take a breath of the air to make sure it wasn't nasty like that back at the oil well site. Thank goodness it was clean and fresh, except for the smoke coming from Raylene. Their landlady was whip-thin, tanned walnut brown, and wore her gray hair in a long pony tail down her back. With her tie-dyed T-shirt and baggy jeans, she could have been a hippie stuck back in the sixties.

"We were told you allow dogs. We'll keep him on a leash." Lucky was impossible to miss since he was answering Butch's barks with his own from the backseat of the truck. Butch was a ten-pound ball of fur but had one of those big egos that made her wonder if he'd attack Lucky just to show him whose turf this was. Megan didn't want to get in the middle of a dogfight, though she thought Lucky could take the fur ball.

"Oh, I allow 'em. On a leash, like you said. Now, I'll need a deposit. Credit card will do." Raylene waited while Rowdy pulled out his company card. "Calhoun Petroleum?" She frowned. "Well, your money spends as well as anyone's, I guess." She lowered her voice. "I got some of those protesters here. You hear about them?"

"Yes. We were told there were some unhappy people trying to shut down the rigs." Megan looked down the dirt and gravel road. No one was out walking around, but she could smell food cooking. Suppertime.

"I should say. Mad as hell is more like it." Raylene shook her head. "The ones here are cousins of Sharon Wallace, that organizer from Waco. If I was you, I'd keep your affiliation with the company to yourself or you'll be hearing from them night and day."

"Oh great." Megan shared a look with Rowdy. "How many are staying here?"

"Well, I'll have to think. I heard in town that Dr. Wallace—that's how she insists people call her—has fifty-three cousins. Can you believe it? When she got herself all riled up about the fracking, I guess she called in the troops. So some are staying with her at her place. Those are the dumb ones." Raylene laughed. "The noise from those wells can be heard clear as a bell there, night and day. And when the wind is right, the smell will knock you over."

"Yes, we stopped by the site a while ago." Rowdy frowned. "So, how many are staying here?"

"The smart ones who brought trailers? Good business for me, not so good for you." She laughed. "I'd say there are twelve RVs, no, make that fifteen. Maybe about thirty people of that bunch staying here." She finished her cigarette, stomped it out, then picked it up and stuck it in her jacket pocket after she pinched it to make sure it was out. "Got to be careful. If you folks smoke, please police your butts. Butch eats the dang things. Don't know why. I'd think they'd taste nasty, but nicotine poisoning almost did him in when he was a pup." She leaned down to pick him up and gave him a cuddle. "Scared me to death."

"We don't smoke, but I'm glad he survived." Megan reached for him and almost lost a finger when he snapped at her.

"Careful, honey. He doesn't take to strangers." Raylene laughed again. "I have to go inside to run your card. I can bring it down to you or you can come by to pick it up. One week, paid in advance. That's the deal."

"That's fine. We'll pick it up after we have dinner." Rowdy nodded toward their RV. "Thanks for making room for us, Raylene. And for warning us about the cousins."

"No problem, honey." She winked at him. "I didn't catch your name, girl."

Megan shifted her feet. If she dodged the question, it would just make this woman even more determined to get the answer. So she'd give her half of one. "It's Megan, Raylene. I'd shake hands, but I'm afraid Butch wouldn't like it."

"Pleased to meet you. Most workers who come out here don't get to bring their gals with them." Raylene looked Rowdy over. "I guess you must rate special treatment." She gave the gleaming trailer an even longer appraisal. "You a bigwig in the company, Rowdy Baker?"

"Nope. Just a lowly engineer, sent here to help clean up the mess that's causing problems." He opened the truck door. "See you later, Raylene. Let's go, Megan, I'm getting hungry."

Megan hurried around to her side of the truck and climbed in. "Way to avoid the third degree."

"It'll come out soon enough when you have to meet with Dr. Wallace." He drove the truck and trailer down the central track between rows of trailers. Many of them had fancy SUVs or pickup trucks parked next to them, most with out-of-state license plates. "She's right about one thing. This parking spot is going to be tight. I think I'll drive straight in, go out onto the flat land, then make a wide turn, so I can aim toward the road again. I may have to drive over some of that prickly pear you're so fond of."

"Smash it all." Megan eyed the challenge he had getting the RV parked. "You want me to get out and direct you? That looks awfully narrow to me." Megan could see the place where they'd plug in had probably been set up for a much smaller trailer. Luckily there would be no other trailers on the end. There was a barbecue grill set up on a concrete slab along with picnic tables and benches that were obviously for the tenants of the trailer park to share.

"Couldn't hurt. Just wave me left or right if I'm in danger of hitting that post or the picnic area." He waited until she jumped out, then slowly moved forward.

Megan realized he really didn't need her help as he expertly fit the trailer into the slot, then turned off the engine. When he began unhooking the RV from the truck, a man appeared, then another, until there were six strangers gathered around offering advice and help. It soon became apparent that these were some of Dr. Wallace's "cousins" here visiting and to lend her moral support.

"Yes, we're going to stay until this fracking thing gets settled. I have to say I've wanted to check out this model RV from that manufacturer. Let me help you get it stabilized, then would you mind if I took a look around inside?" This from Bert, who hailed from Oklahoma.

"This has got to be right off the lot. I think they just came out with it in August." Harley from Kansas also wanted "just a peek" inside. He and his wife were RV fanatics and had jumped on the chance to help out Sharon, since they hadn't hit the Davis Mountains and West Texas yet in their travels.

"It's brand new. Our company had to replace the one we started out in after ours got totaled. We barely survived a tornado in South Texas a week or so ago." Rowdy must have realized something was up when everyone went still.

"Your company?" Amos from Orlando, Florida, stepped forward. "That wouldn't be Calhoun Petroleum, would it?"

"Afraid so." Rowdy quit fooling with the RV and faced the men. "We're here to see what we can do to clean up the mess that's been made at the well site. You can pass that on to Dr. Wallace, if you will." He smiled. "Megan and I want to be sure the environment is safe from the worst that fracking can do. Isn't that right, Megan?"

Megan had been walking Lucky away from the men, not sure she was ready to get involved yet. Now she had no choice but to step up. "Rowdy's right. We're open to listening to all of Dr. Wallace's concerns and to seeing that they're addressed. I'll be calling on her myself. Probably early next week, as soon as Rowdy has gathered all the facts at the site. Then I'd like to see us hammer out a solution to the problems she's had."

"Sharon's problems are also this beautiful land's problems." Art from Arizona waved his hand toward the distant mountains. Too bad the land where they stood was just flat desert with not much to recommend it except a few scraggly bushes and cactus. "Oh, I see your face. Listen. Do you hear birds singing? I don't because that damn noise from the wells your company is drilling has run them off from their natural habitat. And don't get me started on the pollution."

"Now, Artie, didn't she just say they were here to help?" Amos, who looked just like Art, might have been his twin. "Shut up. I want to see inside this trailer. We're not here to fight with these folks. Are we, boys?"

"No." It was a resounding chorus.

"Bully," Art muttered. "I see you both studying us. Yes, he's my twin. Born a couple of minutes sooner and always trying to run my business. That's why I live half a country away from him."

"No, you live half a country away because your wife has family there and she bosses you around worse than I do." Amos poked his brother in the ribs. "Doesn't hurt that Janet is a looker."

"You always did want her for yourself." Art grinned. "But I saw her first."

"How about that tour?" Rowdy moved over to the trailer door. "I'm still learning things about this trailer." He pulled out a tablet. "Look at this. I just use this app to activate the pop outs." He touched the screen and parts of the RV began to move. That got the men clustered around him. "If any of you have done research on it, maybe you can help me figure out some of these other features. Did you know we have a washer and dryer?" He gestured, and the men hurried to follow him inside.

"Well, I see you handled the cousins all right." Raylene was carrying Butch when she walked up next to Megan. "Let's see if our boys will get along. What's his name?"

"Lucky." Megan squatted down and held Lucky, who was growling at Butch. "Now, Lucky, play nice."

Raylene set Butch on the ground and he trotted over to give Lucky a good sniff. To Megan's surprise, Lucky let him do it and settled down, finally wagging his tail.

"I do believe they're going to be just fine. Yours is just a pup, isn't he?"

"Yes. I found him on the side of the road, but the vet said he was about three months old. We just got him all his shots." Megan stood and watched the dogs nose each other. "He's going to be much bigger than he is now."

"Yep. But he's fine for Butch to socialize with for now. If you want to leave him with me when you two go to work, I'll watch him for you. No charge. It's good for the dogs to have a playmate." Raylene lit up a cigarette.

"Why, thanks, that will be a big help. I'm supposed to be helping Rowdy at the rigs. And with the Wallace situation." Megan shook her head. "That was only six of the cousins. And one of them was already pretty worked up about the environment. Is it true the birds left because of the noise?"

"Of course. You said you stopped by there. Would you nest where that racket was going on?" She cocked her head. "It's very faint, but you can still hear it, when everything else is still. And at night the glow from their flares makes the sky light up on the horizon." She pointed with her cigarette. "They say when all the wells are done and just pumping, it'll be better, but I don't believe it."

Megan couldn't deny that her skepticism was probably warranted. "There's a lot of animosity toward the oil companies. And throwing money at it doesn't seem to count for much." Megan took a deep breath of the clean air.

"You're right, honey. People are glad enough to lease their oil rights and rake in the money from it, but then reality hits. I see you enjoying our fresh air. Where are you from?"

"Houston." Megan smiled. "Lived there most of my life except for time away at school."

"Ha. Was there forty years ago. No desire to go back. Houston's a big city. Too much traffic, so the air's full of car exhaust. Then there's those chemical and gasoline plants spewing God knows what near the Ship Channel. Bet you never breathed air quite like this before." Raylene took her own deep breath, which came out more like a wheeze.

"Well, a lot has changed since you were there. Stricter emission laws have made cars run cleaner, though traffic is still horrible. The Ship Channel isn't as bad as it used to be, either, from what people tell me. But you're right." Megan took another deep breath and almost felt dizzy. "This air is incredible."

"Imagine growing up with this every day, and then the oil companies come in and send it all to hell." Raylene took a drag on her cigarette. "I know, I know, I'm pollutin' my own air, and that's a damn shame. But it's my choice. People who're stuck here with nowhere else to go are miserable about what's happened and money can't fix it."

"Let me do some research on that." Megan remembered some of the articles she'd read on the Internet. "This well site can be cleaned up. There may be some things that money can help fix, too. They do make sound suppressors, things like that. So, wait and see." She turned when the trailer door opened. "Here come the men. I hope Rowdy has made them happy. We sure don't need to come home each night to hostility."

"That may be inevitable. Sharon Wallace is doing her best to work up a real hate around here for anything to do with Calhoun Petroleum. That's a new truck you drove in, so I guess they didn't have time to put the logo on the door. Good thing." Raylene put out her cigarette, stomped on it, then picked it up. "The super on the job here has had his truck vandalized a couple of times because of his logo. Windows shot out. Tires slashed. People see Calhoun and go crazy."

"That's a shame." Megan wondered what would happen when

they found out her last name. She wasn't in any hurry to announce it, but it was inevitable, too.

"Well, if you're here to fix things, then more power to you. Just hurry, is all. I think Wallace is planning something big for weekend after next. That's the Marfa Lights Festival. She knows there'll be a lot of people here for it, and the press always comes in to cover it."

"I've heard of Marfa. How close are we to it?" Megan wanted to see the mysterious lights it was famous for. They were a twinkling show along the horizon above the mountains that some claimed were alien lights. They'd been seen around the town of Marfa for more than a century.

"Ninety miles. Which is nothing around here." Raylene put her cigarette butt in her pocket and picked up Butch. "Mark my words. Wallace plans to do something to get the press to notice the situation over here that weekend. So calming her down before then would be the smart play."

"No pressure. I have a week and a half to take care of a problem that's been brewing for how long?" Megan patted Lucky when he pawed her leg. He obviously wanted to be picked up, too. She finally gave in, even though he was getting pretty heavy.

"Almost a year, hon. Sharon Wallace retired from Baylor a year ago May, bought the old Weimer place, and settled in right before the first well was started." Raylene cursed when Butch bit her hand. "Damn it, you're not getting down. We need to get home, and these folks need to eat supper." She dug in her pocket and pulled out Rowdy's credit card and receipt. "Give this to your fella, Megan, and good luck. I heard Wallace sank her retirement savings into buying her place. Big mistake. Now no one will want it, and she was stupid enough not to check to see if she got the mineral rights in her deal. She didn't. So someone could come on her land to drill and she couldn't stop them." Raylene cursed again. "Damn dog, quit biting or I'll put you in your crate. Anyway, guess who owns her mineral rights?"

"Not Calhoun?" Megan felt Rowdy's hand slide around her waist. For once it didn't give her ideas. She was too worried about what was coming.

"Nope. But the people who do own them worked out a deal to let Calhoun lease them. No one knows who the owners are, so Calhoun is the easy target. Ow!" Raylene popped Butch on his butt. "That's it. Time-out for you."

Lucky barked and strained toward Raylene and Butch as they walked off.

"Lucky made a friend." Rowdy rubbed Megan's back. "And the guys loved our RV. Seems like you and Raylene had quite a talk."

"You have no idea." Megan turned in his arms and buried her face in his shirt. God, he smelled good. "Where can we buy a bulletproof vest? Because I may have to start wearing one when these people find out my last name."

"We'll check online. I asked the guys. Raylene's Wi-Fi is high speed and rock solid. I know you're anxious to research the situation here." He raised Megan's face until he was looking into her eyes. "Can I get a smile?"

"No." She dragged him toward the trailer. "But I'll let you take my mind off my troubles. Which bedroom would you like to do first?" She jerked open the trailer door. "Fore or aft?"

Rowdy kissed her until he felt like he was in danger of losing himself. Yet he couldn't get enough. They'd come together fast, the bunk under them not nearly big enough or long enough to give them the room they needed to play the games Megan liked. She finally just laughed and braced her feet on the ceiling. When she shouted his name and came apart in his arms, Rowdy let himself go, too. What was it about this woman that turned him into some kind of superstud?

"Wow. I'd heard that phrase 'the earth moved,' but I never believed it before." She smiled lazily up at him.

"No, this is serious." The bed trembled and Rowdy could hear the dishes in the cabinets rattling. Cabinet doors popped open, and the one above them released a load of sheets on their heads. "We've got to get out of here."

"What? We're naked." Megan grabbed the sheet when he jumped up and picked his jeans up from the floor.

"Wrap yourself in that sheet and come on. The trailer could roll." He managed to get into his pants, hopping down the aisle while making sure Megan was behind him. He had to dodge pots, pans, and food cartons that kept falling in front and on top of him. "Be careful!"

"It's an earthquake?" Megan had made a toga out of the sheet and ran into his back as he struggled to get the outside door open. It was jammed.

Lucky was barking, and she dashed forward to let him out of the front bedroom. They'd closed the door when he'd tried to make it a threesome. So not in their wheelhouse.

Rowdy put his shoulder to the door and it screeched open. An awning above the door had come loose and fallen in front of it, blocking their way. Once he ripped it off, they ran outside. Other people were standing in the middle of the road, trying to keep their balance as the earth continued to shake for another minute or two. He kept his arm around Megan, who trembled beside him.

Finally everything was quiet.

"Are you two all right?" Amos hurried over to them.

"Yes, we were trapped by that awning. I'll have to get it fixed." Rowdy looked around. No one was going back inside their RVs. "How about you?"

"We're okay. This isn't the first time this has happened." He waved at his brother.

"Is it over?" Megan adjusted the sheet, which Rowdy could see was embarrassing her. It wasn't late. In fact, it wasn't quite dark.

"Not yet. There might be aftershocks. That's what we're waiting for. It's smart to wait for about thirty minutes or so." Amos smiled. "Guess you two skipped dinner." He glanced over at his own trailer. "Young love. I remember those days." He walked back to his wife and whispered in her ear, then gave her a kiss. She laughed and hit his arm.

"Earthquakes. Aftershocks." Megan looked at Rowdy with big eyes. "It's because of the fracking, isn't it?"

"Afraid it could be. Check your research, but I don't think they had any earthquakes out here until the fracking started." Rowdy looked back at the trailer, then at Lucky, who was headed down the road toward Raylene's trailer. "I'd better catch the dog. You want to go get his leash?"

"Go back in the trailer now?" She looked horrified.

"Never mind. I'll get it. You stay put." He glanced at his watch. "We've got twenty-five minutes before the all clear. You okay alone while I take care of the dog?"

"Yeah. Go ahead." She sat on the ground. "If you're going inside, would you bring me a blanket? And get yourself a shirt and jacket. It's cold out here."

"Good idea." Rowdy leaned down and gave her a long kiss. "For the record? The earth did move for me."

"Aw, shit." Her eyes filled with tears. "Don't you dare be nice, Rowdy Baker. Not when I feel like things are going to hell around me."

"You can handle it, Megan." He ran inside, got what he needed, and came out again, buttoning his shirt and sliding into a jacket. He'd stuffed his feet into tennis shoes, too, not willing to hit gravel barefoot. He carefully wrapped a blanket around Megan, then headed down the road. He was almost to Raylene's when the earth did move again. He ran full tilt back to Megan's side and got there in time to hold on to her until it was over.

Chapter 13

"I heard on the news that the earthquake last night was about a 3.1." Clint Stephens greeted them with stacks of papers and a smile. If he had something to hide, he sure didn't seem worried about it. "No big deal."

"Felt like a big deal to me. Scared me to death. Do those things hit often around here?" Megan had lost her appetite after they'd run for their lives. She'd wanted nothing more than to go to bed with the covers over her head. That had left Rowdy to clean up the mess in the RV and fix himself a sandwich for dinner. She couldn't even work up any guilt over that. She'd been pretty sure it was late when he'd finally slid into bed next to her and taken her into his arms. He'd obviously been exhausted and had just kissed her on the cheek before falling asleep.

"About once a month or so. Of course, they're blaming it on the wells." Clint shook his head. "A car has a blowout around here, Calhoun caused it. Doesn't matter that the truck had bald tires." He pulled a can of tobacco out of his back pocket and stuck some in his cheek behind his lip. "I'm damn sick of it."

"Science shows we could be responsible if we've got disposal wells that are on a fault line. Where are you injecting your wastewater?" Rowdy held his hard hat. "How far away is it from the site?"

"Far enough. But I'm sure you're gonna want to 'inspect' it, so let's go." Clint opened the door to the outside. "We need to drag Ms. Calhoun out to the desert while I show you the site or can she stay here in comfort?"

Rowdy stood in the doorway. He looked like he was considering it.

"If you think I need to see this, I'll go. But I just started on these reports." Megan waved at the pile of papers in front of her. It was chilly this morning, and she'd hoped to stay in the trailer with the heat on while Rowdy did what he needed to do on the well site with Clint Stephens. Rowdy had told her he wanted her to examine accident reports to look for a pattern. She'd already noticed there was no big board posted outside the trailer with the number of days since the last accident.

"Stick with what you're doing. We shouldn't be gone long." Rowdy let the door bang closed behind them.

Megan worked her way through what looked like a pretty serious number of accidents. She couldn't forget that Vince Claypool's site on the Rocking S had made almost a year without a single mishap. It seemed like hardly a week went by here without one. Yes, some of them seemed minor. A man had smashed his finger with a hammer while trying to get a bolt loose from a pipe fitting. That had resulted in a trip to town for a doctor's visit, an X-ray, and a hand broken in three places. Maybe not so minor. Could a hammer really cause a broken hand? She put that report aside. She'd like to talk to the man involved. Or the doctor. Things didn't add up on that report.

Much worse was a head injury when a man had been hit by a length of chain. He'd gone to the hospital in a coma. It didn't say the chain hadn't been laid down right, but Megan remembered how she'd seen it arranged on the rig at Vince's site. If handled properly, the chain never should have hit anyone in the head. She was relieved to see in a follow-up that the man had recovered but was still on disability. The company had covered his hospital bills, of course, but she wondered if he'd ever get back to work. The doctor's report mentioned possible brain damage. She set that paper aside, too.

She made notes on the tablet computer Rowdy had given her to use. Soon she had a long list that convinced her this site was dangerous. Broken bones, falls, even a few chemical burns that made her shudder. Clearly there needed to be a serious overhaul in the practices here. Seemingly preventable accidents were not only endangering the workforce, but they were costing the company money. It didn't take reading that enormous safety book to figure that out.

The door flew open, and Rowdy stepped inside. "I have to see the geological surveys to be sure, but I think he needs to find a new place for disposal." His face was grim when he strode over to the small refrigerator and pulled it open. "I need some water, it's dusty out there." He stared into the fridge, then turned to Megan. "You're kidding me." He gestured. "Did you look in here?"

"Yes. I got a bottle of water earlier." Megan knew what made him wrench open the outside door again and yell for the supervisor. Beer. A case of it chilling in the fridge. It was against company policy. That was just common sense, even if Rowdy hadn't already mentioned the ban on alcohol on any well site.

"Stephens! Get the hell in here!" Rowdy yelled it from the porch. He slammed the door as he came inside again. "I can't believe it. What did you find in the accident reports?"

Megan told him. "Maybe some of them could be attributed to drinking on the job, but there was no mention of that. What I'm sure of is that there are way too many things going wrong. At least compared to Vince's operation. Just yesterday a man fell off the scaffolding and broke his leg. Cause of the accident was listed as railing failure. Why would a well-constructed railing on the platform fail?"

Rowdy held out his hand and she placed the report in it. "A railing shouldn't fail. Not if you took the time to build it properly. Shit. Now I've got to inspect all the platforms to see if they're built to safety standards."

"In the meantime, we've got another man on disability." Megan jumped when the office door flew open.

"What the fuck, Baker? I don't appreciate being yelled at like that in front of my crew." The super was obviously ready for a showdown. "The concrete truck is late, and we're waiting to set up the Christmas tree on rig number four. I don't have time for your inspection shit right now."

"My inspection shit is what's going to decide whether you keep your job or not, Stephens, so I suggest you think twice before you go off on me." Rowdy didn't wait for Clint to respond to that before he opened the refrigerator. "And I want to know what the fuck a case of beer is doing on this job site?"

"Oh, that." Stephens actually laughed. "Is that what's got your panties in a wad? Hell, Conrad Calhoun himself told me about a little tradition he had when he finished a well, back in his early days." He winked at Megan. "Your daddy was a real fine man, Ms. Calhoun, a true old-school oilman. Came up when it was every man for himself. He said he had to work hard to keep good men on his crew between jobs. So when it came time to bring in a well and put on the tree, he threw a little party. Beer for everyone."

"What do you mean 'the tree'? You said there was a Christmas tree?" Megan came out from behind Clint's desk, where she'd been working. "It's September."

"Not an actual tree, Megan. It's what they call the apparatus they put on top of the platform when the oil starts to flow. It pumps the oil to the pipeline. It's got a string of lights on it that gives it the nickname 'Christmas tree'. It's been called that for decades." Rowdy handed her the accident report. "That means number four is about done. At least that's good news." He shook his head. "But I can't believe Conrad encouraged you to give the crew beer here, on the job, to celebrate."

"Well, believe it. You ask any of the old-timers around here who worked for him and there are a couple. They'll tell you. He inspired loyalty. Gestures like that helped. It also motivates the guys to work fast." Clint spit into a nasty-looking cup Megan had noticed he kept behind his desk. "And, relax, it's only a case. Split among the crew, that's not nearly enough to even give the guys a buzz. The men on that rig will get the rest of the day off, too, once we're sure the tree is on good and everything's running like it should." Clint pulled his phone out of his pocket and frowned down at it. "Now, if you're through, I'm calling the concrete people to see what the hell's the holdup on my delivery. We need that shipment."

"Go ahead, make your call." Rowdy shut the refrigerator. "Beer on the job. I'd never have allowed it." He walked over to look through the reports Megan had sorted into piles.

"These the most serious?" He picked up the smallest stack and read through them. "Damn, I sure hope so."

"Yes. The others are minor injuries." She glanced at Clint, who was cursing and looked ready to throw down his phone. "What is it, Clint?"

"Would you believe those damn protesters have blocked the road into the site and won't let the truck through?" He stormed out of the office. "Sharon Fuckin' Wallace. I swear, someday I'll make her sorry she ever crossed my path."

"Wait, what's he going to do?" Megan ran outside after Clint, Rowdy on her heels. "Clint, stop!" She saw him with one foot on the running board, about to climb into his truck.

He turned and glared at her. "I'm going down there and help that truck get through. I need that concrete. Without it, my job is at a standstill. My men are standing around with their thumbs up their asses waiting, and it's costing us money. As a Calhoun, I'd think you'd be on board with doing whatever it takes to get this job rolling." He jumped into the driver's seat.

Megan ran to keep him from closing his door. "No, wait. Stay here. We'll go." Megan glanced at Rowdy. "I didn't tell you this before, Clint, but I was sent here to handle the problems with the protesters. So, I'll go down to talk to them. I'm pretty sure I can get them out of the road peaceably. How were you going to make them move?"

"Drive right at 'em, of course. Tree huggers aren't willing to die for the damn environment. Not unless they're crazy, and these folks don't seem to be. They'll move and the concrete truck will come on through." He jingled his keys. "Why do you think talking to them will work? These people love to talk. So they'll jibber jabber. But when all is said and done, they'll still just stand or sit in the road and sing 'Kumbaya' or some such shit like they're at a rally for the spotted owl or white buffalo."

"Clearly you've had your fill of them." Megan tried to show some sympathy. "I get it. They've really been a nuisance, haven't they?"

"Damn right they have." Clint hopped out of the truck to spit in the dirt.

Megan looked away from the tobacco stain on the ground. One of the environmentalists would have cringed.

"You should see the abuse my truck has taken." He pointed to pockmarks on his bumper. "Bullet holes. I'm lucky I wasn't in the truck at the time. And this is my third windshield. I'm not getting another one until I can't see through this one at all anymore." He pointed at a spiderweb crack on the passenger side. "Second set of tires, too. I have to pay my landlady extra so I can park in her garage and lock the truck in at night." He leaned against the fender. "Of course it's billed to the company, all of it. So maybe I shouldn't get so worked up about it."

"Still, I can see that it's stressful. So let me deal with these protesters. And you can go wait for your concrete on the rig." Megan put her hands on her hips. "I also suggest you make sure no one gets hurt while you're doing it. It might be a good idea to check the railings, too. I read the report on that accident last week. Not a good mark on your record."

"*My* record?" Clint's face turned red. "You're blaming me for a hand's carelessness?"

"Maybe the man who built the railing was careless, but it's your responsibility to make sure he did the job right. Or am I mistaken, Rowdy?" Megan turned to him. He'd stayed back, watching her and letting her deal with Clint. She appreciated it.

"No, Megan's absolutely right. Take care of your site, Stephens. You've had too many accidents here. That could be grounds for dismissal right there." He walked to his truck. "Ready to go, Megan?"

"Yes, indeed. I'll handle this situation and be back before you know it." She stepped back when a stream of tobacco juice almost hit her boot. "And by the way, Clint? I report everything I see and do here to Calhoun Headquarters. If you aren't cooperative, then Rowdy's right. We can call in a supervisor who will be easier to work with." She nodded toward the oil rigs. "And who takes better care of his crew." She left Clint sputtering to walk around Rowdy's truck and get in.

"That was impressive. You've got *me* scared for *my* job and I'm your boss." Rowdy started the engine. "I just hope you can follow through on that promise to handle the protesters."

"Watch me." Megan was determined to show confidence, even if she wasn't totally feeling it. She'd done lots of research in the hours since she'd been handed this assignment. It was good news that yet another well was about to be completed. That meant less noise right away. Sharing that with Dr. Wallace and her cohorts should help. She also had a few other tricks up her sleeve. She pulled out her phone as she shivered and reached for the heater vents. They were at a high altitude and fall had arrived. She wasn't ready to pull out her heavy coat, but her jean jacket wasn't quite enough. She needed layers. Her fingers were clumsy as she put in the phone number that fortunately had been easy to memorize.

"Who are you calling?" Rowdy made the turn onto the road that led to the job site.

"Listen and find out." Megan waited for the operator to answer.

"Reeves County Sheriff's Office."

"Yes, I want to report an incident on a county road." She read the number off the sign they passed. "There's an obstruction blocking the road and it's a real hazard. I'm afraid someone's going to get hurt if a patrol car doesn't get here right away."

"Any idea exactly where on that county road the obstruction is located, ma'am?" The operator seemed to be taking her seriously. "That's a long track that crosses into Pecos County. It might not be in our jurisdiction."

"It's a few miles west of that place where they're drilling those oil wells. On Sharon Wallace's land. You know the place I'm talking about? Isn't that in your county?" Megan knew it was. Part of her research.

"Yes, it is. I'm dispatching a patrol car now. Please stay on the line so I can take down your information."

Megan hung up instead, because she could see that there were people strung across the gravel right-of-way ahead. Rowdy slowed the truck, then came to a stop well back from the group that stood arm in arm so the big concrete truck couldn't get through. They'd made a chain the truck driver was clearly not willing to break. The people weren't singing "Kumbaya," but they were obviously excited and talking to each other. The truck's mixing drum rotated, churning the concrete to keep it ready to pour. The driver and his helper stood beside the truck, one of them smoking a cigarette while the other was on the phone.

"Now what?" Rowdy watched the scene, obviously letting her call the shots here.

"Turn the truck around so I can stand in the back, in the bed. I want to be above them when I talk. Like I'm on a stage. I haven't done a lot of public speaking, but I know I want them to see me." Megan cleared her throat. She should have brought a bottle of water with her. It *was* dusty, and the wind had kicked up. If only this were as simple as standing on a stage in front of her pals at a fund-raiser for animal rights. That was a friendly crowd with open pocketbooks. She could feel animosity rolling off of *this* crowd already, and she hadn't even stepped out of the truck yet.

She took a steadying breath and held on to the door handle, ready to jump out. She was going to handle this and show these people that a Calhoun was willing to listen to their complaints. But she wasn't stupid, either. She'd gone into this year hoping to make her father proud. Now that she knew he'd been deceitful and had robbed people, her focus had to change. It was important to her to prove that the next generation of Calhouns would always deal fairly with the public. Too bad "fairly" in the oil business usually cost a lot of money.

Rowdy maneuvered the truck until he'd backed it close to the people. The protesters had gone quiet and were all staring now. When Megan and Rowdy hopped out of the truck and he helped her climb up onto the tailgate, the whispering started. Of course, the men they'd met in the RV park recognized them.

Megan held out her hands and everyone shut up and stared. "Hi, I'm Megan Calhoun."

There were gasps, then a woman stepped out from the line and faced her. "And I'm Dr. Sharon Wallace. Really. You're a Calhoun?"

"Yes, my father was Conrad Calhoun."

"You could have told us that yesterday." Amos, along with his brother, Art, was front and center.

Several rocks sailed toward the truck where she was standing. Thank God they fell harmlessly to the ground next to them. Rowdy leaped up on the bed next to her.

"The next person who picks up a rock will be choking on it." He glared at the protesters. "You don't believe me? Try it." He had the tough-guy attitude down, and his size matched even the largest of the men standing in the road. They heard a couple of rocks drop and Rowdy nodded.

Megan straightened her spine, determined not to let them see how those flying rocks had scared her. "I'm here to see if I can address your concerns about the drilling on your land, Dr. Wallace." She didn't bother to smile. The animosity radiating from the woman told her it would be wasted. Sharon Wallace must have retired fairly early from her teaching career. She looked like she was still in her fifties with carefully styled blond hair, a trim figure, and pressed jeans with her cotton shirt and leather jacket. Her boots were dusty but high fashion. It made Megan wonder where she did her shopping.

"I'm happy to see you got one thing right. It *is* my land. And you people are defiling it." This got a round of boos from the people behind her. Catcalls ranged from "Polluters!" to "Bird killers!"

Rowdy jumped down from the truck and advanced on a man who kept yelling and had even taken a step forward. "Let the lady speak, or I'll shut your mouth for you." That got the crowd quiet again.

"There's no need for violence. Or to have this conversation in the middle of a county thoroughfare." As if on cue, Megan heard a siren in the distance.

"You called the police?" Wallace looked behind her. They could all see the sheriff's car kicking up dust as it bounced down the gravel road with its lights and siren going.

"Of course. You're impeding traffic and we have to have this concrete delivered right away so we can continue our work." Megan saw the driver and his helper jump into their truck. "You'll be happy to know that a fourth well is about done. That should abate some of the noise you're so concerned about."

"Nothing Calhoun Petroleum does makes me happy." She turned when the sheriff's deputy strode up to her. "Calvin."

"Dr. Wallace, you and your crew are going to have to get out of the way. Let the traffic flow." He was a man about the professor's age and assessed the situation with a keen gaze. Nobody had moved yet. Obviously they were waiting for a signal from their leader. "Who made the call, if I may ask?"

With Rowdy's help, Megan hopped down from the truck's tailgate and extended her hand. "I did, Officer. Megan Calhoun. Sorry I hung up, but we came upon the scene, and I guess I got flustered at the sight of so many people blocking the road."

"Deputy Calvin Rydell." He shook her hand. "Ms. Calhoun. This is a surprise. So the company sent one of the owners here." He turned to Dr. Wallace. "Now, Sharon, this is good news. Stand down and see what comes of this." He turned back to Megan. "Are you here to talk? Help make this situation better?"

"Of course. I'm sorry if I didn't make that clear enough, Dr. Wallace. I just got here. I'm assessing the situation now and hope to set up a meeting with you next week." Megan still couldn't smile when faced with such a stony reception. Sharon Wallace had hated her on sight, or at least she hated what Megan represented. "This is Roland Baker. He's an experienced engineer with the firm. He will be personally inspecting every aspect of the operation and making sure things are done correctly and with the least impact on the environment."

"We've heard that before." Wallace shook her head. "Words. Meaningless without action."

"Well, Dr. Wallace, I'm going to tell you one more time, then you're not going to like *my* action." The deputy shifted his gun belt. He wore a sand-colored uniform shirt, black trousers, and a shiny silver badge on his chest. He was fit and looked like he'd have been at home in the Old West with his wide-brimmed Stetson shading his eyes. He certainly seemed to mean what he said. "Get these folks out of the road right now, or I'm calling for a van and taking you all in to lock up for interfering with a public roadway. Do you understand?"

Dr. Wallace nodded. "Okay, people. We've made our point for today. Meet back at my house for lunch." She dug into her jacket pocket and handed Megan a business card. "Here are my numbers. I want that meeting sooner than next week." She turned and headed down the road to where there were a number of trucks and SUVs parked on the shoulder.

"Thanks, Deputy Rydell, for your quick response." Megan jumped when Rowdy tugged on her hand. "We've got to move our truck so the concrete can be delivered."

"I hope this issue between Sharon Wallace and Calhoun Petroleum can be settled amicably." The deputy made serious eye contact. "She's the ringleader and the most vocal, but not the only person around here who's not happy with the way things are going out there at your well site. Look at this road." He pointed to a pothole that a Smart Car could get lost in. "Wasn't like this before your crew started using it for heavy equipment. And there's been no compensation for the damage. This county sure can't afford to fix it when your vehicles will just tear it up again."

"I understand. I'll see what I can do about that, Deputy." Megan smiled. "Seriously. I want to make things work here. There is a limit to what we can afford, of course. If oil were still at a hundred dollars a barrel, I could do a lot more. But please pass the word in town that I'm here to help." She pulled her own card out of her pocket. "Here are *my* numbers. I have a new one that's written on the back. Address complaints to me, and I'll see what I can do."

"All right, then." He tipped his hat. "And next time you call us, please leave your name. We may not like Calhoun Petroleum out here, but we will certainly always come to your aid when you need us." With that, he turned on his heel and walked back to his cruiser.

"Let's go." Rowdy slammed the tailgate closed, got into his truck, and waited until Megan was inside before he pulled out of the way so the concrete truck could go first. They followed it back to the well site. "You did a good job back there. I just have one complaint."

"Oh?" Megan knew what was coming.

"You had to give them my real name? I didn't think you even knew it." He grinned. "Don't ever say it again. I'm not too crazy about it."

"You've just given me ammunition, you know. And of course I knew it. Research. I'm learning I'm pretty good at it. As for handling Wallace and her crew? Thanks. I wasn't sure talking to them would work, but I had to try. The rock throwing surprised me. I was glad you were there." She patted him on the thigh. "At least they backed right down. Being outnumbered . . ."

"I wasn't about to let them get away with that. And I didn't figure they'd do anything too bad in broad daylight with witnesses. Calling the cops on them was genius." He frowned and hit the brakes. "I've got to stay well back from that concrete truck. Look at the rocks that thing is kicking up. I'd hate to get this new windshield dinged."

Megan stared out at the road as they crept along. How much would it cost to repair some of the damage they'd caused? Everywhere she looked, there was something that would be a drain on the company's resources.

"Good to know the sheriff's department will back us up." Rowdy pulled into the job site and shut off the engine.

"Oh, sure, they will. But only if we're in the right. You notice Calvin called our professor 'Sharon'?" Megan had picked up on that right away. "I bet they have some kind of relationship, though he was trying hard not to let it show."

"She's an attractive woman, and single, according to the background information I was given. He might be available, too, and he seems about her age."

"No wedding ring, either." Megan opened the door and hopped out. "But I still wonder why a woman like that would have come out here by herself to retire. It's so isolated."

"Some people like to be where they can enjoy nature. Imagine how she felt when her dream of living on unspoiled land fell flat." Rowdy stood next to her, but his eyes were on what was happening on rig number four. "And being alone doesn't have to mean you're lonely. Maybe she likes the isolation."

"A woman with fifty-three cousins? I doubt she gets to be alone too often. Not with so many of them liking to use their RVs." Megan laughed. "Oh, go watch the Christmas tree action. I can see that's where you want to be. I'm going back to my research. I want to know more about Dr. Wallace and the land around here."

Rowdy grinned, looked around to make sure no one was watching them, then patted her bottom. "Okay. I need to make sure they're doing things right up there. See you in a while. Lunch. I'm getting hungry."

"Good idea. We should go into town and see what there is to eat. Maybe pick up some gossip about the situation here." Megan ran her hand over the backside of his well-worn jeans, too. "Let me know when you can leave." She headed back into the office and got on her computer. A professor who had suddenly retired to the back of beyond. Why? And she'd bought the land quickly without doing decent research on it or she'd never have made the basic mistake of buying without owning the mineral rights. It wasn't something an intelligent woman with a doctorate should have done.

Megan began her Internet search, trying different combinations of words until she finally hit pay dirt. It wasn't anything she'd use to get Sharon Wallace to back off in her complaints against Calhoun, but it certainly explained a lot about the woman's current attitude. Well, well, well. The lady had a past. Too bad it had ruined her career and sent her into hiding.

* * *

Rowdy figured Megan had been right about the food on this trip. He'd paid little attention to what he ate when he'd been by himself. Throwing together a ham and cheese sandwich on the run had been pretty much the norm for him. No wonder he'd been on the edge of burnout. But here he'd just devoured another excellent meal in a little town café and was feeling pretty good about his job. He could make a difference. Clean up a bad situation. All in all, it was an important assignment.

Of course, what made the difference this trip was the good company of the woman across from him. Clearly word had spread that they were working for Calhoun. One look at their shiny new truck parked in front of the café and their waitress had barely spoken to them. She'd delivered the food efficiently enough for a tip, but her folksy manner was reserved for the tables around them, which had cleared out until they were now an island in an almost deserted restaurant.

Rowdy sipped his second cup of coffee. He'd need it or he would fall asleep on the job. It had taken him hours to get the RV in order the way he liked it after the earthquake. He certainly hadn't wanted to ask Megan to help him. She'd been too freaked out after the third aftershock and gone straight to bed. So he was tired. Clint would probably be happy if he and Megan didn't come back right after lunch. Maybe a nap . . . He realized Megan had just dropped a bombshell.

"Wait. Wallace came here because she had an affair that ended badly? How'd you find that out?" He leaned forward after glancing around. Of course, no one could hear them.

"The Internet is my playground, Rowdy. You just have to keep digging. Apparently it was hushed up, but I finally found a little article in the college student newspaper. Frankly, I'm not sure she had the affair at all. Sharon Wallace was accused of sexually harassing a student. He was no kid—twenty-something—but he claimed she came on to him. She fought his allegations all the way to the faculty senate, and won, because it was a case of he said, she said. Then the student wrote a book about it. Called it fiction and masked the names just enough to avoid a lawsuit. *Dr. Wallabe and her Study Bunny.* Can you believe it?"

Rowdy shook his head. "Doesn't seem fair."

"You're right. The book became a steamy online sensation with tales of how they had wild monkey sex on her desk in her office, all over campus between classes, and in her car. No wonder she ran away. I feel sorry for her. The student was a loser and a user. Bitter because he flunked her class."

"Wow. I admit she's attractive. But a sex scandal? She doesn't look the type. I hope it doesn't follow her here." He studied Megan as she dove in to her dessert.

"I sure wouldn't tell. Like I said, I'm on her side. He was obviously out to get her." She grinned. "I might order a copy of the book, though. For ideas. Steamy? I like the sound of that."

"You think you need new ideas?" Rowdy finished his coffee and frowned. "Or do I?"

"Never hurts to broaden our horizons." She winked and offered him a bite of her lemon meringue pie. "Try this. Delicious."

"You finish it. I'm stuffed." He watched her lick the fork, and his body kicked into gear. "Stop that."

"What? Enjoying my dessert? You should know by now that it's my favorite part of any meal." Her eyes twinkled as she took another bite and licked her lips. "Do we have time to go back to the trailer after lunch? I feel a nap coming on."

"I was just thinking the same thing. And you tempt me. We need to finish what we started last night. We have a lot more territory to cover in that RV. The other bedroom, that padded bench in the dinette, the shower." He was hard and getting harder.

"Ah. So, you do have ideas. But the shower?" She laughed. "Even if we can both squeeze into that tiny bathroom, I doubt we'd be able to move once we got in there." She reached for his hand. "But I'm willing to try."

Rowdy held on and sat back. What the hell was happening to him? He could not, *definitely* could not, fall for Megan Calhoun. She was from a completely different world. When he'd walked into the office trailer after they finished with the concrete, she'd been on the phone pricing repairs for that county road. And had already gotten authorization from Headquarters to offer money to the county commissioners up to a dollar amount that made his head spin. Only a Calhoun could have managed that.

He wasn't stupid. He knew she'd grown up with every advantage.

In San Antonio they'd been talking about school field trips when she'd dropped the name of the exclusive private school she'd attended in Houston. He knew the tuition for that place cost as much as a year at most colleges.

Then there were the clothes she kept pulling out of her duffel. He'd been with Cassidy long enough to recognize quality goods. Cass had saved for months to buy just a few pieces like those Megan seemed to take for granted. Everything Megan owned was the best. Even now he knew the pale blue shirt she wore that matched her eyes was of the finest cotton because he'd felt it when he buttoned her into it just this morning. Now he wanted to peel it off her again. It was soft, almost as silky smooth as her skin when he touched her.

He raised his hand and the waitress ambled over. "Can we have a couple of pieces of that lemon meringue pie to go? For later." He smiled at Megan. "And the check."

She flushed, clearly getting the picture. "Why do I think you're having even more of your own ideas?"

"Because I am." As soon as the waitress set the Styrofoam box down in front of him, he glanced at the ticket, threw money on the table and jumped up.

"Come on, let's get out of here." He didn't need to look at his watch. He was going to make time for what he wanted and to hell with responsibility.

Chapter 14

"I hope we both can fit in that shower, because I have lemon pie in the most interesting places." Megan grinned and dragged herself off of Rowdy's chest. She sauntered down the short hallway to the bathroom, then turned on the shower. The water took a while to heat up, but that gave her time to slide a plastic cap over her hair.

"You know we have to go back to work." Rowdy followed close behind her. "There are still several hours left in the workday."

"I know." Megan stepped onto the bathroom's wooden floor with a drain in it. She grabbed a washcloth and the shower gel and got busy. She wasn't surprised when Rowdy pushed aside the shower curtain and got in with her. "Seriously? You really want to try this now? After the performance you just gave? You must have eaten your Wheaties this morning, big guy."

"I am nothing if not an overachiever." He took her washcloth and the gel and slid the cloth over her backside. "You're right. That lemon filling is everywhere."

She squealed when he got particularly interested in searching for more. "You do that again, and I'm going to have to turn around and see what you might have up your—"

She didn't finish the sentence because he turned her to face him anyway, his mouth on hers. Where, oh where, did this come from? This desperation to have him? To have each other? She'd never been this insatiable before. Megan ended up out of the shower and on the tiny counter, her butt almost in the sink before she linked her ankles behind him and he thrust inside her. God. Had she ever felt so complete?

The washcloth fell to the floor and the gel landed on the back of the toilet. The water grew tepid but they couldn't seem to part. Megan held on to his broad shoulders, sliding her hands down and around him, eager to feel every inch of his skin, his taut muscles, his . . . everything. He was doing the same, his hands lingering where she gasped or called his name. The water finally sputtered into icy cold and they laughed, giving in and pulling apart. He turned off the faucet, his wicked grin making her kiss him again.

How much was too much? Megan didn't know, but she hadn't found it yet with Rowdy. He handed her a towel from the cabinet above her head and took one for himself. They dried each other, still reluctant to leave the bathroom. A knock on the door to the outside broke the spell.

"Rowdy? Megan? I've got someone here who wants to see you."

"God. It's Raylene. I guess she saw our truck." Megan finally stepped out of the bathroom and reached for the robe Rowdy had stuck neatly on a hook. "I'll tell her we have to go back to work."

"Wish we didn't." Rowdy had grabbed fresh jeans and was already pulling them on when there was another knock. "I'll get it." He tugged a shirt over his head and opened the door. "Raylene, I'm sorry we didn't stop by your place when we drove in. We just came home for lunch and a quick nap. Megan didn't get much sleep last night. Too upset by the earthquake."

"Oh, I'm sorry, honey." Raylene had Butch in her arms and Lucky on his leash. "I can take them back."

"No, that's all right. I'm working in the office today. Why don't I take him with me this afternoon?" Megan went to the door to grab Lucky's leash. He was so excited to see her he jumped around. She lost her balance and he managed to pull her outside. She finally picked him up. When she rubbed his head with her nose, she almost sneezed at the interesting smell clinging to him. "I hope he wasn't too much trouble."

"This sweetie pie? Good as gold." Raylene must have noticed Megan's nose twitch. "Bet you thought that pup would come out of my trailer smelling like an ashtray, didn't you?"

"Well, I know you smoke." Megan sniffed Lucky's fur again. "What *is* that smell? Rowdy, take a whiff." She smiled. "It's nice."

Rowdy leaned over to give the dog an ear rub and sniff his fur.

"Smells like something my mama likes to put in our bathroom back home. Not an insult, Raylene. It does smell nice."

She pulled a can out from the pocket of the apron she wore over her jeans. "It's my secret weapon. I just knew the cigarette smell would bother you folks, since neither of you have my bad habit. So I gave Lucky a good spritz with my lavender-scented air freshener before I brought him back to you." She squirted it in the air a couple of times. "See? Sweet as can be."

Lucky sneezed, then barked. Butch barked, too, and they were soon doing a doggy duet, even after Megan set Lucky down and told him to hush.

"Quiet now." Raylene put Butch on the ground and gave him a spritz, too. "Gets jealous if I leave him out." Instantly both dogs were quiet and sat down beside each other. "Isn't that cute? I can't get over how they've bonded."

"It's amazing. We'll let you keep him again, of course. Every day until we have to leave the area. We really appreciate it." Megan exchanged glances with Rowdy. "I have something to tell you. Should have done it right away. I had a run-in with Sharon Wallace today. And some of the cousins."

"Not surprised. They don't like anyone who works for Calhoun Petroleum." Raylene scowled as a couple of trucks and an SUV drove into the park. "Some cousins are back now and just look at them kicking up dust. I have a posted speed limit for a reason. And they're claiming to be all about the environment?" She bent over to pick up Butch again. "I'm going to give them a piece of my mind."

"Wait. You need to know something about me. Before they tell you." Megan laid her hand on Raylene's thin arm covered in an old, well-worn army jacket. It was several sizes too big for her. The name stitched across the pocket was Sadler. Was that hers? A husband's? Boyfriend's? Or had she just found the jacket at a thrift store?

"Megan?" Rowdy nodded. "Raylene is waiting."

"Oh yes. Anyway, I didn't give you my last name, and you didn't ask for it." She recognized Amos in one of the trucks that had pulled up nearby. "I'm not married to Rowdy. Maybe you assumed . . . Anyway, it's Calhoun. I'm Megan Calhoun. Conrad Calhoun was my father."

Raylene's mouth fell open. "Seriously? No wonder you arrived in the Cadillac of RVs." She cackled. "I'll bet Sharon Wallace about shit her drawers when you told her that." She got serious and looked back at the vehicles that had parked and were unloading people. "Honey, what the hell happened today?"

"Megan faced us down, that's what happened." Amos strode over to stand next to their landlady. "Could have knocked us over with a feather. Here we'd been in their trailer, everyone so friendly, and she's a *Calhoun*?" He shook his head. "But we're not stupid. I'm here to tell you, Megan, that most of us want to have a dialogue with the company. Sharon said it's too late. She claims she's tried to be reasonable and nothing happened so it's time for drastic action."

"I'm sorry it came to that. She needs to give me a chance to see what I can do now that I'm here." Megan sighed. "This hasn't been handled well so far."

"It's just that Sharon came out here for a reason, and things have gone wrong ever since. I think it's got her so worked up she's not thinking straight." Amos turned when Art joined him. "We came when she called saying she needed help, but the family—many of the cousins, anyway—believe that it's better to try to work out problems. We're determined to get her to see that. We think that the company sending you here, Megan, is a good sign."

"Yes, yes, it is." Megan held out her hands to the two men. "I want to work with her. Please tell her that." They shook hands. It was awkward, but a start.

"I tried to tell her, too, that she might not like the kind of publicity she'll get." Art exchanged looks with his brother. "Sharon usually avoids the press. If you can do something about the noise and the smell around her place, I'm pretty sure she'll back off fast. She really doesn't like to talk to reporters."

"Then pulling stunts like blocking a road or staging protests isn't a good approach." Rowdy finally entered the conversation.

"Well, at least it did get the attention of Calhoun's head office." Amos smiled. "Now, I'm confident Megan will get this all straightened out and we can head on back home or finish our travels." He glanced back at his RV. "The wife has a real urge to go on to the Grand Canyon."

"Keep in mind that Megan wants to help Dr. Wallace. But within reason, gentlemen." Rowdy cleared his throat. "Ms. Calhoun is a representative of a company that has a board of directors and stock-holders to whom she must answer. She's not authorized to give away the farm, if you know what I mean."

"No, of course not." Amos nodded. "And clearly she's got other things on her mind, as well." He nudged his brother. "Raylene, we've interrupted these two lovebirds. Can't you see that?"

Megan looked down at her robe. She obviously had nothing on under it and was barefoot. As a representative of Calhoun Petroleum, she was a joke. She pulled the lapels together and tightened the cloth belt to make sure she was decently covered. The robe was a thick terry, thanks to the spa shop at the hotel in San Antonio, but she still felt at a distinct disadvantage. Crap. She jerked off her plastic shower cap.

"Gentlemen, Rowdy's right. I'll act in good faith, but there is only so much I can do. Your cousin has ownership for the surface of her land only. There are limits when you don't own the mineral rights underneath. While our company has certain responsibilities when we use the land, so does the landowner. The state of Texas is very clear on that. I will be asking Mr. Baker to go over her property to examine her compliance with state laws. If you don't know what her obligations are when wells are drilled on her land, I suggest you look them up."

"We certainly will." Art whipped out his smartphone.

"Good." Megan really wanted to go back inside and get dressed, but she needed to make one more point. "It's unfortunate that Dr. Wallace was apparently sold acreage she knew so little about. What's the saying? 'Buy in haste, repent at leisure'?" She didn't bother to smile; the men were clearly thinking hard and weren't happy.

"I think that's 'marry in haste', hon, but it applies here to this sit-uation, as well. The girl was swindled when she bought the land and that's a fact." Raylene turned to the twins. "You folks need to talk to her about that. She should turn some of that anger she's got fester-ing inside toward the right person. Whoever sold her the land in the first place is at fault. I'm sure there was no disclosure about what she could and couldn't control since the mineral rights didn't come with it."

"We need to look at her initial contract. When she bought the property," Amos said to Artie, who nodded.

"You do that." Raylene looked around them, at the rows of RVs and the land beyond. "Hell, I had an offer for the land I'm standing on here not more than eighteen months ago. I turned it down flat." She nodded. "Lot of money on the table, too, just for the mineral rights. But I paid attention. Read the fine print. Didn't like the terms and didn't need the money." She shook her head. "But some things are supposed to be explained to the buyer anyway. Don't you think?"

"Good point, Raylene. We'll get right on that. You don't know it, but we're both lawyers. Not licensed in Texas, but we can find someone who can act for us here." Amos nudged his brother, and they both walked away, Art still working his cell phone.

"Thanks, Raylene. I was afraid you'd be mad at me for not telling you my name right away." Megan shivered. Clothes. She needed shoes, at the very least.

"Why would I be mad? I don't poke my nose into other folks' business. I rent to people who come through here all the time. They might pay in cash, and sometimes I don't even get a first name. I don't care as long as they treat my place with respect." She smiled down at the dogs, who were asleep next to each other.

"In this part of Texas, we're a little funny about people getting into our personal business. That's probably why Sharon is here. In my experience, people who move out here by themselves are looking for some privacy. When Calhoun Petroleum moved in practically on her doorstep, she lost a good bit of it. I'd say if you can promise she'll get it back, you might get more cooperation from her." She reached down to rouse Butch from his nap. "Come on, pup. I'm still going to chew out some drivers who think my road is a raceway."

"Privacy. You know, Raylene, you might be on to something. Thanks for watching Lucky. We'll bring him by again in the morning." Megan gently woke the dog and picked him up before she stepped back into the trailer. Warmth. It felt good. She put Lucky on the floor, then collected their dropped towels and hung them up to dry.

"Sorry we got interrupted." Rowdy slid his arms around her waist. "You are continually surprising me."

"How?" She snuggled against him. When Lucky tried to squeeze between them, a command to "sit" took care of that. He really was a smart dog. She stepped back, opened her robe, and enjoyed Rowdy's growl before he pulled her close again.

"Quit trying to distract me. I'm making a point here." He smoothed the cloth over her back. "Seriously, Megan, you handle people really well. Me, for sure."

Megan laughed. "Oh yeah? I thought *you* were handling *me*." She pulled his fingers off her breast.

"Okay, I'll stop that." He moved his hands to her shoulders. "I mean it. First Clint Stephens, then those protesters. Even Raylene. I haven't caught you making any missteps yet." He smiled and touched her chin. "Is this something you've always been good at?"

"I've always been a good talker, anyway. Who knew it could be useful?" Megan leaned against him. "Maybe I'm finally figuring out my place in the scheme of things. All my life I've jumped from one interest to another, never giving any one thing a chance to stick. But now . . ." She looked up at him. "I'm doing something worthwhile by trying to save my family's company. It doesn't hurt that you're backing me. It feels good to know you're with me."

"Every step of the way." He leaned down to kiss her, then put her away from him. "Now, get dressed. There are men drinking beer on our rigs, and I want to get back and see what's happening. I let my need to be with you cloud my judgment today. I should have gone straight there after lunch."

"Sorry. That's the old Megan. The Bad Influence Megan. I'll do my best to be good from now on. I'd hate for you to get in trouble with the company." She grinned and threw off her robe. "Where are my baggy jeans and sweatshirt?"

"God." He gave her a good, long look, then shielded his eyes and groped for Lucky's leash. "Come on, pup. Bad Megan is in the house, and if we don't leave now, I'll never make it back to work." He dragged the reluctant dog out of the trailer.

Megan sank down on the foot of their bed.

She was falling in love with him. For some reason, the thought didn't scare her. Instead she couldn't stop smiling as she got up and found one of his huge sweatshirts and pulled it over her naked body. It smelled like him. She sighed and picked out a pair of the thong panties he loved. He could do a treasure hunt for them later.

Next went on those baggy jeans and heavy socks, then the ugly work boots she hated. No one she knew would believe this was Megan Calhoun actually looking forward to going to work. She didn't quite believe it, either.

A week went by before Megan could set out to meet with Dr. Sharon Wallace. She had research to do and a plan to implement. Then she found out the coming weekend was the Marfa Lights Festival. Since Raylene had also passed on the same rumors Clint had mentioned about a big planned demonstration, Megan realized she had a deadline. So she'd called to set up the appointment with the professor, ready or not. Rowdy was going to drive her to the Wallace ranch, which wasn't far from the well site.

Her next call was to get the okay from Mason MacKenzie. There were things that needed approval both from her evaluator *and* from the company if this was going to work. After she told him her idea, he was quiet for so long she was beginning to think she'd blown it.

"Go ahead. Ever since these protests started, I've been studying the area where you and Baker are working," Mason finally said. "What I found surprised me."

"Really? I can make the offer?" Megan just hoped this would be enough for Sharon Wallace.

"Yep. I know Conrad had his faults—"

"Faults?" Megan heard her voice crack. "Mason, Daddy has turned out to be a liar and a thief."

"Okay. He was in his early days. But he was also what my grandfather called one of the best oilmen he'd ever known. He had a nose for finding oil that was hard to beat. That's how he built one of the most successful oil companies in the world."

Megan thought about that. It hurt even more, then, that her daddy had cheated to get there instead of just relying on his God-given talent.

"Megan? You still there?"

"Yes."

"Listen to me. Conrad was out there in Reeves County over a year before he died, wasn't he?"

"Yes, the supervisor here at the well site even met him."

"That's because Conrad was buying up land out there, most of it with the mineral rights intact. That piece on Wallace's land was an exception. Most of what he bought is uninhabited." Mason laughed. "You're not going to believe this, Meg. Hell, I couldn't believe it myself. I knew your daddy had the nose for oil, but he stumbled on one of the biggest new oil fields the industry has seen in years. He bought thousands of acres. I've got the geologist's reports here in front of me. I only got it because Cassidy talked her board into making the development of the new field into a joint venture with Texas Star."

"You're kidding." Megan wished Rowdy was here with her to hear this instead of out on the rig.

"No, I'm not. That property is sitting on billions, that's with a *b*, billions of gallons of oil, Megan. Yes, it's not easy to get the oil out of there, the place is pretty damn isolated. But with a partnership, like with my own company, it can be done and very profitably. It couldn't have come at a better time for both of our companies."

"Mason, you mean Texas Star and Calhoun really will work together on this?" Megan knew they'd always been rivals. She was shocked their board of directors was going along with this.

"I brought some things to the table that made a joint venture attractive. One of them is that I proved I've got a line on some tax credits that will even make it worth our while to recycle our wastewater out there. It costs a lot, but with those federal credits, we can make the environmentalists happy and avoid more earthquakes." Mason couldn't have sounded prouder.

"Wow." That was all Megan could think to say. "Could—could that discovery make a difference for Calhoun? Keep us from going under?"

"You'll have to ask Cassidy about that. She's still trying to figure out how much it will cost to pay off the people your father defrauded." Mason sighed. "But it will bring in a lot of money, even at the price of oil now. Our hope is that this new field can save your company and mine."

"I can't believe it. So I can present my plan to Sharon Wallace?"

"In light of what's coming? Her field is insignificant. Cass got permission for you to do whatever you think is right. So go ahead." And he hung up.

Megan sat back. Good news for a change. And good to know that her father had been doing some clever thinking near the end of his life. With that crazy will she'd been having some real doubts.

At last they were on their way to see Sharon Wallace. Megan was glad to get it over with, but she was also afraid she was going to throw up before they got there. The road was smoother but still not without its bumps and dips. *Suck it up, Megan.*

"It's interesting. We go down the same county road the well site is on, but then the entrance to her place is on another little offshoot that is little more than dirt and gravel," Rowdy said when he turned at a stop sign. "So when Wallace looked at the place with a Realtor, she wouldn't have had a clue that the wells were probably already getting started. The prep work isn't as noisy as drilling and doesn't smell."

"Right. It's one of the points I'll make. She didn't take time for her own due diligence when she bought the place. Surely whoever sold her the land owed her more information up front, too." Megan shifted in her seat, fighting the case of nerves.

Rowdy patted her leg. "You have a folder full of papers. You're ready for her. Relax, you can do this."

"We'll see. Of course, we know that lizard she's so crazy about isn't even endangered. So, she can take her Texas horned lizard and shove it." Megan had printed out a picture of the thing that could actually spit blood out of its eyes. She hoped she never ran into one. She couldn't imagine an uglier creature.

"That's my girl." Rowdy laughed. "What else?"

"Wait and see." She'd decided to surprise Rowdy with her plan. "Just feel free to jump in if I get in a bind, especially if one or more of the cousins look like they want to rumble."

"I have faith in you, baby. But if a cousin goes ballistic, you can count on me." Rowdy grinned as he stopped at Wallace's gate. "You'd think she'd have this open since you called ahead." He waved when a man walked out from behind his truck. "Oh, it's Bert, or was it Ernie? One of the cousins." He rolled down his truck window. "We have an appointment to see Dr. Wallace. She's expecting us. Megan Calhoun and Rowdy Baker from Calhoun Petroleum."

The man just nodded and pushed a button on his side of the gate, which began to slowly swing open. There was no friendly smile or greeting.

"Gee, why do I have a feeling we're going into enemy territory? At least he's not carrying a gun." Megan turned around and saw the gate closing behind them as soon as Rowdy drove the truck inside.

"Want to bet? I think I saw a bulge under his jacket." Rowdy drove down a dirt and gravel driveway.

At the end was a large log house that had a contemporary feel. Trees surrounded it, and someone had arranged flower beds with the types of native plants that managed to flower even when there was a drought like the one that had plagued the region for months. There were big windows and a slanted roofline that helped Megan understand why Sharon Wallace had fallen in love with the place and jumped to buy it. Especially since records showed she'd gotten it at a bargain price.

"I see at least a dozen cars and trucks. RVs, too." She sighed as Rowdy stopped the truck. "We're sure going to be outnumbered. Maybe you should pull your gun out of the glove compartment and stick it in your pants."

"Go in there armed? That's just asking for trouble." He squeezed her hand. "You can't be serious. Just stick to your research, and it'll be fine. As a fallback, play hardball. Calhoun doesn't owe Wallace a damn thing. We're here as a courtesy. Is that what your daddy would have said?"

"My daddy would have done a lot of things I won't. Like bring up her problems back at the university. I won't play dirty. Something my dad was known for in his early days in the oil fields." Megan couldn't look at Rowdy. She'd already said too much. The ball of nerves in her stomach tightened. Yes, she knew now that her father wouldn't have hesitated to do whatever it took to get his way. He'd have loved to sling the mud and see what stuck. She wasn't going that way. Surely a well-educated woman could be made to see reason. She took a breath, then opened the truck door. Rowdy was right there to help her get down.

"Smile. You've got this." He stepped back and walked behind her to the front door of what was a seriously beautiful log house. The door opened before Megan could push the doorbell.

"Ms. Calhoun. Come in. I hope you're not going to waste my

time." Sharon Wallace turned and walked into an open-concept living area. A fire blazed in a soaring stone fireplace that had a colorful woven art piece hanging above it. There were many chairs and two long sofas facing it. People sat or stood in clusters around the enormous room.

"Of course not. And I hope you agreed to meet me with an open mind." Megan didn't bother to count the number of cousins in the room, but she felt every eye on her as she sat in the straight-backed dining chair the woman indicated. Apparently no one had saved a seat for Rowdy, so he stood behind her. She kept her papers in her lap and waited for Wallace to sit in an easy chair a few feet away.

"I won't offer you refreshments." Dr. Wallace glanced around the room. Most of her guests held coffee cups or soda cans. "This isn't a social visit."

"Of course not, since you seem determined to be belligerent." Megan leaned forward. "But could I trouble you for a glass of water? Or is that too 'social' for you?" She knew this was pushing it, but she'd be damned if she'd let this start on Wallace's terms.

"Amos, would you mind?" Wallace waved her hand. "I'm not belligerent. I'm just fed up. Since I moved here, I've put up with lies from your company and empty promises. If you're here to give me the same, you might as well leave."

Megan waited until Amos handed her a bottle of water.

Wallace jumped to her feet. "Oh no, Amos. I'm sure Ms. Calhoun wants to taste our delicious well water." She jerked the bottle out of Megan's hand, then rushed out of the room and came back with a glass. "Try this. If you dare." She thrust it in Megan's face.

She took it, trying not to wrinkle her nose at the whiff of rotten eggs coming from a liquid the color of weak tea.

"Why aren't you drinking?" Wallace sat back down. "I've been assured it won't kill me. At least not in the immediate future. Of course, the trace of carcinogens in there will eventually build up in my system and—"

"You've made your point, Dr. Wallace." Megan handed the glass over to Rowdy.

"Have I? Have I, really?" Wallace leaned forward. "How would you like to shower in that? Brush your teeth with it?" She looked around the room when her cousins begin to move, one of them shouting, "That's right!" Another said, "You tell her, Sharon!"

Megan stood. "Hold it!" Her voice rang out and, to her surprise, everyone got quiet. "Let's get something clear right off the bat. I don't think Calhoun Petroleum owes you a thing. You have a beautiful home that you bought without a lot of forethought. We own the mineral rights and are asserting those rights as we are certainly entitled to do. If your well water is bad now, I'm sorry. Show me proof that it was uncontaminated before we started drilling, and I'll see what we can do about it." She waited while Sharon looked around.

"Artie? Where are those papers?"

He was going through a file folder. "Nothing here, Sharon. Just the readings after Calhoun started the first well."

"Moving on." Megan wished she had the bottle of water Wallace had taken back to the kitchen. Her mouth was like cotton. "Dr. Wallace, have you bothered to read the statutes concerning the rights of landowners as set out by the state of Texas?"

"Of course." Wallace leaned forward. "What are you trying to pull now?"

"I don't think you have read them. Or you wouldn't have built a three-car garage so close to our pipeline." Megan pulled out a paper and passed it to the person sitting next to her, who gave it to Wallace. "As you must know, we have the right to build a pipeline across your property. Which we have done."

"That ugly thing! You can bet I had plenty to say when trucks tore up my land putting it in." Wallace started to crumple the paper, but Art grabbed it.

"I'm sure you've been told that you have no recourse or say-so as to where we place it." Megan ignored the curse one cousin muttered a few feet away. "Then, according to rules set out by the state of Texas, you must keep your buildings a certain number of feet away from it. Or that building will be considered a safety hazard." She waited for silence when there were more curses and murmurs around the room.

"It seems you violated those guidelines when you built a brand-new garage as recently as four months ago. Then there's the shed—or is it a barn?—you also managed to set right next to the pipeline." She passed another paper around the room. Amos stopped it this time and read it. "Those are both potential hazards, and don't bother claiming you didn't notice the pipe."

"She's right, Sharon. The statutes are clear. Ms. Calhoun, are you going to make her tear the buildings down?" Amos finally passed it to Sharon.

"It's possible." Megan smiled. "But then it wouldn't be our decision if the state board was contacted about it, would it?"

"That's a threat." Sharon Wallace jumped to her feet.

"No. Not yet." Megan pulled out another paper. "Your concerns about the local wildlife are duly noted. The Texas horned lizard is protected in this state, but not endangered. Close, but no cigar, Dr. Wallace."

"But the noise from your fracking has run off all the birds!" This came from Amos's wife, and several other people chimed in about the wildlife and the noise.

"That *is* a shame." Megan nodded. "You'll be glad to know that well number four is complete and we're close to finishing wells five and six. There are noise abatement measures we can take that should help minimize the sound in the pumping stations that will be left when we're done drilling here. Research shows that the birds will come back to nest once the fracking is completed." She paused. "Of course, we could decide to drill more wells. Engineering specs and geological surveys show that we have enough allowable space and a promising formation that make this property attractive to drill, oh, a dozen more. This has already been a very profitable field for us."

"No!" At least five people jumped up then. The discussion got so loud that Rowdy finally had to shout for quiet.

"I have some power over that decision. Whether to drill more wells or stand down. As do you, Dr. Wallace, about whether these protests you're planning will go forward. Do you understand what I'm saying?" Megan pulled out yet another paper, this one a map. "Here's where we can drill next, if we decide to do so. You'll notice the site is quite close to the fence line on the other side of your property." She passed it on around.

"That's where I plant my vegetables!" Wallace almost wailed. "You people are deliberately torturing me. It's inhumane!"

"No, we're in business." Megan sat back while different groups huddled around the papers she'd given them. "I don't want to despoil your property. And measures are being taken to clean up every bit of your land that's been damaged by our drilling and pipeline operations. In compliance with state guidelines."

"I saw that the county road is being repaired," one of the cousins spoke up. "When Calvin came by yesterday, he said Calhoun Petroleum paid the county commissioners a good chunk of change to get the job done. That's a promising start."

"Don't listen to her! You really think her company is going to follow through on any of the good things she says?" Sharon was on her feet. "I don't trust you, Megan Calhoun."

"I'm not surprised you have trust issues. Whom did you buy this place from, Sharon?" Megan stood and faced her. "The party who sold you this place is a matter of public record. That's Comstock LLC. Digging out who exactly is behind the corporation is a little more complicated. But what's clear is that Comstock chose to sell this place cheap, because the royalties from the mineral rights are making them rich. Comstock would like nothing more than for us to drill a dozen more wells right here next to your house. I fielded a call from a representative of theirs just this week asking about it."

"Comstock. Bastards." Sharon looked around the room. "I needed to get away, and the house was so beautiful. The air was clean and fresh then, too." Tears filled her eyes. "Now if the wind is wrong, all I smell are those damn chemicals."

"I'll be working on a way to fix that, Sharon." Megan put her hand on the woman's arm. "You need to sue Comstock and whoever is behind it for deceptive practices. I looked it up. If you weren't notified of the proper terms when you bought this property, they will have to buy it back, with interest."

"No, no more bad publicity. And I do love my house." She shook her head. "I made a stupid decision, and I have to live with it." She sat down. "Can you really clean things up? Stop drilling more wells? Will the chemical smell go away when you do?"

"Yes, the chemicals are only used when we drill. No more drilling, no more chemicals."

"You'd give up the chance to make more money with more wells just to keep us from protesting?" She looked around the room. Many of her cousins were shaking their heads. "How can I believe you?"

"We have our reasons for thinking that your land isn't worth the hassle. And Calhoun owns other uninhabited properties in the area that will be much easier to develop." Megan saw she'd surprised them with that news. "Now, what if I put our agreement in writing? Got our lawyers to draw up a contract? Would you believe me then? I have reason to believe that our contracts can be made binding and we can't wiggle out of them." Megan sat, too. Everyone had stopped talking, waiting to see if this could be settled.

"A contract with all those points you just made. But my garage and barn. You won't tell the commission about them?" She glanced around the room again, looking for reassurance. "I knew I was taking a chance putting them where I did, but the garage is so convenient with access to the road and the barn is next to my garden. It's where I keep my tiller and my tools." Her hands were shaking as she pushed back her hair. "I can't lose my garden, too!"

"I won't tell the commission, but that doesn't mean the facts might not come out anyway. You'd be smart to move both buildings while you're not subject to fines and a time crunch." Megan looked back at Rowdy, who'd been quiet the entire time. "What are the problems with buildings being so close to a pipeline, Mr. Baker? Sharon, you remember our engineer. He's been checking into your situation here for the company."

Rowdy looked serious and very professional in a yellow shirt with the company logo on his chest. "It's dangerous. The contents of the pipes are flammable, of course. There are signs posted with that information all along the pipeline right-of-way. With the drought you've been having, if anything close catches fire, you could have an explosion that could cost you a lot more than the garage and barn. Even this beautiful home." He gestured toward the fireplace. "And it is a great house. No wonder you bought it."

"Yes, I love it." Sharon held out her hand. It was steadier, as if she was finally calming down and ready to be reasonable. "Give me whatever papers you have. I need to study them. And tell your lawyers to get busy. Once I see what the contract says, I'll decide." She looked at her cousins. "Artie, Amos, you're lawyers. Will one of you stay long enough to look over what the company sends me? Advise me?"

"Sure, Sharon." Amos walked over and held out his hand. "Megan, just give those papers to me."

Megan passed them over, glad she'd been so thorough.

Sharon stood and faced the people in the room. "Well, folks, I guess we're not going to rally like we planned, but Marfa is still a nice trip. I hope some of you will go over there and enjoy the music, food, and film festival."

"I've heard the lights are interesting. Sounds like a fun weekend."

Megan stood. "I look forward to hearing from you once those contracts come in. I'll try to make sure they expedite that. But one more thing." She raised her voice and made eye contact with as many people in the room as she could. "I need all of you to listen to me. Everyone involved in the protests and you, Sharon, must sign a nondisclosure agreement. This is important. Calhoun is bending over backward to accommodate you, but we are not going to set a precedent. If any of you feel like this is your opportunity to go to the press and start bragging that the environmentalists have won over big oil? If the details of her contract leak? Well, then, Sharon's contract will be null and void. Am I clear?"

Sharon Wallace waited until the angry buzz died down. "She's not being unreasonable. If this goes through the way she's promising, I'm willing to keep my mouth shut. I hope you'll do the same." She walked Megan to the door. "They'll calm down, as a favor to me. They know I've had a rough couple of years. But I have a question: Once the wells are complete, will there still be Calhoun workers on my land?"

Megan turned to Rowdy. "Will there?"

"No regular crew. There's electronic monitoring of the pipeline and pumping stations, and someone will do a visual check from time to time." Rowdy nodded. "I think I can safely say you'll have your privacy back, though. There will be no more big crews on the well site for you to worry about, and no one should be bothering you at the house here. Never should have been."

"That's a relief. That man, Clint Stephens, came by several times when they first started drilling." Sharon shuddered. "I was beginning to think he had an interest in me." She grabbed Megan. "He's not a bad-looking man, but when he spit tobacco on my yucca plant . . ."

She seemed to realize she was squeezing Megan's arm and let go. "I told him to leave and never come back."

"Of course. I'm sorry he bothered you." Megan frowned. What had the supervisor been thinking? Of course, Sharon Wallace *was* attractive.

"I admit it made me a little scared to be alone out here after that. It was also a convenient excuse to call for reinforcements when I decided to come after Calhoun. Can I call you Megan?"

"Of course." Megan almost smiled. This was real progress.

"Well, Megan, I don't like the way your company came in and spoiled my land. But at least you seem reasonable. That's more than I can say for the man running the show out there at your oil wells. When I did go out there to complain about the noise and smell, all I got were vague promises, then curses and threats." She opened the front door. "Thanks for coming out here. A Calhoun in West Texas. I heard your father was here last year. Before I arrived. Do you think he would have helped me?"

Megan laughed. "Never in a million years. I loved him, but Daddy was all about oil production. He was more like Clint. Though he didn't touch tobacco. Once the wells are complete, the supervisor will be gone. Maybe sooner, if Rowdy and I have anything to say about it." She stepped outside. "And we do."

"Be careful. I've seen his temper." Sharon looked back when someone from inside called her name. "But I'll be glad when he's no longer on my property. Now I have to calm the family." She shut the door.

"I think we can call that a win." Rowdy slung his arms around her shoulders. "You were brilliant. But those were big promises you made. Did you check all this out with the head office?"

"Yes. I'll tell you the details once we're out of here. You're not going to believe it. But Sharon's right. We do need to get rid of Clint. It's past time." Megan paused. She could hear the noise from the last two wells clearly. The roar of the generators wasn't as horrible as being on the site, but it wasn't peaceful, either. Rowdy had made good progress in getting Clint to clean up out there, but she could still smell the chemicals when she took a deep breath. And that well water! She wished she could do something about it. Research. Time to hit the computer. If there was a way to remediate . . .

"Clint goes as soon as the last well is done. No sense in changing supers this close to the end." Rowdy held open the passenger door for her and helped Megan inside.

"But if there's another serious accident?" She kept thinking about Clint's temper. She'd seen it in action herself.

Rowdy frowned. "Then he's gone."

Chapter 15

"I can't believe you're giving in to those do-gooders. I know your father expected to get more wells drilled on this land." Clint was livid. "He's probably twirling in his grave."

"First, you don't know what my father is doing in his grave." Megan was clearly not happy. "Second, I made the decision, and Headquarters is fine with it. You have any idea what the price of oil is this week? We're not drilling any new wells right now. Here or anywhere."

Rowdy was ready to step between them, but he knew Megan liked to fight her own battles. She sure had taken care of the Wallace group. In the two days since they'd met with Sharon, her cousins had already started leaving for parts unknown. Half of the RVs in Raylene's trailer park had taken off this morning. The few that were left had moved down by the showers and the building with the washers and dryers next to Raylene's trailer. That left Rowdy and Megan with their end of the park to themselves.

Clint dug more tobacco out of his tin and reloaded. "This contract you're having drawn up. What about when oil goes back up to a hundred dollars a barrel? You can't promise to never again drill more wells here. That's just plain stupid. And isn't fair to the people who own the mineral rights."

"People who buy mineral rights are gamblers. They take a chance that someday oil will be found and drilled on their property." Megan was being surprisingly patient, but Rowdy could tell she was about to lose her temper. "And I really have no respect for the holder of these rights. Comstock basically took advantage of Sharon Wallace when they sold her that land. If they lose out on the rest of the property, tough shit."

Clint took a step closer, his fists tight. "What the fuck do you know about it, missy?"

"Hold it right there, Stephens. You need to remember whom you're talking to." Rowdy stepped in front of the supervisor. "Don't you have work to do on rig number five? It looked to me like it's about time to push on it."

"Yeah. I'm waiting on a chemical delivery now. Clearly I'm wasting my time here." With one more sour look, he strode out of the office and slammed the door.

"We need to give him time to cool off." Rowdy picked up his tablet computer and gestured at Megan's laptop. "Why don't you give the research a rest for now and let's take off early. That festival in Marfa sounded like fun. What do you say we go back to the RV, change clothes, and head over there?"

His reward was her beaming smile.

"Seriously? We can take the afternoon off?" She threw her arms around him and gave him a deep kiss that made him want to lock the office door. "Thanks, Rowdy. I've been wishing we could go. I was trying so hard to stay Good Megan."

"There's nothing bad about wanting a little time for ourselves. Turn off that damn computer and let's get out of here." He didn't have to tell her twice. He knew they'd been buried in their work for too long. He was used to it—the mud, the men, and the noise. He could see that it had been wearing on Megan, though she hadn't complained.

Instead she'd thrown herself into settling what he'd privately figured was a losing proposition. When you went up against the anti-fracking mob, you really didn't have many arguments you could win. Not when your well site hadn't been following good procedures. Megan had done a great job ferreting out just the arguments she'd needed to win over Sharon Wallace and her crew. They were at least listening now. And trying to be patient as he kept after Stephens to get his act together. It hadn't been easy. The man was all about speed over efficiency. He didn't give a damn for the environment.

Rowdy waited on the porch while Megan printed out some pages she said she wanted to take back to the RV with her. It was strange.

Stephens was up there yelling at his crew now. It was almost as if he had a personal stake in the outcome from this well. Rowdy felt the door hit his back as Megan came out behind him.

"You doing any of your research on our super there?" He nodded toward rig number five. "What's his background?"

"Funny you should ask." Megan waved her papers in front of him. "It's all right here. I found something very interesting."

"Am I going to like it?" Rowdy followed her to the truck.

"Probably not. So I think I'll wait until after we enjoy the festival to tell you." She had that twinkle in her eyes that matched the dazzling blue of the sky over their heads. Rowdy figured she was planning her own special brand of fun in Marfa and he couldn't wait.

He wanted to kiss her right there, in front of the crews on both rigs. They hadn't laid off the men from rig number four yet, so there were a lot of guys still here. Stephens had insisted they keep them on so they could complete the last two rigs faster. His excuse had been that it would make Dr. Wallace happy to see this work done quickly. Rowdy had gone along with it.

He helped Megan into the truck, something he realized he should do more often, then looked back at the busy site. He knew the railings were up to code now and that everyone had been warned to be careful. He'd be damned if an accident happened while he was around. Maybe leaving right now wasn't such a good idea. But then, this was an experienced group of workers and he shouldn't have to babysit the job. So he walked around and climbed in. Damn it, he also shouldn't have to work seven days a week. He needed a break as much as the next guy, and he was going to take one.

Megan was happy to be in clothes that showed off her figure for a change. She knew when she came out from the extra bedroom wearing the white outfit she'd bought in San Antonio that Rowdy appreciated it, too. They'd decided to leave Lucky with Raylene so they could enjoy the festival without worrying about the dog. The landlady sent them off with her blessings and a list of "don't miss" sights to see.

"I feel like a kid playing hooky." Megan grinned at Rowdy once they were on the road. "Are we being naughty, boss man?"

"Hey, we've worked our tails off. Time to take a break." He drove fast, following directions from the navigation system, then reached over to capture her hand. "What do you want to do first?"

"Listen to music. Raylene said there's always a good band in the lineup. You like to dance?" She rubbed her thumb across his knuckles. She loved his big hands.

"I can manage. Depends on what we find. I'm pretty good at a two-step. If you don't get too fancy on me, I can usually hold my own." He grinned. "But this time *I* did research. They're featuring a Latin artist. You into salsa?"

"Oh my God. Tell me you'll try it." She almost bounced in her seat. If she'd found a man who would salsa dance, she was going to marry him. She froze. She did not just think that. Thank goodness she hadn't said it out loud.

"Not only will I try it, little lady, I'll slay it." He tapped a button on the steering wheel and roamed through stations until he found Latin music. "Getting you warmed up."

Megan sighed and leaned back. "Where, oh where, did you learn to salsa?"

"Cassidy and I took lessons." He concentrated on the highway when the navigator told him to prepare for a turn. "I realize now it was an act of desperation. We weren't getting along too well. I'd been out on the road for a long trip, and she felt like we'd grown apart. So we came up with something we could do together when I was home on a break. She picked dancing." He glanced at Megan and smiled. "I liked it."

"And I know for a fact that you have rhythm." Megan's face heated. "Oh, me and my big mouth."

"I appreciate the fact that you noticed my excellent rhythm." He touched her cheek. "You're cute when you blush. For an uninhibited woman, you do get embarrassed."

Megan grabbed his hand again. "Yes, when my mouth overloads my brain." She kissed his knuckles. "And thanks for telling me about Cassidy. So you'd been having problems for a while."

"Before she dumped me, you mean?" He rubbed her chin with the back of his hand. "Yeah. The dancing lessons helped for a month or two. We both enjoyed them. But we *had* become distant with each other, not the close couple we'd been when we were younger. My work schedule and her job demands kept pulling us apart. Even if

Mason hadn't come along, we were going to have to admit soon that we'd grown up and changed since we'd first met. We tried to keep our relationship working, but you shouldn't have to *try*. You know?"

"Not really. I bail so quickly on any connection I make with a guy that it's never gone that far." Megan wished the truck didn't have a massive console between them. She'd like to sit closer to Rowdy so she could rest her head on his chest. "I have no idea how to make a relationship work."

"You think we have one? A relationship?" He glanced at her again. He was serious.

"Yes, I guess we do." She kept holding his hand. "And for some reason I don't feel like running. Wonder why."

"Maybe you're still having fun." He slowed the truck. "I know how you are about fun."

"That could be part of it." Megan was afraid to say more. Instead she noticed the city limits sign. "We're here. Already."

"Yep. Doesn't take long when you can drive so fast." He dropped her hand and put both of his on the steering wheel. "Detour signs. It looks like they're having a parade on the main drag." He punched off the navigator. "I'm turning down a side street so I can find us a place to park. Then we can walk over to the pavilion where the stage and music are set to start in about an hour."

"You really did do your research." Megan smiled at him. "I'm impressed." She sat back and let him take over. Soon they were parked and started walking. He had the blanket he'd thrown into the backseat over his arm and they could hear the band tuning up. There were vendors everywhere and they bought spicy tacos and cold beer to take to the grassy area where they could have a picnic and still see the stage.

"This is great." Rowdy was on his second taco. "What do you think?"

"Mmm. Delicious." Megan wiped off her hands and drank some of her cold beer. "Look, the music is about to start. That's a dance floor next to the stage. Finish eating. I want to test your skills."

"Isn't there a rule about waiting an hour after you eat before dancing?" He finished the taco and polished off his beer.

"That's swimming. I think you'll survive if you dance a few steps on a full stomach. Unless you're chickening out?" She stood and twirled in her skirt. She'd be right at home on the floor among the other women already dancing with their partners.

"But what about dessert?" Rowdy took her hand and pulled her down next to him. "We always have dessert."

"Later. When it's dark and the Marfa lights come out." Megan laughed and looked around. "Come on, or I'll think that whole story about you and Cassidy dancing was bull."

"No bull. I don't know what you have on your mind. But I was thinking more along the lines of some sopapillas and honey from that vendor over there for dessert." He groaned when she dragged him to his feet. "I think you only like me for my body, woman."

"You may be right." Megan kissed his cheek and pulled him to the dance floor, winding her way through the many people picnicking on the lawn. Soon they were dancing among the other couples in the crowd. Rowdy hadn't been lying. He pulled her close then swung her out, his hips moving to the beat as he proved he'd mastered the salsa. Of course, neither of them could hold a candle to the people who'd obviously made a serious study of the exotic dance, but they were laughing and having fun.

When a slow tune played, they clung to each other, breathless by the time the song ended. The Latin beat and swaying to the music made Megan think of foreplay, and she pulled Rowdy's face down to kiss him. Whistles broke them apart and their faces were red, but the good-natured laughter around them soon got them over any embarrassment. By the time it was dark, they'd danced to a dozen songs, had two more beers, and even hit the dessert vendor.

"I need a place where I can wash the honey off my hands." Megan looked around. "There. Public restrooms."

"Fine. I'll meet you back here in five minutes. Make that ten." Rowdy took off into the darkness with their blanket under his arm.

Megan decided he must have had stomach issues with the tacos to be in such a hurry. She was glad she still felt good. She quickly cleaned up, then wandered around the different vendors, looking over the displays of crafts and homemade food items.

"Here you are." Rowdy appeared next to her at a stand for salsa and chips. "Surely you're not eating again."

"No, but I wouldn't mind taking some of this salsa home. They gave me a sample. Taste. Don't worry, it's not too hot. I know you're a scaredy cat when it comes to chilis." She held out a chip and he tried it.

"That *is* good. I'll get it." Rowdy dug in his pocket and paid the woman behind the counter. "*Gracias, señora.*"

Megan laughed. "Not bad for a man who sucks at languages." She took his arm. "What now?"

He took the bag with the jar of salsa and pulled her toward the parking lot. "I have a surprise and a plan. You like surprises?"

"Love them." She let him lead her through the crowd. It was darker in the parking lot, and she waited next to the truck while he wrapped the salsa in Lucky's towel. He set it on the floor in the backseat, then threw the blanket on top of it. After he slammed the door, he took her in his arms.

"I've been waiting all afternoon for more of this." His kiss was deep and urgent.

Megan melted against him. When he finally eased back from her, she ran her hands over his chest. "Me, too. I want you, Rowdy Baker. How long will it take us to get back to that RV?"

"Too long. But I told you, I have a plan." He pulled open the passenger door and helped her inside. "Trust me?"

She tugged on his shirt until he was almost lying on top of her in the front seat. "More than you know." She kissed *him* this time. Only the fact that the dome light in the truck cab let anyone passing by see their action made her pull back. "Show me what you have in mind." She shoved him out of the truck and slammed the door.

Rowdy drove out to the place he'd been told about. It should be perfect—isolated and with a good view of the well-known Marfa lights. He had a little something in his pocket that he hoped would make this night even more special. Had he lost his mind? Probably.

By the time he parked the truck, he was sweating. Yeah, he had a bad case of nerves. No big deal if he just kept his mouth shut. But his heart was full and, damn it, he had something to say tonight. He felt like if he didn't get it off his chest, he'd explode. Would Megan try to put him down gently? Or laugh it off like he was joking? Either of those reactions would surely kill him.

"Where are we?" Megan leaned against the dashboard and looked around. "Are we lost? It sure is dark out here."

"Nope. I made a friend in the men's room. Hector. He swears this is a great place to see those mysterious lights you've been telling me about all week." Rowdy smiled at her. "You know, when you weren't researching something else."

"Don't mock my research, pal." She opened the truck door. "I want to see them. People have been reporting these lights for a century. You saw all the souvenirs in town. Some claim they're alien spaceships. Others think our own country has secret experiments going on in the mountains west of here."

Rowdy hopped out of the truck and grabbed the blanket from the backseat. "Well then, I think it's worth a look. But, you're right, it's black as pitch out here. Wait till I turn off the lights on the truck so our eyes can adjust."

Megan ran around to hold his hand. "Okay, now do it." She leaned against him when darkness surrounded him. "It's a little spooky now." She jumped. "What's that sound?"

"You mean the silence?" Rowdy laughed. "Relax, close your eyes, it'll help. And be glad we aren't listening to fracking for a change. There aren't any wells near here."

"Oh, you're right. And, hey"—she paused—"yep, that was definitely a bird chirping. At least Marfa still has some wildlife."

"Open your eyes. Can you see to walk now? To the top of that rise?" Rowdy pointed to the mound about a hundred feet ahead of them. "Watch your step, but there is a path. I don't think we're the first couple to find Hector's hideaway."

"Yes, I see it." Megan tugged on his hand. "And look up. There are about a million stars. Surely those aren't the lights they've been talking about."

"No, the alien lights are all colors and move across the sky at the horizon. Some people used to think they were just headlights on a highway. But there's no road there. Wait and see." Rowdy pulled her up to the top of the hill and got the blanket stretched out to his satisfaction. He bowed and gestured. "My lady."

"Ah, a gentleman. Thanks, I believe I will." She sat in the middle of the blanket, then lay back so she could look up into the sky. "It's beautiful here." She got up. "Ouch." Reaching under the blanket she pulled out a rock and tossed it away. "I see cactus, too. I'm glad you didn't put us near that."

"I know how you feel about cactus spines. I think it's turned into a full-blown phobia." Rowdy sat beside her, then pushed her onto her back again. "Relax, Megan. Take it all in. We're just tiny specks in a vast universe."

"I know. It's intimidating." She rolled to her side and propped her head on her hand. "Do you really think there could be aliens out there?"

"I'd be surprised if there weren't intelligent civilizations thriving on other planets. I mean, what are the odds we're the only ones who've managed to do what we've done?" Rowdy couldn't look away from her.

"You mean pollute and ruin it? That's what people like Sharon Wallace would say." Megan took a deep breath, then settled her cheek on his chest. "I think she has a point. Right here is perfect. You can't do this on her land anymore. Listen to birds singing or inhale without coughing."

"Can we forget the fracking controversy for tonight?" Rowdy ran his hand over her soft hair. "Look! I think I see what they're talking about. Colored lights, moving from east to west over there."

Megan gasped and held on to him. "They're beautiful."

They both lay there for a long while watching an incredible light show. Finally the sky was back to normal, just the stars and an almost-full moon that had risen in the sky. The old man looked like he was watching them.

Rowdy kissed her then, starting something he'd been thinking about ever since he'd put the blanket in the truck. Maybe he was a horndog. Didn't matter. Megan was right there with him, pulling off the shawl she'd thrown over her sexy top, then shoving his jacket out of the way. He carefully unclipped her silver belt and set it aside, then ripped that white top up and off over her head. No bra. He'd been watching her breasts moving under the cotton all evening. He knew he'd never get tired of seeing and tasting them. She dragged his shirt up and off, too, pressing kisses over his chest before working open his belt buckle.

"Slow down." Rowdy couldn't believe he'd said it. The air was chilly, and fast would warm them up. But he liked this part almost as much as the big finish.

Her eyes twinkled as she leaned over and pulled down his zipper with her teeth. "Is this what you mean?" she asked as she slid his belt out of his jeans and dropped it in the grass. When she unbuttoned him she didn't pull the jeans off, just laid them open and used her lips to find him hot and ready.

Rowdy didn't say a thing. Couldn't talk when her mouth closed over him and she let her tongue drift up and down his shaft. He knew slow wasn't going to be an option now. He slid his hand up her bare leg and found that, praise God, she hadn't worn panties. He probed her with his fingers. Of course she was slick and ready for him. He started a rhythm that made her press urgently against his hand. She was still being too damn clever with her mouth, and Rowdy was afraid he was going to lose it any second.

"Did I say slow?" He rolled on top of her, pushing her to her back and bunching her skirt around her waist. "You make me crazy, woman. I can't wait." Entering Megan was like coming home. Rowdy sank into her and paused, taking a moment to just savor being held inside her. She clung to him and looked up. Trust him? It was there in her eyes. She smiled and waited, content to let him set the pace. Suddenly that pace was urgent. He wanted to claim her, to take her higher than she'd ever been before. He didn't give a damn if she'd had a hundred men before him. He wanted to be her best, her last.

They climaxed together, their shouts echoing in the empty land. Megan hid her face against his damp shoulder, still shuddering with the aftershocks. She finally kissed his skin and fell back on the blanket.

"God, Rowdy, how do you do that to me? Every time?"

He managed to roll her on top of him and felt her shiver again. "It's a gift." He patted her bottom. "Damn it, you're freezing." He grabbed his jacket and her shawl and pulled them across her. "You should have said something."

"What? I was speechless most of the time." She leaned down and kissed him, licking her way into his mouth until they were both breathing fast again. "You're amazing."

"Takes two to salsa, *chica*." He kissed *her* this time, determined to ease up, to keep it tender. Yeah, he could go another round, crazy that he'd already begun to stir again. But he wanted this night to be about more than sex, as great as it was between them.

"You keep throwing around Spanish words and I'll think you're finally trying with the language thing." She fell off of him and lay back to stare at the sky again. "Look, the lights are back." She laughed. "Do you think the aliens watched us?"

"If they did, they learned something."

Megan laughed. "So did I, lover."

Rowdy dug in his jeans and for the box that held what he'd bought at the craft show. "I have a surprise for you. I told you I did, didn't I?"

"I thought coming out here was it." Megan sat up, her shawl wrapped around her shoulders. "A present?" She took the box. "What have you done?"

"Don't panic. Are you thinking this is a proposal?" Rowdy watched her closely. What did that expression mean? He couldn't read her.

"Well, is it?" She grinned. "Would it kill you to make an honest woman out of me?"

"You already are an honest woman." Rowdy relaxed. "I have no doubt about that." Uh-oh. Her face fell. What had he said? "Open the damn box."

She pulled off the lid. "Oh, it's beautiful." She pulled out the silver bracelet with the intricately carved cactus dangling from it. Small flowers centered with turquoise and coral stones bloomed on the stems.

"It's a souvenir of our time together." Rowdy waited while she clasped it around her wrist. "I'll never forget taking those cactus spines out of your butt. You still have a small scar where the biggest one got you."

Tears filled her eyes, then she launched herself at him. "I love you, Rowdy. You're too good for me." She sobbed against his bare chest.

"What the hell?" He didn't know how to take this. On the one hand, she'd said she loved him. He wanted to pick her up and dance with her around the hilltop. On the other, she was crying as if her heart was breaking. "Megan! Talk to me, baby."

"Don't call me baby. It's too sweet. I don't deserve it." She leaned back and wiped her streaming eyes with the back of her hand.

"Where is this coming from? I know I didn't say it first, but can't you tell? I love you, too." Rowdy fell back when she jumped up and almost hit him in the chin with her foot. She grabbed her clothes and headed for the truck. "For fuck's sake, what did I do wrong?"

"Shut up, Rowdy. You're only making this harder for me." She crammed her feet into her sandals, clearly not thinking straight since she dropped her shawl on a cactus. She pulled her top over her head. "Shit." She shook out the shawl, then opened the door and threw it in the truck.

"Don't just sit there! Get dressed and drive us home!" This was a screech like he'd rarely heard from her. It was as if Megan was in a panic.

"Fine. Whatever you want. I will not call you 'baby,' and I sure as hell won't throw out an 'I love you' if that's the reaction I'm going to get." Rowdy pulled on his jeans, then got his shirt over his head, though it was backward on the first try and he had to do it again. He grabbed his jacket, stuffed his feet in his shoes, and snagged the blanket, giving it a good shake in case a tarantula wanted to ride home with them. There were a few other things he picked up, then he stalked over to the truck.

"I will never understand women. Never in a million years." He slammed the door and started the engine. "You just sit there, Megan Calhoun, and don't say a fucking word. Not while I'm driving. But when we get back to the RV, I want an explanation for your behavior." Rowdy wheeled out of his parking spot and down the track to the highway. He was pissed. All his planning, a beautiful night, and it had somehow gone to shit. And, to top it off, Megan was over there against her door sniffling.

"I'm sorry, Rowdy." She said it quietly.

"Don't want to hear it. I said save it for when we get back. You will not go straight to bed. You will not refuse to explain. No bullshit. So, sit there and think. Pretending to fall asleep won't fly, either." He took a breath, relieved that it didn't come out rough or watery. "I know why I'm not good enough for you. Anyone with half a brain knows that. I decided to get over it and have faith we could figure things out together. But when you look at me and say you don't deserve me? Well, that's going to require an explanation. So, get ready." He punched on sports talk radio. Football. At least he understood the rules of *that* game.

Chapter 16

Megan dragged herself out of the truck when Rowdy stopped in front of Raylene's trailer. She needed some time and a walk to the RV. When Lucky bounded up beside her, she reached down and took his leash.

"Lucky and I will meet you there." She kept walking.

"You bet you will." Rowdy still sounded furious, but he drove slowly past them when Lucky stopped to water a light pole.

"You probably should have spent the night with Butch and Raylene, Lucky. It's going to be no fun in our place." Megan sniffed. She knew crying was a weapon she could use. Maybe not for forgiveness, but at least he might soften a little. She sighed. Oh, who was she kidding? He shouldn't forgive or forget that she'd known since the day they'd left Houston that her family had wronged his. Better for her to just tell him now than for him to find out from someone else first.

The letters had gone out to the injured parties more than a week ago. Had his mother thought it was a hoax and tossed it? It wouldn't surprise her. Who would believe in a sudden windfall from an oil company for mineral rights lost long ago?

Megan arrived at their RV and opened the door. Lucky waited impatiently for her to take off his leash, then went searching for Rowdy. The dog barked and Megan followed the sound to their bedroom. Rowdy was lying on his back, petting Lucky and waiting for her. He'd left on his clothes but kicked off his shoes. He still looked impossibly good to her, and he'd said he loved her tonight. Tears filled her eyes as she turned away.

"Where are you going?" He didn't yell, just asked the question.

"I want a bottle of water. And I'm putting Lucky to bed. Come on, boy." She slapped her thigh and Lucky followed her. She refilled his water bowl, then sat on the bed in the extra bedroom. They had a ritual at night. She put his favorite toy in the bed and they played a little tug-of-war with it. Then she kissed him on the head and told him good night before she turned off the light and closed the door.

She decided to hang up her outfit in the hall closet and put on her robe. No matter where this conversation went, she needed to be comfortable. The white looked like it needed to be hand-washed, but not tonight. When she started to take off the top, she realized she didn't have her silver belt.

"Rowdy! I must have left my belt on that hill." She tried to re-member exactly what she'd done when they'd left. No, she hadn't picked it up. "That was a signed piece by an artist. It cost a bundle."

"I'm sure. So I picked it up. It's still in the truck. In the backseat with the blanket. You need it tonight?" He stood in the bedroom doorway.

"No. I just had a moment of panic, that's all." She pulled off her top and dropped her skirt, turning away from him to slip on her robe. Then she carefully hung up the two pieces.

"Not surprising you forgot it. You freaked out there at the end." He sat at the dinette table. "Grab your water and sit down here. Let's talk."

Megan pulled a cold bottle out of the fridge and sat across from him. "I'm sorry about that. The panic."

"So I'm waiting for an explanation." He looked over at the cabi-net, when a phone buzzed. "It's my old phone. I left it here since we rarely have decent reception in this area. Let me see who this is."

"Don't." She grabbed the phone and looked at the screen. "Oh, it's your mother. Isn't it kind of late for her to call?"

"Yes, it is. So I should take this. Give me my phone, Megan." Rowdy held out his hand.

"You can call her back after we talk." Megan dropped the phone into her lap. "It will be better that way."

"Hand me the fucking phone. My mother has had cancer. It might be about a relapse." He got up and came around the table. "Don't make me take it."

"Cancer! I didn't know. Of course." Megan almost threw it at him.

Now she felt even worse. What if life-sustaining treatments hadn't been available when his mother had needed them because she and Rowdy couldn't afford it? Not only was her father a swindler, but he could have very well caused people to die from neglect or inadequate care. Oh, the repercussions of what Conrad Calhoun had done didn't bear thinking about. She dropped her head into her hands, then looked up again. She had to see how he reacted to what his mother told him.

"Mom, you're up late." Rowdy sat across from her again. "What's up? How are you feeling?" He listened and finally smiled. "Oh, that's good. You scared me, calling so late."

Megan sagged in her seat. At least illness hadn't been the problem.

"You have? I'm sorry. This phone is almost useless out here. I got a new number now. A satellite phone." He paused. "Yes, finally. You have something to write with? Here goes." He rattled off the number. "You can always reach me on it."

Megan knew this was the call she'd been dreading. She decided she didn't want to sit here for it after all. She walked into the bathroom and took a shower, even washed her hair. That should give Rowdy plenty of time to hear about the evildoings of Calhoun Petroleum and Conrad Calhoun. She could only pray that he'd give the monster's daughter a chance to explain how they were trying to make things right for them.

But would they really be able to follow through on the promise implied in that letter? The last word from Cassidy hadn't sounded good. The company was being reorganized, and most debts were being paid. But the big looming debt was the compensation owed to the people whom Conrad had defrauded early in his career. She had no idea how many wells had been drilled on the land owned by Rowdy's family or if they'd been profitable. But even if only a few came in successfully, with penalties and interest . . . The numbers had to be significant.

Megan blew her hair dry, then put on her robe again. She couldn't stay in the tiny, steamy bathroom another minute. She felt sick, and it wasn't just because she couldn't breathe in the enclosed space. She threw open the bathroom door.

"Megan, you finally through hiding in there? Sit down." Rowdy's phone lay on the table. When she hesitated, he slammed his fist next to it. "I said sit the fuck down!"

"What did your mother have to say?" She picked up her water and then couldn't manage to open the top. He grabbed it, unscrewed the cap, and thrust it into her hand. He kept staring at her as she took a swallow and almost choked. "Well?"

"Are you seriously going to sit there and pretend you don't know why she called? She got a letter, Megan, from Calhoun Petroleum." His laugh was bitter. "Signed by Cassidy herself as acting chief financial officer." He stared down at his phone. "Isn't that a kick in the nuts?"

"Rowdy. You know this all happened before Cassidy, me, all of the kids were born. We didn't—"

"I know that." He met her gaze. "Don't you dare fucking cry, Megan Calhoun. I don't blame you for something your lying, stealing father did. But I sure as hell hate the fact that you knew about this and didn't say word one to me this whole trip." His lips were tight, like he was holding in a lot more words that he knew would wound her. "You did know, didn't you?"

"Yes." She closed her eyes, hating the way he was looking at her. No, too cowardly. She met his gaze head-on. "We were sworn to secrecy. But I know that's no excuse!" She didn't dare reach for his fist, lying there on the table, but God, she wanted to touch him. "Cassidy's still trying to figure out how to pay what we owe. It's . . . it's a lot."

"Forgive me if I don't give a flying fuck if it sends you and your high-living family to the poorhouse." This time he was the one who looked away. "You have any idea what that money could have meant to *my* family? Thirty long years Calhoun has been using mineral rights that belonged to first my grandmother, and now to my mom." When he finally turned back to face her, his eyes were actually bright with tears he would never shed. "My grandma had Alzheimer's, Megan. So your daddy tricked her into signing away her rights when she was incompetent. She would sit on her front porch and watch your father's company drilling wells. Used to say it was too bad they were messing up her pasture. But she never could remember how or when she gave someone permission to do it."

"I'm learning that my father was ambitious. Too much so. It made him greedy and dishonest in the early days of the company. It's why Cassidy's mother cut her off from her father. Made him sign away his parental rights when they divorced." Megan took another drink of water, her throat tight with emotion.

"No wonder Cass's mother never remarried, with an asshole like that for a husband. But Liz should have turned Conrad in, reported what he did to the authorities back then. Tried to make things right." He just kept staring at that phone. "Shit. She's almost as guilty as he was, keeping Cass to herself and letting that man go on about his lying, cheating business for thirty years."

"I don't know why Elizabeth Calhoun chose to behave the way she did." Megan could have told him what a wonderful dad her father had been when he hadn't been off working to build his huge company. He certainly hadn't let his kids see his unethical side. Instead he'd provided them with a lavish lifestyle. Using tainted money.

"She was better off not knowing him." Rowdy scowled and flexed his fingers. "Sorry if that hurts your feelings."

"No, I get it." He was upset. She couldn't blame him for lashing out. "But didn't you or your mom ever look into who owned the mineral rights on your grandmother's land?" Megan didn't want to make him mad, but she'd learned that much in her research. People had to take care of themselves when it came to land ownership and what did or didn't belong to them.

"I was a kid, Megan. Mom had her hands full with her mother losing her mind. It started small with missing papers, paranoia, then she didn't know us anymore. Mom finally had to put Grandma into a nursing home and it wasn't a good one. We didn't have money, so we had little choice, even after we sold the land where Grandma had lived most of her life. The nursing home was state-funded and the care was for shit. I spent many hours after school there with Mom making sure Grandma was clean and fed. The staff meant well, but the people were overworked and really didn't have time to see to all the patients under their care."

Megan had nothing to say. She couldn't imagine spending her childhood in that situation. But she did remember seeing her mother in a mental hospital when Missy'd had one of her bad spells. It had left scars she'd carry forever. And that was despite the fact that her mother had always received the most expensive care available in a private facility.

"I still worry that my mom or me will end up like Grandma, losing our minds someday. It's a special kind of hell." He shook his head. "But I'm getting sidetracked. This is about you and me."

"Is there? A you and me?" Megan held her breath.

"That's what I'm trying to figure out here." He finally reached across the table and Megan put her hand in his. "I can't blame you for what your father did. And I'd met you what—twice?—before that day in Houston when we headed out of town. I understand why you wouldn't break your family's trust by telling me what your father had done then."

"I couldn't. But as I got to know you, it ate at me. Keeping this secret." She held on tight. "I don't know how much money we're talking about, Rowdy, or if there will be *any* money when all is said and done." She bowed her head, the shame of admitting that weighing her down.

"I've always made my own way, Megan. I'll survive no matter what. But having financial security would mean a lot to my mother. She's worked hard all her life with little to show for it. I'd like to see her able to retire and take it easy." He let go of her hand and leaned back. "I told her we need our own lawyer. To fight for what's owed us."

"That's a good idea. Since we're clearly on opposite sides of this, maybe we should change the subject." Megan stood, really ready to talk about something else. "I didn't get to tell you what I found out about Clint Stephens." She grabbed the papers she'd brought home with her from the job site and laid them on the table. "I wouldn't bother you with this now if it wasn't important. You need to do something about it, probably tomorrow."

"What is it?" He picked up the pages. "More of your research, obviously."

"Yes. Clint is from Virginia City, Nevada. Does that ring any bells with you?" She pulled the last page from the pile.

"It's a mining town. Site of a big silver find back in the eighteen hundreds." He scanned the pages, then dropped them back on the table. "Just give me the bottom line."

"Well, the major discovery of silver found in Virginia City was called the Comstock Lode. Seems our supervisor named his own little company Comstock."

"No kidding." Rowdy frowned. "Clint Stephens is the person who sold Dr. Wallace her place? And kept the mineral rights?"

"That's correct." Megan handed him the last page. "Look when he bought it. It was right about the time my dad started buying up land in this area. I don't know whether Clint was acquainted with the geologist or just got lucky. Maybe he heard gossip on the job site where he was working for Calhoun Petroleum at the time, but Clint had inside information."

"He sure as hell did." Rowdy scanned the page. "Which is why it's against company policy for an employee to work on a project where he has a financial interest." He threw it on the table. "I'll be damned. No wonder Clint is all about speed. In a big fucking hurry to bring in those wells. And he went ape shit nuts when you admitted you'd told Wallace we wouldn't drill any more wells on that property. That represents a huge loss of income to the mineral rights holder."

"Exactly." Megan found her phone and checked her e-mail. "I asked Cass to send me the account so I could see what we've paid Comstock so far in royalties on this site. Check it out." She passed Rowdy her phone.

He read the numbers and then closed his eyes. "You can't be serious. That much?"

"And we haven't completed all the wells yet. Can you imagine how much it will be once all of them are in and the price of oil recovers?" She reached for his hand. "Rowdy?" He was pale, as if he might faint. Impossible. He was way too tough for that. "What's wrong?"

"If that's what he made on just three wells in a couple of months, what in the hell could you owe my family after decades and what I counted once were a dozen wells on our property?" He grabbed her water bottle and drained it. "And you don't need to remind me that the price of oil for some of that time was double what it is now."

Megan got up to put her arms around him. She was relieved that he didn't push her away. She leaned against his back as he sat there, clearly unable to take it all in.

"Do you see now why I panicked in Marfa? This secret . . . it's huge. And I knew what it could have meant to you." Megan just breathed, wishing he would say something. Finally, she couldn't stand the silence. "You see why it's taking Cass so long to figure this out? My brother Ethan has been working on it, too. It's almost impossible to put an exact figure on what we owe each person involved. Some wells go dry. Others are put idle for one reason or another. Like when the price per gallon bottomed out. Anyway, coming up with the totals is a nightmare."

"But it'll still be in the millions, won't it?" He got up quickly, stepping away from her. "How many people did your old man do this to, Megan? Steal their mineral rights? How much of a disaster is this for your family's company?"

"Over a hundred." She swallowed, really nauseated as it hit her again, the sheer disgusting truth of it. And her mother had been in on it, too. Missy had the excuse of mental illness, though she'd bragged about pushing Conrad when he'd finally had an attack of conscience. Her dad? He must have been the one to have started the scam. The man with the nose for oil. No excuse worked for him. Rowdy stared at her, incredulous.

"Yes, you heard me right. He defrauded over a hundred innocent people." She didn't know how long she could stay on her feet, the sheer impossibility of their making good on this finally hitting her. "Disaster? Rowdy, this is probably the deathblow for Calhoun Petroleum."

"Oh no. Declaring bankruptcy is the coward's way out. It's one of those tricks rich people use to get out of paying their debts." He gripped her shoulders. "Tell me they're not going to do that."

"We had a family meeting before I left town. We promised each other that we'd do whatever we could to avoid it." Megan wanted to move in and lean against him but held off. He might not welcome that. "But as you reminded Sharon Wallace's cousins, it's not up to us. We have that board of directors and the shareholders who ultimately may call the shots. If it becomes too expensive to put things right, we may not have a choice."

"But who are the majority stockholders?" He stared at her until she had to answer.

"The four of us. Conrad's children."

"So, I'll know who is really to blame if the company calls it quits." He let her go and looked at the bedroom they'd shared every night since they'd picked up the RV. Then he stared at her. "I've got to think, Megan. I need time to process all of this. Maybe you'd better sleep with the dog tonight." His face was bleak. "I'm sorry. I know you didn't create this mess, but I can't forget right now that your name is Calhoun and that you were raised by that duplicitous son of a bitch." He stepped into the bedroom and closed the door behind him.

Megan held on to the table, afraid to move for fear of falling to the floor. How had a glorious night gone so completely to shit? She was sure Rowdy was wondering exactly the same thing. She finally did move and found her purse. Maybe she should call one of her sisters, get an update. If she had some promising news to give Rowdy . . . She laughed softly. Who was she kidding? She'd seen the numbers. There was little likelihood that he and his mother would be compensated even close to what they were owed—if they got anything at all. The oil in the fields out here could come up by itself and run to the refineries, and they still wouldn't make enough capital to pay everyone like they should.

She slipped into Lucky's bedroom and crawled under the covers. The dog's weight against her back provided a little comfort. But not nearly enough to keep her from crying herself to sleep. She wanted a different male in her bed, one that didn't have a wagging tail and a wet nose.

Rowdy woke up dry-eyed and numb. He didn't know what to do with what Megan had told him. Her father had done something so abhorrent he couldn't get a handle on it. His sweet grandma had never harmed a soul. She'd worked in her garden and enjoyed planting a corn crop in the acreage behind her house. After Grandpa Roland died, she'd sometimes leased it to neighbors for their horses. Yep, he'd been named for his grandpa.

When Grandma's mind had started going, they'd kept her in her own home for as long as possible. There'd been a friendly church lady and a hired nurse stopping by at least twice a day to make sure she was all right. He and his mom had been there daily, too. He'd loved his grandma and her homemade cookies. When they'd started tasting funny, he'd pretended to eat them anyway, slipping them under the porch when she wasn't looking. It had been a fall and a broken hip that had persuaded them she couldn't stay in the house any longer. The oil wells were already pumping, but selling the house had brought to light that the mineral rights were long gone. His mother hadn't questioned it.

Rowdy showered, the smell of coffee letting him know that Megan was up, too. He'd missed her last night. Maybe it hadn't been fair to push her into the other bedroom. But he'd been so confused, so damn hurt, he'd just reacted. He walked out of the bathroom with a towel around his waist and stopped next to her where she was sitting at the dining table. She was dressed and ready for work.

"I'm sorry, Megan." He pulled her to her feet. "I know you didn't make this mess. Forgive me?" He looked into her eyes, rimmed with red. Shit, she'd been crying.

"No, *I'm* sorry. I wish I could promise to make things right for your family, but I don't know if I can." She stepped into his arms. "If there's any way to get something for your mother, so she can retire, we'll see to it. Okay?"

"Forget about that now." He kissed her. "I missed you last night." He picked her up and tried to carry her into the bedroom. The narrow doorway into the bedroom almost made that impossible, but he managed. "I'm beginning to hate this RV."

She smiled up into his eyes. "How can you say that? I have very fond memories of this deluxe model." She laughed shakily when he dropped her on the bed and whipped off his towel. "Why, Mr. Baker, I believe you intend to ravish me and make me late for work."

"I believe you're right, Ms. Calhoun." He fell on top of her, running his hands under her sweatshirt to find her breasts. "Did anyone tell you about our dress code? Workers of the female persuasion should wear appropriate undergarments at all times."

"Oh really. Then it's your duty to always check to make sure I'm wearing or not wearing them. Right?" She ran her hands over his chest. "Guess I failed today. You going to punish me?"

He shoved the shirt up to her chin and grasped a breast in one hand. "Have to." He took her nipple in his mouth and devoured it, making it more pleasure than punishment.

"Oh, I'm feeling very sorry for breaking your rules." She moaned when he turned to the other breast. "You haven't checked for my other undergarment yet. If you do, you might find I'm *barely* following your rules."

"Barely." He grinned and made quick work of her jeans. "Ah, I see what you mean. This scrap of lace hardly qualifies as a panty. I think you must take it off and find a more appropriate item in your wardrobe." He slid his hand under the triangle of lace. "Or wear nothing at all."

"Mm. You're making me really sorry I didn't follow the dress code." She kicked her jeans off the rest of the way and widened her legs. "Rowdy." She looked up at him, suddenly serious. "Make love to me." Her whisper hit him right in the heart.

"All you had to do was ask." He raised her hips and plunged into her, cursing when he bumped his head on the low ceiling. "Well, that wasn't too smart."

She laughed and pulled his face down to kiss him. "I'm beginning to understand why you're sick of the RV. We need to settle this deal at the site and get the hell out of here. Surely they'll either let us come home or stop in a big city for a few days. I have dreams of a hotel and a king-sized bed." Her eyes closed when he pushed into her again. "But enough talk. Take me higher, lover. You just need to watch your head while you do it."

Rowdy held on to her and moved, loving the way she wrapped her arms around him and whispered his name. When they both came together, it was a miracle of sensation he knew he'd never forget. Finally they lay side by side. The cool air on his back reminded him that he needed to either cover up or get dressed. Instead he leaned over her and looked into her eyes.

"I love you, Megan. Do you believe that?"

"I'm trying to. But after all—"

He shut her up with a finger over her lips. "No buts. Just accept it."

She nodded. "I love you, too, Rowdy."

"All right, then. Let's get dressed and go kick some butt. I can't wait to fire Clint Stephens, and you gave me the ammunition to do it. I really don't like that asshole."

Megan shoved him out of bed. "Then, let's get going. You can fire him, but I get to watch. Remember who found all that dirt on him. And I'm not through looking." She wiggled out of bed, giving him an arch look as she pulled on her jeans without panties under them. "Ah, dress codes. Who would have thought they could be so much fun?"

Rowdy groaned. "Fun? I think they may be torture." He chased her down the hall, then realized Lucky was barking from the front bedroom. "Get your dog and walk him down to Raylene's. I'll meet you there."

"Yes, sir." She pulled on a sweatshirt and a jacket. "I love it when you order me around, boss. Just remember, though, that when my year is up, I won't let you do it ever again."

Rowdy stopped and stared after her. It was the first time either of them had mentioned any future beyond this year together. He didn't have a chance to comment before she was out the door.

A future with Megan. Was it possible? With the giant elephant in the room called Calhoun Petroleum and her thieving father? Rowdy picked up her computer and his jacket and headed out, locking the trailer behind him. People claimed love could conquer all. Maybe it was true, but he'd never tested it. He put the computer in the backseat and climbed into the truck. He needed to be optimistic. A retirement for his mother. That wasn't much in Calhoun terms. Surely it could happen. He saw Megan waving at the end of the road, a smile on her face. Damn it, they would make it happen. Together.

Chapter 17

"I see you've made good progress on well number five." Rowdy held the papers Megan had printed out about Comstock and was ready to lay down the law.

"Yep. And got that pond cleaned out like you asked. Smell better to you, Ms. Calhoun?" Clint spit into his tobacco cup.

"Sure. I'd think everyone working here would appreciate being able to actually take a breath without choking." Megan just shook her head when Clint laughed.

"Hell, we get used to it. Isn't that right, Baker?"

Rowdy didn't answer that question. "I see we're getting more chemicals. Is that for number six?"

"Sure is. And we're about ready to order concrete for five. Maybe day after tomorrow. So we can put up the Christmas tree." Clint smiled proudly. "You can't say I don't know how to get things moving."

"No, I'd never say that. You've been all about speed on this job." Rowdy sat on the edge of Clint's desk. "You got a hand who could take over for you if you had to, say, take a trip somewhere?"

"Why? You got another site that needs my expertise?" Clint took off his hard hat and chuckled. "You don't say much, but I knew I was impressing you." He turned to Megan, who still sat in the chair behind his desk. "What do you think, Ms. Calhoun? You letting them know back at Headquarters how this site's coming together?"

"You can be sure Headquarters knows all about this site." Megan had her laptop open. "I was glad to see there haven't been any more accidents since we arrived."

"I had a strong talk with the crew. Let them know I'd lay off the next man who was careless." He hit that hat against his muddy jeans. "But, Baker, I really don't want to leave here. I'd like to see a job through to the end, if you know what I mean. It's important to follow through." He headed to the door. "Now, if that's all . . ."

"Seriously, Stephens, give me a name. I might need for you to turn things over to a qualified hand." Rowdy was having a hard time keeping his shit together. A "strong talk with the crew"? Hell, most of the accidents were because the supervisor had been cutting corners, too focused on getting the job done fast. God, but he couldn't wait to kick this man out on his ass.

"Dave Rodriguez is a good guy. Been around a long time. I suppose he could complete the last two if push came to shove." Clint stepped closer. "What's this about, Baker?"

"It's about Comstock, Stephens. That name ring a bell?" Rowdy watched the other man quickly school his features, but he hadn't covered his surprise fast enough.

"Don't know what in the hell you're talking about." Clint dug his tobacco tin out of his back pocket.

"Playing dumb won't work here. Though you seem to have a natural aptitude for it." Rowdy jumped up when Clint tried to throw a punch. Luckily he threw his can of chew instead. It hit the wall and bounced to the floor next to them.

"Listen, you son of a bitch. I don't have to take that from nobody, certainly not from an asshole who came out here eager to cave to a prissy environmental agenda. Don't make it go down any easier that you're obviously enjoying perks like that fancy RV because you're fucking a Calhoun daughter." The supervisor's face was red.

Rowdy slammed him back against the door. "You keep your filthy mouth shut about Ms. Calhoun. Got it?"

"Right. Owners can do whatever they want. It's always been that way." He shoved Rowdy away from him. "Now, what's this about? You claiming I have something to do with Comstock?" He picked up his tobacco tin from the floor. When he stood again, he smiled, showing his stained teeth. "Prove it."

"No problem," Megan said. "This is the paperwork you filed in Nevada setting up your LLC. Then there's the paper trail that shows you bought the property that you later sold to Sharon Wallace. Minus the mineral rights, of course. You'd already leased those to Calhoun Petroleum the month before."

"Okay, you got me. So what?" Clint scowled. "Dumb bitch fell in love with the house. Never asked a thing about what was under the ground. So I outsmarted her."

"Yes, you can claim that. But now we're going to tell you what's going to happen here." Megan hit a button on the computer, and the printer in the corner stirred to life.

"Oh, save it. You think I don't know? Conflict of interest. Whatever. But I'm here to tell you that you're going to regret that promise you made Wallace to stop drilling on this property. We're sitting on a pool of oil. Millions of gallons. You can't fucking refuse to drill for it. And I'm not going to sit idly by while you screw me over." He slammed a fist down on the desk that made the computer jump. "No way in hell."

"You've got no choice, Stephens. We've fulfilled the terms of your lease agreement. You can waste your time and money suing the company, but it'll do you no good whatsoever." Rowdy slapped the papers against his hand.

"What the hell are you talking about?" Clint looked from Rowdy to Megan and back again.

"You were so busy hiding your connection with the company that you made a mistake when your agent signed that lease with Conrad Calhoun." Rowdy was looking forward to this part. "I'm surprised an experienced hand like you didn't look over the lease more carefully. Of course, you were in a hurry. Just like you always are. And you were pushing to be named superintendent on this site at the same time. So you let Calhoun get away with such a long-term deal that you'll be dead and buried before the terms on this lease expire. Check it out. The wells already here more than satisfy any requirements laid out in your agreement." Rowdy held out the papers in case Clint wanted to reread his own lease.

"Get that fucking paper out of my face. What the hell do I care, anyway? I'm already making more money than I know what to do with. You want to fire me? Go ahead. You can take your company policy and cram it up your ass. At least I got to push the rigs through in record time before you caught on." He spit on the floor, narrowly missing Rowdy's work boot. "Almost got them finished, too. Shit. Just a couple more days. A week at most." He gave Megan a hate-filled look. "That's why I arranged Comstock through my home in Nevada. Took you a while to figure it out, didn't it, missy?" He threw his hard hat on the floor, where it bounced and came back to hit his own leg. He kicked it aside in a fury.

"Watch it, Stephens." Rowdy moved closer to the man.

"*You* watch it. And, Ms. High and Mighty Calhoun? You're right. These well sites smell like shit and are a muddy mess. You think I'm sorry to walk away? Fuck, no. I spent years saving my money, wait-ing for a chance to make a score like this one. When I heard Conrad Calhoun was out here buying land, I knew my time had come. Hell, little lady, I even arranged to meet your old man to seal the deal." Clint laughed. "He liked me because I was old school, just like he was. Didn't give a rat's ass about some stupid lizard or earthquakes. All he cared about was that I knew how to bring his wells in on time."

Rowdy watched him carefully. He didn't like the wild look in Clint's eyes or the way he stared at Megan, who had jumped to her feet at the mention of her father.

"Then those tree-hugging do-gooders just got worked up over the environment. You think I give a shit about that?" He waved the hand that held his tobacco tin. "But you and your company caved in to them at the first squawk. Un-fuckin'-believable. Your daddy would be downright ashamed of you. He'd have never made that deal."

"If you'd done your job right, kept this site decent, maybe Wallace and the environmentalists wouldn't have gotten so worked up, Stephens." Rowdy kept himself between Megan and the super.

"Oh, what does it matter now? I'm done. These wells are already making me rich anyway, and I'm getting richer with every well we complete." Clint poked Rowdy in the chest. "So, who's stupid now?"

Rowdy shoved Clint away. "Don't you fucking touch me again."

Megan rounded the desk after a stop by the printer. "Settle down. You're right, Clint. These wells are productive. In fact, we know ex-actly how much money you've been making here." She waved the paper in Clint's face. "But it doesn't look like the state of Nevada was aware."

"What?" Clint took a step toward her. "What the hell are you talking about?"

"Back off, Stephens." Rowdy slapped a hand on the man's chest to make sure he gave Megan room.

She smiled at Rowdy. "You know I just love living in Texas. One reason? No state income tax. But Nevada? They find it necessary and are careful to collect it. And they sure hate it when someone doesn't report income. So does the IRS. So I sent them both a copy of your recent windfall, Clint. I'm sure you'll be happy to get straight with them. To pay what you owe. Since you insist that's your permanent residence. And the papers you filed for the Limited Liability Corporation make it official." She slapped the paper she held against Clint's chest. "Look. I just got a nice thank-you note from your home state. They tack on penalties and interest for failure to report, you know. I may get a reward as a whistle-blower."

"Why, you bitch!" He lunged at Megan.

Rowdy tackled him before he could reach her and wrestled him back. "You touch one hair on her head and I'll kill you." He slammed Clint against the door again. "Now, get off of this well site. And be sure to leave that company truck when you go."

"You motherfucker." Clint shoved back. "How the hell am I supposed to get to town?"

"Catch a ride with that chemical truck that's fixing to leave here." Rowdy pulled open the door and whistled. The truck that was about to pull out of the yard stopped. "Hurry now. Because if you miss it, you'll have to walk the ten miles."

Clint spewed obscenities as he staggered out of the office and down to where the truck idled. He said something to the driver, then stopped by his pickup and pulled some things out of the backseat and glove compartment. Rowdy stood on the porch, watching until the truck with Stephens aboard finally rumbled out of sight.

"That was intense." Megan came up behind him.

"When did you come up with the income tax thing?"

"This morning. It was bothering me that he had created his corporation in Nevada. Of course, he did it to hide the ownership, but I had a feeling it could be useful. The reason it took me a long time to find out who was behind Comstock in the first place was because there was a little mix-up with his Social Security number. He used a bogus number. So, he's looking at tax evasion, too. I'm sure that's why he's really upset. I can't believe he thought he could get away with that. He'll owe a ton of money to the IRS and to Nevada and may face federal charges. He'll still get plenty of money from Calhoun in the future, but he may have to spend a lot of it on lawyers."

"He was furious and he's a bad enemy to have." Rowdy looked toward the rigs. "I need to go find this guy Stephens recommended. If I don't think he can handle the job, I'll have to make some calls." He'd been watching the men work for a couple of weeks now. He had a pretty good idea which ones knew what they were doing, but he hadn't learned all their names.

"Good luck." Megan sighed. "I don't know about you, but I'm feeling relieved. I never liked that man."

"Me, either. Tonight let's celebrate. Dinner in town, then a private party in the RV."

She grinned. "It's a date."

"Well, that was a surprise. Who knew you'd find such fantastic Italian food in a little West Texas town?" Megan was happy and just a little too full after a delicious meal.

"And veal piccata. That's always been one of my favorites." Rowdy held her hand as they drove toward home. The county road was much smoother after crews had been out doing some repair work. With the wells almost complete, it would probably stay that way, too.

"Yet another thing we have in common." Megan sighed and thought about unbuttoning her jeans. Not because she wanted to get something started with Rowdy, but because the Italian cream cake she'd eaten for dessert had been a little too much. She really did need to start doing more exercise than just what she and Rowdy had been doing in bed. She said as much to him.

"What? You like to run? Go to a gym?" He grinned and tried to tug her closer. It was impossible with that stupid console between them and the seat belt holding her into her seat. "Maybe our bedroom exercise hasn't been vigorous enough."

She laughed and reminded him to watch the road. "It's the trailer. How wild and crazy can we be with so little space?" She saw the RV park ahead. "We have to stop and get Lucky. Which reminds me.

How long do you think we're going to be here, now that this protester thing is settled and Clint Stephens is gone?"

"I need a few more days to be sure Dave Rodriguez will work out, but we could leave as early as next Monday. Of course, you need the Wallace contract signed." Rowdy stopped next to Raylene's trailer. The park was almost deserted, except for just a few trailers near the entrance. Those were occupied by Amos, Art, and a couple of the workers on the well site.

"She'll sure miss Lucky." Megan bit her lip. She'd been thinking about the upcoming year and had arrived at a decision. "What would you think if I offered to let her keep him?"

"Seriously?" Rowdy stared at her. "You were so dead set on making him your dog."

"I know. But he's getting bigger and, living on the road like we do, well, I can see it's not fair to him and it's impractical for us." She stared into the dark landscape. "I'll miss him. He's so sweet. But he's really happy here. And she loves him."

"You do what you want." Rowdy held her hand. "I'll support you either way."

Megan sighed. "Let me think about it." She realized actually giving up the dog was going to be harder than she thought. "I'll sleep on it."

"Good idea. Now, go get him." Rowdy nodded. "I'll drive on down and you can walk off your dessert and let him do his potty stops."

"Fine. See you in a few." She opened her seat belt, then leaned across and kissed him. "Have I told you today how much I love you?"

"Maybe this morning. But I can't hear it enough." He grinned and smoothed her hair back from her face. "I love you, too, Megan Calhoun. Now, smile or Raylene is going to think something's wrong."

"Hey, something usually is. But tonight I'm feeling pretty good. You know, looking over his lease agreement and seeing what Clint Stephens gets from those wells reminded me that the company gets seven times what he does. Calhoun does have money flowing in from wells all over the world. And we have the Reese County bonanza to look forward to now. It may be that we'll survive this mess my father made." She opened the truck door. "I'm going to think positively about that."

Megan collected Lucky and warned Raylene that they'd be leaving the next week. The landlady's reaction made her realize just how attached the woman had gotten to Lucky.

"I know he'll miss you, Raylene. We'll miss you, too." Megan dragged Lucky away from the landlady's trailer. She shivered, wishing she'd put on more layers in the chilly night air. She noticed a couple of the lights were out between the small cluster of RVs and their site. The darkness began to bother her. It must have spooked Lucky, too, because he growled and barked at the edge of the barbecue area.

"What do you see, boy? Is there a rabbit out there?" She held tight to his leash. "I'd let you chase him, but then I'd never be able to catch you. And there could be a rattlesnake. I know you're a brave boy—" She yelped when he almost jerked the leash out of her hand. "Stop it!"

The door to the RV opened. "What's going on out here?" Rowdy came down the steps. "Lucky, behave yourself!"

"He thinks something interesting is out there." Megan passed off his leash and examined her hand. "He got me when he leaped after it."

"Let me see." Rowdy pulled her under their porch light. "You skinned your palm. I think you'll live, but we'll put some salve and a Band-Aid on it." He glared at the dog, who'd kept barking. "We'd better get him inside. I think they can probably hear him down at Raylene's. It's almost ten o'clock. The hands living down there have their lights off. They're trying to sleep."

"Pull him inside." Megan looked around at the darkness. "Did you lock the truck?"

"Not yet." He pushed the dog inside and closed the door.

Megan could hear Lucky scratching to be let out. "Get the gun out of the glove compartment. I'm spooked. Maybe there's a rattlesnake out there. Whatever it is, I'd feel better if we had the gun in here with us."

"Anything to make you happy." Rowdy pulled her close for a kiss. "Am I allowed to call you 'baby' now?"

"I guess so." Megan smiled and waited until he was back beside her again. "Sorry for that outburst. I actually love it when you call me that."

"You know some guys call every woman they're with the same pet name. So they won't have to take the chance they'll call the wrong name when they're in the middle of the action." Rowdy opened the door, and they both shoved Lucky back when they stepped inside.

"Really? Did you just share inside information with me? Break the 'guy code'?" Megan laughed and took the gun from him. "All loaded?"

"Of course. Put it in that cabinet next to the dinette. I'm figuring it's a good time to christen that spot. What do you think?" Rowdy looked down when Lucky whined and hit his leg. "Dog, what the hell's the matter with you? I don't care what it is, you're going to bed." He walked him down to the front bedroom. "His toy in here?"

"Yes, it is. Hurry. I'm pulling out a sheet. If this is happening, I'm covering the table. We do eat on this thing."

Rowdy looked back and grinned. She was setting up the space topless. Oh boy, but he was just as lucky as this goofy dog, who was bringing him a stuffed mouse Raylene had given him. By the time he'd turned out the light and shut the door, Rowdy was pulling off his shirt and kicking off his shoes. The lights in the RV were all off, except for one small night-light in the bathroom. It made the woman stretched out on the table look perfect and ready for love.

He stopped and just took her in—her golden hair spread out around her head on the blue sheet, the way she'd posed so that one hand lay on her breast, the other on that silly and sexy tattoo he couldn't wait to kiss.

"Rowdy, what are you waiting for?" Her voice was husky, and she dragged a fingertip down from that tat to where he knew she'd be wet and welcoming.

"You're beautiful. I'd like a picture of you like that." He almost reached for his phone.

"Don't you dare. Stuff like that has a tendency to show up where you don't want it to. Quit looking and start touching, *Roland*." She grinned, sure that would get him moving.

"That's my grandpa. You want me over there, call me by my name."

"Rowdy. Come play with me." She sat up, then frowned. "Lucky's barking again. And do you smell something?"

Rowdy sniffed. "Diesel? Or is it a propane leak?" He headed back to the dog. "Lucky, what is it, boy?" As soon as he opened the door, Lucky raced to the front bedroom and went crazy, digging into the carpet with his paws.

"What is it?" Megan was up and had pulled the sheet around her.

Rowdy had followed the dog. "Smoke. God, Megan, we've got to get out of here. The RV is on fire and the fuel tank could blow any minute. Grab the gun, I'll get the dog."

"Put him on the leash. I don't want him running out into the desert." She had the gun in her hands and was sliding her feet into the shoes she'd worn to dinner.

Rowdy tossed her a coat and grabbed one for himself. "Come on, we need to run." He clipped the leash on Lucky, who had to be dragged from the corner by the bed, and threw open the door. The smoke smell was strong outside and he looked behind him to be sure Megan was with him.

"Where the hell are you? Megan!"

She finally appeared with her purse under one arm and her computer under the other, all the while struggling with that sheet wrapped around her. The gun was sticking out of the purse. "A woman knows what's important."

"Screw that. If the thing had blown . . ." He grabbed her hand and pulled her well away from the trailer. "We need to get behind the truck!" Thank God he hadn't taken off his jeans yet and his cell was in his pocket. He fumbled it out and hit 911. Then he heard a *pop* just before the RV exploded into a ball of fire.

Megan screamed and pulled him down to the ground, the truck acting as a shield against the worst of the blast. When fiery debris began falling from the sky, they crawled under the back end to avoid being hit. Rowdy could hear heavy pieces of the trailer hitting the truck for endless seconds. The heat was intense, and he realized he couldn't hear the 911 operator who'd answered his call.

"Emergency. Fire. Ray's RV Park." He'd be damned if he could remember the address or the proper name. "Need help." He gave up and held on to Megan and the dog. Both of them were trembling against him. He tried to organize his thoughts. Brand-new RV. Fuel tank. Leak? But a *pop*. What did it mean? He heard screaming and looked out behind the back of the truck. People were running toward them from the other end of the park. Of course they'd heard . . . The fire . . . lighting up the sky.

"Stay there. We see you. Are you hurt?" Raylene had a phone in her hand. The people behind her stood and stared at the blaze like they were watching a movie.

Rowdy took inventory. *Was* he hurt? Didn't know. He tried to ask Megan how she was but couldn't get a word out. All he could do was hold on to her. Who was shaking harder—her, the dog, or him?

Megan realized the fire must have died down, because a man in a firefighter's slicker was trying to coax them out from under the truck.

"Rowdy. Are you okay? Can you move?" She passed Lucky's leash out to the man and the dog ran to Raylene, who was crying. Ray picked him up even though it made her stagger. "Rowdy?" Oh God, what was wrong with him?

"Megan?" He finally moved his arms, which had been wrapped tightly around her. "I think I'm bleeding. How about you? Okay?"

"Me? I'm fine. You protected me." She felt his chest, then his head. There. A wet spot. Some falling debris must have hit his head. "Can you crawl out now? See the flashing lights? I think there's an ambulance, paramedics. Let them find out what's wrong. Please?"

"Give me a minute. You go out first. I want to see that you can move." He shoved her toward the fireman who still squatted at the end of the truck. "Check her out."

"Will do, sir." The man waited patiently, finally pulling Megan out when she got close enough for him to reach her. "She seems fine, sir. Now it's your turn."

"Do it, Rowdy. Come on, baby. See? I can call you that, too. Crawl on out here. I'd hate for you to bleed to death under there." Megan wiped away a tear. "Damn it, move!" Finally he crawled slowly toward them.

By the time Rowdy had been helped out and was lying where they could work on him away from the ruined truck and the still-smoldering RV, it was clear he'd been hit on the head by something large. He probably had a concussion. He seemed confused and kept falling asleep. The paramedics loaded him into the ambulance and promised Megan she could ride with him to the regional hospital.

"Megan, honey, take this with you." Raylene caught up with her before she got into the vehicle. It was a bundle of clothes. "You can't run around in a sheet all the time." She laughed but it turned into a sob. "The sheriff found a bullet hole in your fuel tank. Someone shot the tank to make it explode. This sure wasn't no accident. You keep your gun handy. You hear me?"

Megan hugged her. "Loud and clear." *Bullet hole?* That fact sank in, and she shuddered. *Someone tried to kill us.* She heard Rowdy call her name. She couldn't tell him this, or he'd try to fling himself out of the ambulance and lead the manhunt. Of course, she knew who had a grudge against them and hated them enough to want them dead. "Tell the sheriff I have a suspect for him. He can talk to me at the hospital. And thanks for the clothes." She climbed into the ambulance. The thirty-minute trip gave her plenty of time to dig in her purse and make some calls. Damn, but she hated being so far away from her family at a time like this.

"That's two RVs and two trucks, Megan. I don't think we can afford for you and Rowdy to stay on the road." Mason didn't laugh. "Seriously, are you sure you're all right? You say Rowdy is still in the hospital?"

"A concussion. He's being released now. We don't have any place to stay." Megan stood outside Rowdy's hospital room. She wore one of Raylene's hippy-dippy T-shirts and a pair of her jeans. Thank God their landlady favored a loose fit or she wouldn't have been able to wiggle into them.

"How's he doing?"

"Fine, except for a lingering headache. So, where should we go, Mason?"

"You need to remain in Pecos until Wallace signs that contract. See if you can find a short-term rental RV." Mason cleared his throat. "You think that asshole Stephens tried to kill you?"

"They found a bullet hole in our fuel tank. The sheriff is taking our allegations seriously, but we don't have proof the man did it. We've been promised that they'll keep an eye on Stephens while he's still in the area. If he's smart, he'll leave town." Megan glanced toward Rowdy's room and saw the doctor go inside. "They're releasing Rowdy now. I've got to go. When will her contract be ready?"

"Tomorrow. All the nondisclosures had already been executed by e-mail, so we're good there. Can't believe you thought of that." He cleared his throat. "We'll make an oilman out of you yet, Meg. As soon as you have Wallace's signature, you can get transportation to the nearest airport and fly home, both of you. I think you've earned a break. We'll talk about how you can spend the rest of your year when you get here."

"Not in the field?" Megan had her fingers crossed. "And what about Rowdy?"

"He works for Calhoun now. I like how he handled the situation out there. With his field experience, I think we have plenty of things he can do for us here in Houston. Conrad's will says you need to learn the oil business. You've been in the field, now maybe you can learn the rest of what you need to learn at Headquarters. From Rowdy. If that suits you."

"Don't tease me, Mason. It would suit both of us very well." Megan was grinning when the doctor came out and tapped her on the shoulder. "Got to go."

"See you soon. Stay safe." Mason hung up.

"He's ready to go. I've given him some medication for those headaches, but they should be gone by tomorrow, the day after at the latest. Let me know if they're not." The doctor handed her a pre-scription. "You can get this filled downstairs in the pharmacy or in town." He looked down the hall. "Here comes a nurse with a wheel-chair now."

"Oh, we have to figure out transportation. And where we're going." Megan looked down at her phone.

"No, you don't." Raylene walked up behind the nurse. She was dressed in khakis and a red leather jacket with fringe. "I've got you all taken care of. An extra RV just came free at my place. You and Rowdy can use it till you leave. And my truck's outside." She ex-claimed when the nurse wheeled Rowdy out of his room. "There's our guy! Lucky's been pining for you, Rowdy."

"Doubt that. You know he wants to be your dog, Raylene." Rowdy reached for Megan's hand. "Where are we going?"

"Looks like back to Ray's Rest." Megan smiled. "Thanks. I was totally at a loss." She walked beside the wheelchair. Raylene chattered all the way to the door, where she'd parked illegally, insisting that she needed the front door to take home her "dear friend." After a stop in town to have the prescription filled and to buy Raylene lunch, they drove out to the RV park. The suddenly available trailer was next door to the landlady and had obviously been hastily emptied. It smelled strongly of her lavender air freshener.

"Sorry about that, kids. He was a smoker. But he's doubling up with his buddy next door now. One of your oil field workers, Rowdy. He don't mind." Raylene hurried to get Lucky, who put on his usual show of jumping for joy. "That's our hero, that dog. Megan told me how he smelled the smoke and went crazy that night. Whoever was out there in the desert must have been waiting to see if the tank would blow on its own because of the fire he set. When you two ran out of there, I guess he got desperate and shot at the tank. *Boom!*" She shuddered, then patted Lucky's head. "Thank God for this little guy. He's a damn fine watchdog. Saved your lives."

"Yes, he did." Megan sighed. "I'm hoping whoever it was has decided scaring us was enough and left town." She helped Rowdy sit in the vinyl recliner that was part of this RV's décor.

"We're going to keep a sharp eye out anyway. I've got my gun and you've got yours. That dog starts a ruckus, we're going after that son of a bitch." Raylene looked Rowdy over. "Hon, you look a little worse for wear. Headache?"

"Afraid so. Maybe I'll take one of those pills and go to bed." Rowdy closed his eyes.

"I put on fresh sheets, and there's bottles of water in that icebox." The landlady headed for the door. "You need anything, you know where to find me." She laughed when Lucky followed her. "No, pup, you stay here. I'll see you tomorrow if these two want to go to work." She closed the door behind her.

"Let me help you." Megan brought Rowdy a pill and handed him some water so he could drink it down. "Bed?"

"I just needed to get rid of her. I don't need a bed. I'm fine here." Rowdy leaned back in the recliner. "Tell me the news. Did they find Clint Stephens? Arrest him?"

"No to the arrest. They don't have proof. He rented a truck, but he still has his room in town. Since no one saw him out here, they couldn't charge him with anything. But they're keeping an eye on him."

"Why's he staying, then?"

"Guess he's in no hurry to go back to Nevada, where they really want to talk to him." Megan shrugged. Then she told Rowdy about the job waiting for him in Houston.

"Really? That sounds too good to be true. This isn't because of our connection, is it?"

"Not at all. Mason has no idea we have anything going on. He likes how you handled the job out here. And how you handled me." Megan sat in Rowdy's lap, sighing when his arms came around her. "I like it, too."

"Well, then. I think it sounds like a perfect opportunity." He kissed her, then closed his eyes. "Those pills make me sleepy. Maybe I will stretch out for a while."

Megan looked around the small RV. "Only one bedroom. We're going to have to get tough with Lucky tonight."

"At least the bedroom has a door." Rowdy pushed her off his lap, got up, then took her hand and pulled her toward the bed. "I need you to help me with something. I have to see whether my injury has had any lasting effects." He dragged her down onto the clean sheets that smelled strongly of lavender. "But be gentle, okay?"

Megan laughed and ran her hands down his body. "Hmm. I think I feel you stirring to life, but I may need to take a closer look."

It was much later when Rowdy heard the dog barking. Damn drugs. He'd slept the day away, and now it was after midnight. Megan had slept with him, because spending the previous night in a chair in the hospital room with him hadn't given her much rest. They'd closed the door on Lucky, but now he was scratching at it and going crazy. Just like he had the night the other RV had blown up.

Rowdy jumped out of bed, even though it made his head hurt, then pulled on his only pair of jeans. He'd be damned if he'd lie there and wait for something to happen. If it was Clint Stephens and he was crazy enough to come after them again, then he was going to find out they weren't passive victims.

"Rowdy?" Megan sat up. "What is it?"

"You hear Lucky?" Rowdy pushed his feet into shoes and shrugged into his jacket. "Where'd you put the gun?"

"Not again." Megan was up, too, throwing on a new white robe and digging for shoes. "It's in the cabinet next to the stove."

"Stay here." Rowdy threw open the door and almost stepped on Lucky. "Pup, you *are* an excellent guard dog. But you need to stay here."

"Rowdy, you can't go out there." Megan was on his heels. She held a small handgun.

"Where the hell did you get that?" Rowdy pulled his own gun out of the cabinet.

"I took a cab to a pawnshop and bought it while you were in the hospital. I told you I can shoot. I'm not going to let you do this by yourself." She shoved Lucky into the bedroom and slammed the door. "Cut the lights, and let's see if we can catch this bastard."

"My woman." Rowdy grabbed her and planted a kiss on her mouth. Then he doused the lights. "Be careful." He eased open the door to the outside. He could still hear Lucky barking.

"I'll go right," Megan whispered.

Damn it, she was too easy to see in her white robe. Rowdy went left, but the sound of a gunshot froze him in his tracks. Megan dropped to the ground.

"I'm not hit. Did you see the flash?"

Rowdy tried to get his heart started again, nodded, then realized she couldn't see him. "Yeah. Stay down."

He moved silently toward the area where he'd seen the gun's muzzle flash. Then something moved on his left.

"Don't shoot me." Raylene waved a shotgun toward the desert where Rowdy thought he saw someone running. "Son of a bitch blows up my park? I'll teach him a lesson he'll never forget." She crouched low and began moving forward, using the bushes for cover as if she'd done that kind of thing all her life.

Rowdy took her flank, marveling at the woman's agility. When she silently signaled, he took off running at an angle. He'd spotted the truck when she did and managed to get to the driver's door in time to catch the man who was about to jump inside. He pressed his gun to the back of his head.

"Don't fucking move or it'll be my pleasure to blow your head off."

"You don't have the balls." Clint Stephens swung his rifle around, trying to hit Rowdy with it before he brought it up for a shot.

Rowdy didn't wait for him to finish the move. He slapped Stephens in the head with his gun butt, then kicked the rifle away when it fell from his hands. "Balls?" He shoved the man against the truck and hit him again. "This from a man who hides in the dark and then runs away?" He realized Stephens wasn't fighting back. *Too easy.* He let go, and Stephens dropped to the ground, unconscious.

"Good job, son." Raylene kicked Clint's legs to make sure he was really out, then pointed her shotgun at his back. "Call the sheriff. I figure we get this bastard for trespassing and shooting at Megan. Maybe his bullet will match the one they dug out of your fuel tank, too."

Rowdy had to take a moment after he made the call. His head hurt, and he needed to come down from the burst of adrenaline. He still wanted to pound Clint Stephens. He watched him carefully. If he made a move, he was going to shoot him. There was a noise behind him, and he swung around, his gun raised.

Megan walked up with her hands raised. "Don't shoot. I'm on your side." She glanced at Stephens. "Good work, you two. I was getting tired of playing dead. And I didn't hear gunshots, so I figured things were settled down out here."

"Never assume." Rowdy put his gun down, still shaky. Damn pain pills. He was blaming them. "Woman, you almost got a bullet between your eyes."

"Hey, I waited and waited. Didn't hear gunfire, so I crept out here, risking God knows how many cactus spines, to see if I could help." She waved her gun toward Stephens. "Sorry if I startled you, babe, but when I saw the bad guy already on the ground, I made enough noise to let you know I was coming. You and I both know that man is too mean to have an accomplice. I bet he doesn't have a friend in the world."

"You're right about that." Rowdy finally relaxed. "Come here." He stuck his gun in his waistband and held out his arms.

"Guess I'm forgiven." Megan smiled and slid one arm around

Rowdy's waist. "I hear sirens. Raylene, you look badass with that shotgun."

"I *am* a badass. Ask any of my four ex-husbands." She grinned and nodded at Rowdy. "Would you let go of Megan long enough to hold this bastard? I need a cigarette." She passed the shotgun to Rowdy, then dug out her cigarettes and lighter, lit up, and took a deep drag. "Ah. Now, that's not as good as sex, but it's about all I'm getting these days."

Megan laughed. "Maybe you need to look for number five, Raylene. There will be a lot of oil action out in other parts of this area soon. You never know who'll show up in your RV park."

"Honey, that's music to my ears. Action of any kind is what I live for." She waved when they saw the sheriff and his deputy striding toward them. There was a moan from Clint Stephens. "Watch this creep try to talk his way out of it. Guess what? I put in security cameras after that fireball the other day. Infrared. I bet we got this loser on tape." She smiled. "Rowdy, you're looking pale. Hand me my gun, and go on back to the RV. I'll tell them to meet you there."

Megan and Rowdy headed back, stopping just long enough to assure the sheriff that they'd be happy to answer all his questions. Rowdy *was* tired, and he collapsed into the recliner with a bottle of water.

"You know, I think we can safely say things are working out here." Megan sat at the tiny dinette across from him after she let Lucky out of the bedroom.

"Really?" Rowdy leaned back in the recliner and let his feet pop up. "So, you're feeling mellow right now?"

"Yep. My man is looking better, the bad guy is on his way to jail, and my evaluator says I can come in from the oil fields. What else could I want?" She got up and walked over to sit on the arm of the chair.

"A ring on your finger?" He took her hand and rubbed her left ring finger. "Would that make you happy?"

"Hmm. It might. Would it make you happy to be tied to one of the horrible Calhouns? Seriously?" Megan gripped his hand, very serious herself. "I know—"

"Yeah. There are problems. But I love you, Megan Calhoun. Marry me and we'll work on them together."

Tears filled her eyes, and she fell into his lap. "All right, then. Together. I might even get that tattoo you want me to have." She pointed to her butt. "'Roland.' Right here."

Want more Heat?

Then keep an eye out for

TEXAS PRIDE

coming in October

and be sure to read

TEXAS HEAT

available now from Lyrical Shine.

ABOUT THE AUTHOR

A nationally best-selling author, GERRY BARTLETT is a native Texan who lives halfway between Houston and Galveston. She freely admits to a shopping addiction, which is why she has an antiques business on the historic Strand on Galveston Island. She used to be a gourmet cook but has decided it's more fun to indulge in gourmet eating instead. You can visit Gerry on Facebook, twitter, or Instagram. You can also check out her latest releases on her website at gerrybartlett.com, where you can sign up for her newsletter and read her series of articles with advice for aspiring writers, "The Perils of Publishing."

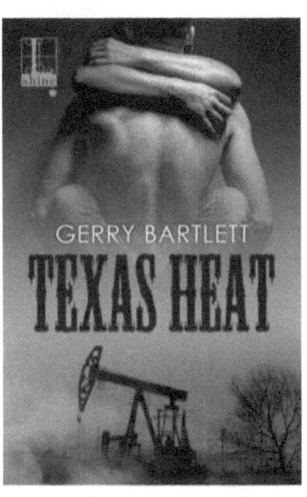

GERRY BARTLETT

TEXAS HEAT

A surprise inheritance. A family of strangers.
And a man she can't avoid . . .

Cassidy Calhoun can't believe she's the secret daughter
of an oil billionaire. This small-town Texas girl
with student loans by the barrel has never gotten a thing
she didn't earn for herself.

The terms of her late father's will say Cassidy—and her spoiled
newfound half-siblings—must work a year at the family's
floundering business before they inherit a dime.
Too bad the only thing Cass knows about oil
is that it makes the junker she drives go.

Mason MacKenzie, the evaluator for their test, will help her
get up to speed. Or will he? Mason is a boot-wearing,
truck-driving Houston hottie who runs Calhoun Petroleum's
biggest rival. The sparks between him and Cassidy
could combust any minute. But the closer they get,
the more strange near-accidents Cassidy seems to be
having. And Mason has plenty of reasons to play up
their attraction for his own benefit.

If she can trust him, the two of them working together
might save a crumbling dynasty. But if she can't,
Cass might just lose both her fortune and her heart . . .